Solitario

STEPHEN ESTOPINAL

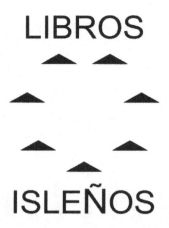

LIBROS

ISLEÑOS

DEDICATION

As always, to the love of my life
Marie Elaine Russell

.

OTHER NOVELS BY THIS AUTHOR

EL TIGRE DE NUEVA ORLEÁNS
(The Tiger of New Orleans)

INCIDENT AT BLOOD RIVER

ANNA

ESCAPE TO NEW ORLEANS

MOBILE MUST FALL

PENSACOLA BURNING

BENEATH THE BONNIE BLUE FLAG

THE MAN FROM RED HILL

CHAPTER 1

Morning was always Mike's favorite time of day, particularly a cool morning on the water. A cold north wind filled the little sail on his work boat, propelling him down a narrow bayou and then out onto the white-capped expanse of Lake Borgne.

The sun had not yet broken the horizon, but an orange glow beneath the pale blue southeastern sky was crowned by a sliver of thin white clouds silhouetting the low outline of a distant shore. He had timed his arrival on the lake correctly. By the time the disk of the sun broke clear, he would be at the small cut in the shoreline that led to his destination that morning.

A flurry of splashes spread out across the water between him and the emerging sun. A flock of waterfowl erupted from the wave tops, running on the water as they became airborne. The birds rose in the air by the hundreds, forming a cluster of dancing specks.

"*Poule d'eau*," Mike muttered to himself as the raft of coot rose in a spectacle of beating wings and splashing feet.

He collapsed the lateen-rigged spar, folded the sail against the stubby mast and lashed it securely with the reef points. The small boat still had some way on her, so he steered with an oar toward the great expanse of low marshland which was the southern shore. He scanned the tall cane, called "roseaux," that grew to the very edge of the vertical two-foot-high bank, searching for any sign of the tiny opening to a narrow waterway leading deeper into the marsh.

The cut he was searching for came into the lake at a sharp

angle, making it practically invisible to travelers on the lake. He was certain he was near the opening when he saw the eddies of a falling tide curling against the bank. He placed the oar in a cradle and picked up a long pole with a wedge-shaped foot on one end. He pushed the long pole against the grassy bottom of the lake, smoothly propelling his wide, squat boat into the narrow opening.

The only sounds he could hear were the gentle lapping of the wavelets against his boat and occasional clogging of his wooden shoes. Birds and other shore creatures had fallen silent, he did not know why. He coasted behind the tall canes, screened from all who may appear on the lake.

He rounded a turn and coasted into a thick fog bank. Suddenly startled, he reflexively slapped his sternum with his free hand and then began to feel feverously for the gas-mask case that should have been there.

"*Mierda*," he said loud enough to cause an unseen duck to quack inquisitively.

He admonished himself. *This is December 1921 in Louisiana, not September 1918 along the River Meuse in France*, he thought. The frequent nightmares of choking, poisonous gas filling shell holes and forcing men up above ground to be raked by German gunfire had become less frequent, but the sudden appearance of the thick, white fog had brought it all flooding back.

He sat on the stern gunnel and willed his heart to stop pounding. In his mind's eye he could see the advancing Germans transformed into hellish monsters by their gas masks, the eye lenses of which were clouded over with a silvery condensation.

The Germans had been practically blinded by their masks as they advanced across no-man's land. The ragged grey files stumbled into shell holes and struggled up slopes, their efforts confounded by the breathing restrictions imposed by their gas masks.

Mike had discarded his damaged mask and had climbed up onto a tall root ball to escape the gas. From this elevated position, he had raked their ranks with blasts from his shotgun, killing a half-dozen men. Because of their hampered vision and the confusion of a night-time attack, only a few of the advancing Germans had detected Mike. Those that did were quickly gunned down.

Mike had purchased an American 12-gauge pump shotgun, likely stolen from an American armory, on the black market in Chaumont, and had tossed away the worthless French Chauchat he had been issued. Later, when the army replaced all the French Chauchats with American produced versions, Mike retained his "trench sweeper." American Doughboys despised the undependable Chauchat automatic rifle so much that any worthless thing was said to be a "shoo-shoo."

He coughed dryly and brought up a brown gob of phlegm. The army doctors had assured him that because of his exposure to the gas he would suffer with weak lungs for the rest of his life.

He waited until the shaking stopped and resumed poling up the narrow but deep waterway. Rounding another tight bend, he pushed out into a small pond, maybe two hundred yards wide.

A clamshell mound several feet high and covering an area of about an acre bordered the pond on the north. For hundreds of years local Indians would visit the lake to collect clams from the water bottoms and bring them to their camp on this mound. After eating, they would discard the shells where they ate. Eventually, a midden of millions of small white clam half-shells crowned with hardy scrub oaks rose above the marsh.

Mike drifted along the base of the mound feeling the bottom

with his push pole and soon detected the hard, rough shape of an oyster reef. He moved along the reef, appraising its size and orientation. Satisfied that the reef was large enough to warrant his attention, he set aside the pole and placed a plank tray across the gunnels of the boat and maneuvered his oyster rake into place.

The rake, called a hand dredge, consisted of a pair of crossed heavy poles each worn smooth at one end and armed with large iron baskets at the other. The toothed open sides of the baskets faced each other and pivoted about a single bolt so that the contraption could be opened and closed by manipulating the smooth ends of the poles.

He worked the dredge over the side of his boat. He would open the rakes, slam the dredge into the reef, close the poles and lift. Each time oysters would be pulled off the reef and collected by the rakes. When enough oysters had been trapped, he lifted the dredge and spilled the contents onto the tray.

He picked through the pile of oysters on the tray. He tossed the large fat "number ones" into the bottom of the boat. Broken shells and small oysters were pushed back onto the reef. He worked like this for several hours until his arms ached, and his lungs burned.

From time to time, he would pause to drink water from a jug he kept in the stern, or open one or two of the oysters and swallow them whole. He would close his eyes and savor the salty taste of oysters so fresh they wiggled as he ate. No need to bring a lunch when your work provided such delicacies.

Several hours of work filled the boat to the gunnels with choice oysters. He lashed the dredge to the gunnel and walked across his cargo, his wooden shoes providing perfect protection from the sharp shells. He poled his boat back into the center of the waterway and out into the lake.

He unfurled the lateen-rigged sail to capture the mild northern breeze. The boat rode much lower in the water, but the open lake had only a mild chop and what little splashed over the gunnels was diverted by the small curb that ringed the edge of the boat.

The northern wind forced him to tack toward the east until he could gain enough sea room to turn west and make a run for Bayou Dupre. The boat, burdened with cargo, wallowed clumsily against the slight chop, but slowly made progress to the northeast.

He had considered adding a motor to the boat but rejected the idea. A motor would consume cargo space and cover everything with a sheen of gasoline and oil. Besides, there was something peaceful and fulfilling about being under sail or rowing along a bayou, even if it did take longer to get where you were going.

*****

Lake Borgne was much busier in the early afternoon than it had been when Mike crossed before sunrise. A few sails dotted the horizon, but most vessels moving about did so under power. A tugboat pushed a barge toward the mouth of Bayou Dupre. Mike would make for this destination as well, as soon as he had the sea room to tack.

Some of the boats were oyster luggers returning from a day of dredging on leased reefs further to the east. The boats did not use the laborious hand dredge but dragged large rakes across the reefs pulled by power winches. Their catch bagged in large canvas sacks and stacked on the open decks six or seven rows high that were walled in with plank grates to prevent them from spilling overboard.

One of the luggers changed course and headed to intercept Mike. Oystermen leased large areas of lake bottom from the

5

state, and they vigorously guarded their leases from poachers. The owners of the large power luggers were known in the fishing community, but a small boat filled with oysters drew suspicion. Mike reached into a box at the stern of his boat and removed a model 1911 automatic pistol which he tucked into his pocket.

The lugger grew close until Mike could read the name on the bow. It was the *Captain Toss*. He knew the boat and her captain, John Donavich. Donavich was a Taco, a descendent of Croatian emigrants who had come to Louisiana decades ago to cultivate and harvest oysters. Donavich's burly form appeared at the bow of the fast-approaching lugger.

"Michael Demill," Donavich hailed as soon as he was close enough to be heard over the chug of his boat's engine. "Michael, I thought it might be you. Did you not know there are no oysters on this side of the lake?"

"It is my specialty, John," Mike called back. "I dredge oysters from where they are not supposed to be."

At a signal from Donavich, the *Captain Toss* killed her engines, turned to parallel Mike's course, and slowed to a drift.

"You did not collect your cargo from one of my leases, now did you, Michael?'

"You can see where I am, John. You have no leases within ten miles of here."

"Just the same. It is a simple matter to dredge a little here, a little there and fill your boat with other men's crop. Loners, like you, are not so careful about where they harvest." Donavich's tone became menacing. "Tell you what I can do. I am a reasonable man. We can add your cargo to ours and I will even pay you for your work."

"I think that will not do, John. I will bring my harvest to the dockside myself," Mike replied. He reached into his pocket and gripped the butt of the .45, a move that was not unnoticed by Donavich.

"You take care, Michael," Donavich said as he motioned to his man in the wheelhouse to start the engine. "One day you will be caught with your dredge on the wrong reef."

"Goodbye John," Mike said, his hand still gripping the pistol in his pocket.

The *Captain Toss* forged ahead and turned sharply, causing Mike's little boat to take on some water. A Loner, that's what Donavich had called him. He didn't know why that bothered him like it did. One day he would be able to afford a proper boat and trawl for shrimp or dredge for oysters in style. He would name his boat *Solitario* – Loner.

Mike made the tack and set his heading toward the mouth of Bayou Dupre. He would enter the bayou in about one hour and make the seven-mile trip from Lake Borgne, along the bayou which merged into the Violet Canal, until arriving at locks which regulated commerce into the Mississippi River in another two hours. The *Captain Toss* was nowhere to be seen. Mike considered it likely that Donavich had taken his lugger through the locks and continued up the river to New Orleans.

Constructed in the mid-19th Century and named for the wife of its main financier, the Violet Canal provided a maritime passage from Lake Borgne and the Mississippi Sound to the Mississippi River.

It was full dark when Mike guided his boat into the slip under his cabin on the canal. He tied the boat off, bow and stern, with enough slack to account for the tide. He hung the push pole and oars on a wall rack and collected his water jug. He turned a white knob on a pile and an electric light winked on. He remembered how amazed he was when he first encountered electric lights as a young boy. He had grown up in a remote fishing village down the bayou, far from civilization.

Everyone in the fishing village, all descendants of Canary Islanders – Isleños - brought to Louisiana in 1778 to fight the British, spoke Spanish. Most had also managed to learn French through contact with neighboring villages. Mike was eight years old when his father brought him up to New Orleans where he first heard English spoken and discovered the electric light.

He walked up the stairs to his quarters, removed his hand-carved wooden shoes and placed them on the landing by the door. He opened the door -- there was no lock -- entered and turned on the single light which hung by a cord in the center of the room. On the far wall there was a cot, to his left was a table and chair next to a wash basin under a window and to his right his entire wardrobe hung from rows of pegs. A wood burning stove and a pantry completed the furnishings.

He laid the pistol on the table and crossed to the pantry where he removed a glass and bottle. Placing the glass on the table, he poured himself two fingers of whiskey and took a sip. He swirled the whisky in the glass, took another sip and set the glass on the table next to the open bottle.

He opened the iron door on the stove firebox and added kindling along with a few pieces of wood. He struck a match and got the fire going. The cabin did not have running water, but a cistern that collected rainwater from the roof was at one corner. He placed a pot under the spigot on the basin and allowed a few cups of water to flow into the pot.

He placed the pot on the stove and opened a can of beef chips which he poured into the pot along with a clove of garlic, some carrot slices, and a few potato chunks.

"Tonight, a feast," he said aloud. "Tomorrow, into town."

*****

In the morning he put on a round bowler hat, selected some

clothes from the row of pegs, and stuffed them into a satchel along with a pair of leather shoes. He stepped out, put on his wooden shoes, and descended to the boat. He placed the satchel in the boat and walked across to a door and out to the small out-house among the willows.

He returned to the boat, cast off the moorings, and standing on the stern of the boat, sculled it out and up the canal with graceful sweeps of a long oar. The dock he approached was bustling with fishermen selling their wares to merchants who loaded their purchases into train cars that had been backed onto a siding next to the dock.

He bartered with a representative of several fancy New Orleans restaurants. The going price at the seafood dock in New Orleans was eight dollars a barrel for fresh number one oysters. But the Violet landing was eleven miles from the New Orleans market and unlike New Orleans, Mike's complete inventory would be taken by one broker. He settled on a price of six dollars twenty-five cents a barrel for his oysters. Dock workers quickly unloaded his boat to fill seven barrels and rolled the barrels into a train car.

He moored his empty boat at an unused corner of the dock, tossed the wooden shoes into the boat and donned the leather shoes he had taken from his bag. With over forty dollars in his pocket, two weeks wages for some, he crossed to the train station, paid the conductor ten cents, and climbed aboard the passenger car of the morning train to New Orleans.

The railway into New Orleans ran through truck farms where occasional stops were made to load produce and pick up passengers. Soon roadways fronted by homes and businesses paralleled the railway on either side. They passed over a new railway and roadway bridge at a huge navigation canal under construction. When Mike had left for the army, the canal was only talked about, but now it was being built.

The new canal had massive locks at the river and would allow barges and coastal steamboats to navigate between Lake Pontchartrain and the Mississippi River. It was called the "Industrial Canal" and would likely put the relatively tiny Violet locks out of business.

He checked into a hotel near the train stop. The room came with the privilege of a bath with hot and cold running water. He dropped the satchel on the single bed, chose the clothes he wished to wear and made his way down the hall to the bath. It was mid-morning, so the bath was open, and he enjoyed a long sit in a hot tub and a clean shave.

He left the hotel wearing high button, polished shoes, a stiff shirt with a bow tie, black coat, and a bowler hat riding square on his head. His six-foot frame and muscular build were accented by sparkling blue eyes and sandy brown hair. He stepped onto a streetcar headed toward the river and enjoyed the sights along the way.

Women in fine dresses, gloves, hats, and parasols walked along the store fronts with their gentlemen escorts. He noticed that a few of the ladies, particularly the younger ones, preferred dresses that were not so full and stopped above the ankles. A bustling city was a sight he had not seen since Paris.

He dismounted when the car stopped at the river and walked along Decatur Street to the Café Du Monde. He walked up to a small, dark man seated at one of the sidewalk tables.

"*Buenos días, Señor* Moreno," Mike said as the man looked up from his paper. The conversation was to be in Spanish.

"Ah, *buenos días, mí amigo*," Moreno said as he stood and offered his hand. They shook hands and Moreno pulled out a chair indicating Mike should join him.

"A coffee?"

"Yes, thank you."

Moreno waved a waiter over and ordered a café au lait with beignets in his heavily accented English. Mike studied the man. Moreno was short, but powerfully built. He had active intelligent eyes and confident mannerisms. He was a man widely known to be particularly ingenious when it came to business and money.

Moreno was a man whose business specialty had been importing goods in a way that evaded duties or taxation. Now that prohibition was the law of the land, he adjusted his importing business only slightly to include smuggling whiskey. The local population in and around the city brewed enough illegal beer and wine to satisfy demand, but hard liquor had to be smuggled.

Moreno, like Mike, grew up speaking Spanish. This proved to be a great asset as almost all the hard drink Moreno "imported" was distilled in Cuba. Mike was known to be very familiar with the intricate web of waterways below New Orleans and Moreno was expanding his business.

"I was saddened to learn of your mother's passing," Moreno said. It was impolite to begin with business straight away.

Mike's mother, Anita Broud, had no other children. She had been from the upriver side of New Orleans known as the Garden District. A strikingly beautiful woman, who enjoyed the attentions of many courters, Anita was suddenly cast out of the polite society of New Orleans because of some business scandal involving her father and the Spanish Consulate.

It was during a time of great tension between the American Government and Spain, a tension egged on by the New York press corps eager for an expression of America's arrival on the world stage. There were accusations of treason. The Spanish-

American War came later, long after Anita's exile from the polite society of the Garden District.

Mike's father, Diego Demill, was the owner of a small fleet of fishing boats and was considered "established," but not wealthy. Cutoff from old money, Anita married Diego to survive and was widowed by Diego's death in 1910. The scandal of the Broud treachery had slowly faded away. In 1916 Anita remarried and moved into New Orleans, bringing Mike with her.

Anita's new husband was an elderly and very wealthy, prominent New Orleans banker, Jacob Wiltz. Anita basked in her return to the elites of the Garden District and old money while Mike, born and raised as a fisherman, tried to fit in.

His French, Anita's preferred language, was perfect, but now he had to learn English as well. He struggled with the language, and developed an understandable, but heavily accented, fluency.

Jacob Wiltz was condescending toward Mike and considered the young man to be an uneducated, backwoods lout. He shunned his stepson and offered him only menial positions at warehouses or docks he controlled. Mike was not fond of his stepfather and his resentment was fully reciprocated.

Mike and his mother became estranged on the day he departed for Fort Oglethorpe, Georgia, with his induction papers in hand to report to the 11th U.S. Infantry Regiment.

Anita had forbidden Mike to register for the draft, and she was determined to use her husband's influence to protect him. She reasoned that many in the isolated communities along south Louisiana were easily over-looked by the government, so Mike, so recently relocated from the isolated marsh village of Bencheque, would go unnoticed as well.

When he was drafted, Anita accused him of defying her and

secretly registering out of spite toward her and Jacob. In truth, he had not registered for the draft, as she had commanded, and yet he was drafted anyway, the notice carried to him by a constable. She remained angry with Mike, even after he returned from Europe.

"Thank you for your concern," Mike replied, his thoughts returning to Moreno and the Café Du Monde. "I hope all is well with your family."

"Oh, yes. All is well indeed. I have a new granddaughter just this week." Moreno looked about and leaned in to speak in low tones. It was just possible someone in earshot could speak Spanish. "I have asked to meet with you, Miguel, precisely because you have no family. *Solitarios* can come and go without notice. You can take long trips, make early meetings and not have to explain to anyone, is this not so?"

"I have no ties, that is so," Mike agreed. "Do you have a position to offer?"

"Yes, I do. I need someone to go to Cuba, see that my goods are cataloged and loaded on a ship. Then I need that person to meet my small boats somewhere around Breton Island, see that the boats are loaded and then sent inland, each by a separate route. If you can do such things for me, Miguel, I will pay you ten dollars a day and one-half a percent of the profits from that shipment."

Mike's head begin to spin. Ten dollars a day was more than most doctors made and a half-percent of a single shipment would be enough to build and outfit a deep-water trawler.

"I will do this," Mike said. "When would you like me to start?"

Moreno handed Mike a steamer ticket to Havana. "Today."

CHAPTER 2

Mike examined the steamer ticket while Moreno sipped his coffee, his eyes never leaving Mike's face. The ticket was a pre-printed form declaring in bold letter across the top "New England Shipping – Passage to Havana." The next line stated, "Steam liner *Ariel* – Modern Accommodations." The form had blanks to be filled in by hand distributed among the print work. The blanks were labeled "pier," "time," "date of departure," and "passenger(s)."

Moreno smiled and nodded as he watched Mike read. A clerk with a broad and scrawling script had written "Marigny Street Warf," "6 am," and "December 18, 21" in the appropriate spaces. The passenger's name was Josef Rodriguez.

Mike folded the ticket and slipped it into an inside coat pocket. He was to depart for Cuba in the morning as Josef Rodriguez. Now that the war in Europe was over, passports or other proof of identity were not required for international travel.

Mike stood and offered his hand to Moreno. "I will conclude some business in Violet and board the *Ariel* in the morning."

Moreno took his hand and shook it firmly. "Good. Once you arrive in Havana, find the docking steward, and ask if he has any messages for you, *Señor* Rodriguez. He will give you further instructions. Good luck."

"Thank you, sir."

Mike made his way out of the Café Du Monde and walked the few blocks to the Rampart train stop at Esplanade. He would catch the last train down to Violet and, with any luck, conclude his business in time to catch the last return train back to his hotel.

*****

Mike stepped from the train onto the passenger coach landing at Violet in time to see the *Captain Toss* locking her way out of the river. He walked down to the dock where he had tied his boat. It was his intention to return to the small boathouse he rented and collect a few items, stow his boat's rigging, secure the boat, and walk back to the train station.

There were two men waiting for him at his boat.

"Well, Demill, we were wondering if you had left town," the smaller of the two men said in the way of a greeting.

"I was gone for just one night, Sonier." Mike responded. Danton Sonier was Mike's landlord. Sonier charged Mike two dollars a month rent for the one room hovel over the boat shed. Sonier was a squat man with rolls of fat under his chin. He had dark eyes that darted about, never looking anyone in the eye during a conversation.

"I have come to pay you one month's rent in advance as I may be away for a few days." Mike began to dig into his pocket. The man with Sonier snorted derisively.

"Keep your money," the second man said.

"What business is it of yours?" Mike asked. The second man was tall, wide, and heavily muscled. He had a full red beard, bushy eyebrows and dark, nearly black eyes which contrasted starkly with his red hair and ruddy complexion. He wore bibbed overalls tucked into tall, rubberized boots and had the large, calloused hands of a deck worker.

"It is my business because I have rented the boathouse."

"Do you have a name?"

"I do," the man said as he crossed his arms, flexing his huge biceps.

Mike smiled, "Would you do me the honor of disclosing that name to me?"

"Folks call me Captain McDae. I am master of the *Isle of Hvar*, one of Mr. Donavich's fleet."

Mike shrugged a gesture of dismissal and turned back to the smaller man.

"Sonier, I have two weeks left on the rent I have already paid."

"Here," McDae snarled as he flipped a silver dollar to Mike. "You have been paid off, now get."

Mike deftly snatched the dollar from the air and slipped it into his pocket. The move caused his coat to open slightly and McDae saw the butt of the .45.

"Pull that hog leg, Demill, and I will crush your head before you can clear your coat."

"Such a thought never crossed my mind," Mike lied. "If I am to be without a place to live on this canal, perhaps I can interest you gentlemen into purchasing a boat, lateen-rigged with a fine set of hand dredges."

"Take your boat off this canal," McDae said, "or eat it. I care not. It is a boat for a loner, a poacher."

"Five dollars? You could tow it behind the *Isle of Hvar* and use it to reach the best number ones. Although, it does require work." Mike glanced at Sonier, "Takes a real man, you see."

McDae bristled, unfolded his arms, and clenched his ham-sized hands. "You better go while you can, boy."

Mike raised his hands and stepped back. Sensing a fight, a crowd had gathered around the three men. Mike kept his hands up, lest McDae could claim he was going for his pistol. Looking around, he recognized one of the men in the small circle of onlookers.

"How are you doing, Francis?" he said.

"To tell the truth, Mike, somewhat better than you, at the moment."

Mike switched to French, hoping that McDae was ignorant of the language. "Francis, I give you my boat and all the rigging aboard her."

"Why would you do that, Michael?" Francis answered.

"Because, when I finish here, I will not be welcomed back."

"I accept your gift. I will pay you the five dollars when I can."

"Good. Now, when I run, shout 'after him' in English."

Mike suddenly bolted toward the train station.

"After him!" Francis shouted.

Instinctively, McDae rushed after Mike, arms wide and screaming obscenities. Mike pretended to stumble, allowing McDae to gain ground rapidly. Just as the man reached him, Mike grabbed an oar that had been laying on the ground, braced one end against the steps and raised the other end to meet the charging McDae in the stomach.

McDae expelled a great "Umph!' The oar snapped cleanly into two pieces and McDae fell to his knees. Mike swung what remained of the oar into McDae's face, and the man crumpled to the ground. The crowd caught up to the action in time to see McDae roll over onto his back, gasping for air.

"Donavich is going to see you answer for this," Sonier said.

"McDae started it," someone shouted.

"Yea, he had it coming," said another.

"Gentlemen," Mike said, raising his hands to quiet the spectators. "I have given Francis my boat and I am square with Sonier, here. If Donavich wants to continue this, tell him to meet me in Saint Louis."

The train whistle gave a last warning toot. Mike sprinted to the landing, jumped aboard, and tossed a dime to the conductor. He looked back at the dock to see men milling about, talking and gesticulating. He saw Francis climb aboard the small boat and begin to scull away from the crowd.

Mike moved forward in the coach and chose a seat across from a frowning woman.

"I saw what you did, young man," she admonished. "I do not recognize you as someone from here. You are just a ruffian and not welcomed here."

"Yes, ma'am," Mike said, tipping his bowler, which had somehow managed to stay on his head throughout the ruckus.

*****

Mike appeared at The Marigny Street wharf at five-thirty. He carried a single satchel containing all his worldly possessions and a tightly wrapped package that Moreno had sent to him at the hotel. He planned to buy two more suits in Havana. Even this early, there were people queuing at the foot of the gangway. The dock steward was positioned behind a kiosk where he booked passengers aboard.

Mike stepped up, following a couple with three small children, two asleep in arms and one holding her mother's skirt, who had been boarded. The steward held out his hand.

"Ticket, please," he said.

Mike unfolded the document and held it toward the man.

"Name?"

"Josef Rodriguez," Mike answered.

The steward referred to the ticket then checked the name "J. Rodriguez" in a logbook.

"Welcome to the liner *Ariel, Señor* Rodriguez." The man stamped the paper, folded it, and offered it to Mike.

"Will you require any assistance with luggage?"

"I travel light," Mike answered in Spanish, lifting his satchel for the man to see. He could feel the package, a tight cube about six inches on each side, bounce against his leg when he lowered the satchel. The messenger had not disclosed the contents of the package to Mike.

"Next," the steward said in way of an answer.

The steamer *Ariel* would have proven to be as advertised had this trip taken place during the 1890s. She sported very modern accommodations for twenty years ago. Each berth (Mike was grateful he had not been booked into steerage) was provided with a single high-railed bunk, a locker large enough for a half-dozen suits, a dresser, a desk, and chair. There was a single overhead light operated by a dial next to the door. A lavatory and a commode were tucked in a curtained alcove. If one closed the curtain, use of both would be in the dark. A single porthole, no more than ten inches in diameter, adorned the bulkhead over the desk. There were showers down the passageway shared by only a dozen berths.

Mike chuckled to himself. The last time he had been on a steamship he had been accompanied by seven hundred men. The facilities for hygiene consisted of facing rows of sinks, twenty to a row, two sets of rows for each deck and three decks for the enlisted. The men shaved or brushed their teeth in platoons. Toilets were in similarly facing rows and most of the daily gossip occurred as men sat facing each other knee to knee. Privacy was non-existent. There were no showers for the enlisted men.

He placed his satchel on the bunk and peered out of the grimy porthole. All he could see were the rooftops of warehouses. He adjusted the .45 tucked in the small of his back and left the berth. The lock to the berth accepted a large iron key that appeared to have only two simple-looking bits. Mike was certain it would require little skill to pick such a lock.

On deck, Mike worked his way to a section of the side rail shadowed by a support structure where he could observe the crowd of well-wishers ashore. Passengers waved and called out to friends and relatives who returned the gestures. He examined the smiling faces and found nothing unusual.

He was about to turn away when he noticed one man partly concealed behind a lamppost who had his hands tucked into his coat and seemed to be scanning the rows of passengers with great interest. Mike moved further into cover, removed his bowler, and studied the man intently.

A whistle sounded causing several aboard and ashore to start. Fore and aft lines were hauled aboard, and the *Ariel* pulled away from the dock stern-first, engines in reverse. Smoke blanketed the passengers and the ship shuttered as power was added to the screws until a hundred yards or more separated the bow from the dock.

Mike could hear the ding of the telegraph as the pilot called for "all stop." A tug appeared and pushed gently against the bow until the ship was pointed downstream. The tug retreated, the pilot's telegraph chimed again, and the *Ariel* surged forward, bound for the mouth of the Mississippi River and then Havana.

*****

They reached the mouth of the river at noon. All the passengers of the upper deck had gathered at the common dining room for lunch. Those jammed in steerage were not served from the ship's mess but had to get by on what they had carried aboard. The run to Havana would only require another day and a half. The seas and winds were light, so, according to the ship's steward, they should see the coast of Cuba before the dinner hour on Monday, the 19th of December.

A deckhand leaned into the dining area and announced that they were officially leaving the river. Many passengers left their places and lined the rail to watch the last bit of Louisiana slip away. A boat came along side to pluck the river pilot from the ship. Once the pilot boat cleared the ship's side the *Ariel* laid on more steam until the decks vibrated and she was doing twenty knots or more. The low, marshy coastline quickly disappeared astern, and people returned to the dining room.

There were thirty-two passengers gathered for lunch, not counting some children. The menu was varied. One could have pork chops with potatoes or pork chops without potatoes. There was water to drink and, as soon as they were three miles out, beer and whiskey was available at sobering prices.

Mike added a beer to his order and was eventually served a room temperature mug of swill. The art of beer making was falling onto hard times, at least at sea. He put the half-full mug next to his plate and forced himself to swallow.

Three young women sat across the table from Mike, and they giggled, their heads together. Clearly amused by Mike's expression, one asked, "Don't like the beer?" Her English betrayed her as an American from the mid-west, probably from Chicago. Most of the other passengers were Cubans returning from or going to visit relatives or business associates.

The speaker was dark-haired, perhaps twenty with fair complexion and a thin figure. She had high cheekbones, slightly round face, and hazel eyes. She was quite attractive, as were her friends, despite their figure-suppressing wardrobes.

All three wore the new tight-fitting tasseled dresses and round, thin-brimmed hats that were becoming popular. The ladies were about the same age, chatted incessantly and made a big show of smoking cigarettes stuck into long holders. Clearly three friends on holiday and daring an adventure to Cuba.

Why had they chosen this second-rate steamer instead of one of the swanky American ships that regularly carried shiploads of Americans between Cuba and New Orleans intent upon enjoying entertainment and legal, quality drinking? The fact that they had addressed a perfect stranger demonstrated an inclination toward reckless independence.

"I have bailed better tasting water from the bottom of my boat," Mike said in English. "I have decided to join the temperance movement, at least until we land in Havana."

This induced a round of giggles from the ladies.

"My name is Annie," the dark-haired girl said, extending her hand across the narrow table. She tilted her head toward the blond on her left, "She's Summer and," her head kicked right toward the brunet, "and this one is April."

"I'm Josef," Mike said, standing to shake hands. He had almost forgotten to use his alias. "A seasonal pleasure to meet you all."

"You mean 'singular,' don't you?" April said.

Annie and Summer laughed. April flicked the ashes from the tip of her cigarette in a way she hoped showed sophistication. "I get it," she snarled.

"Your accent, are you French?" Annie continued.

Mike had grown up using French, his mother's preferred language. He spoke Spanish with his father and most others in their little fishing village on Bayou La Loutre. As a result, the English he learned during his time in New Orleans reflected a hint of his mother's French. His Spanish, on the other hand, was perfectly accented *Isleño* and nearly identical to the Spanish spoken in Cuba.

"You are most perceptive. I am but recently in America from Verdun." He omitted the detail that his time spent in Verdun was along, and across, the Meuse River as an infantry soldier assigned to the American 11th Infantry Regiment.

"Oh my," Annie said, her hand to her mouth. "How has your city fared?"

"It is rubble, and I am here."

"Were you in the war?"

"I will make a guess and say you all are from Chicago," Mike said. Annie perceived that he was changing the subject.

"Close enough," Annie laughed. "Cicero. It is like Chicago, just more sophisticated."

"And why would three ladies from Cicero travel to Cuba on a second-rate bucket? The Havana lines cater toward such sophisticated Americans."

"We wanted to see the real Cuba," Summer said. "The American hotels in Havana could just as well be in New York, except the booze is better."

"If the real Cuba is what you desire, how is your Spanish?" Mike noticed the question solicited a round of embarrassed expressions.

"*Puedo hablaba Espinol*," April said.

"Nearly," Mike smiled. "Perhaps you should hire an interpreter, I do not think your version of Spanish is spoken in Cuba."

"Well then, how is your Spanish, *Monsieur*?" April said, somewhat testily.

"*Puedo hablar Español como un Cubano*," Mike answered.

"You're hired!" Annie exclaimed!

"No, I have other business in Cuba. I suggest you ladies go to the Hotel American, enjoy your visit safely and forget about 'seeing the real Cuba' idea. Or at the very least, hire a guide recommended by the hotel."

"There is no fun in that," Summer said with a theatrical pout.

"There is no fun being bound, gagged and tossed on a slow boat to Arabia either." Mike said.

"You exaggerate the dangers, Josef. This is the Twentieth Century," Annie said. "You sound like my father. We can take care of ourselves." Annie turned to her friends. "Let's go to the bow, ladies." She tugged on her companions. "We can feel the wind in our hair and freedom."

The ladies filed out; Annie last. She glared at Mike as she stepped through the door. "Goodbye, *Monsieur* Josef," she said.

Mike shook his head. Until now, he had not given much thought to how the change in fashion and women's suffrage had produced a sort of reckless wildness among some young women. It was as if there were no longer any restraints at all. Three young ladies exploring Havana without an escort was, to his mind, courting disaster.

*****

It was two in the afternoon when the *Ariel* was warped into her berth in Havana. Mike tarried in his cabin until all the other passengers had joined the queue at the gangway. When he stepped into the rear of the line, he noticed Annie and her friends were already on the landing where they were being questioned by the dock steward. Stacks of luggage had been piled near the steward's kiosk where cab drivers and porters awaited to assist passengers.

They will require the services of two cabs, Mike thought. Most of the cabs for hire were horse-drawn carriages or open wagons. There were a few Ford Model T's modified with racks attached to the rear to accommodate luggage.

Mike watched as Annie directed stacks of luggage toward a wagon and, with exaggerated gesticulation and the uncertain help of April, directed the driver to follow a motor cab. The ladies piled into the Model T and the cab began to work its way through the congestion at the dock followed by the wagon. Mike hoped they would follow his advice.

The rest of the upper deck passengers had been processed through the dock steward's station, followed by those who had passed in steerage before Mike stepped into the last place in line. Those in line in front of Mike looked at him curiously as they did not recognize him. Everyone in steerage had become well acquainted, even on such a short trip.

"I think you no here," the dock steward said in broken English. "Rodriguez on list, no come out."

"I delayed so that we could talk," Mike answered in Spanish.

The steward, visibly relieved at not having to use English, said, "I am called Lucas. I will finish my logbook and return it to the office. Meet me at the cab." He tilted his head toward the lone horse-drawn cab on the dock. It was one of those London-type cabs where the driver rode on an exterior exposed seat above the enclosed passenger's cab.

Mike, carrying his single satchel, walked to the driver who was watering the horse. The driver looked up inquisitively.

"Lucas and I will be your fare," Mike said.

"*Señor*, please climb in," the driver said as he scurried to open the cab door. A burly man occupied the rear-facing seat. Mike's hand went to the .45 at the small of his back.

"*Monsieur*, there is no need for that," the man said in French as he flipped the coattail from his lap to expose a pistol pointed at Mike. "Step up. I will holster my revolver once you are seated. We will wait for Lucas. Our conversations will be in French. I am advised you are comfortable in French. Lucas and our driver here," he gestured with the pistol, "are pitifully ignorant."

Mike climbed up into the cab and took the forward-facing seat opposite the Frenchman, who returned the revolver to a holster inside of his coat. Mike pushed over until he was against the shuttered window to make room for Lucas. Should Lucas accompany them, Mike would need to share his seat, for the Frenchman was huge and spread across the rear facing seat.

The cab rocked, and Lucas clambered aboard. He sat next to Mike as the driver poked his head into the doorway.

"We go," Lucas said.

"Yes, sir,"

The driver closed the door, twisted the latch and the cab rocked again as the driver ascended to his seat. The Frenchman turned aside slightly and pulled back a sliding panel which revealed the back of the driver's boots.

"*Castillo de Malecón*," he said. He closed the port before the driver could answer.

Lucas cleared his throat, "*Señor* Josef Rodriguez, it is my pleasure to introduce you to *Don* Philippe Dugas."

Dugas extended his hand. "My pleasure, *Señor* Rodriguez," he said with a smile.

Mike shook Dugas' hand. "My pleasure, *Don* Philippe Dugas."

Dugas opened the small port once more. "Stop," he called out to the pair of boots. The cab shuttered to a stop and the driver climbed down and opened the door. "What is the matter?"

"*Señor* Lucas needs to get down here," Dugas said. Lucas paused for only a moment before struggling through the door past a curious driver. They had stopped in the heart of the city. Once on the street, Lucas turned to face Dugas. "Good night, *Don* Philippe."

"Good night, my friend," Dugas said. "Drive on." This last was snapped at the driver, who jerked into action, closed the door, and clambered up to his station. The driver whistled and slapped the reins. The cab lurched into motion.

"You may call me Philippe. I am not a *Don*. May I call you Michael?"

"Simply Mike will do."

"Good," Dugas grunted with a slight chuckle. "There should be no formalities between coworkers, do you not agree?"

Mike tried to place the accent and decided Philippe Dugas was a Parisian.

"Is that what we are?"

"Clearly, as far as this transaction is concerned. Once we arrive at the *Castillo de Malecón*, I will explain the full extent of our working relationship. You do have the package Moreno sent?"

Mike reflexively placed his hand on his satchel, cursed himself for being so easily drawn out, and replied. "I have it."

"Did you count it?"

"I have not opened the package."

Dugas smiled. "Moreno assured me you were worthy of my trust. You did not succumb to curiosity. That is good. I find that an inquisitive nature can be dangerous in our line of work."

"I have been sent to be observant, not curious."

"Indeed, Mike. Succinctly put." Dugas placed an envelope in Mike's hands. "Peruse these papers. They convey a business arrangement between our employers. You may open the window curtain now that we are away from the port. We have a quarter hour of travel time remaining. I suggest you familiarize yourself with the particulars."

Mike pulled the chord to raise the window curtain, slit the envelope open and removed a single sheet of legal-sized paper. Leaning toward the light, he began to read. The figures "$25,000.00" and "1,000 cases" seemed to leap from the paper.

CHAPTER 3

The *Castillo de Malecón* proved to be a walled hacienda situated on the western bank of a small river named the Almendares. The driver directed his horse along the narrow road that meandered between the river on the right and the *Castillo* on the left. The road made a sharp turn to the west, and the river was replaced by the wide expanse of the Gulf of Mexico.

The tall stucco-covered windowless walls met at guard stations on the corners and dominated the western point of the tiny bay that was the mouth of the *Río* Almendares. In the distance, about a mile or more across the river, Mike could see the silhouette of an ancient signal tower, serving as a beacon for the forts bracketing the entrance to Port Havana.

The driver stopped the cab at the only opening in the wall, tall double solid timber doors with a pedestrian entrance set in the right gate. The cab rocked as the driver jumped down and opened the cab door, placed a small box at the bottom of the last step and moved back to allow the passengers to climb down.

Dugas nodded for Mike to exit first. After reaching the ground, Mike moved aside to allow Dugas room. The driver offered Dugas a hand, which was accepted, and the huge man maneuvered the two steps required to get down. He grunted with the effort required to reach the ground from the box. The light was fading, but enough remained for Mike to make an assessment of Dugas that was not possible in the darkened, cramped cab.

Rising to his full height, Dugas had to have been over six and a half feet tall, powerfully built and weighing well over two hundred-fifty pounds. The man wore a wide-brimmed black fedora pulled low. The collars of his overcoat were turned up, though the weather was only slightly cool. A full, dark beard concealed what Mike assumed were heavy jowls. Dugas' dark, tiny eyes seemed alert and deeply perceptive as they peered out from under the fedora's brim.

A noise behind him caused Mike to turn. The pedestrian door in the right gate creaked open and a slender man in a butler's uniform stepped out. He looked at Mike and Dugas and inquisitively raised an eyebrow.

Dugas spoke in Spanish, "Good afternoon, Esteban. I am here with Miguel Demill to see *El Señor* Sebastian O'Neil y Madrid," as he brushed and straightened his overcoat.

"You are expected," the servant said as he stepped aside. "Good afternoon, Señor Dugas. It is good to see you well. Please come in and I will bring you to *El Señor* O'Neil."

Mike entered the pedestrian door after Dugas and both men paused a moment while Esteban followed them in, closed the door and moved across the courtyard, motioning the pair to follow.

The courtyard was over one hundred feet wide, separating the high wall from the house, with gardens, fruit trees, a fountain, and stone walkways. Mike could see that the wall had an encircling walkway between guard posts, forming a fortress-like parapet accessed by stairways at the corners.

Esteban led them along a winding stone path bordered by ponds to a recessed doorway. Wrought iron gates covered the double entrance doors recessed a dozen feet into the house. There were small slits on either side of the recess. Mike glanced up to see more slits in the ceiling. *Murder holes*, Mike thought. This place was built to withstand the assault of an army.

The inner doors were pulled open by a maid, and Esteban opened the iron gates. The maid withdrew a few steps, her head bowed as Esteban shepherded the guests into the house.

Dugas removed his hat and overcoat and Mike, having no overcoat, only removed his bowler. Esteban took the hats and coat and reached for the satchel, but Mike pulled it back with a shake of his head. Esteban handed the hats and coat to the maid, who scurried away with them to another room.

Esteban pointed to a bristly pad next to the door. "Gentlemen, please wipe your shoes." Dugas and Mike complied by scraping their shoes on the pad and stomping their feet.

Evidently satisfied with the effort, Esteban said, "Please follow me to the library. *El Señor* O'Neil will see you now." He led them along a hallway divided on either side by matching pairs of varnished oak doors. The floor was paved with marble tiles, and busts or figurines adorned pedestals along walls hung with oil portraits. Stopping at the doors in the right wall, Esteban rapped a knocker, opened one door, and announced, "Phillipe Dugas and Miguel Demill, *El Señor* O'Neil."

"Come," said a voice from within the room.

"Gentlemen," Esteban said as he stepped back and indicated the men should precede him into the room. Once

Dugas and Mike were in the room, Esteban remained in the hall and closed the door.

"Welcome to my home." A tall, slender man, perhaps thirty years old, stood from behind his desk. "Please, come in, sit."

The room was enormous. Bookshelves lined three walls from the floor to the ceiling. A well-worn step ladder on casters occupied one corner, an indication that the books were not simply for decoration. Behind the desk a wide picture window dominated the fourth wall, providing a view of an elaborate garden. A fountain sending a cascade of water down a stone-lined stream was centered on the garden. Mike could see iron rails along the window frame beyond the glass. He was certain this was to guide a steel shield that could be lowered to protect the window should the need arise.

El Señor O'Neil walked from behind the desk to offer his hand to his visitors. He concentrated his greetings toward Mike. The man had a significant limp and a clearly misshapen right leg. His smile seemed sincere as he guided Mike to one of the two large captain's chairs facing the desk. He nodded for Dugas to take the other chair.

O'Neil wore a frilled shirt and tight trousers tucked into fine polished, knee-high boots. A large silver buckle was centered on his narrow waist and he sported a jet-black moustache and goatee. Mike thought the man a caricature of a Spanish nobleman, until he noticed one of the pictures on the wall.

It was a framed billboard promoting a bull fight. The stylized painting was of a charging bull in a shower of roses, brushing past a man in a suit of lights. Above the scene were the words "Today, in Plaza de Toros de la Real Maestranzade Caballería de Sevilla" and below "We proudly present El Señor

Sebastian O'Neil y Madrid." The poster was dated September 15, 1919.

O'Neil noticed Mike's interest in the poster. "A lifetime ago, I think. Now, please sit down. *Señor* Demill, no need for introductions. I have a complete dossier on you. We have much to discuss." O'Neil returned to his place behind the desk and sat, adjusting papers and an elaborate pen set as Dugas struggled into the captain's chair and Mike sat, placing the satchel on his lap.

"May I address you as 'Mike?' I understand that is a common nickname for 'Miguel' in the American language." O'Neil's Spanish was perfectly accented Castilian.

"If it should please *El Señor*," Mike answered.

"Good. If we are to be business associates, there should be trust. Is that not so?"

"I am in the employ of Manuel Moreno. Does that make us business associates?"

"Ah! You see, Phillipe? Mike makes no promises quickly. It has been my observation that a man who is reluctant to embrace every new commitment is a man who values his word."

"Yes, I can see that, *Don* Sebastian," Dugas answered in a bored tone.

O'Neil smiled at Mike. "My friend and associate here thinks I am too quick to trust you. *Don* Moreno sent you and I value his judgment. Please address me by my Christian name."

"Yes, Sebastian," Mike said.

"*Don* Sebastian," Dugas corrected.

"Yes, *Don* Sebastian."

"The formalities are done," O'Neil said. "Let us get to business. Have you had an opportunity to read the instructions Phillipe gave you when you met?"

"I have, *Don* Sebastian."

"Do you recognize the hand?"

"Yes, *Don* Sebastian. The note was written by Manuel Moreno."

"Good. Now first, according to our agreement, please present me with the – compensation."

Mike opened his satchel, moved some clothes aside, removed the tightly cord-wrapped bundle and placed it on the center of the desk with an audible "thump." He began to untie the knot for one of the cords when O'Neil slid a dagger across the table, butt first.

"This was crafted in Toledo from the remains of my sword, broken in my last fight."

Mike caught the handle and slipped the blade under the cord, which parted without much effort. The second cord parted as easily, and Mike rolled the bundle free of the butcher paper, which proved to be only the exterior wrapping. The inner wrapping was of white cloth, folded and sealed with red wax bearing the impression of an American silver dollar.

"What is the year on the seal?" O'Neil asked.

Mike squinted and read the reversed date. "It appears to be '1898.'"

Mike tried to remove the cloth without breaking the seal. This proved to be impossible. The seal fractured, and where it was pulled from the cloth it left a red stain.

"A seal on cloth cannot be sweated away as is possible on paper," O'Neil commented. Mike was not certain what constituted "sweating away" a seal. He continued to unroll the cloth until bundles of twenty-dollar bills spilled onto the table. He counted twenty-five packs of bills. The paper strapping for the packets were labeled as "$1,000" and "First National Bank of Illinois."

"Excellent," O'Neil said. "Phillipe, please accept the compensation."

Dugas produced a cloth sack. He thumbed each packet, ensuring that all were the correct denomination, placed the strapped bills into the sack and pulled the opening closed. He nodded to O'Neil.

"Now, Mike, my product." O'Neil opened a drawer and withdrew a folder. He handed it to Mike who opened it to reveal heavy-stock papers within. He spread the five separate papers onto the desk. Each paper carried the letter head of the Cuban Ministry of Commerce, with official-looking seals and signatures in the lower left corner.

"Those are export grants, Mike. Each is for two hundred cases of rum. A case of rum is six, two-liter bottles. That is twelve thousand liters of *Toro Negro*, the finest rum in the world. A bargain if you were to buy the rum at our distillery in Artemisa at twice the price and before paying export duties."

A little over two dollars a liter was less than a bargain price, but once in Louisiana, the rum would be worth five dollars or more a liter to upper-class downtown speakeasies and likely ten dollars to Garden District swells. Swanky customers would pay a dollar a shot and be glad to have it over the swill spilling from most backroom establishments where the whisky offered was so vile it had to be mixed with citrus juices into "cocktails" to become palatable.

From distillery to barkeep, everyone was going to make a great profit. Mike tried to estimate his cut of the transaction, but it made his head swim. He collected the documents and placed them back into the folder.

"Phillipe will bring you to your property, so you can inspect the shipment." O'Neil stood, walked to a cabinet, and took out a large bottle. He handed it to Mike. "Here is a two-liter sample of our rum. My gift to you. It is identical to the bottles that will be turned over to you."

Mike accepted the bottle and examined the label. It pictured a black bull on a red field, its head tossed high and one fore hoof on a broken sword. Included in the labeling were the words "Two quarts of Cuba's finest rum."

Mike glanced up at O'Neil who chuckled. "Our American label. A liter - a quart the difference is about five per cent." Mike shrugged. He was not interested in labeling. He placed the bottle in his satchel.

O'Neil walked around his desk and offered his hand to Mike. "I believe this concludes our business. It has been my great pleasure to meet you. Phillipe, inform Esteban to bring you both to *La Abeja*. There you will allow Mike to inspect the cargo to his satisfaction. Explain the transfer arrangements and have me informed if there is any problem."

"I have one question, *Don* Sebastian," Mike said as they walked to the door of the library.

"Of course. Your question?"

"In previous transactions with Manuel Moreno, who dealt with you?"

"Ah, yes. *Señor* Moreno and my father, and now myself have been transporting beverages from Cuba to Louisiana for a dozen years or so. Long before the foolish Prohibition. The profits were small before Prohibition, for we only avoided the taxes on the products.

"The man who filled the role you have now was Juan Pena. Last year an ally of one of *Señor* Moreno's competitors was elected to a local government post, District Attorney I think it is called. Pena's son was involved in a brawl at a speakeasy. A man was killed and the District Attorney, Ira Roberts, told Pena he would not prosecute the son if Pena turned over a shipment to this competitor.

"What father would not comply? Pena could never be trusted again. Roberts could charge Pena's son at any time so now he owns the man. *Señor* Moreno decided he would recruit a *solitario* as a replacement."

*****

Esteban led Dugas and Mike through a back gate and across the road between the hacienda and the river onto a long pier that jutted out into the *Río* Almendares, ending in a wide dock. A coastal patrol boat with the name *La Abeja* across the stern was moored on the down-river side of the dock, which was piled high with crates.

Mike examined the boat. He had never seen anything like it. "Esteban, what sort of boat is *La Abeja?*"

"Ah, *Señor* Demill," Esteban smiled with obvious pride. "She had been an Italian torpedo boat during the Great War, what the Italians called an MTB. *El Señor* O'Neil acquired her as surplus. She has been refitted for our special needs. The torpedo launchers and a deck gun were removed, and cargo spaces introduced. She is very fast, very fast."

"Are those gun mounts I see?"

"You are most observant. We carry three of the new American anti-aircraft guns - I think they are call 'fifties' – the captain will only have them mounted if needed. The machine guns give her a sting. That is why she is named 'The Bee.' I will introduce you to her master, Captain Solis. That is him, directing the loading of the cargo."

Captain Solis was a wide, squat man. He wore matching khaki long sleeved shirt and trousers tucked into over-sized rubber boots. A weathered black coat with gold-striped epaulets hung on a post next to the Captain. A black service cap with gold and blue piping was pushed down firmly on the man's head with wisps of exposed white hair.

"The Captain commanded a Cuban coastal patrol boat during the Communist rebellion in '16 until well after the Americans sent their Marines to protect the sugar plantations. But two years ago, Captain Solis had a - uh – disagreement with a Marine officer. The American was sent to the hospital and Captain Solis was removed from the Cuban navy. Since then, he has been in the continual service of *El Señor* O'Neil."

Solis was directing deck hands in the placement of wooden cases onto cargo nets that were spread out on the wharf next to *La Abeja*. Three separate nets were arranged to receive the cases of rum, and men were transferring the cases from a large stockpile to places on the netting.

"Captain Solis," Esteban hailed as they approached the man, who was concentrating on the loading, and barking commands to the workers. "Captain, may I introduce you to the shepherd for this cargo?"

Solis turned a weathered face toward Mike. Heavily tanned with squint-lines radiating out from the corners of large brown eyes, he stepped forward and offered his hand. "José Solis, at your service, *Señor.*"

Mike took the offered hand, as calloused and weathered from a life at sea as his own. "Michael Demill, Mike to my friends. A great pleasure to meet you."

"Are you Cuban, *Señor* Demill?" Solis asked. "Your accent says so."

"No, I am an *Isleño* from Louisiana. Please address me as 'Mike.'"

"Mike, would you like to inspect the cargo before I have it hoisted aboard?"

"Yes, please."

Solis stepped aside and waved his hand. "Then do so, Mike."

Mike set the satchel at his feet and withdrew the bottle of rum O'Neil had given him. He walked to the stockpile and pointed to a case under several others. "May I have this case opened?"

Solis ordered some hands to remove the top cases and place them on the cargo net to expose the case Mike had indicated. Another series of orders and the top was pried off the case, revealing the tops of six bottles padded with straw.

Mike removed one of the bottles, noted it was identical in every detail with the one O'Neil had given him, down to the fake tax stamp seal covering the knobbed cork stopper. The tax stamp was a leftover from the time rum was legal in the United States and smuggling was simply a way to avoid taxes.

Mike placed the bottle from his satchel into the case. "Captain, please have the case closed."

While a deckhand insured the case was properly closed, Mike broke the counterfeit stamp and pulled the cork. He took a draw on the bottle and swished the rum around in his mouth. Having never had the need to evaluate rum before, Mike performed the actions as if it were his profession.

The rum burned as he swallowed and the fumes from it flowed out of his nostrils. It was indeed very smooth, fine tasting and high proof. Much superior to the homemade rum with which he was familiar.

"*¡Estupendo!*" Mike exclaimed.

Dugas laughed, "We knew it to be so. You will have clients clambering for more. Captain Solis, now that Mike has approved your cargo, please resume loading."

Mike returned to the group and offered his hand. "A great pleasure to meet you, Captain Solis. I look forward to working with you."

"As do I," Solis said, accepting Mike's hand, and clicking the heels of his rubber boots."

"Come, Mike," Dugas said. "We must review the details of the shipping arrangements." He led Mike to a small building at the corner of the wharf and dismissed Esteban before stepping inside with Mike. The building was a one room affair with a central table supporting a single burning kerosene lamp, four chairs, and waist-high, pigeonhole cabinets all around. Banks of windows provided unobstructed views in every direction. Dugas pulled a chart from one of the pigeonholes and spread it out on the table.

"This is the Havana harbor, our location, and these are the coastal beacons we will be using." Dugas indicated symbols on a chart of the northwest coast of Cuba.

Mike was to return to Havana and take a room reserved for Robert Stone at the Hotel Americana. At 1:00 a.m. in the morning, December 21st, two nights hence, he was to go to the Jesus Maria wharf and board the Portuguese-flagged coastal steamer *Garanhão do Mar*. There he would present documents to the ship's Captain, Alfonso Peres, detailing the rendezvous with *La Abeja*.

Three miles off the mouth of the *Rio* Almendares, when the magnetic bearings to three coastal lights coincided and well within sight of the towers at the O'Neil hacienda, they would stop and wait for the *La Abeja*. Peres would use the on-board cranes of the *Garanhã* to bring aboard three cargo nets of cases from *La Abeja*. Mike could inspect the cases as he saw fit as they were secured on deck.

The *Garanhã* would then steam to a point between Horn Island, Mississippi and Hewes Point of the Chandeleur Islands, Louisiana. Another set of coastal light bearings would be matched to a location well out of the shipping lanes. The *Garanhã* would stop engines and wait for three shrimp boats.

Cargo would be transferred to the boats, each receiving five tons. Mike would transfer to one of the boats, the *Captain Robin,* and the *Garanhã* would steam away to the south. Once aboard the *Captain Robin*, the business with *El Señor* O'Neil would be concluded.

At eight p.m., a motor cab stopped at the foot of the pier. There were no lights about, save that of the cab's driving lights and a sliver of a moon. The driver climbed out, walked to the passenger door, and looked about expectantly.

"Your transportation has arrived," Dugas said. "Let us not keep the man waiting." He gave Mike a leather document case, pulled the lamp from the table and walked with him to the cab. The driver opened the door and offered to take the case. Mike shook his head, transferred the case to his left hand and offered his right.

"A pleasure doing business with you, *Don* Phillipe."

"And with you, Robert Stone," Dugas said. Mike realized the alias just given him needed to be confirmed by the driver. "I look forward to continuing our profitable enterprise."

Mike climbed into the cab and Dugas slipped several coins into the driver hand and said, "Hotel Americana."

The driver nodded, pocketed the coins without counting, slipped into the driver's seat and executed a tight U-turn. They bounded and puttered along the river road only slightly faster than the horse-drawn cab had managed coming to the hacienda.

"*¿Habla Español?*" the driver shouted over his shoulder.

"No," Mike said.

*****

The cab dropped Mike at the front doors of the Hotel Americana. Two United States Marines with bayonetted Springfields bracketed the entrance. The doorman, assuming Mike was an American, spoke in an English that was only slightly accented.

"Welcome to the Hotel Americana, Sir. I am John. Let me take your bag."

"I can handle the bag. Why the guards?"

"Oh, a North American admiral is visiting the casino upstairs. May I have your name, Sir?"

"Robert Stone."

"Yes, Mister Stone. We were expecting you. Allow me to show you to the registration desk."

They strode through a wide lobby with cushioned chairs in various locations. Some were occupied by uniformed Marine officers, some by ladies dressed in the modern American style. The Marines had been sent to Cuba at the end of the Great War to help the new Cuban government put down a Communist-inspired rebellion in the east. The rebellion was successfully suppressed and the American forces in Cuba had been decreased to a few thousand Marines who guarded the embassy and American wharfs, and assisted sugar plantation owners in resisting small remnant rebel bands that had been reduced to common banditry.

Music and the raucous sounds of gamblers drifted down from the second floor, which was accessed by matching staircases on the left and the right. Mike could hear the clicking sounds of a marble seeking a slot in roulette wheels mixed in with the hum of activity. There was little laughter. It had been Mike's observation that few laughed in casinos.

The doorman escorted Mike to the front desk. "Mister Robert Stone is checking in."

The desk clerk increased his already wide smile. "Welcome Mister Stone. A room has been reserved for you." The clerk turned to a rack of letter drops behind him. He pulled a key and a thick envelope from the one labeled "300" and gave them to Mike. "Your room is number three hundred. It faces the street and has a balcony with a view of the bay. You go up the stairs to the casino, which is on our first floor, cross to a stairwell and continue up to the third floor. Your room will be on the right as you exit the stairwell. Our restaurant is on the ground floor, this floor, through the archway to my left. It will be open until midnight."

Mike had become accustomed to the European system of identifying floors by starting with the ground floor, the first floor and so on when he was in Paris before being sent to the trenches. Then came the wounds, hospitals, and confusing transfers across France. He did not fully recover from the bullet and shrapnel wounds for nearly two years. He still had a recurring cough, the result of his exposure to poison gas.

He glanced into the casino as he crossed to the stairwell. Mixed in with the crowd at a craps table were Annie, Summer and April, interspersed among well-dressed gentlemen with slicked-down hair and a Marine Lieutenant.

"Welcome to the real Cuba, Annie," he muttered to himself sarcastically. He paused to observe the ladies for a moment. The men were betting, and the ladies were watching, occasionally puffing on cigarettes in long holders. April and Summer were laughing, and Annie looked bored. Mike felt an unexpected pang of jealousy, shook it away, and continued up to his room.

Room 300 was a corner room with a balcony that wrapped around the west and north sides of the top floor. The room had a separate bathroom with running hot and cold water, including a bathtub. Mike marveled at the luxury. *This is the way to live*, he thought. No trips down the hall to a common bath.

He placed the .45 next to the sink. It had been days since he had a decent bath. He tested the water faucets, discovered hot after it ran a few minutes, and began to fill the tub. He retrieved a clean set of clothes and laid them out on the bed, stripped down and climbed into the tub.

Refreshed and dressed in clean clothes, Mike left the room and descended the stairs. He was quite hungry, thirsty, and thoroughly tired. He paused at the first-floor landing to glance in at the casino. He saw Annie and a Marine Captain chatting in a corner. Annie was sipping at a drink. The Captain set aside an empty glass and lifted a replacement.

It was only ten or so in the evening. He had been in Cuba for less than seven hours, yet it seemed as though he had arrived days ago. Mike continued down to the restaurant looking forward to a fine meal followed by a full night's sleep.

CHAPTER 4

Mike finished his meal of *Arroz con ropa vieja*. It was the simplest dish on the elaborate menu, clearly created with vacationing North American swells in mind. The thick gravy from the shredded beef was a perfect combination for the steamed brown rice. The robust red wine suggested by the waiter was just right. He had the feeling that Manuel Moreno had recruited him into a version of the importing business that would suit him just fine.

He had taken his time with the dinner. It was nearing midnight and, save for himself, the restaurant was empty. He waved the waiter, who had been hovering hopefully nearby, over to pay the bill. Twenty dollars, by far the most he had ever paid for a meal, covered the bill with some left over for the waiter.

"Sorry to keep you waiting," Mike said in Spanish.

"*No, es nada, Señor.* Will there be anything else?"

"No," Mike said as he stood, surprised at how stiff he felt. "Good night."

"Good night, *Señor.*"

Mike climbed up the staircase to the first floor where the casino was still in full operation. He did not see Annie or any of her friends at the tables. He crossed to the stairwell and, feeling bone-tired, trudged up to the second-floor landing. He was rounding the landing to continue up to his floor when he was stopped by the sounds of argument in the hall to the north.

"I will not," said a muffled female voice. "Billy, let go of me now."

"You're coming with me," slurred a male voice, who Mike assumed was Billy.

"Please, let go of me now! I will not let you do this-,"

There was the sound of ripping cloth and Billy laughed drunkenly. "I will have to fix that," he said.

Mike stepped into the hallway and peered south. The view down the long hall alternated with gas-lit bright islands and dark stretches. He saw two figures struggling in the shadows. Before he could take another step, he heard a subdued "pop – pop" and the larger shadow slumped down against the wall. Mike ran forward and confronted Annie, a smoking derringer in her hand. Her make-up was streaked with tears, her face bruised, and her dress torn at one corner.

"Are you alright?' Mike asked.

"What? Josef? What are you doing here?'

"Never mind that. Are you hurt?"

"Only a little, I think." She looked down at the uniformed man lying against the wall. "Oh, God." Annie exclaimed. "Did I kill him?"

Mike knelt next to the man, felt for a pulse, and pulled open the uniform coat. "No. He has two bullet wounds in his right side. One just scraped the ribs and the other is so shallow I can feel the slug under his skin. He's not dead, just passed out drunk. His thick belt must have blocked the shots."

"What am I to do?" Annie asked. "We have to leave tomorrow to go back to New Orleans. I will be in prison. I don't know anyone here. I can't even speak Spanish."

Mike knew Annie was in a tight spot. Cuban authorities would not care how many foreigners shot each other, but the Marine Corps would insist on taking her into custody. Even if she were found to have acted in self-defense, it would be weeks and the hearing would be before a court of less than objective naval officers.

"Who knows you have a gun?"

"What? Why, no one."

"Not even your traveling companions?"

"No. They don't know. My dad said I should never advertise that I am armed."

"A wise man. Give me your gun," Mike said.

"Why," she asked as she place the pistol in Mike's hand. It was a tiny, two-barreled derringer, the kind commonly called belly-busters. The belly-buster was .22 caliber, easily concealed and with no recoil, it was the kind of weapon a woman often carried for protection. She had fired both barrels.

"Do you have any cartridges?"

"Yes, a small box in my room."

"Go get them and bring them here."

Annie scurried away. Mike noticed she carried her shoes as she trotted away, her white cotton stockings flashing in the uncertain light.

Mike lifted Billy's hand, pried open the fingers and pulled out a piece of Annie's dress. He stuffed the rag in his pocket, put the derringer in Billy's hand, closed the fingers on the gun and tucked it under the Captain's coat. Billy groaned, gritted his teeth, and then began to snore. Annie came padding back with a half-full box of .22 rimfire cartridges.

Mike took the box and stuffed it into Billy's front pocket. He looked up and down the long hall. Amazingly, no one had appeared. Apparently, scuffles in the hall were not uncommon.

"Are Summer and April in your room?"

"Yes, both are asleep."

"Go to your room. Get dressed for bed. Nothing happened, understand? Billy dropped you at your door. That is all you know."

"What are you going to do, Josef?"

"I am going to get some of the Marines downstairs and tell them I found a drunken officer who had accidently shot himself. It is very important for you to remember this: Billy escorted you to your door and then left. He was very drunk. Nothing else, no gun, no argument, don't embellish anything."

"Why are you doing this?"

"When are you scheduled to leave?"

"Tomorrow afternoon. We have passage on the *Cuban Star* for New Orleans. We will then take the train back to Chicago and be home for Christmas." Annie put her hand to her lips and stifled a cry as she realized she might not ever see home again.

"Get up in the morning as if this never happened. Board that ship and get home."

"But why are you doing this?"

"Just get to your room before someone comes along."

Annie dashed back to her room, driven by the overpowering fear of being discovered. Mike watched her go. Why was he doing this? As far as any of the ladies knew he is Josef Rodriguez, a Frenchman from Verdun with a Spanish name. His exposure was minimal. Perhaps his concern stemmed from his experiences during the Great War where he witnessed abuses of the women trapped in combat areas. In the small towns, soldiers met the desperate widows of brave Frenchmen killed in the trenches, women forced to sell their bodies to survive.

Mike had used his fluency in French to take advantage of such desperate women. There was something about a young man facing death that stirred an overpowering need to lay with a woman. Guilt he had not felt at the time haunted him. He ran to the stairs and down to the casino.

Two other Marine officers, both Lieutenants and only moderately drunk, were still at the tables. Mike walked quickly up to them. "Lieutenants, I need to talk to you."

"What about, my good man?" slurred the shorter of the two.

"Marine business. Step over to the stair landing. It is important, and you will not want others to hear."

"Come on, Johnny," the officer said suspiciously. "Let us hear what this man has to say."

Both left the table. Evidently, they had no bets down. Carrying drinks in one hand and Mike between them, they escorted him to the stair landing. They stopped at the foot of the stairs up to the second floor, out of sight of the casino. The shorter officer, probably the ranking one, looked back to assure no one had followed.

"This better be important," he hissed. "If you are trying some trick, I warn you, we will pound you into the ground."

"Gentlemen, I am trying to save the Corps from some embarrassment," Mike said, holding up his hands innocently.

"What is it, man?" Johnny said, taking a sip from his glass. "Get on with it. I'm starting to sober up." Both men laughed.

"One of your officers, a captain, is upstairs lying in the hall."

"I told you Captain Frank would never get to his room with that girl," the shorter Lieutenant laughed as he poked Johnny with the hand that held his drink, slopping some of it onto the man's coat.

"Damnit, Jack. Mind your drink."

"Gentlemen," Mike whispered more loudly. "The captain has shot himself."

"What!" Jack said, suddenly quite sober. "The devil, you say. Shot himself! Show us."

"You lead," Jack said. He pushed Mike up the stairs and followed with Johnny close behind. "If this is some trick, you're dead."

They reached the second-floor hallway.

"This way," Mike said, pointing down the hall. When the officers saw Captain Billy Frank's large body, both dropped their drinks and rushed past Mike to kneel next to the man.

"He is alive!" Jack exclaimed as he put an ear to Billy's mouth. Jack rocked back, fanning his hand across his face. "Pooo! And drunk as a sailor."

"He isn't bleeding much. All I can find are these too little scratches on his side," Johnny said as he opened the captain's coat and examined the wounds. "And this." He opened Billy's hand and removed the derringer.

"Shit! Why would he have this little piece of fluff?" Although wearing their dress blues, all three of the Marine officers carried .45 pistols in white holsters at their sides. Cuba was still considered a combat zone and they had been there under the pretext of guarding the Admiral.

"What are we to do?" Johnny asked. "This will ruin Frank's career."

"Let's get him to the room. The Admiral won't be back and looking for us until noon. Maybe we can fix him up enough for him to stand muster then."

They managed to rouse Billy enough to get him to stand and each officer looped one of Billy's arms over a shoulder.

"Up an' at'm, boys," Billy mumbled.

"Thank God we only need to get him to the far end of the hall," Jack said. "He is as heavy as a barrel of rocks."

They had gone a few steps toward the opposite end of the hall from Annie's room when they paused, and Jack glared at Mike.

"What's your name?"

Mike had to think a bit. "Robert Stone."

"Not a word of this, boyo," he said. "Blab about what you found, and it will be a blanket party for you. Understand?"

"Not a word, sir," Mike responded. "You can count on me." Mike knew that a "blanket party" was barracks justice. The "party" consisted of several soldiers, in this case, marines, wrapping a miscreant in a blanket and beating the hell out of him.

He watched as the men lugged Billy down the hall and, after fumbling in the man's pockets for a room key, unlocked the last door on the left and half carried, half dragged him into the room. Jack stepped back out into the hall to pick up several small items from the floor. *Cartridges fallen from Billy's pocket when they dug for the keys*, Mike thought.

Mike turned and looked toward Annie's room. Satisfied that all was quiet, he went to the stairs and up to his room. With luck, the drunk would not remember what happened. If he did, it could be a problem. Perhaps, instead of helping Annie, he didn't even know her last name, he had gotten her into more trouble.

Mike undressed and climbed into bed. "Shit," he said, thinking he would never go to sleep, but he did.

*****

Pounding on the door startled Mike from a deep sleep. He had been dreaming of a treeless, pitted field. The Germans were "walking" an artillery barrage toward his position, a water-filled shell hole, each subsequent burst nearer to him than the last. The explosions were timed with the pounding on the door.

"Mister Stone," a voice called from beyond the door. "Mister Stone, some men are here with questions for you."

"What?" Mike shouted. "Give me a moment. What time is it?"

Somebody else beyond the door shouted. "This is Major Reston, United States Marines. We need to talk to you now. Come to the door or I'll have the clerk let me in."

"I'm coming, Major. Give me a moment to pull on some clothes."

"Be quick about it."

"Yes, sir. I'm dressing now."

Mike pulled on his trousers, a shirt, tucked his .45 under his belt behind his back and stumbled, shoeless to the door. He cracked it open to see a red-faced Major flanked by two sergeants. Lieutenants Jack and Johnny hung in the back against the far wall.

"Are you Mister Robert Stone?" asked a short, thin Marine Major who was blocking the doorway.

"I am."

"Did you find a wounded Marine Captain in the hall on the second-floor last night?"

"I did."

"Can we come in? We have some questions for you."

"Yes, come in." Mike backed away and sat in the only chair in the room, his back against the wall. Reston took a position directly in front of Mike. A Marine private with a pad and pencil stood to the Major's right, the sergeants wedged themselves to either side and the Lieutenants, lacking space in the now crowded room, leaned into the doorway.

"I am Marine Major Adam Reston. I am leading the investigation into the shooting of Marine Captain William Frank." Ruston, staring at Mike intently, paused for a response.

"Good morning, Major. Is the captain in good health?"

"He has had some difficulty communicating this morning. I want to hear what you have to say."

"Is he still drunk?"

Reston's face flushed. "Never mind that. I will be asking the questions."

"Sorry, sir."

"Did you find a Marine Captain lying wounded in the hall on the floor below?"

"Yes, sir."

"Tell me how it was you came to find him?"

"I had just finished supper in the restaurant downstairs. It was near midnight. I came up past the casino, crossed to the stairwell and was on my way up to this room. When I made the turn on the floor below, I heard two muffled popping sounds. I stepped into the hall and saw a man slumping against the wall."

"Was there anyone else there?"

"No, sir. Just the one man. Captain Frank, you say. Only I didn't know his name, I could see he was a Marine Captain."

"And then what did you do?"

"I went over to him and asked if he was alright."

"What did he say?"

"Nothing. He was unconscious."

"What did you do then?"

"Shook him, trying to wake him up. He stank of whiskey."

"Don't write that last thing down," Reston snarled at the clerk.

"I then saw that his coat was open, and I could just make out a trickle of blood," Mike continued. "Not much, just a trickle. Then, when I looked for a wound, I found a pistol in the captain's hand. Drunk as he was, he must have shot himself accidently while trying to put the pistol in his belt. Then I went down to the casino and found a pair of Lieutenants and told them about what I had found. I brought them to the captain, and they carried him to a room down the hall."

"What did you do then?"

"I came here and went to bed. What time is it?"

"You say the captain was alone when you found him?"

"That's right."

"And how long was it between when you heard the shots and you saw Captain Frank lying on the floor?"

"I heard the shots and immediately stepped into the hall and saw the captain. I was right at the landing, you see, making the turn to come up to the third floor. Two seconds, no more."

"Are you certain there was no one else in the hall, maybe standing in a door to a room?"

"I did not see anyone else."

"Witnesses say Captain Frank was escorting a lady when he left the casino. Did you see a lady in the hall or on the staircase?"

"I did not see anyone else in the hall or on the staircase."

"What did you do after you determined Captain Frank had shot himself?"

"I went back down to the casino and found those two," Mike pointed at the Lieutenants at the doorway.

"How long did that take?"

"Less than a minute."

"And the three of you came directly back up to Captain Frank?"

"That's right."

"That will be all for now, Mister Stone. How long will you be here in Cuba?"

"Two weeks, until the next ship to New York."

"Which ship is that?"

"I don't know. I haven't booked the trip yet."

"Well, don't go anywhere outside of Havana until I release you."

"Yes, sir."

"Gentlemen, let us go," Reston said.

Mike's visitors exited the room, Major first, and marched down the hall. Mike rose from the chair, adjusted the pistol tucked behind his back and went to the door. He watched as the Major and his entourage trooped down the hall. No doubt they will talk to every guest on the floor and the one below to ask if they had heard anything. He wondered if lying to a United States military investigator during an investigation in Cuba was a crime. He closed the door and noticed the clock by the bed. It was 6:00 a.m.

Mike quickly brushed his teeth, shaved, washed his face, combed his hair, and dressed. He hurried down to the second floor in time to see Reston and his people knock on the door next to Annie's room. If one of the Lieutenants saw Annie, they would finger her as the lady Frank was escorting.

Mike moved forward to blend into the rear of the cluster of men following Reston. The hotel clerk knocked on the door to Annie's room and one of the girls within asked, "Who is it?" in a frightened voice.

Reston pushed the clerk aside and boomed out, "This is Marine Major Adam Reston. I need to talk to you."

"The clerk whispered to Reston, "Three ladies are registered to this room, sir."

"We need time to dress, please," said the voice behind the door.

"Don't dawdle, ladies. This is official business."

"We are hurrying!" came the response.

In a few moments, much sooner than Mike expected, Summer opened the door slightly to see a mob of men in the hall.

"Oh, my," she said.

"Madam, may I come in," Reston said.

"Yes," Summer stepped back.

Reston turned around, "Just Private McGregor and the Lieutenants are to come in with me. The rest of you, stay in the hall."

Reston went in with the clerk and the two other officers, but the door remained open. Mike could see Annie in the back of the room. She was wearing a dressing gown and sleeping cap. It struck him how pretty she looked, even roused out of bed so early in the morning.

"That's her," Jack said, pointing accusingly at Annie. "That's the trollop Captain Frank was bringing to his room."

"You," Reston barked, "come here."

Annie edged forward clutching her robe tightly about her neck.

"What is your name?"

"Ann Norwak of Cicero, Illinois. My friends call me Annie."

"What do you do?"

"I am a telephone exchange operator."

"Why are you in Havana?"

"My friends and I are on vacation."

"On an operator's salary?"

"We saved for two years to make the trip."

"You all work at the same exchange?" Reston looked at the other two ladies, who both nodded vigorously.

"Do you, Miss Norwak, know Marine Captain William Frank?"

Annie glanced about, fear showing in her eyes. "Do you mean Billy?" she asked in a trembling voice.

"Yes, yes. Captain William Frank. Do you know him?"

"I met a Captain last night down in the casino. He said his name was Billy."

"Did you leave the casino with Captain Frank?"

"Well, yes. He escorted me to my room."

"What time was this?"

"Near midnight, I expect. He wanted me to go to his room, but I declined so he dropped me here." Anne's eyes were wide and flitted from face to face questioningly.

"Why did you not want to go to Captain Frank's room with him?"

"I am an honest woman, Major. A fact you should be able to ascertain for yourself, were you a gentleman."

Reston's face flushed, but he kept his composure. "He dropped you here, at this door?"

"Yes. He stood in the hall while I unlocked the door. I said good night, thanked him for escorting me, closed the door, locked it and went into the lavatory to prepare for bed."

"Did you hear anything occurring in the hall after you closed the door?"

"No. I was trying to be quiet because my friends were already asleep."

"You are certain you heard nothing else? Voices maybe. In the hall?"

"No, nothing."

"How long will you be here in Havana?"

"We have passage this afternoon on the *Cuban Star* for New Orleans," Summer interjected.

"I wasn't talking to you, miss."

"We are traveling together, Major. We are booked to board the *Cuban Star* at five p.m., just after the siesta," Annie said.

"You will not depart without my permission, Miss Norwak," Reston rose to his full height as he said so. "Your friends may go, but you are confined here until further notice."

"But I must be home for Christmas, Major. My steamer ticket is paid for and I can't afford to stay here," Annie said.

"We will make accommodations for you in our brig, if need be. You may not leave Havana. Your friends will board this afternoon under armed guards. In the meantime, you stay here until I say otherwise." Reston turned to go.

"Major?" Annie said.

"Yes, miss," Reston replied impatiently.

"Why all these questions about Billy?"

"Have you not heard? Captain Frank was shot last night. He was found not twenty feet from this door. It is a wonder you heard nothing."

"Oh, God!" Annie covered her mouth. "Is he badly hurt?"

"He is expected to make a full recovery, but as of yet, I have not been able to get much out of him. Until Captain Frank has recovered enough to tell us what happened, you are restricted to this hotel."

Reston turned abruptly and stormed down the hall, his people scrambling to keep up.

Mike remained until the mob trooped down the stairway. He looked at Annie, who was standing in the open door, Summer and April behind her looking over her shoulder. Her eyes were filled with worry.

"Mister Rodriguez," Summer said. "Why are you here?"

"They woke me too, asking questions."

"What are we to do?" April asked.

"Prepare to leave this afternoon as planned," Mike said. "I am certain it will all be fine." This last sentence he spoke directly to Annie.

CHAPTER 5

Mike entered the restaurant looking for some breakfast. It was early, particularly for a hotel full of tourists. He selected a table with a good view of the entrance and sat with his back to the wall. A boy, perhaps ten years old, came from the kitchen and arranged a table setting for Mike.

"I would like you to do a favor for me," Mike said.

The boy looked up, startled that he was being addressed. "*No hablo Inglés, señor,*" the boy muttered.

Mike switched to Spanish. "That is even better. How would you like to earn an American dollar?" American dollars were accepted across Cuba and exchanged through a very active black market. The Cuban government, eager for cash, turned a blind eye to such activities.

"What would I have to do, sir?" The boy said, clearly suspicious. He had never been addressed by a guest before.

"I would like to send a note to someone that is a guest here. Can you do that?"

"Yes. This I can do."

"There are three young ladies registered in room 212. Do you know the room?"

"Yes, sir. My mother is a maid. Sometimes I help her clean the rooms."

"Good. Go get me a pencil and paper."

The boy returned with a pencil and a scrap of butcher paper torn from something in the kitchen. It would have to suffice. Mike scribbled, "meet me in the restaurant for breakfast – now. Josef."

"Give this to the young lady in 212 named 'Annie.' Say the name back to me."

"Ann-y," the boy said.

"Good. If there are men in the room, don't give her the note, come back to me."

"Yes, sir."

"What is your name?"

"I am called Conejo."

"Then hop to it. This is for you, and another when the ladies join me." Mike put a silver dollar in the boy's hand. It was a fortune far beyond anything he had ever dreamt about. A week's wage for his mother.

The boy hurried off. A waiter appeared. Mike told him he would be joined by some friends and he would wait until they arrived.

Conejo trotted to Mike, his head scanning the room. The boy must have run all the way there and back.

"The lady called Annie sends this note. After she read what you sent, she said 'Ok,' I know what that means, sir." He placed the note in Mike's hand.

It read: "We are all packed to leave. We will come down, have our luggage stored at the reception desk and come into the restaurant."

"Here," Mike said. He placed another dollar in Conejo's hand. "Stay close by. I may need some other chores."

"Yes, sir!" The boy rushed into the kitchen. A few minutes later, another boy emerged and began to place table settings for the breakfast crowd. Conejo reappeared and stood in a corner watching Mike intently. Arrangements to accommodate the Spanish speaking North American had been made.

Annie, Summer and April appeared in the restaurant doorway. They scanned the room, which was beginning to fill, saw Mike and hurried over to him.

Mike stood and indicated the chair to his right as the ladies approached. "Good morning, ladies. Join me, please. Annie, if you would sit here."

The waiter appeared instantly. "May I take your order?"

"Coffee for now. We need to discuss the menu." Mike said.

"Certainly, sir. Cream? Sugar?"

"Please," Summer said, her voice shaking.

Mike waved Conejo over and placed another silver dollar in his hand. "I am a man of my word. Do not go far."

Conejo nodded and drifted back to his corner.

"How much have you told your friends?" Mike whispered to Annie.

"They know it all. If they are questioned now, I cannot ask them to lie for me."

"I understand. April, please go to the reception desk and get Annie's day bag and bring it back here." All ship passengers would have a small day bag containing toiletries, a change of clothes, money, and other items they would not care to have stored with the luggage.

"What are we going to do?" Summer asked.

Mike was impressed when Summer said "we." These were close friends. But every friendship has limits.

62

April returned and gave the bag to Mike, who set it on the floor next to Annie.

"When Billy becomes sober enough to remember what happened last night, he will accuse Annie of trying to rob him. The navy is quite accustomed to ladies of the evening robbing sailors and Marines. There will be a presumption of guilt. Self-defense, though it be true, will take time to prove. It will require Annie prove her lineage and purpose for being in Havana. If she is to stay and fight this, you all will have to stay. Lawyers, good ones, are expensive, even if one can be found to argue before a military court. None of you have the time or the money and Annie will be risking it all on a fair trial."

"So, what do you suggest we do?" Annie said. "I will not put my friends at risk."

"I suggest that Summer and April have all of the luggage brought to the *Cuban Star* and board her early. They will stay on board until departure and return to New Orleans as scheduled."

"And Annie?" April asked.

"Annie will come with me. I am booked on a coastal freighter bound for New Orleans scheduled to arrive some eight hours after the *Cuban Star*. Do you have rooms reserved in New Orleans?"

"Yes, we have reservations at the Hotel Grunewald," Summer said.

"The Hotel Grunewald!" Mike exclaimed. "Perhaps you do have the money needed after all."

"It was all planned and strictly budgeted," Annie said through clenched teeth. "We were going to have one last adventure before dumping our lives into tedium."

Mike, taken aback by Annie's fervor, placed his hand on the table in front of her. He would have touched her hand, but she had both clutched in her lap.

"If it is adventure you were looking for, I would say you have found it. Summer and April will return as scheduled and check into the hotel. Annie will arrive about eight hours later. After a good night's sleep, you all will be on schedule for the return to Chicago and a life of tedium."

The desk clerk, carrying a small bundle, appeared at the door of the restaurant, saw Mike, and rushed over.

"Good morning, ladies. Pardon the intrusion, but I must talk to Mister Stone for a moment. Mister Stone, the package you sent for has arrived. You asked that I bring it to you immediately."

"Yes, Juan. Thank you," Mike said. "For your trouble." He placed a coin in Juan's hand.

The moment Juan was out of ear shot, Annie asked, "Who is Mister Stone."

Mike smiled slightly, "I am Robert Stone when I am in this hotel."

"What happened to Josef Rodriguez?"

"That was on a ship to Havana. That is not important. You need to decide now. Do you trust me?"

Annie reached down and picked up her day bag. She placed it on her lap, took a deep breath and, all the while looking intently into Mike's eyes, said, "Summer, you and April need to board the *Cuban Star* now. I will see you in New Orleans."

"Are you sure?" April asked. "You don't know this man."

"Who are you really? Josef Rodriguez or Robert Stone?" Summer said. "Don't lie to us."

Mike reached into his pocket, took out his wallet and removed a folded piece of paper. He handed it to Annie. She opened it and read aloud, "Automobile Operator's Permit. Issued to Michael Demill, Polymnia Street, New Orleans, Louisiana."

"I have not lived there for some time now." Mike said.

Annie stood, causing the rest at the table to rise as well. She hugged Summer and April. "Go now." She turned to Mike. "How are we going to get out of here? The hotel is being watched."

*****

Lieutenant John "Jack" Donnigan stood in the lobby of the Hotel Americana. He had been charged with the responsibility of insuring Miss Ann Norwak remained in the hotel until Major Reston could determine if she were to be charged in the assault on Captain Frank. How Frank had been so foolish as to get himself shot by some little floozy was beyond him, but orders were orders.

He watched as Miss Norwak and her two roommates entered the restaurant and had coffee with the man, Stone, the same man who claimed to have found Frank in the hall. It was all clear now. Stone managed the girls. When Frank resisted being robbed, Stone or Norwak shot him and then tried to make it appear as if Frank had shot himself. Neither one was going to get away with it.

He watched as the three ladies finished their coffee, said goodbye to Stone and returned to the stairway.

"Follow them," he snapped to a private he had detailed to shadow Miss Norwak when she moved about the hotel. The private moved out briskly, keeping the ladies in view the entire time. Donnigan had posted a guard in the rear as well. Thinking he had better check on the rear guards, he stormed through the restaurant and out the back door. Two men bracketed the back door. They snapped to attention when Donnigan approached.

"Anything?"

"Nothing, sir. Just the spics loading food stuffs into the restaurant. No sign of Miss Norwak. We know what she looks like, sir. You pointed her out this morning."

The three were asked to step forward as a wagon laden with vegetables was pushed back to the rear door. A swarm of employees began to unload the wagon amidst a cascade of rapid Spanish.

"Right. Keep a sharp eye."

"Yes, sir."

Donnigan returned through the restaurant and noticed that Stone was gone. He continued to the lobby and took his position by the front entrance. It had begun to rain turning the roadway surface into slick mud and wet manure-coated cobblestones. It was a steady, slow rain - a winter rain - instead of the torrential downpours for which Cuba was notorious.

Soon the ladies, followed by their shadow, appeared in the lobby. They directed the hotel staff to load their luggage into one of the two covered horse drawn cabs that waited at the curb. All wore rain slickers. He recognized Miss Norwak as she chatted with her friends.

He stepped forward. "Miss Norwak?"

"Yes, Lieutenant?" Annie turned to face him.

"Remember, you are not to leave this hotel."

"I remember, Lieutenant. We are going back to the room now to ensure nothing has been left behind."

The three ascended the stairway in file, their shadow close behind. They soon returned, stopping on the landing above the lobby. Two wore traveling capes and all were weeping, handkerchiefs to their faces and embracing each other repeatedly. Finally, the two in capes put their hoods up and continued down to the lobby.

Donnigan stopped them and pushed back their hoods. He recognized both ladies, red faced and teary eyed, as "the others." He nodded them forward. Following a cab driver, the pair left the hotel and climbed into a cab.

Donnigan realized he had been distracted when he verified the identities of the ladies he had permitted to leave. He quickly looked back to the landing to see Miss Norwak, weeping into her handkerchief, and waving with her free hand. Her marine shadow was standing against the wall. She turned away and left the landing followed by the marine private. Growing impatient, Donnigan went up to the second floor and met his guard in the hall.

"Anything to report?"

"No, sir. The lady went straight into room 212, locked the door and has been in there crying ever since."

Donnigan put his ear to the door. He could hear sobs.

"Good. If she should come out without my permission, arrest her, and bring her to me. I'm going to check the back."

"Yes, sir."

Donnigan descended to the lobby, which was now crowded with guests coming and going. He crossed through the restaurant to find his rear guard in place and alert.

"Anything to report."

"No, sir. We checked every wagon in and out, sir. Nothing other than hotel people have been by here. We checked them all."

Donnigan returned to the lobby just in time to see the man, Stone, get into a motor cab.

"Your time will come, Mister Stone," Donnigan hissed under his breath. "The trollop first, then the fish monger."

An hour passed before a staff car screeched to a halt at the hotel entrance. Major Reston exited and sprinted for the doors.

He charged into the lobby and Lieutenant Donnigan snapped to attention and saluted.

"Good morning, sir," he said as he held his salute.

Reston returned the salute. Barely concealing a smile, he announced, "Captain Frank has regained consciousness. He says while escorting Miss Norwak to her room, she produced a pistol and attempted to rob him. He resisted, and she shot him. The woman is still here, I presume."

"Yes, sir. In room 212. I have it under guard."

"Excellent, let us go arrest the bitch."

The officers stormed up the stairs to the second floor where they saw the private guarding the door to room 212.

"She still in there?" Reston barked as he automatically returned the privates' salute.

"Yes, sir. Still weeping a bit, sir."

"I will give her something to cry about," Reston said. He pounded on the door. "Open the door, Miss Norwak. I am here to arrest you for robbery and attempted murder of a Marine officer." He rattled the handle. "Open the door, damn you, or I'll have it kicked in."

He heard the latch key turn. Impatient, he pushed the door open, knocking the room's occupant back onto the bed.

"What? Who are you?" Reston roared.

"*¿Qué?*" responded the lady, now sitting on the bed. She was dressed in the "flapper" style. Donnigan recognized the clothes as being very like the outfit Miss Norwak had been wearing the last time he saw her.

"Where is Norwak?" Reston asked.

"*¿Qué? No hablo Inglés, Señor.*"

Reston rounded on Donnigan. "How," he started and then he noticed there were two Marine privates gawking into the room. "Give us this floor," he growled at them. They rushed down the hall and disappeared into the staircase.

"How could you not complete such a simple task? All you need do was watch one little girl, and she just waltzes out of this hotel right under your worthless nose." He stepped back a moment as the lady from the room eased past him. She disappeared down the hall.

*****

It had all been so simple. After finishing their coffee, Annie, and her friends, followed by their shadow, returned to room 212. Mike and Conejo's mother, Maria Lucia, ascended to the third-floor stair landing, waiting there until the ladies and their guard passed below on their first trip to the lobby.

Mike and Maria Lucia hurried to room 212, let themselves in and waited. When the ladies returned, leaving their guard in the hall, Annie and Maria Lucia went into the washroom and exchanged clothes.

Summer and April donned their capes, pulled up their hoods while Maria Lucia pulled down the decorative veil of the narrow-brimmed hat she wore, worked up a good cry and covered her face. Summer, April, and Maria Lucia left the room amid exaggerated weeping and headed for the stairs, the guard dutifully following.

Mike waited long enough for the diversion to reach the landing at the casino before he and Annie, now dressed in Maria Lucia's work clothes and covered by a riding cape, went to the stair landing and up to the third floor.

Once they heard Maria Lucia, sobbing louder than ever, pass the second-floor landing, Mike and Annie went down past the second floor to the casino landing above the lobby. As luck would have it, not only was it raining, giving Annie a reason to pull up her hood, but Lieutenant Donnigan had left the lobby and disappeared into the restaurant.

Annie pulled up her hood and she and Mike went down to the lobby, out the front doors to a waiting taxi. Annie climbed in first and scooted over to make room for Mike. As Mike climbed in, he glanced back to see Donnigan re-enter the lobby and glare at him. At that moment, Mike feared the Lieutenant would come out to check if Mike were alone, but the man did not.

*****

"Café Marinero Feliz, near the Jesus Maria wharf," Mike said. He leaned forward to talk to the cabbie to block any view of Annie from potential watchers in the lobby.

The café was a two-story affair with a combination bar and eatery on the ground floor and rooms to rent, by the day or the hour, on the next. Mike negotiated a room above the entrance with a clear view of the moored freighter *Garanhão do Mar* across the road and wharf.

It was noon. They sat in chairs facing the open windows to the balcony, a small table between them with two cups of steaming coffee. The activity in the bar below and along the wharf faded into an occasional buggy or pedestrian. The rain continued in a gentle hiss, water dripping from the awning over the abbreviated balcony attached to the room.

"What do we do now?" Annie asked.

"We wait until one in the morning, or I can contact Captain Alfonso Peres, master of that freighter you see. Then, we go aboard her, and you will disembark in New Orleans."

"What about you?"

"I have my business to attend, then I will return to New Orleans as well."

"You still have not told me why you are doing this?"

Mike paused. Annie, thinking he was not going to answer, reached in her purse for some cigarettes.

"Please don't," Mike said. "The smoke bothers my lungs."

"Oh, sorry. Of course," Annie said, stuffing the pack back down into her purse.

"There was a time, in Verdun, on a rainy December day in 1918, a day like today, only colder, much colder, when I had the opportunity to help a young widow with a little girl."

Mike leaned back in his chair, his eyes focused beyond the balcony, beyond the freighter.

"You might say I helped her in a way. I gave her some food I had taken from the mess and a few francs I had pilfered from corpses. But I could have done more, instead I just lay with her all night and then was gone in the morning, never to see or hear of her again."

"You told us you were from Verdun and that you were in the war."

"I was in hell. The rest of the world called it a war. I'm not a Frenchman from Verdun, I was an American soldier in Verdun, the American 11th Infantry Regiment, 5th Division; the Red Devils."

Mike's face was dark, foreboding. He didn't look at Annie as he spoke.

"Did you ever have to kill anyone?"

Mike looked back into Annie's eyes. "That question, Miss Norwak, should never be put to a soldier."

"I'm sorry, but, for the first time you frighten me a little."

"Oh, forgive me." Mike's mood changed suddenly. "I forgot. I have something for you." He dug through his day bag and retrieved the parcel the desk clerk had brought to him that morning. He unwrapped it slowly to reveal a small box and a pistol. He laid both on the table.

"It is a .38 Police Special, 2-inch barrel. Perfect for carrying in a purse. Let me show you how it works."

"I'm familiar with the .38," Annie said. She picked up the pistol, expertly thumbed the latch, flipped it open and spun the empty cylinder. Digging into the box of cartridges, she loaded the five chambers, and flipped the cylinder into the closed position.

"I felt I should supply you with a replacement for your belly-buster." Mike said. He leaned back, clearly reassessing Annie.

"Thank you," Annie said. She slipped the pistol into the small purse she carried strapped across her body. "How much do I owe you."

"Use it wisely, and I will be well paid. It is your turn to tell me how it came to be that a telephone operator from Cicero wound up in Cuba."

Annie laughed. "It was silly, really. Summer, April, and I worked the same exchange. It was demanding work, rarely a break, and monotonous. We would lunch together. I came up with the idea that we would save our money for a year and tell our folks we were going to visit New Orleans. Once there, we could hop a steamer to Cuba, spend two days here and go back home.

"We would have been free, if only for a few days, and in an exotic foreign country. Anything to escape the dreary four walls and spider web of wires that were consuming us. We just needed to breath."

She held the cup of coffee to her lips and blew softly. "We were – are so foolish."

"Believe it or not, I think I understand."

"Do you? No, you are just making fun of me."

"That, I would never do. I can understand the loneliness created by working hard every day just to survive. I don't blame you for wanting to escape. So, now what do you want to do?"

She laughed softly. Mike thought the sound of her laughter was magical. "Provided I manage to get back to New Orleans and catch the train to Chicago. I truly don't know. The thought of walking into the phone exchange and donning headsets after all this makes my skin crawl."

Mike put his hand on Annie's. "Look, coming down the gangway," he said, pointing at the *Garanhão do Mar*. "I think that is the ship's master now."

A tall man hunched into a Macintosh, his cap pulled down to keep out the rain, was coming down the gangway suspended from the ship's deck to the wharf. Two sailors who had been working at the landing, stopped their labors, stood, and respectfully made room for the figure as he stepped ashore.

"He's coming here," Annie said.

The man hurried across the wharf clearly intent upon entering the café.

"Wait here, I'll go down and see if it is who I think."

"And if it is the ship's master?"

"Then we will board now and not wait until 1:00 a.m. as planned. I don't like the idea of sitting in this café while there are people out searching for us. It won't take them long to start visiting every ship in Havana. Captain Peres was prepared to hide me if need be. He will have to hide us both."

Mike went out and Annie locked the door behind him. She went back to the window and sat. She knew she should have been filled with doubt, but for reasons she could not explain, she felt thrilled.

There was a tapping on the door. Annie crossed the room, pulled the pistol from her purse, and asked quietly, "Who is it?"

"Mike."

She opened the door and Mike slipped in, closing it quickly behind him.

"It was Captain Peres," He said. "Everything is set. We will go down to the entrance. Peres will cross to the gangway landing and wait for you. You will cross, and he will send you up to the deck. Then I will cross. He wants to do it this way because there are Marines up the street and a crowd crossing in the rain will draw attention. Once on the ship, we will be safe. It is a Portuguese flagged ship, and the Marines cannot board her without permission of the port master, which they will not be able to obtain."

Mike and Annie went down to the café where Captain Peres was enjoying a mug of ale. He had a dark complexion, weathered by years at sea. He had bushy eyebrows, a full beard and dark, wavy hair. He spoke English in a voice that was gravelly and heavily accented.

"A pleasure to welcome you aboard, Miss Norwak. It will be no trouble accommodating you, provided you are willing to share a cabin with Mister Demill."

"Thank you, Captain. I will make do," Annie said. The realization of the living conditions began to sink in. *Too late for a change of heart now*, she thought. *Mike must think me a tramp.*

"Wait for my signal," Peres said. He pulled up his collar and walked quickly across the street and wharf to the gangway. He stopped to talk to the two sailors working at the landing, stood and motioned Annie over.

When Annie reached the landing, Peres sent her straight up with one of the sailors. He signaled to Mike.

As Mike crossed, he looked left and right down the street. A cluster of Marines were crowded around the front of a building two blocks away. They were clearly conducting a search. Had he and Annie waited, they would have been caught.

"Up you go," Peres said when he reached the gangway. "Nuñez is waiting with Miss Norwak in the hatchway at the top. Didn't want her looking over the side, you see."

Mike joined Annie, and Nuñez led them to a small cabin just behind the Captain's cabin. It had a bunk hanging from one bulkhead, hooks along another, and an interior hatchway opposite from where they entered. A writing desk was hinged from the bulkhead next to the entrance below a porthole. There was a single armless chair.

"I will bring a hammock," Nuñez said, and he left.

"Mighty spartan," Mike said.

"It will have to do," Annie said, her mind racing ahead to the sleeping conditions. Mike seemed so trustworthy, so sincere, but was she being a fool? She looked around. She was on a foreign ship, in a foreign port, with a man she just met, running from arrest and no one else knew where she was. Had she been a fool all along?

CHAPTER 6

Annie's concern about the sleeping arrangements were erased as soon as the *Garanhão do Mar* reached the open Gulf of Mexico sometime shortly after 1:00 a.m.

The interior door proved to be a small head with a toilet and a wash basin. Annie had discovered that fact earlier, but now the roll of the ship and the claustrophobic space of the tiny cabin found her racing for the toilet, which she embraced and began to toss away the coffee, ham and cheese Peres had brought them for supper.

Mike was sympathetic and assured Annie that the sea sickness would pass. The smaller size of the coastal steamer and the increase in seas had just taken her by surprise, he said. Annie no longer cared about escape, or who anyone was, or even why she was kneeling at a steel toilet in a Portuguese ship. Nothing matters except breathing and not having her insides get outside.

"I'll lock the door when I go out and only knock twice when I come back in," Mike said. "I'll see if I can get you something for the sea sickness." Annie looked up from her position, pulled a strand of hair away from her face, nodded and returned to heaving.

Mike went out, locked the door, and stepped the few paces forward past the Captain's berth and into the wheelhouse which stretched completely across the width of the ship. It was all windows, with steel hatches that could be locked over each window should the need arise to protect the glass. This night, all the windows, fore, aft, port and starboard were uncovered.

Mike could see a rugged shadow that was the coastline of Cuba sliding along the port side. Lights were scattered along the coastline, most were villages. The nearest looked to be over three miles away. A few of the lights were brighter and higher than the others and they winked on and off at a regular pace. Mike knew these were rotating navigational lights with a narrow beam which caused them to appear to blink. The lights were identified by the frequency with which they seemed to blink, their color, and the relative location to other lights.

"Is your friend unwell?" Captain Peres asked.

"Seasick," Mike said.

"I have something," Peres went to a small drawer under one of the windows. "Sometimes my helmsman here will feel a bit queasy." He leaned closer to Mike. "And me too," he whispered.

He retrieved a small medicine bottle. "Have her take a short sip of this when she has a break from heaving. It may help. If it works, she will be able to join us here."

"What is it?"

"I do not know. It works, that is all that matters."

Mike accepted the bottle. "I will be right back."

He knocked twice, unlocked the door, and entered. He had to turn on the light. Annie must have switched it off. "I have something for you."

Annie's sweat-streaked face appeared. "What is it?"

"The Captain gave it to me. He doesn't know what it is, but he swears it works.

Annie crawled forward and held out her hand. "I will take it."

"Only a sip. It might be potent."

"I am certain little of it will stay down," Annie said. She pulled the cork, put the bottle to her lips and tilted it back."

"Only a sip!" Mike took the bottle from Annie and held it up to the light to gauge how much was left. He could see about half of a bottle remained. He admonished himself for not noting how full the bottle was before he gave it to Annie. Worry of a possible overdose was lessened when Annie returned to another bout of vomiting.

"I will be in the pilot's house a few steps forward. The Captain said you could join us there if you feel better. If not, I will be back here in an hour or so. Don't forget. Two knocks." Annie nodded in recognition of Mike's instructions, heaved again, then spit away strings of drool.

"How is the lady?" Peres asked as soon as Mike stepped into the wheelhouse.

Mike gave the bottle back to Peres. "She thanks you for this."

Peres held the bottle up and shook it gently. "I would say she has taken enough. If the sickness does not stop, she will be miserable until we touch land. No one can tell these things."

There were two sailors in the wide wheelhouse in addition to the helmsman. Each man was peering through the sights of auxiliary compasses mounted next to windows on the port and aft bulkheads. The man facing aft called out, "Captain, I have Castillo de Los Tres Reyes heading one hundred nine and one quarter degrees." The ship's crew spoke Portuguese, a language Mike could sometimes understand, but could not speak.

"Helm come to two eight nine," Peres said. "Two eight nine," repeated the helmsman.

Peres pulled the stopper from a speaking tube and blew into it. He waited a moment and then shouted into the tube, "All ahead slow."

"All ahead slow," came a voice from the tube.

"Quibu light?" Peres asked.

"Two zero two," came the answer from the sailor manning the port auxiliary compass.

Peres walked around the ship's compass mounted before the helm. "The bearings will match soon," he said in English. When the directions to specific shore beacons matched predetermined values, they would be at the rendezvous point.

The new heading put the ship head-on to the long rollers coming from the northwest, reducing the sickening roll of the ship. *That should help Annie a bit*, Mike thought.

"Two hundred," said the port observer. Mike knew when they reached one ninety-nine and one quarter, they should meet the *La Abeja*.

The helmsman glanced toward the starboard hatch and pointed with his head. Mike turned around to see Annie braced in the hatchway.

"Come in, Miss Norwak," Peres said. "I hope you are feeling better."

"Yes, Captain," Annie said weakly. "I am most grateful for the medicine."

"Yes, it usually works. Next you will be sleepy, and you will wake ready to – how is it the Americans say? – eat a horse."

Annie walked up to Mike and took his arm to steady herself against the pitch of the deck. "Why have we slowed down?"

Mike looked at Annie and prepared to gauge the effect of what he was going to say. "We are going to meet another boat with some cargo I'm bringing to Louisiana."

Annie was silent for a long time, then she said, "What kind of cargo?"

"Do you remember the bottle I have in my day bag?"

"Yes, a large bottle of rum. I was wondering if you were a drunkard."

Mike smiled. She was playing with him. He could tell she was going to make him say it.

"My cargo is one thousand cases of rum."

"Ah," Annie said as if the revelation had suddenly hit her. "You are a rum-runner."

"Yes, I am. That is the reason for the many aliases. I am bringing about fifteen tons of rum to a thirsty city."

"And all this time I worried that I had fallen in with a bad crowd," Annie said. Her reaction puzzled Mike. He had expected something quite different. What kind of woman did he have here?

"One ninety-nine and a quarter," announced the sailor observing the light called "Quibu."

"All dead slow ahead," Peres said into the speaking tube.

The *Garanhão* slowed until she had only enough way on her to keep steerage.

"Dark," Peres ordered and suddenly every light on the ship went out. A blacked-out ship at night was a dangerous situation. Other vessels steaming along, some going as fast as twenty knots, would not be able to see the *Garanhão* until it was too late to avoid a collision. The hairs on the back of Mike's neck tingled. He noticed that every person in the wheelhouse, and probably every sailor on the deck below, was scanning the sea about them very intently.

Gradually, Mike's eyes adjusted to the darkness. He was able to distinguish the sea from the distant land. The stars in the sky became a wide swath of white. He saw a shadow move on the surface of the sea to the starboard side, the side away from land.

"Boat to the starboard," said one of the sailors in a conversational tone.

Peres held a speaking trumpet to his mouth and shouted through an open window, "Nuñez, man the crane. Prepare to bring cargo aboard."

"*La Abeja* is here," Peres said in English. He had been giving the orders in a mixture of Portuguese and English depending upon who was being addressed. "If you would like to supervise the loading of your cargo, go to the deck next to the crane."

"I will go to watch. I am confident Mister Nuñez knows his business." Mike turned to Annie. "Would you like to come with me?"

"Yes, I would like that very much. I have learned so much in the last two days, why stop now?"

They descended to the cargo deck and went to the starboard rail next to the buttress for the upper decks. The *La Abeja* was clearly visible below them as she maneuvered to parallel the freighter. She looked very small as she came along the side of the coastal freighter. Mike could see machine guns atop mounts both fore and aft. The Bee had her stingers out.

Captain Solis was facing aft from the wheelhouse. He was shouting to his deckhands as they pulled the hatch covers away to reveal what appeared to be a bundle of netting. One of the hands signaled and Nuñez swung the arm of the crane and lowered an iron ball with a great hook toward the boat below.

The *La Abeja's* deckhand caught the ball as it swung across the open hatch, expertly connected the hook to some netting, and stepped back as he signaled by placing one fist on top of the other and then switching them back and forth. It was the signal that the load had been hooked.

Nuñez raced the engine of the crane and a huge cargo net filled with crates lifted out of the *La Abeja*. He brought the load up and across to hover above the cargo deck of the *Garanhão*. Men raced out from the shadows and hooked long poles to the netting. Nuñez lowered the load, and the deckhands, pushing and pulling on the poles, guided it into a location on the deck.

The first load was being lashed down while the crane swung back for the next. Soon the three large mounds of cargo covered in netting were lashed in place.

Solis looked up and saw Mike standing at the rail. He waved in acknowledgement. Mike waved back. Solis ducked into the *La Abeja's* wheelhouse and the boat roared to life, her lights winking on as she sped away. The *Garanhão's* running lights came on and her engines rumbled to life. It had all taken less than fifteen minutes.

Mike and Annie walked forward to one of the cargo mounds. Mike moved the netting aside a little and checked the markings on the crate.

"Is everything here?" Annie asked.

"It does seem so. Let's go back to the bridge. The ship is picking up speed and the air is cold."

"Is your cargo secure?" Peres asked as they stepped into the wheelhouse.

"Yes, everything is well in hand," Mike answered. "When do you expect to reach Hewes Point?"

"About sunset tomorrow, I would think."

"And from Hewes Point to New Orleans?"

"Another 10 – 12 hours," Peres replied.

Mike turned to Annie. "That puts you in New Orleans on the morning of the 23rd. The *Cuban Star* was scheduled to dock at eight in the evening of the 22nd. You will have caught up with your friends and then it is on to Chicago."

Annie had an odd look on her face. "Yes, I will be back to Cicero, Illinois, and all of this will be behind me."

The ship began a slow cork-screw motion as it reached cruising speed. The heading to Hewes Point was just to the port of the long, deep groundswell coming from the north.

"If you could excuse me, gentlemen, I think I shall retire. Suddenly, I am most tired," Annie said weakly.

"It is the medicine, Miss," Peres said. "You will sleep for several hours and awaken quite starved."

"Captain, I cannot imagine ever eating again."

Mike walked with Annie to the small berth. Nuñez had rigged a hammock on the bulkhead opposite the cot.

"I'll step outside to give you a minute of privacy," Mike offered. "Open the door when you are ready, and I will help you up into the hammock once you are ready."

"Why do I get the hammock and not you?" Annie asked.

Mike's face had the hint of a smile. "Two reasons. Hammocks are more comfortable in a rolling sea. You should sleep better. I'll be just on the other side of the door." He put his day bag on the bunk.

"And?" Annie asked.

"And what?"

"And the other reason I should have the hammock?"

"It is not possible for two to fit in a hammock."

*****

83

Mike watched her as he marched with his platoon toward the front. He tried to remember her full name. It was Ynes Marie –. It wouldn't come to him. She held the hand of her little girl, Camille. The sack of canned goods he had stolen for her from the mess tent lay at her feet. Mike knew he would never see her again - never know what became of her or little Camille.

Ynes called to him. "Mike - Mike, wake up."

Annie was shaking him awake.

"What? What is it?" Mike asked sleepily. It seemed as though he had just gone to sleep. Annie was up and dressed. The skirt and blouse she had borrowed from a Cuban kitchen worker she had been wearing when Mike last saw her had been replaced by a fashionable dress complete with frills. A thin-brimmed hat with a decorative veil was pinned to her head.

"I am sorry to have to wake you, Mike. I am starving and I'm reluctant to search for the dining room on this boat."

Mike shook away the fog in his mind. "Peres said you would wake up hungry. What time is it?"

"I don't know. It's daytime, I can see that through the porthole."

"Give me a second and we will go in search of the mess." Mike said as he threw aside the covers and swung his legs to the floor. He had worn his trousers to bed but was bare-chested. He slipped on his shoes, picked up his day bag and, rubbing his face, went into the little washroom. He closed the door.

Annie had barely managed to stifle a gasp. Although Mike was broad shouldered, muscular, and appeared to be fit, his left side was a mosaic of ugly scars. Some were raised, jagged, meandering ridges, others were pits in the center of puckered depressions. She listened as Mike ran water in the small sink and waited.

When Mike emerged, he had shaved, combed his hair, and donned a new shirt. "Let's find the galley," he said.

Mike opened the hatch to the walkway along the starboard side of the freighter. He stepped out into a bright, clear day. The sea sparkled a deep blue. The waves were short and choppy, but without white caps. The groundswell that had the ship corkscrewing when they had retired had subsided into a smooth roll.

Nuñez, one of the few deckhands who could speak a version of English, stuck his head out of the wheelhouse. "Good morning, my friends," he said. He looked back into the wheelhouse and said something and joined Mike and Annie at the rail.

"I think you look for something to food," he said.

"Eat," Annie corrected. "Yes, please."

"Come this way," Nuñez said, his head bouncing.

He led them aft, down two flights of steps and into the galley. The smell of bacon filled the air. He said something to a greasy man wearing what might once have been a white shirt and trousers, who pointed at a long table surrounded by a half dozen chairs. A cup containing an assortment of forks, knives and spoons occupied its center.

"Sit here," Nuñez said, "and Adão will serve you breakfast."

"What time is it?" Annie asked.

"It is three hours after dawn." He looked at Mike, "After you eat, Captain Peres would talk with you."

Adão arrived with two large plates covered with scrambled eggs and fried ham. Annie closed her eyes and chewed the ham slowly. "That is good," she said. "How do you say that in Portuguese?"

"*Delicioso*, I think?"

"What, that might as well be English." Annie looked at Adão when he brought two glasses of wine. "Adão. *Delicioso!*" She said.

Adão beamed, "*Obrigado, menina.*"

"You have made a friend," Mike said.

After the breakfast - Annie had two servings - they stepped out onto the cargo deck. The ship must have been making twenty knots and a cool wind swept the deck. Annie had been wise enough to bring a shawl. She wrapped it around her shoulders and stepped against Mike's side.

Mike's netted contraband lay in three stacks on the cargo bay hatch covers. Lines ran across the mounds securing them firmly should they experience rough weather.

"Why did Peres not place the cases into the hold?"

"We will be offloading them in only a few hours. The holds are already filled with cargo, raw sugar ingots for the refinery in New Orleans. That is where you will go ashore. Captain Peres will see to it that the refinery will provide you with a car to take you to the Hotel Grunewald."

Annie looked at Mike, not certain she had understood. "Will you not be with us when we dock?"

"No. I must leave this ship with my cargo and see it safely ashore. I am certain you understand."

"I am not certain I do. I am not comfortable being alone on a ship filled with strangers, few of whom speak English. What guarantee do I have that I'll not be abducted?"

"Captain Peres is a businessman, not a criminal. His personal take for this little side delivery is more than he would normally make in a year. The prospect of repeat contracts is very high. The deck hands will also receive a considerable bonus. You are quite safe." He tapped the purse she carried across her body. "Besides, I know how you deal with unpleasant men."

"That is not amusing," Annie said coldly.

"I am sorry, but it cannot be otherwise. I will ask you for a favor."

"Which is?"

"My transfer to my smaller boats will be at sea, during the night and while underway. I would appreciate it if you would bring my day bag with you. You can leave it at the front desk of your hotel if I am unable to see you before you have to catch your train."

"I suppose I can do that, if I'm not sold to a harem," she said.

"My hat will be in the bag."

"Then you must really trust me," Annie said. The realization that tonight she might be seeing Mike for the last time unexpectedly saddened her.

They spent the rest of the day touring the ship and talking about their lives before they met. Mike did not speak of his experiences in the Great War but went into great detail as he reminisced about life as a shrimp boat deckhand for his father and his struggles to learn English when his mother moved back to New Orleans.

Annie talked about her job as a telephone operator, and her prior adventures with her friends Summer and April. Annie was the last of seven children, the only girl. Her mother had died of influenza leaving her the only woman in the family. Her brothers had all married, so she moved out on her own.

They talked about nothing for hours. They had taken a late and full breakfast, so the noon meal passed without their notice. Before either of them realized it, the sun began to set.

"We had better visit Adão one more time," Mike said. "Soon, I will be very busy, and it will be the last time I can eat today or tomorrow morning."

Adão cheerfully greeted Annie when she and Mike entered the galley. He heaped their plates full, but Annie had lost her appetite and she picked around the edges of her fish, much to Adão's disappointment.

Later, Mike brought Annie back to the berth. "Get some sleep," he said. "You have not fully recovered from the events of the last few days."

"Promise you will come and get me when it is time for you to go."

"I will. And you will see why you must go with the ship to New Orleans."

*****

Annie woke to the sound of knocking on the hatchway. Mike had dropped her at the berth, and she latched the door from the inside. The sea had calmed so she decided to sleep in the bunk instead of the hammock. She had slipped off her shoes, lay her head on the pillow, the same pillow Mike had used, and had fallen into a deep sleep.

The seas had increased considerably, and the tossing berth momentarily confused her until she became fully awake. There was another pair of knocks.

"Who is it," she called out as she slipped on her shoes.

"Mike."

"Coming." Annie straightened her dress and opened the door. Rain and wind met her. Mike squeezed in.

"Better put on that rain hood," he said. "You can watch things from the dryness of the wheelhouse."

"What time is it?"

"Midnight. We have made good time."

"Midnight when - I mean - what day?"

"It is the morning of the 22nd day of December."

I arrived in Havana on the 19th! How could so much have happened? Annie thought.

She followed Mike, holding his coattail, as wind and rain whipped around her until they both ducked into the wheelhouse. The wind was from astern and Peres had ordered the glass panes in the forward-facing windows lowered for a better view.

The night was black but speckled with dancing dots of lights here and there on the horizon. Mercifully, the rain ended abruptly. The cloud bank slipped to the south, its outline distinct as the moon and stars began to appear.

"We can see the beacons we need," Peres said.

Mike and Annie watched intently as the watchmen called out bearings until Peres ordered the engines slowed.

"I can see a boat," Annie said, pointing toward the port bow where a small shrimp boat bobbed into view.

"Good eye," Peres commented.

Two more boats appeared and maneuvered toward the lee side of the ship. The deck crane roared into action. The forward-most of Mike's netted cargo had already been attached and it lifted away and over the side.

"How can you load such a small boat in this sea?" Annie asked. "The waves have the little boats bounding about. Surely the cargo will crash through their decks."

"Yes," Mike said. "That is why there is a buoy attached to the netting. Nuñez will drop the cargo in the sea. The little boat will retrieve the buoy and tow the bundle to the lee-side of an island and, once in calm water, transfer the crates from the netting to their hold."

The crane was returning for another load.

"I must go now," Mike said.

"How will you get into one of the boats? You are not going to dive into the sea, are you?"

"Watch. I'll make the transfer with dry feet."

Mike held her arms in his hands. "I must go now."

Annie instinctively kissed him lightly on the lips and Mike slipped out of the wheelhouse and down to the cargo deck. Nuñez had delivered the last bundle of netted crates into the sea. Mike grabbed onto the cargo hook and Nuñez swung the crane over one of the boats.

He slowly lowered Mike over the shrimp boat's deck as it pitched violently up and down. Mike watched the deck beneath him. It raced up, then fell away. One time, the deck touched his toes before falling away. Mike stretched his arms and bent his knees. The next upward pitch slammed into his feet. He released the cargo hook just as the deck fell away, Mike firmly aboard.

Annie had been watching from the wheelhouse. She did not realize she had been holding her breath the entire time Mike was suspended over the little boat.

The shrimp boat veered away. The long line to the submerged cargo grew taut. Peres called for the engines, came about and in moments, the sea was empty.

"We will be in New Orleans by six this evening," Peres said.

Annie looked back at the empty sea.

"I will make my train with ease," she said. She felt empty.

CHAPTER 7

Mike stumbled about the deck of the shrimp boat as he tried to catch his feet. The transition from hanging from a relatively stable cargo hook to a pitching deck was sudden and difficult. It was his first attempt at such a maneuver, and it was much simpler in his mind than it had proven to be.

The edge of the iron ball above the cargo hook had slammed against his chin as the deck and Mike fell away. The next swell pushed the shrimp boat back up toward the cargo hook, but Nuñez had quickly swung the crane away and it barely missed Mike's head. Mike made a mental note to never again attempt such a thing.

Mike recovered his feet and grabbed one of the trawl braces to stabilize himself. He rubbed his aching chin and looked up at the *Garanhão* from the pitching deck of the *Captain Robin*. He could see Annie at the rail standing next to Peres. He hoped she had not seen the fiasco of him stumbling about to catch his feet and resisted the urge to wave.

The *Garanhão*'s engines roared to life and she surged ahead as the little shrimp boat veered away from the ship's side. The *Captain Robin* swung quickly away only to be dramatically slowed by the partially submerged cargo net. The young deckhand positioned himself at the stern with a hatchet ready to cut the line should the cargo be sucked toward the *Garanhão*'s screws.

After a dramatic moment, the potential threat passed, and Mike was able to look up toward the freighter's rail. He could see no one and moved back toward the rear of the shrimp boat's cabin and watched the wake wash over the dark bulge of the cargo.

The *Captain Robin*'s single deckhand had removed the buoy from the line attached to the mostly submerged cargo net, threaded it through the stern guides and doubled it around a power capstan mounted just aft of the cabin. The hand pulled the free end of the line taut causing the capstan to draw the cargo closer to the stern.

"*Atar*," came a shouted command from the cabin.

The deckhand kicked a lever, removing power from the capstan and looped the line around a cleat, tying it off. He was young, maybe fifteen. His feet were bare, though the weather was quite cold, and he wore ragged trousers and a loose flannel shirt. The boy's hair, dripping with seawater, was matted to his head. Mike didn't recognize him, but he looked familiar.

"*Hola, Miguel*," The boy said. "You do not remember me? I am your cousin, Pedro."

Mike remembered the name. The last time he saw Pedro Demill was at the funeral of Mike's father, Diego Demill. The boy had been three years old and spent most of the time hiding behind his mother's skirts. Mike was only fourteen and vaguely remembered details of the extended Demill family. Pedro was the last child and only son of his father's oldest brother.

"Pedro Demill? Of course, I remember. You have grown too much for me to recognize you. How is your family?"

The boy shrugged. "Father is at the wheel."

Mike ducked into the boat's cabin to see his uncle Geronimo piloting the shrimp boat through the rough water toward the lee side of a low island. It required a lot of skill to keep the tow line tight enough to prevent significant slack which could snap taut violently, and at the same time, not overload the tow line. Either error could damage the boat or cause the cargo to break free.

"Tío Geronimo," Mike said, "I am glad to see you well."

Geronimo released one hand from the wheel and gave Mike a modified embrace.

"It has been too long, *sobrino* (nephew)." Geronimo returned his attention to the wheel. He spoke over his shoulder. "Manuel told me he had recruited you. I could not believe it. Did you grow tired of the Garden District and fancy women? Last I heard, there was one fancy woman in particular."

Mike wondered why anyone in the fishing village of Delacroix Island should be gossiping about him.

"There was an unpleasant parting," Mike allowed. "Manuel Moreno found me dredging oysters as a *solitario*. Enough of that. How are Tía Isabella and the girls?"

"They are all well."

"Give them my love."

"I will do that. Better, you can do that yourself."

Mike wondered if he would return to the life of a fisherman.

Geronimo slowed the boat's engines. They had rounded the tip of a flat island and the seas were calm. The island was more of a treeless sand-dune. The waves broke in rollers on the windward side not three hundred yards from where the *Captain Robin* anchored.

"Give us a hand, *sobrino*," Geronimo said. "Three can store these crates below in half the time. If we are quick about it, we can make the docks before sunrise."

Protected from wave action by the island, they began to unload the netting one case at a time. As the load was reduced, Pedro would winch more net to the fantail to access the rest of the cargo. It required a full hour to stow the three hundred and forty cases in the hold reserved for shrimp.

The empty netting and tow line were jettisoned, and the *Captain Robin* headed through a narrow pass between shoals into Chandeleur Sound. Mike could see the dark shapes of the two other shrimp boats transferring their loads.

Free of the narrow pass, Geronimo pushed the throttle forward until the boat was running at top speed.

"We will make for Chicot Island," he shouted to Mike over the roar of the engine. "If it is not light enough to run in from there, we will wait for the others at Twilight Harbor."

Twilight Harbor was a harbor in name only. The mouth of Bayou La Loutre at Chandeleur Sound was sheltered by a finger of marsh to the north. Generations of fishermen had driven poles and rigged catwalks along the sheltered side of the island, forming a convenient anchorage for boats waiting out bad weather.

"If the light is good, and it might be sunrise by the time we make Chicot Island, we are going to continue up La Loutre, cut across to Lake Borgne, up Bayou Bienvenue to the landing at Fisherman's Canal."

Fisherman's Canal ended at a railroad that connected New Orleans to Lake Borgne. A crude narrow clamshell roadway wound along the bank of the canal. Dotted with camps, commercial seafood landings and crude piers isolated into clusters by thick stands of brush and cane, it was an ideal location to unload cargo onto trucks unnoticed, even in full daylight.

Warehouses and a railway loading dock crowded the land between the end of the canal and the railroad. Once the trucks joined the commercial traffic along the service road next to the railroad, they would be indistinguishable from the dozens of other trucks hauling seafood and farm products. It was less than a mile from the boat landing to the city.

"Manuel has trucks waiting at the warehouse next to the railroad," Geronimo explained. "Pedro will run up the road and call the trucks to us. Ten, maybe twenty minutes and we will be free of our cargo. Manuel wants you to ride in the first truck back to the city where he will meet you."

"What about the sheriff's people or city police?" Mike asked.

"The sheriff will have all of his people well away from the area. The city police have been instructed not to stop any trucks. There should be no problems."

*****

It was full daylight by the time they reached Chicot Island. Geronimo reduced speed as they passed Twilight Harbor and its forest of posts. They passed two boats coming down Bayou La Loutre less than a mile inland. Geronimo maintained a reduced speed to minimize his wake. He and the other captains, as tradition demanded, exchanged waves as they passed.

Running in the bayou at a reduced speed was a comfortable change from the open water. Mike began to feel the accumulated effects of lack of sleep and stress. He stifled a yawn and closed his eyes.

Geronimo elbowed Mike. "Get some sleep," he said pointing to a pair of cots below the forward deck. Pedro was already asleep on one of the cots. "Wake Pedro and send him up. We need to tidy up things around this boat."

Mike did as Geronimo suggested. He managed to pull off his shoes before collapsing into the cot and into a deep, dreamless sleep. Even the transition from bayou to the open water of Lake Borgne failed to wake him. Mike finally stirred when the engine fell to idle. He rolled out of the cot and searched for his shoes. Geronimo had been asleep in the other cot, which meant Pedro was at the wheel.

"What time is it?" Mike asked groggily.

"Near to five in the afternoon," Geronimo replied. "We had to spend some time trawling in Lake Borgne. There were some boats about that looked to be suspicious to me, so I decided to drag a net for a while. Manuel's other boats caught up with us and they did the same. Once we had a ball of shrimp, we hoisted the net and dumped them into the hold on top of the cases. The others will be along after they catch enough to cover their cases."

"I thought the sheriff was taken care of."

"He was, but there might be some hijackers about. No need to invite problems."

They were in the Fisherman's Canal. It was straight and populated by only a few moored boats. Mike could see the horizontal line of the railroad at the far end of the canal. Tall cane and heavy brush dominated both banks except where a small pier or camp bordered the water's edge. Geronimo took the wheel and sent Pedro forward to prepare for docking.

"Who would dare hijack one of Manuel's boats?" Mike asked. This was the first he heard of hijackers as a potential problem.

"Some boys out of Texas," Geronimo said. "The gang is run by two brothers, the Hadens. They used to steal cattle in west Texas, but a bigger and better cattlemen's association made that trade less profitable. They got pushed east and are now teamed up with D. A. Roberts and bootlegging. Manuel thinks they are behind the hijack of Hildago's last run which left the man hospitalized."

Teaming up with local authorities was standard practice. If the sheriff was on your side, there were never any arrests. If the D. A. was your man, arrests never ended in convictions. The ideal situation would be a partnership with both. Any competition could be arrested and convicted out of business and your people could operate with impunity. State Police were a different matter unless you could guarantee a block of votes for the governor.

"Who do the Hadens have working for them?"

"Bunch of hard cases from Texas. No one local that we know of."

Geronimo shifted the transmission into neutral and guided the boat toward a pier set well back and hidden by brush overhanging the canal on both sides.

"I've got to let some water," Mike said. He exited the rear of the cabin and made his way to some rigging at the stern where he could steady himself. The trawl nets were hanging on either side where they had been set to dry. Mike had just finished and was buttoning his trousers when Geronimo reversed the engine and the *Captain Robin* bumped gently against the pier.

"Come on out," someone yelled in English.

Mike ducked down behind the cabin and caught a glimpse of Pedro standing at the end of the pier, his hands in the air.

"Get over by the kid, old man," the same voice ordered.

Mike pulled his .45 from the small of his back and crept across to the side of the cabin where he had a clear view of the pier. He saw two men with shotguns. The man nearest him was doing the talking. He could not see much of the other man standing on the speaker's right. Mike made a quick glance around the bank and over to the road. He saw a car, the doors were open, and the engine was running, but no other people were about.

"Who are you?" Geronimo yelled in heavily accented English.

"Don't you worry about that, old man. This is your last haul." The speaker raised his shotgun to his shoulder.

Mike stepped around the boat's cabin and fired three rapid shots at the speaker and then shifted to the other man who dropped his shotgun and sprinted for the road. Mike put two more rounds toward the sprinter, but instead of making for the car, which Mike expected, the runner turned left at the road and disappeared behind the brush.

Mike bounded onto the pier, glanced toward Geronimo who had been shielding Pedro with his body.

"Check on that one," Mike yelled pointing at the man he had shot. "Make certain he is down." Mike ran to the edge of the brush line, stopped, peeked around the corner, and immediately pulled his head back. His quick glance had assured him the other man had not checked his retreat. Mike stepped out onto the road and watched as the running man disappeared around a turn.

Mike went back to the pier to Geronimo who was squatting at the side of the gunman.

"Do you know who he is?" Mike asked. Geronimo shook his head.

"Pedro alright?"

"He is over there. He is not hurt." Geronimo pointed toward the bow of the *Captain Robin* where Pedro knelt on the pier, his hands on the boat's bow and vomiting into the canal.

The wounded man groaned. Mike gave him a kick in the thigh. "Who are you? Who do you work for?"

The man's eyes fluttered open. "What happened?"

"You were going to shoot my men. I shot you first."

"I thought the kid shot me. He was so nervous, I thought he accidently shot me instead of the Dagos."

Mike gave him another kick. "Who are you? You had better tell me or we will find out if you are in a condition to swim."

"Shit," the man said. "You have already done kilt me. What do I care?"

"Who are you?" Mike asked, followed by another kick. The man groaned, and his eyelids fluttered.

"I'm Karl Portman. Everybody calls me Porkins." Portman did not appear to be any larger than average to Mike, but one cannot tell when it comes to nicknames.

"The kid with me was Billy Thigpen, a runaway from Mississippi. This was his first job with us."

"I don't think little Billy will quit running until he gets back to Mississippi," Mike observed.

"I hope he stays," Portman said. "He ain't cut out for this kind of stuff."

"Who do you work for? I can see you are not the law."

"I run with the Hadens. We was supposed to take each boat as it came in and hijack the load."

"Why did you make to shoot these people?"

"Figured each boat had a two-man crew. Six men would be too much to watch. Six dead men are no problem."

"Tío Geronimo, get his arms. I'll grab his feet and we can put him in the back of the car. I'll drive up to the hospital and leave him and the car."

As they worked their way toward the car with Portman sagging between them, the man convulsed violently, vomited blood and died. They continued to the car and placed the corpse on the rear seat. Mike searched the body, found a wallet with two ten-dollar bills in it and a .38 revolver in a shoulder holster. Mike pocketed the money and gave the revolver to Geronimo. He tossed the wallet onto the body.

"Wait here and I'll send the trucks down from the warehouse," Mike said as he slid into the driver's seat. Geronimo nodded and closed the car door. Mike turned the car around and headed up toward the railroad, half expecting to run into Billy Thigpen waiting in ambush. He turned into the loading dock of the warehouse and got out of the car.

The men waiting inside had not expected a car. Five armed men surrounded Mike the instant he closed the car door.

"I know you were expecting Pedro. I'm Mike Demill. Pedro and Geronimo are at the landing. We were ambushed."

A burly man separated from the others. "You're Mike alright. What happened? Are the goods there?"

"We shot up the hijackers. One ran away and the other is in the back of the car, dead. Geronimo and the rest are waiting for the trucks."

"Roll the trucks," the burly man said as he circled his hand over his head. He looked back at Mike. "I'm Manuel's trucker, George Leeds. Get inside and we will call Manuel now. He needs to know what is going on."

George got Manuel on the phone then handed the set to Mike. "Careful what you say," George cautioned. "Use Spanish. Anybody could be listening."

"Hello, Josef," Manuel said when Mike held the receiver to his ear. "Tell me what you have."

"We have a good catch. All boats are being unloaded now."

"Any rough weather?"

"Some thunder, but all is quiet now. I have a new car."

"That is good news. Wash your new car carefully before you park it. I will see you when you get home."

The line went dead.

"Do you have some gloves and rags?" Mike asked.

George pulled open a drawer and took out several pairs of workman's gauntlets and rags. Mike put on a pair of gloves and took the rags. He went to the car and wiped it down thoroughly, including the wallet. He had heard that it was possible to identify people through fingerprints. It was not likely that the local police had that capability, but he wanted to take no chances.

Still wearing the gloves, he drove the car into New Orleans until he reached a side street intersection with Canal Street. He parked the car, a 1920 Packard Twin, on the side of the street, left the keys in the switch and closed the door. He walked to Canal Street in time to catch a streetcar bound for the river.

The streetcar was sparsely populated. It was after six and growing dark. Night workers were on their way into town. Mike took a bench and slipped off the gloves. He tucked them into the edge of the seat against the car's frame. He rode to Liberty Place, got out and walked the half block to a small office.

Lights were beginning to be lit along the main streets when he knocked at the door to 137 Liberty Place. A black man opened the door and stared at Mike wordlessly.

"Mister Demill to see Mister Moreno," Mike said.

"Come this way, please. Mister Moreno is expecting you."

They walked down a short hall. The man stopped, knocked on a door and said, "Mister Demill is here, sir."

"Show him in, William." Mike recognized Moreno's voice.

William ushered Mike into the room and left, closing the door behind him.

Manuel Moreno was standing next to his desk. He offered his hand. "I am sorry you had problems, Mike. We live in a changing world. Time was, a man could conduct business in peace."

"I had to kill one of the hijackers," Mike said. "What kind of problem does that create?"

"What did you do with the body?"

"It is in a car parked on Sixth Street."

"Good. It will be a long time before it is noticed. Do you know who is responsible?"

"Before the man died, he said he was working for the Haden brothers."

"Did you get his name?"

"He went by Porkins."

"Ah," Moreno nodded. "That is one of Danny Haden's top men. He will be upset."

"Does this mean war?"

"Perhaps, perhaps not. The Hadens will confer with District Attorney Roberts before they act. Roberts will not want a war. Elections are around the corner." Moreno shrugged. "At any rate, I owe you your fee for a job well done. Depending upon conditions, we should make another such transaction in six months or so." He handed Mike a heavy envelope.

"Thank you, sir." Mike took the envelope. "I will await your call."

"Do so. Goodbye, Mike."

Mike stuffed the envelope in his coat pocket and stepped into the hall. William showed him to the door. He pressed the pocket containing the envelope to his chest as he began the walk to the Hotel Grunewald. It would be seven in the evening by the time he would arrive.

*****

Annie watched as Mike managed to establish himself on the deck of the little shrimp boat. She was terrified he would be knocked into the sea. The boat turned away and disappeared into the darkness before she had the opportunity to wave a goodbye to Mike.

"We will make the port at New Orleans before 4:00 tomorrow afternoon," Peres said. "You might as well take some supper and sleep the morning away."

Tomorrow would be the 22nd of December and the tickets she had were for the seven-thirty train the following day. This was cutting things very close.

Annie went to the galley where she was served baked fish and a potato dish she did not recognize that was simply delicious. Adão shown with joy as Annie exclaimed *"Delicioso!"* She had forgotten the Portuguese word for "thank you," so she used English.

"Belcomb, Belcomb," Adão said, beaming.

She returned to the berth, locked the door, and turned to face the room. She braced the single chair against one of the locking levers for the hatch, just in case. The porthole over the desk had a black-out shield, which she swung in place and went into the lavatory to prepare for bed.

She dressed for bed and contemplated another night in the hammock. Deciding the seas were sufficiently light, she pulled back the covers on the bunk. It smelled of Mike. She lay down, put her purse containing the .38 next to her and closed her eyes.

As she fell asleep, she wondered if she would ever see Mike again.

*****

Banging on the hatchway brought Annie out of a deep sleep. She grabbed her pistol and went to the hatch stumbling slightly as the ship rolled. Light shown around the black-out plate, she had not locked it down in place.

"Who is it?" She shouted at the closed hatch.

"It is Nuñez, miss. The Captain says it is time for you to come on deck and get something to eat. You have been asleep for ten hours."

Ten hours! Annie felt as if she had just closed her eyes.

"What time is it?"

"It is an hour or so before noon, miss. Adão has prepared a special stew for you. The Captain will join you."

"Tell the Captain I am coming. Thank you."

Annie returned to the lavatory. She stripped and washed herself as well as she could with a hand towel. She had only one dress aside from the clothes she had switched with Maria Lucia.

She applied lipstick, brushed her hair, and arranged her hat. She paused as she looked into the tiny, dirty mirror above the steel sink. The woman that looked back at her seemed years older than the one that dashed away with her friends looking for adventure.

She packed her day bag with everything she had, including her high heeled shoes, the little flats Maria Lucia had given her were much more comfortable for ship wear. She slung the strap of her purse across her body and placed the revolver in it where she could easily reach it.

She pulled the chair from under the hatch and opened the doorway to step out on the deck. Nuñez was waiting, the wind blowing what hair escaped his cap.

"Did you sleep well, miss?"

"Yes, thank you."

"The Captain will meet you in the galley. He wants to talk to you before we take the river pilot aboard."

"Are we that close to the river?"

"Oh, yes, miss," he pointed toward the bow of the ship. "That is the pilot boat coming now."

Annie squinted in the direction indicated and saw a small bump on the horizon.

"The pilot will be aboard and ready to guide us into the river in about twenty minutes. Please hurry."

Annie stepped into the galley to see Adão placing a bowl of stew and a cup of coffee on the table. He motioned for her to sit, which she did. Captain Peres sat across from her.

"Good morning, Miss Norwak. I hope that you slept well."

"Yes, Captain. I am well rested."

"That is good. When the river pilot comes aboard, I shall be too busy to speak with you, although you are invited into the wheelhouse. It is a very entertaining trip up the Mississippi River."

"Thank you, Captain. I would like that very much. When we came down the river the weather was very bad, and we could not see much."

"Then I am confident you will enjoy the sights. The day promises to be – how is it you North Americans say – a blue bell day."

Nuñez appeared at the galley door. Peres nodded at him and looked back at Annie. "I must go now. Enjoy your meal. I think that Adão will weep when you go ashore. He tells me you remind him of his youngest daughter."

The stew was wonderful. Annie thanked Adão using the few Portuguese words she knew. She got up and impulsively hugged the cook before heading to the wheelhouse.

The Captain was indeed busy. The ship had not yet entered the river's mouth to Annie's understanding, but the tension in the wheelhouse was palpable. There was a stranger standing next to the helmsman. Annie guessed him to be the pilot.

"Captain," the stranger said, "I recommend we reduce speed to one quarter."

Peres said something into the speaking tube and the engines slowed.

"I recommend one point to the starboard."

Peres said something to the helmsman who moved the wheel clockwise slightly while concentrating on the compass. In a moment, the helmsman said something and straightened the wheel. Commands were passed from pilot to helmsman and back in this manner for the rest of the run up the river.

The banks of the river appeared. Low marshlands dotted with clumps of brush commanded both banks to be replaced by cypress forests and then, after more than an hour's run, farmlands appeared with green fields spotted with cattle. Soon villages appeared with people working vegetable patches or sugar cane mills with tall brick chimneys spewing smoke. Horse drawn wagons were replaced by motor cars and trucks.

"Come look, miss," Nuñez said, sticking his head into the wheelhouse.

Annie stepped outside. The light was fading and in the distance across the treetops she could see the lights and distant roof tops of the city of New Orleans.

"We will be docking at the Chalmette Slip," Nuñez advised. That is where we will deliver you and several thousand tons of raw sugar."

*****

The Chalmette Slip proved to be a very active industrial site. The tug had pushed the *Garanhão do Mar* to her mooring station where a legion of dockworkers swarmed her decks.

Annie followed Captain Peres down the gangway carrying her and Mike's day bag. She stopped Peres as they passed the shipping clerk's desk. There was a telephone standing on the corner of the desk.

"Captain, a moment please. I must call my friends at the hotel and tell them I have arrived."

"Certainly, Miss Norwak," Peres said. "I will be just outside."

Annie was able to reach Summer, who burst into tears when she heard Annie's voice.

"Summer, what is the matter?"

"We thought we would never see you again," Summer managed to say between sobs. "How could we tell your father?"

"Well, I will be at the hotel in half an hour, we can talk then."

Annie walked out to where Captain Peres had hailed a motor cab from the several parked near the exit to the dock. Laughing and animated seamen lined the curbside in clusters of three or four. The groups, clearly destined for a night on the town, vied for cabs and negotiated fares.

"Thank you so much, Captain Peres," Annie said as she embraced the man.

"I hope to see you again Miss Nowak." He placed the bags in the cab and held out his hand to assist Annie into the vehicle.

Annie's cab brought her to the Hotel Grunewald. A uniformed doorman opened the cab door as Annie paid the fare. He took the pair of day bags and led Annie through the massive doors to the front desk. Annie gave the doorman a quarter, which he pocketed with a smile.

"Welcome to New Orleans, Madam," the registrar said.

"I am Ann Norwak. I and my friends have a reservation for tonight."

"Yes, Miss Norwak. Your friends are already here. They said they were expecting you. They are waiting in the cafeteria for you. There has been a change in plans, I am afraid."

"A change in plans?"

"Yes. Your friends have canceled the reservation. They say they will catch the train for Chicago tonight. It leaves in one hour."

"Oh, my. I did cut it close." She put Mike's day bag on the counter. "Could you hold this bag for a friend? He should be by later today or tomorrow morning."

"Certainly, madam. What is his name?"

"Michael Demill," Annie said. *Or Josef Rodriguez or Robert Stone*, she thought.

The clerk wrote the name on a slip of paper and tucked it under the grip of the day bag. He placed the bag behind the counter.

"Will there be anything else?"

"Yes. Do you have a telephone I might use for a long-distance call?"

"Yes, madam. I must place the call and reverse the charges. Once your party is on the line, I will give you privacy."

He placed a handset on the counter at the end away from the entrance doors.

"What city?"

"Chicago."

"And the number?"

"Cicero 3223."

"And who is the call from?"

"Ann Norwak."

The clerk spun the crank and spoke to an operator. He repeated the required information.

The clerk held the earpiece away from his ear, so Annie could hear the process. After two or three switches, Annie could hear the receiving ring tone.

"Office of the Cicero Chief of Police," said a female voice.

The operator in Chicago said, "Collect call for anyone from Ann Norwak. Will you accept the charges?"

"My goodness yes," came the reply.

"Your party is on the line, sir."

The clerk handed the phone set to Annie and walked to the other end of the counter where other guests were waiting.

"Annie! Is that you?"

"Yes, Meg. It's me."

"Your father was so worried. Why haven't you called sooner?"

"Is the Chief very angry?"

"He is steamed. I'll get him." Annie could hear Meg, the Chief of Police's receptionist, call across the office. "Chief, come to the phone. It is Annie."

CHAPTER 8

The walk to the Hotel Grunewald brought Mike across Canal Street, named so for a planned, but never constructed, canal linking Lake Pontchartrain to the Mississippi River. The wide right-of-way set aside for the canal now accommodated broad sidewalks (locally called banquettes) along store fronts, roadways for wagon and motor traffic as well as four railways for streetcars and narrow-gauge trains.

The street also divided the "French Quarter" from the "American" sector. During the uneasy time following the acquisition of Louisiana by the American government, those wishing to retain their European roots clung to the French Quarter while the brash Americans occupied much of the City above, that is upriver of, Canal Street. The rail lines and median along Canal Street divided the two unofficial districts and became known as the "neutral ground," claimed by neither American nor Creole.

The light of the day had faded quickly, hurried along by a cloudy sky and a cold misting winter rain. Mike worked his way across the Canal Street neutral ground, picking his way between manure piles, mud puddles and slick iron train rails. He turned the collar of his trench coat up to keep out the cold mist and wished for his hat. The open sea transfer to the shrimp boats had been so blustery that he had placed his bowler in his day bag under the care of Annie.

Cold rain and wind hurried Mike along the upriver side of Canal Street until he reached Baronne Street where he entered the foyer of the hotel. The dryness and warmth of the hotel lobby was a welcome relief. It seemed as if it had been weeks, not days since he first boarded the ship for Cuba. It was not just the comfort of the lobby, but the anticipation of seeing Annie again that lifted his spirits.

Mike approached the desk clerk, who looked at him with some distain and said, "May I help you, sir?"

"Yes, thank you," Mike said, suddenly aware that he was unshaven, wearing a disheveled trench coat and hatless, his hair a tangled mess. "It has been a tiring trip. My name is Michael Demill. I am here to meet Miss Norwak. Could you send word that I am here."

"Oh, yes. Mr. Demill. Miss Norwak and her two friends have already departed. A change in plans, it seems."

Mike felt both disappointment and relief. Annie had made it safely to the hotel, but now it seems he would not see her again. He managed to say, "I thank you, sir," and turned to go.

"Wait, Mr. Demill. Miss Norwak left this here for you." The clerk reached under the desk and produced Mike's day bag. He placed it on the counter with an audible "thunk." The image of Annie standing on the wet, windswept deck of the *Garanhão do Mar* as he swung over the side flashed into his mind.

"I thank you again, sir," Mike said as he hefted the bag from the counter. It did not seem as heavy as he remembered, but he shrugged off the observation. He carried the bag over to a guest reading area and sat down, placing the bag on his lap.

He unbuckled the bag's cover and opened it. His bowler was on top. Relieved that he would not have to make the trip back to his room bareheaded, he pulled the hat out of the bag and a note came along with it.

Mike recovered the note and slipped the envelope Moreno had given him into the day bag. Then he noticed that the half-gallon of rum was not in his day bag. He smiled to himself at the thought of three ladies from Cicero, Illinois, sharing a half gallon of rum on a train bound for the frozen north.

He read the note:

"I owe you for the sample of your imports. If you wish to collect, contact me by telephone or come in person.

Annie Norwak, 2315, 50th Avenue. Cicero, Illinois. Phone Cicero 5756."

He pocketed the note with a smile. He would definitely call. A trip to Cicero was not out of the question. He re-buckled the day bag and made his way out to Baronne Street, bundling up against the cold rain.

He crossed Canal Street to a streetcar stop. A newsboy huddled in the lee of a storefront near the stop.

"Paper, mister?"

"Yes, what do you have?"

"The Item. Only three cents, sir."

"I will have one." Mike tossed the boy a quarter and the boy withdrew a newspaper from under a make-shift canvas awning intended to keep the papers as dry as possible. The boy began to make change for the quarter.

"Keep the change," Mike said.

"Gee, thanks, mister. That's swell of ya."

Mike folded the paper under his arm just as the streetcar trundled to a stop. He boarded the crowded car and made his way to the rear. It was just after seven in the evening and a cadre of day laborers were headed home. No seats were available, so Mike stood near the rear door contemplating what he would do first at the hotel: open the envelope Moreno had given him or take a bath.

*****

The hot bath was marvelous. It seemed to soak away the days of cramped ship berths, Cuban hotels, cafes, and dodging Marines bent upon revenge. He walked back to his room wrapped in a hotel towel and carrying his dirty clothes bundled in another towel. In the morning he would put his dirty clothes in a bag and set it next to the door for the laundry service.

Once in his room, he slipped on underpants, placed his day bag on the bed, and opened it. He transferred the envelope from Moreno to the center of the small desk next to his bed. He sat at the desk and opened the thick envelope.

It contained three bundles of twenty-dollar bills. The paper strap on each bundle was marked "50." Three thousand dollars. Mike was astounded. He had hoped for half of what the envelope contained. There were also four loose ten-dollar bills.

Ten dollars a day, Mike thought. Had it only been four days since he contracted with Manuel Moreno? The man had a strong reputation as an honest man and this payment confirmed everything Mike had heard about Moreno. The man was an honest smuggler.

Mike opened the newspaper and turned to the real estate section. He could hardly go down to the bank tomorrow and deposit three thousand dollars in cash. He did not trust banks, anyway. If a bank folded, which had happened, he would lose his money.

Land was something else. Land was permanent, dependable, and rental property was income-producing. He scoured the "for sale" columns for bungalows and duplexes. One that caught his eye was a duplex on the corner of Leontine and Laurel, just on the upriver fringes of a neighborhood known as the "Irish Channel." The seller was asking two-thousand five hundred. He copied down the phone number.

There were some single residence bungalows priced in the range of fourteen hundred or so, but he decided he did not want several properties widely spaced about the city. With the duplex, he could live in one side and rent the other for about sixteen dollars a month. The Irish Channel was a working-class community and local housing was in high demand. He would call tomorrow and visit the property.

Annie's train had departed New Orleans about 7:00 p.m., almost the same instant he was entering the lobby of the Hotel Grunewald. With the additional stops along the route, the travel time from the Chicago terminal to Cicero and other factors, Mike did not expect Annie to make it home before 7:00 p.m. tomorrow, Friday. Saturday was Christmas Eve, so he decided a call Monday afternoon would be best.

He circled several residential properties for sale and a few used automobile advertisements. In the morning, he would go to the hotel reception desk and use the house phone to make a few calls.

He climbed into bed and, for the first time, thought about killing Porkins. The war had made him insensitive to killing when it was necessary. Had he not shot Porkins, his cousins would have died. No regrets there. The police were another matter. He had no desire to have to prove he was justified. He had no doubt that every person in the fishing community where Geronimo and his family lived knew the truth. That was enough.

He closed his eyes and fell into a dreamless sleep.

*****

The morning calls had been very productive. His first call was to Manuel Moreno. Mike asked for a recommendation for an attorney.

"Criminal or civil?" Moreno asked.

Mike didn't know there were such specialties. "I might need both," he admitted. "I am planning to buy some rental property."

"It is wise of you to invest in land," Moreno said. "I use John Eiseman." He gave Mike a phone number. "His partner is Joshua Meyer. Meyer would be the one for other problems. If you want, I will call Eiseman and recommend you to him."

"Thank you, sir. Please do so. I will call him later today for an appointment next week."

He then called the realtor and made arrangements to meet him at the double on Laurel Street.

Mike took the Saint Charles streetcar to a stop a few blocks from 5332-5334 Laurel Street. It was a cool, dry morning and the walk allowed Mike the opportunity to assess the neighborhood. Geographically, it was not far from the Garden District home he had shared with his mother and stepfather before the Great War, but in terms of economics, it was worlds away.

He passed pedestrians, mostly housewives on their way to the market, and overheard snatches of heavily Irish accented

English. These were working people and Mike knew he would fit right in. He wanted to disappear for a while, and the Irish Channel was just the place.

A man was standing on the corner clearly waiting for someone when Mike crossed Laurel Street.

"Mister Robert Viguerie?" Mike asked.

Viguerie reacted with surprise. "Yes, Mister Demill, I assume. I expected you to arrive by automobile."

"Please call me Mike. I wanted to see the neighborhood."

"Yes, of course. We can go in 5334, but there is a tenant in 5332 and they are both at work. He is a dock worker, and she is a domestic. The present owner tells me they have always been prompt with the rent."

"Why are they selling?"

"The original owner died, and his children are selling most of his rental properties. If this one does not appeal to you, I can show you several others. Most are in the Channel."

After a walk through 5334 Laurel, Mike decided the property was precisely what he needed. The realtor quoted the asking price of two thousand, five hundred dollars.

"I will pay two thousand, two hundred and fifty. Cash."

"Mike, I will have to go to my owners with the offer," Viguerie said, but his eyes suggested the offer was going to be accepted.

"Naturally. My attorney is John Eiseman. Call him at Main 5597 if your owners accept. He will make the necessary arrangements."

"I know John Eiseman well. He has conducted many sales for me."

Mike walked with Viguerie to the man's car, which was parked around the corner on Leontine Street. It was a new

Packard Twin. Likely the car cost more than the double he had just offered to buy.

"Can I bring you anywhere?" Viguerie asked.

"Thank you for the offer, but no. I want to see more of the neighborhood."

"There might be a counteroffer. I will call Eiseman either way."

"If my offer is not accepted, there will be no sale."

Viguerie climbed into the Packard and drove away.

Mike walked back to a market on Saint Charles, found a public phone and called Eiseman. Moreno had made the promised contact and the attorney was expecting Mike's call. They discussed the potential real estate transaction and Eiseman promised he could prepare an act of sale for Monday afternoon. As it happened, Eiseman was the notary for the sale of that same property to the present owner, so necessary documentation was already in his notarial archives.

Mike then rode the streetcar to a used car lot and bought a 1919 Ford one-ton truck. It had a bench-seat cab and an open flat bed. He wanted transportation that could be used for deliveries. He bought the truck for two hundred seventy-five dollars. A truck would not look out of place when parked on Laurel Street.

Mike walked out of the car sales office with the registration papers folded in a heavy envelope. He opened the truck's door and put the papers in a leather case strapped to the steering wheel's shaft. He lifted the seat to reveal the gasoline tank. Opening the filler cap, he peered into the tank. He had less than a quarter of a tank of fuel. He checked that the parking brake was set, which also placed the transmission in neutral, and that the switch was set to "off."

He went to the front of the truck and deployed the crank handle. He pulled out the choke knob located just under the radiator. He rotated the crank handle until he felt it engage with the engine. Using his left hand and careful not to close his thumb around the handle, he pulled up vigorously. If, for any reason, the engine kicked back the crank handle would be pulled from his hand, not jammed against his palm and wrist, or break his thumb.

The engine was still warm from the test drive and Mike could smell the gasoline that primed the engine. The procedure was not necessary with a warm engine, and the truck would have likely started easily using the electric starter, but Mike wanted the practice.

He returned to the cab, switched the ignition to "magneto," slightly advanced the spark, a lever on the left side of the steering wheel, and set the throttle lever, on the right side of the steering wheel, to one third. This time, when he pulled up on the crank, the engine fired immediately and ran roughly. He pushed in on the choke until the engine ran more smoothly.

His experience with gasoline engines in the army had taught him the basics of starting by hand. None of the army trucks had electric starters. This truck, a model 1919, was the first year such Model "T"s had been equipped with an electric starter and battery.

Mike drove around several blocks to familiarize himself with the vehicle. He experimented with spark and throttle settings. There was another choke knob on the dashboard, and he was pleased to learn the engine ran well with the choke pushed into the leanest setting.

There were three pedals on the floor. The left pedal was forward, the middle pedal reverse and the right pedal was the brake. The parking brake lever next to the driver's station had three settings. All the way to the rear locked the rear wheels and set the transmission to neutral.

The middle setting released the brake but left the main transmission in neutral. In this setting, depressing the left pedal forward would engage the transmission in slow forward. Depressing and releasing the left pedal allowed it to pop up and set the transmission to moderately forward. If the parking lever were pushed all the way forward, the operation of the left pedal would engage the transmission into higher gears.

He stopped the engine several times and restarted it using the electric starter. Once, to prove the engine was well tuned, he switched the key to the battery setting and advanced the spark slowly until the engine started without engaging the starter.

There was a service station and repair shop on the corner of Saint Charles and Napoleon Avenues, not far from the house on Laurel Street. He bought seven gallons of gasoline, which filled up the tank, for the outrageous price of two bits a gallon. He then drove back to his hotel and stowed his gear in his room.

He hid his envelope of cash on top of the armoire in his room, put twenty dollars on the desk and stuffed twenty in his pocket. If his room were broken into while he was gone, he hoped the twenty on the desk would distract a burglar.

He locked the room and headed for a speakeasy located in the rear of a warehouse not two blocks away. It was said that a boy standing on any street corner in New Orleans could throw a baseball and hit a speakeasy. Mike believed that to be true.

*****

Saturday morning was also Christmas Eve. Mike drove his truck through the Irish Channel to get a feel for the neighborhood. His short time living in the Garden District, not a half-mile from Laurel at Leontine, had not included excursions into the

Channel except for an occasional drive or buggy ride up Napoleon Avenue to the ferry at the Mississippi River.

He was back at his hotel by noon, in time for the twenty-five-cent stew provided to guests. Most of the residents were seamen or other migrant workers who, lacking homes or kitchens, depended upon the hotel for meals. This was particularly true for such holidays as Christmas when markets, diners and restaurants were closed.

After lunch, time dragged by so slowly that Mike finally decided a call to Annie could not wait until Monday. He dug out the note she had placed in his day bag.

He went to the house phone and, since this was a long-distance call and he did not want to reverse the charges, he gave the clerk two dollars to cover the call. "You have five minutes," the clerk said. "After that, you pay me another two dollars, or I disconnect the call." Long distance calls were a common occurrence at this house phone. Often the caller was a person of very limited means and the clerk was well versed in preventing uncollectable charges.

"You will not disconnect. If I run over five minutes, I will pay another two dollars." Mike showed the clerk two silver dollars before pushing them back into his pocket. The clerk made a sweeping gesture toward the phone attached to the wall next to the counter. Evidentially, privacy was not included in the hotel's policy.

Mike lifted the earpiece from the cradle and gave the charging handle a quick spin. He could hear a clicking noise in the earpiece indicating connection to a switchboard.

"Number, please." The switchboard operator had a local accent.

"Long distance, please. Cicero, Illinois," Mike said.

"One moment, please."

There were some clicks, and another voice said, "Chicago exchange. Number please."

Mike half expected the local operator to say something. He paused a moment, then realized he was expected to provide the number. He had not specified person to person, so there was no need for further intervention by the local operator.

"Cicero 5756," he said. He heard several clicks and then two short buzzing sounds as the receiving phone rang. The two closely spaced buzzes meant that CI 5756 was a party line.

The receiving phone was picked up after three sets of double rings.

"Hello?"

"Your party is on the line, sir," said the Chicago operator as she clicked off.

Mike did not recognize the voice. "This is Mike Demill. May I speak with Miss Annie Norwak, please?"

"Who did you say was calling?"

"Michael Demill."

"Just a moment, Mister Demill." The phone was muffled, and a few seconds passed.

"Hello? Mike?" It was Annie's voice. She was breathless as if she had run to the phone.

"Hello, Annie. I am happy you made it home from your adventure."

"Oh, Mike. I was beginning to worry about you. I ran down the stairs when the house mother said I had a telephone call. I am quite out of breath." Mike realized that the address she had given him was a ladies' boarding house and the telephone she was using was likely as public as the one he had in his hand.

"It was not my intention to cause you concern. I had to give you time to get home, or I would have called sooner."

"Yes, I know that. The last time I saw you, the weather was quite rough." Mike was certain the house mother was hovering nearby. The better ladies' boarding houses were run by strict matrons, often called house mothers, who staunchly protected the residences from any possible indiscretion.

"Are others nearby?" Mike asked.

"Yes."

"I have some contact information for you."

"I am ready."

"For the next week, I will be at the Rampart Hotel, a boarding house. The telephone number is Edgewater 8745. After that, I will be moving into a house I bought at 5334 Laurel Street."

"Mike! You bought a house?"

"I do need a place to live. I won't know the phone number until I move in. In the case of an emergency, contact John Eiseman at Main 5597 here in New Orleans."

"Who is he?"

"He is my attorney. He will know how to get in contact with me if you cannot reach me for some reason."

Annie repeated the telephone numbers for confirmation and then said, "I will be at my father's house for Christmas. Please write when you can."

"I will do better than that. I will call as soon as I move into the house I bought, or at least will buy. I'm signing the papers Monday."

"Mike, I am so sorry I did not see you again, but April and Summer were so very anxious to get home they practically forced me to catch the early train."

"I understand. The experience must have been quite harrowing. Did you all enjoy the trip home?"

"Oh, yes. Some enjoyed it too much, I think."

"Did April and Summer make it to their homes safe and sound?"

"They both live here. As a matter of fact, they both want to talk to you."

Mike laughed. "Put them on."

After April and Summer had the opportunity to chat with Mike, Annie came back on the line.

"You must come to Cicero, Mike. I insist."

"That is a possibility. I have some business dealings here I must complete first," Mike said. *Such as preventing a murder charge.* "I will call again when we can have a private conversation."

"Yes, I would like that, very much."

The hotel clerk reappeared. "One minute," was all he said.

"I must ring off now, Annie. I will talk to you again soon."

"Goodbye, Mike. How is it in French, *adieu*?"

"Only for a little while, Annie." The line went dead.

*****

Mike awoke late Sunday Morning. He had missed breakfast but went into the kitchen where the cook was cleaning up and managed to wangle a half-loaf of bread and a few slices of baked ham. It was enough to keep his stomach from complaining.

He went out to a cold and clear morning. The unsettled weather of the last few days had passed. He started his truck using the hand crank without even attempting to use the electric starter. He had not developed a trust in its reliability.

He drove along an almost deserted Canal Street until he reached a newsstand. He bought a copy of the Sunday New Orleans Item, drove to a side street, and pulled to the curb. He switched off the engine and opened the paper. He noted an article on the third page with the headline, "Known Gangster Found Dead."

It read:

"Police made a gruesome discovery on Christmas Eve. The body of Karl Portman was found in an automobile parked in front of 234 Sixth Street. The vehicle was registered to Daniel Haden of Saint Bernard Parish.

"The resident at that address, who wishes to remain anonymous, reported to police that he noticed the automobile, a black Dodge touring car, Friday morning and, when it had not been moved by the next day, he looked into the rear window and saw a man slumped on the rear seat.

"The police were summoned. Officers broke into the car to confirm the conditions within. Details of the crime are being withheld. It was reported that Mr. Portman had several gunshot wounds which appeared to be the cause of death. Persons who may have witnessed any activity associated with the Dodge touring car are urged to contact the New Orleans Police Department."

Mike folded the paper and placed it on the seat next to him. He switched the ignition to "battery" and slowly advanced the spark until the engine started. He switched back to the "magneto" setting and pulled away from the curb. He drove slowly to Canal Street and turned back toward his hotel.

The possibilities of the police investigation played across his mind. The police knew the victim was from Saint Bernard Parish, a jurisdiction politically hostile to the present New Orleans leadership. It was also known that the Hadens were close to District Attorney Roberts, a political ally of the Governor, therefore a political opponent of the New Orleans mayor.

The New Orleans Police Department would very much like to determine the actual murder occurred in Saint Bernard Parish, clearing the case from their books. The Saint Bernard

Sheriff's Department, opponents to the D.A., would want the case to be investigated by the New Orleans Police.

There was no indication, other than the residence of the victim and the registration of the Dodge touring car, that the murder had happened in Saint Bernard Parish. If the case were pursued in Saint Bernard Parish, D. A. Roberts, a political enemy of the Sheriff, could use it to his advantage.

Mike formed the opinion that Portman, a man who was a Texan imported as a gunslinger for Haden, would not be missed by the citizens. It was likely the investigation would die for lack of enthusiasm.

After the act of sale Monday, Mike would have a talk with Moreno and possibly make an appointment with attorney Joshua Meyer.

CHAPTER 9

At 9:30 Monday morning, Mike walked into the law offices of Eiseman and Meyer on the second floor of 225 Common Street. The receptionist, a young woman, sat behind a desk against the right wall. Opposite the desk were two stuffed chairs and a small table with an ashtray. Opposite the doorway Mike entered through was a wall with a pair of doors. The one to the left displayed a plaque engraved with the words "Mr. John Eiseman, Esq." The door to the right had a similar plaque engraved "Mr. Joshua Meyer, Esq."

"I am Michael Demill," Mike said. "I have an appointment with Mister Eiseman – an Act of Sale."

"Oh yes, Mister Demill," the receptionist said with an accent that faintly hinted of German. "I am Hilda," she said as she rose from the chair and walked around to the front of the desk. Hilda was a tall woman, perhaps five feet eight, and hinted at a tendency to be plump. She wore a full dress that nearly brushed the floor, a style reminiscent of the 1890s. Her blond hair was braided and coiled around the back of her head.

"If you could wait here for a moment, I will tell Mister Eiseman you are here. He would like to talk to you before the sellers arrive."

"And when will that be?"

"They are scheduled to be here at a quarter to the hour. Would you like some coffee?"

"No, thank you."

"Please make yourself comfortable. I will be just a moment." Hilda crossed the room and gently tapped on the left door. A voice within said, "Come."

Hilda entered and closed the door.

Mike looked around the room. There was a small, almost hidden door behind the receptionist's chair. When Hilda had offered coffee, Mike had not noticed any indication of a coffee pot or service in the room. He surmised that the hidden door led to a kitchenette.

Hilda opened the door and held it as she stepped back. "Mister Demill, Mister Eiseman will see you now." She gestured for Mike to enter and, once in, announced, "Mister Demill."

Eiseman stood and came around his desk with his hand outstretched. "Mister Demill, I am John Eiseman. A pleasure to meet you, sir. Our mutual friend has told me much about you." Eiseman was a tall, slender man with a full head of black hair and a wide moustache. His face had a smooth, tan complexion and he wore a suit along with a stiff, high-collared shirt. His dark eyes were bright and intelligent. Mike took him to be about forty years old.

Mike shook Eiseman's hand. "Thank you for seeing me and especially for arranging this Act of Sale on such short notice and during the Christmas Season," he said as he took the designated chair. It was well stuffed and quite comfortable.

"You are welcome, sir. It was no effort at all, I assure you."

"Hilda, coffee, please. How do you take your coffee, Mister Demill?" Eiseman took the remaining chair so that only the small coffee table separated them.

"Black, please. No cream. No sugar." Mike resigned himself to accepting coffee in the interest of politeness.

"Yes, Mister Eiseman," Hilda said and swished out of the room, gently closing the door behind her.

"Mister Demill, before continuing with this Act of Sale I would like to go over some particulars pertaining to the residence and the additional services we offer. First, the house was constructed in 1880 and renovated only once when the present owner acquired the property in 1911, or more correctly, the ancestor of the present owners. Electrical lighting was added at that time, as well as indoor plumbing. Telephone service was installed last year."

Mike had noticed the wiring throughout the house. Black wiring had been stapled to the underside of the crown molding, down the walls to electrical receptacles and across the ceiling to light fixtures. Cast iron sewer pipes were mounted on the exterior walls along the sides of the house from the kitchen, past the bathrooms, washrooms and diving down into the ground just behind the rear porch.

"The water is supplied by the city."

Mike remembered the agent pointing out the water meter at the street and the webbing of water pipes under the house which sat on piers two feet above the ground.

"And there are indications that municipal sanitary sewerage collection will be implemented, at which time you will be expected to abandon the septic tank and connect to the municipal system at your own costs," Eiseman continued. "I assume you have made a thorough inspection of the property."

"Yes, the real estate agent escorted me around the entire property, and we walked through the vacant half of the double. There were some minor maintenance things, such as loose bricks in the piers, a broken porch railing, nothing I cannot easily repair."

"Good. The sellers live in Mississippi and have never seen the property. They will be represented by an attorney, Mister David Rothschild, who will conduct the sale, so we can hardly query them for details."

There was a tap at the door and Hilda entered with a tray containing a coffee pot, creamer, sugar bowl and several cups and saucers. She placed them on the table.

"Will there be anything else, Mister Eiseman?"

"No. Please tell us as soon as Mister Rothschild arrives."

"Yes, sir." Hilda gently closed the door as she left the room.

"Do you have any questions, Mister Demill?"

"Thank you, I have no particular questions at this time," Mike said. In truth, ownership of property, particularly property with electrical service, indoor plumbing and telephone service was new to him. When he had lived with his mother and stepfather in the Garden District, he had taken all these things for granted. Since returning from the war, he had lived without such modern facilities.

Eiseman handed Mike a small folder containing papers for the utility services, recurring expenses, property taxes and telephone number. "Once we conclude the sale, I will provide you a copy of the deed and I will have the original recorded."

Eiseman poured a cup of coffee for them both. Mike noticed that Eiseman did not add cream or sugar to his coffee either.

"I am led to believe you may be in the market for additional properties," Eiseman said as he sipped his coffee.

"It is a possibility, depending upon business opportunities."

"That is wise," Eiseman said. "Land is the safest investment, I believe. Many today, particularly bankers, are urging people to invest in the stock market, even to the point of mortgaging their properties to buy paper. Pardon my unsolicited advice, but the practice does not seem wise to me."

"Nor to me," Mike replied. "I am of the old school and do not trust banks beyond such accounts that are necessary for business convenience."

"We are kindred spirits in that regard, Mister Demill."

Mike looked around the room as they conversed. In addition to the chairs and table they occupied, there was a wide, mahogany desk with a high-backed chair against one wall. A louvered window was behind the chair.

Opposite the door through which Mike had entered was another door. Clearly it was an exterior door for it had a dead-bolt lock, a private entrance. Another interior door was in the wall behind the desk. It could only open into Mister Meyers' office. A huge ceiling fan circled slowly overhead, though the room was quite cool.

There was another tap at the door. Hilda came in. "Mister Rothschild is here." Mike reached into his coat pocket for an envelope containing cash.

*****

Mike drove back to his new home. He decided to drive along Saint Charles Avenue. It would have been faster had he taken one of the streets closer to the river, but he hadn't spent much time in the Garden District since returning from France and he wanted to look at the neighborhood. He didn't know why.

The house where he had lived with his mother and stepfather was decorated for Christmas. He had no idea who had purchased the house. His mother had refused to allow him to return to the house and Mike had to find a room in a seaman's boarding house. Eventually, he moved to the Violet Canal village where he rented a boatshed and bought a one-man dredge boat.

The further upriver he traveled along Saint Charles, the more expensive and upper-class surroundings became. He stopped at the corner of Saint Charles and Audubon Place. This is where the truly wealthy had their city homes. Though not strictly in the Garden District, it housed the very wealthy, mostly descendants of Protestant Carpetbaggers, or so he had been told. He looked down the street for a moment before turning around and driving to his house, a trip of less than two miles.

5334 was a corner house and he parked on the side street. He decided that he would make a crossing for the ditch that paralleled the street and build a carport for his truck, maybe a garage. He jumped the ditch and went up to the back door – his back door.

He walked through the house. There was one long hallway that went from the rear washroom to the front of his side of the duplex house. It dawned upon him that he would need to buy some furniture. There was a wood stove, an old bed frame … and nothing else.

The previous tenant had even removed the light bulbs from some of the fixtures. The electricity was on and the telephone was working, both thanks to Eiseman's assistance. Mike would not have known where to start.

He would need to make one trip to collect his things from the boarding house and buy some bedclothes. He would get a newspaper and see what was for sale. When he occupied a one room hovel over a boat shed, he never contemplated such niceties. He checked the front door lock to be certain the key worked, then returned to his truck.

*****

By five in the evening, Mike had the rudiments necessary. A mattress, bed clothes, a table, two chairs and a rickety chest of drawers. He placed a phone call to Annie, hoping she would be in.

"Mike, I am so glad you called," Annie said after the house mother had fetched her to the phone.

"I have had a busy day," Mike said. "There is so much involved in setting up a house. I had no idea."

"That is what wives have been saying for generations," Annie laughed. "It takes two to run a home."

"I will be looking for work tomorrow. Sixteen dollars a month from my tenant isn't going to feed the bulldog."

"What is it you are going to do? I know you long to have your own shrimp trawler, but how does that work with a house in the city?"

"The trawler will have to wait. I will need more money than I have now to even get started. Today I have a truck and I live in a city. Everything must be hauled in. I think I will start in the hauling business. After all, I do have some experience in importing."

Annie paused for a long while, then she said, "Write me, please."

Mike understood. "You have ears about?"

"Everywhere."

"I will write to you tomorrow. It can't be tonight for I have no stationary, envelopes, pencil or stamps," Mike chuckled. "You have my address, write me."

"I will do that very thing," Annie said. "It is important that I hear from you soon. Now Summer and April want a few words with you."

"Good, my letters will have two parts. The last will be for you only." When overseas, letters from home were so valued that soldiers often read them aloud to their bunk mates. Mike never received any letters from home, though he wrote many — at first. The memory hurt, and Mike shoved it aside.

"Hello, Summer!" he said cheerfully.

*****

Mike's first trip in the morning was to a lumberyard. He had intended to buy some rough-cut lumber to build a box culvert to cross the ditch into his back yard. He would question the lumberyard owner of any drayage opportunities. In a port city there were always short haul needs. Most were mule wagons, but deliveries to locations further from the river could require the better speed provided by a truck.

The lumberyard was a beehive of activity. A rail line served the yard and a dozen workers danced around a single steam-powered crane unloading timbers from the flat-beds and preparing them for the mill. The logs, all fresh cut cypress, were huge. Nine logs filled a railcar flatbed to capacity.

A crane would pull a log from the pile and a tractor called a "Popping Johnny" would cradle one end of the log and drag it toward the mill. Instead of large steel rear wheels, these John Deere tractors had articulating tracks, similar to those on battle tanks, that afforded more traction on the packed mud of the transfer area.

Three tractors were circling the off-load location, feeding logs to the mill. When the tractors pulled heavy loads, the engine would make loud "popping" noises as the cylinder fired.

Logs were fed into one end of the mill and rough-cut lumber was removed and sent to the kiln shed in a steady stream.

On the other side of the yard, dried lumber was stacked thirty feet high. These rough-cut slabs of wood would be milled into planks, poles, and slats. The entire city of New Orleans, that which was not made of bricks, was made of cypress lumber. Huge logs, hundreds of years old, felled by lumbermen living on barges and pulled from the surrounding swamps through a network of canals by steam powered pull-boats to rail lines snaking through the swamps.

No one, it seems, had given a thought to the disappearing resource. The lumber yards simply shipped in cypress logs taken from swamps further north and deeper from civilization. If a rail line could be laid or a canal dredged to gain access, the trees would be taken.

Mike drove to the front of the yard where a steady stream of wagons loaded with fine milled planks flowed onto the rutted dirt road. He parked the truck and began searching for a salesman. No one seemed interested in helping him, so he pulled a worker aside and asked how he could buy some lumber.

"Dis here yard serves only contractors," the man said.

"How about some drayage work?"

"See that fat guy over there yelling at a teamster?" The man pointed toward a very fat man in a full-dress suit screaming words and spittle at a black man sitting on a wagon pulled by two mules. "That Mister Cotton. If you get to talk to him, it will be a wonder."

"Thanks, pal."

"No thanks needed."

Mike approached the argument at an angle where Cotton, who was almost incoherent, could not see him.

"I'm telling you now, you have been giving me two – two - trips a day to the Dryades Shop. Those people need lumber, and you are not keeping up."

"Master Cotton, dat shop is eight miles from here and I gots to unload by myself, and the days is short. I will unload in the dark this second trip."

"Agh," Cotton said. "Then get a move on." He slapped the nearest mule on the rump. The only reaction the animal made was to lift its head. The driver slapped the reins, and the mules pulled the wagon forward, the axles grinding.

"What you have there, Mister Cotton, is a lazy load," Mike said. He almost laughed as Cotton started and turned, wide eyed.

"Who in God's name are you?"

"I am Michael Demill, Mister Cotton. My friends call me Mike."

"Well, Demill, I am going to toss you off my property in two seconds." Cotton moved toward Mike but stopped. Usually when Cotton moved toward someone, they showed a little fear. This man was different.

"What did you mean by a 'lazy load'?"

"That wagon was stacked high with only two mules pulling. It would be a miracle if he could make two miles in one hour. A lazy man, fearing many trips, overloads himself and staggers under too heavy a burden."

"Can't use more mules, fool, he's hauling through city streets."

"Take a third off the load and he could make three, maybe four trips a day."

"Where are you from that you know so much about hauling?"

"I'm from down the bayou, but I learned about hauling in France with the 11th Infantry Regiment."

Cotton said nothing. He was clearly thinking, a challenge for him. Mike decided to take advantage of the opening.

"Or you could hire me to bring half of that load at a time and make six trips a day."

"You got a truck of some kind? Those big trucks cannot travel most of the city streets. They got to go the long way around."

"All I got is a flat-bed model T. But I can take the shortest route to and from, fifty minutes one way."

"How much?"

"Three dollars a load."

"Done. Pull your truck up here and we'll see if she'll take a half load."

The truck took a little more than a half load. While the workers were piling the lumber on the truck, Mike supervised the loading to balance the load. At the same time, he discreetly asked where the "Dryades Shop" was located.

With the cargo properly lashed down, Mike fired up the truck and started out in the lowest gear. The steering wheel bucked violently as he fought his way over ruts and onto the clamshell-surfaced roadway of Florida Avenue. He was able to shift up to second gear without trouble and set the throttle, so the truck ran comfortably at ten miles an hour, fighting a bucking steering wheel to stay in the wagon ruts.

Less than halfway to Dryades Street, he passed the mule team with the great stack of lumber. He made the delivery, unloaded the truck, and passed the wagon on the way back to the yard. At this rate, he would make twelve dollars a day. Enough to cover days when the roads were washed out, or the truck needed repair. If a guy couldn't live on sixty dollars a week, shame on him.

When Mike came back from the last run of the day Cotton met him at the gate. Mike handed over the delivery receipt and Cotton made a show of examining it under the lamp.

"You did good, Mike. The Dryades Shop called. They said you were not slow about unloading as well. Five trips at three dollars a trip is fifteen dollars."

Mike held out his hand and Cotton counted out three five-dollar bills. "I could have done six loads, if I had a full day."

"Be here in the morning and we will see."

"Mister Cotton, see that stove-up wagon over there?" A heavy freight wagon lay on its side, axle broken and wheels missing.

"Yea, been there for months. The feller that supposedly owns it just abandoned it there when the axle broke."

"Can I have it?"

"Sure. Beats me having to pay to get it hauled off."

Mike drove over to the wagon. He pulled a crowbar and sledgehammer from his cab and began to disassemble the wagon, neatly piling the salvaged timbers on the flatbed. It took over an hour of hard work, but he headed home with enough to begin the driveway into his backyard and the beginnings of a garage.

That night he washed his clothes in the bathtub and hung them up to dry in the washroom. His next purchase was going to be a washtub and wringer. He crawled into bed dead tired. The only time piece he had was a beat-up pocket watch. He figured sunrise to be about six and he kept checking the watch through the night. He added alarm clock to his growing list of things to get.

Two more days of hauling and between Mike and the mule skinner, Johnson, the Dryades Shop was getting more lumber than they needed. Cotton changed things around. Johnson would continue hauling from the yard to the shop, at half loads, and Mike would begin delivering to job sites. Construction contractors were expected to pick up their orders, but for a small fee, the Dryades Shop would deliver.

Mike's last site delivery of the day was to a new house under construction on Pine near Hampton, not two miles from his house. It would be an easy three dollars. After fuel and other expenses, Mike was clearing eight to ten dollars a day, more money than some doctors.

He found the building site and a man, likely the job foreman, waved him to drive onto the site and unload next to the foundation under construction. Mike unloaded the lumber with the assistance of two carpenters and approached the foreman with the bill of lading for signature. He waited while the foreman verified the delivery, checking off items on the bill of lading as a carpenter called them out.

"Mister Baird!" someone shouted from behind Mike. "Why have you not raised the walls?"

"Mister Kienson, we have not finished with the joists," Baird answered.

Mike turned around slowly. Kienson was climbing out of the rear of his touring car, a great cigar clamped in his teeth. When was the last time he had seen Kenton Kienson? Must have been three days before the draft notice arrived. He wondered if the man would recognize him.

Kienson, a wide man who, in his youth had been quite an athlete, now sported a balding head covered by a silk hat, struggled through the construction materials to reach Baird. He was wearing a tuxedo, everyday wear for the man.

"Mister Baird," Kienson began and stopped abruptly when Mike turned to face him.

"Michael Demill?" he said, his voice filled with astonishment. "You are Michael Demill, are you not?"

"Hello, Mister Kienson."

"We -we thought you were killed in the war."

"I was, but it did not stick," Mike said, almost smiling.

"I never knew you returned to New Orleans. My condolences over the loss of your mother." The man was stuttering, clearly flustered, perhaps embarrassed. He looked around and finally stuttered, "Are you a carpenter now?"

"No, sir. I am in the drayage business."

"Oh. That is a good trade."

"Tell me, sir, how is Chastity these days? Married, no doubt?"

"Not married but promised."

"Will you tell her I asked about her?"

"Yes, of course. She will be greatly pleased to learn the reports of your death were false."

"Only premature, sir," Mike replied. Something in Kienson's demeanor was off. It was more than his meeting the son of a friend who was now a laborer, more than the surprise of meeting a man thought dead. Kienson appeared to be genuinely frightened.

"It would not be wise, Mike, to present yourself to Chastity now. She is engaged, and your return will only serve to upset her."

"Why is that? I wrote her many times, but she never reciprocated, not once. Clearly, I am not, nor was I ever someone special in her life."

"That may be, but I say you are to stay away from my daughter. She is to marry into one of the richest families in this city." With that, Kienson stormed back to his car. The chauffer, expecting his boss to be at the construction site longer, had to scramble to open the door. Kienson barked an order that Mike did not understand. The chauffer helped Kienson into the car, retrieved the man's top hat, which had been knocked into the gutter, closed the door, and glared at Mike as he drove away.

"What was that all about?" Baird asked.

"For the life of me, I cannot say," Mike said.

"How well did you know his daughter?"

"Not well at all," Mike said. *We were lovers,* he thought. *I believed I knew her well, but I was deceived.*

CHAPTER 10

Friday provided a slight break in Mike's drayage opportunities. The morning brought incessant rain. Both lumber mill and construction sites stopped work. The construction driveways and work yards were muddy quagmires. Most of the main city roads were paved with bricks, ballast stones or macadam, but many secondary streets, particularly in developing areas, were clamshell, planks, or packed dirt.

An empty truck could maneuver easily, but a heavily laden truck would quickly bog down. It was one of the few times when heavy hauling was done exclusively by mule and ox sleds. Everything slowed to a crawl along the docks and drayage routes.

Mike took advantage of the time to complete his shopping. He added several sets of work clothes and one suit to his meager wardrobe. He added a washtub, a small icebox, kitchenware, flatware, some china, and an armoire from an eviction sale. On his last stop he added several grocery staples. The previous owner of the truck had converted it from an open canopy top to a closed wooden cab, for which Mike was very grateful.

The rain ceased at three in the afternoon and Mike took the time to disassemble the old wagon and use the timbers to build a culvert and planked crossing, enabling him to park in his back yard. He staked out the location of his planned garage. If the weather cooperated, he would begin the garage Sunday.

At five the light began to fade, and Mike quit his yard work. He climbed the back steps to his washroom, stripped down and tossed his filthy clothes into his new washtub. He checked the temperature of the gas hot water tank in the corner of the washroom. He had lit the heater before starting his yard work. No need to keep water heated all day. Someday soon he would sell the old wood burning stove and buy one of the new gas ones.

He walked naked to his bathroom and filled the bathtub. The long bath had become one of the high points of the day for Mike. Warm, soapy water felt particularly good on those old scars that had healed in raised ridges. If he had been shrimping or dredging oysters, a warm soothing bath would have to come at the end of a week, not every day. He wondered if he was becoming too much of a "city boy."

He shaved, except for a full mustache which he had been cultivating since Cuba. He dressed in his new suit, bowler hat and high-topped shoes. Tonight, he decided he would visit the Orion Lawn Tennis Club.

Tennis was sometimes played on the courts next to the club, but primarily the Orion was a speakeasy for the very wealthy. The clientele drew from the Protestant elite businessmen of New Orleans. Jews were banned and only the wealthiest of Catholics were barely tolerated. Mike did not fall into any of these categories, but he was going to see if he could bluff his way in.

He parked his truck on Saint Charles Avenue, two blocks from the Orion. He walked to the corner and waited. A large Cadillac sedan pulled up to the front canopy of the Orion Club and several flappers and college boys poured out, laughing, and pushing each other. Mike walked up to the rear of the group and followed them into the club.

The first young man out of the car had laughingly accosted the doorman, throwing an arm around the man, and bragging that he had recommended the Orion Club. Mike squeezed by the cluster of celebrants unnoticed. Once inside, he drifted to the darker end of the bar.

The bartender wiping the bar eyed him suspiciously. "What will you have?"

Mike looked at the display of bottles on the shelf. They were certainly confident they would not be raided. There was no attempt to hide the true product that made the Orion such a popular "Tennis" club. A bottle of "Toro Negro" adorned the top shelf. It appeared to be full, and Mike wondered if it was one from his recent shipment.

"I will try a shot of that," he said, pointing at the Toro Negro.

"Are you certain? It is five dollars a shot."

Mike blinked. Five dollars a shot would mean the club was pulling in $160.00 a bottle for which Moreno had paid $4.20 to *El Señor* Sebastian O'Neil y Madrid, a 3,800 percent increase. Bootlegging produced a waterfall of money and everyone along the way had his cup out collecting what he could.

"I will try a shot," Mike said.

"Show me your money first. I don't know you."

Mike pulled out five silver dollars and placed them on the table. The stack of coins was replaced by a shot glass. He tasted the rum. It was Toro Negro alright, watered down about 20 percent. He nursed the drink as he turned to face the crowded club.

The gaggle of young partyers he had followed in occupied about a quarter of the tables. They were drinking beer, joking, laughing. The girls were flirting, the boys were showing off. American kids having fun and without a care in the world.

The front door opened, and another group of young adults flowed in. He saw her instantly, Chastity Kienson. She was the reason he had made the trip to the Orion Club. It hadn't been in existence when he and Chastity were — *What? Lovers? Friends? None of the above?*

Chastity, always fashion conscious, had enthusiastically embraced the flapper look. She wore a silvery dress that stopped a few inches below her knees. It seemed to shimmer and was decorated with beaded tassels that emphasized her every move. Her raven-black hair was hidden by a small-brimmed cup of a hat with a decorative veil.

Mike felt a pang, a nostalgic shadow passed in his mind of a carefree time of lawn parties and secret meetings. That past, as carefree as today was to the revelers across the club, died on August 15, 1917. The draft notice was hand delivered to Mike when his mother's maid called him to the door. "A man's here to see you, Master Michael," she had said.

Mike finished the shot in one gulp and ordered a beer.

"That will be five cents," the bartender said.

"More to my taste." Mike tossed his nickel on the bar. He scooped up the mug of foaming something the bartender slid to him. The man with Chastity escorted her to a table. He was a handsome, tall man, tending toward skinny. When he removed his straw skimmer, blond hair tumbled over his ears. He was about the same age as Chastity, a little over twenty. Mike mentally named him "Stork."

Mike moved down the bar to a seat closer to the table. Stork helped Chastity to her chair and sat opposite her, with his back to the bar. Mike sat behind the man, so he was facing Chastity across the table and over Stork's shoulder. He lifted the beer to his lips and sipped slowly.

Mike pretended to watch the people at a table to his right as he studied Chastity out of the corner of his eye. She might not recognize him. He now had a moustache, a weathered, mature face, and haunted eyes. His blue eyes had changed forever in France. He now had the thousand-yard stare.

A waitress came to Chastity's table and Stork ordered a bottle of champagne. "Put it on my tab," Stork said.

"Yes, Mister York," the waitress said.

So, the Stork's name was York, York the Stork. Mike decided he preferred Stork.

The champagne arrived, delivered by a waiter instead of the waitress who made a big show of opening the bottle. The cork was shot to the far wall and wine bubble over the waiter's hands as he poured foam and some liquid into a pair of flutes.

Stork offered a toast that Mike could not hear, and he touched glasses with Chastity. She lifted the flute to her lips and, in doing so, looked over Stork's shoulder into Mike's eyes. She put the glass down.

Stork noticed the sudden change in Chastity's demeanor. "What is the matter, dear?" Stork said.

"Nothing, the wine is quite bubbly." She looked at Stork, but her face carried a puzzled expression.

"I should think so. It costs twenty dollars a bottle," Stork said. He was not convinced it was bubbly champagne that created the sudden change in Chastity.

Mike looked directly at Chastity, smoothed the beer foam from his moustache and smiled.

"Do be a dear," Chastity said. "I am suddenly quite cold. Could you get my wrap from the car?"

"I told you to bring it in and I don't know where the driver is."

"I know. Silly me. André will be parked where he can see the door. He always is. It won't take you a minute and I would be so grateful."

"Very well." Stork stood up and placed his skimmer on the table in front of his chair, lest someone take the notion that Chastity was unescorted. There were some ladies about who came in by themselves, but none would leave alone.

Stork walked out the door. Chastity stood and slowly came around the table until she faced Mike.

"I do not intend to be forward, but you remind me of someone," she said, squinting her eyes.

"And who might that be, Cass?" Mike replied, using her nickname.

"Michael Demill! Is it really you? I thought you had been killed in the war!"

"Your father told me the same thing when I saw him earlier this week. He said nothing to you?"

"No. Nothing."

"Well, it is me, Cass. Mike back from Gay Par-ree."

Chastity threw the champagne into his face. "You son-of-a-bitch!" she yelled, loud enough that people in the club turned and stared.

Mike was shocked but maintained a calm face. One of the waiters came over and Mike pulled the towel from the waiter's arm and wiped his face.

"Miss, is this man bothering you. I will have him removed," the waiter said, nervously eyeing Mike.

"No," Chastity hissed. "He will be leaving."

"This is not the reception I was expecting, Cass," Mike said, rubbing the towel across his moustache.

"You abandoned me. You joined the army and traipsed off to France for some 'great adventure.' Did you think I would just

146

say, 'Oh, welcome home my little vagabond, did you have a fun time?'"

"I did not have a choice. I was drafted."

"Like hell you were. Daddy has a friend on the draft board. He said you filled out the draft card – something you could have avoided - many did. – and you sent a letter to the board begging to be the first drafted."

"That is ridiculous. If I had wanted to go into the army, I would have joined. That war in France was nothing to me."

"You were afraid your mother would prevent you from joining, so you used the draft to escape blame. Daddy explained it all to me. He saw the letter. You were among the first to be drafted, just as you wanted."

A voice boomed to Mike's left. "How dare you address my fiancée?"

Mike turned to see Stork. He was holding a shawl, rage playing across his face.

"I thought we were old friends," Mike said. "I was mistaken."

Stork pushed the shawl into Chastity's hands.

"We shall take this outside," he said, his chin jutting out as he looked down his nose at Mike.

"Chip, don't. It is alright," Chastity said. "He was just going."

"We have not been introduced," Mike said. "Allow me. I am Michael Demill, late of Bayou Terre Aux Boeufs, and you are Chip York-the-Stork, fresh off mama's breast." Mike held out his hand.

Stork threw a quick left jab at Mike. The man was fast and clearly trained in boxing. Mike slipped the first punch and blocked the following right. He made no attempt to counterpunch.

Rough hands grabbed Mike from behind and Stork threw another left that glanced off Mike's cheek. Other bouncers grabbed Stork and he stopped swinging.

A man in a tuxedo, apparently the manager, appeared. "Mister York, sir, please restrain yourself. This is a gentleman's club."

"John," Stork said through clenched teeth, "I demand you throw this bum out immediately."

The man made a flipping motion with his hands as if he were sweeping out trash. The burly pair holding Mike lifted him off his feet and carried him toward a side door, followed by a third giant of a man. Good clubs did not toss bums out the front entrance. It might interfere with arriving customers.

Mike looked at Chastity's eyes as he was being pulled toward the door. She glared back until he and his beefy escorts disappeared into the alley.

The bouncers holding Mike pulled him into the alley and forced him to turn and face the third man. The man was huge. He completely blocked the alley leading to the street. He punched Mike in the stomach. Mike would have crumpled to the ground had not the other two held him up. Mike coughed violently and spit up a gob of brownish goo. The smoke in the club had aggravated his lungs and his breath came in gasps.

"You ain't never coming back to the Orion Club. Hear me?" The mountain roared.

Mike spat and nodded. "At five dollars a shot for watered down rum, no fear of that," he said.

It seemed as if his head exploded.

*****

Mike blinked and tried to make sense of the spinning world. Grimy water dripped from his eyelids – sideways. He was lying down. A rat squeaked then ran to the base of a wall where it followed the edge to disappear behind a box. It was dark, but a glimmer of light came into the scene from somewhere.

He remembered. He was in an alley behind the Orion Club, at least that is where he was when last conscious. He sat up. Pain coursed around his chest. *Broken ribs*, he thought. He tried to gauge the time. It was still dark, but he didn't know which day.

He managed to stand by crawling up the nearest wall. He coughed and spat up more brown goo. His chest heaved and burned. The beating had aggravated his chemically injured lungs. The world slowly stopped revolving, and he took stock of himself.

The pistol he kept tucked behind his back was gone. His pockets were turned inside out and were empty. He had lost a tooth on his left side. At least one rib was broken or very badly bruised.

He felt a desperate urge to urinate. He leaned against the wall with one hand and relieved himself only to see a stream of bloody piss splash over the broken crate at the base of the wall.

He attempted to walk a few steps but was forced to use the wall for support. He saw his key ring laying in a puddle. Stooping to pick it up, he lost his balance and would have fallen had he not been able to catch himself on the wall.

He stumbled toward the street. It must have been very late, for no music was coming from the club and the only traffic on the street was a slow-moving wagon filled with refuse. He walked toward where he had parked his truck hoping it was still there.

His truck was where he had left it and he crawled into the driver's seat. He was most thankful for the electric starter, for he was certain he would not have been able to crank the engine.

He started the truck, put it in first gear and began a very slow drive home.

He pulled into the area he had designated for his garage and turned off the engine. He rested in the cab for several minutes before climbing down and going into his back door.

He found some matches and lit the hot water heater. He stripped off his clothes and saw with disgust that his new suit had been torn beyond repair.

He stumbled to the bathroom, turned on the light and looked into the mirror. His face was swollen, both eyes blackened, and his upper lip protruded like a shelf over his mouth. He sat on the toilet with his head in the sink and ran cold water over his head.

After a few minutes, he drew a cold bath. The hot water heater had not had time to even warm the water. He soaked in the tub and fell asleep.

When he awoke, it was daylight outside. He surmised it was Saturday, but he was not yet certain of the day. Saturday was normally a workday, but not this Saturday. He managed to climb out of the tub and dress. Every muscle and bone hurt.

Remembering the hot water heater, he went to the washroom and filled the washtub with scalding hot water. He put what remained of his clothes in the tub and turned off the hot water burner. There was a knock at the door.

Dressed, but barefoot, he stumbled to his front door. Without his pistol close at hand, he hesitated before reluctantly opening the door.

A young man, perhaps twenty, was standing in the doorway. He had dark hair, short and was rail thin.

"Mister Demill," he said. "Good God, sir. What has befallen you?"

"I have met a rough crowd, thank you for your concern."

"Mister Demill, I am Patrick Doon, your tenant. I have the rent, sir."

"In that case you are most welcome. Come in. Do forgive my condition. I am certain it is temporary." Mike stumbled to one of the only two chairs in the room and sat down heavily, his head in his hands.

"Stay right there, Mister Demill. I will fetch my missus." Doon went to the door and called out, "Mary, come here quick, darling."

Mike heard some doors slamming, and a small, thin woman swam into view.

"Saints preserve us, Dorn," she said. "But this man has had a wondrous beating."

"Put yourself in our hands, Mister Demill. Mary here is well versed in mending men. We Irish are no strangers to troubles."

"Please call me Mike. I would be most grateful for any doctoring you can provide."

"Mike, it is then. My friends call me Dorn, Doon the Dorn, that's me. Mary and I are here straight off the boat from Cork City. We came here to escape the Black and Tans."

"Dorn, stop chatting and help me get his shirt off," Mary said. Once the shirt was off, Mary assessed Mike's injuries. She gently felt his sides and examined his jaw.

"I do not think you have any broken bones, except for one rib which may be cracked. Your jaw had been dislocated, but it is in place now. One tooth is gone. You have a wide cut on your head that will need stitches. Everything else is bruises or minor cuts. Rest is your best remedy. As for your old wounds, I cannot tell if anything has been aggravated."

Mike did not know about the cut on his head and gingerly felt the back of his head. Mary slapped his hand away.

"Leave that be," she scolded. "All will heal with time. I will go get my kit." Mary scurried out and returned in moments with what appeared to be a doctor's case. She cleaned Mike's wounds, stitched his head, and wrapped his chest tightly.

Mike stood and stretched his arms. His chest felt much better now that it was bandaged. "I thank you, Mary," Mike said. "Send me your bill."

Mary laughed, "I will do that very thing."

"I told you she is as good as any doctor," Dorn said. "Pulled me through when the Brits put two slugs in me side."

Mary pulled a flask from her medical kit, opened it, and handed it to Mike. "Take a pull on this. Doctor's orders."

Mike took a swig without hesitation. "Now that is some very fine medicine."

"And getting rarer every day," Dorn said.

Mike smiled. "Perhaps I can help with that."

"If you can, I know where you will be greeted with cheers," Mary said as she capped the flask and returned it to her kit.

Mike was beginning to feel much better. He attempted a deep breath and decided he didn't feel that much better, yet.

"Tell me, Patrick Doon the Dorn, what does 'Dorn' mean?"

"In the old tongue, Dorn means 'Fist,'" Mary said proudly. "Dorn is wanted by the Brits. Has a price on his head, he does."

"Before you go getting ideas, Doon is not the name on the warrant, and many Irish in New Orleans are Sinn Féin." Dorn said.

Mike had read newspaper accounts of the Irish Republic. It had been the Irish Rebellion Government outlawed and crushed by the British army. A treaty signed a few months ago created the Irish Free State, the Saorstát Éireann, essentially retaining

Ireland within the British Empire. The Sinn Féin opposed such an accommodation.

"Reward never crossed my mind," Mike said. "I think we can do some business. How much hard drink do you think you can use?"

"Good God, man. That is a foolish question. The Irish Channel can absorb all you can get. We have a few sources, but the quantity is little, and the quality is nothing as fine as Mary's medicine."

"Rum I can get tomorrow," Mike said. "Irish whiskey, maybe. Beer, you will have to brew yourself. Mind you, now. I don't want to go up against any Irish providers."

"No one will go against Sinn Féin," Dorn said with a laugh.

"I will need to visit a friend," Mike said. "Then I can tell you more. But, during the meantime, I wonder if I could make a purchase from you, Dorn."

"From me? I am just a day laborer."

"One result of the condition you find me in today," Mike said, "is that I have been relieved of my Colt automatic."

"That is a shame. You should take better care of such valuables." Dorn looked over to Mary and raised his eyebrows.

"I was deceived. It will not happen again," Mike said.

"If you were to happen to have thirty dollars laying around, you might find a fine German Luger, a device with which you may be familiar," Dorn said.

Mike nodded. "Just a moment, my friend." He walked into his bedroom and returned with the cash. He opened the envelope of Dorn's rent money and stuffed in a few bills.

"That is sixteen dollars for doctoring and thirty for a German - souvenir."

Mike's telephone rang. Two short rings between long pauses.

STEPHEN ESTOPINAL

"That's your call," Dorn said. "We're on your party line. Single rings are for us."

Mike went to the wall and picked up the earpiece from the cradle. He looked at Dorn and Mary as he spoke. "Hello?"

"Mike! Where have you been? I called several times last night. I was worried."

"Hello, Annie." Mike's face broke into a broad smile.

"We will go now Mike," Dorn said. Mary collected her things and the Doons let themselves out as Mike waved goodbye.

"Am I interrupting something," Annie asked.

"No, not at all. My tenants were dropping off the rent. Are you able to talk now? I didn't hear your house mother."

"I can talk, Mike. I am at work and I just put a call through to New Orleans, so I had the exchange ring your number. One of the advantages of being a switchboard operator."

"I am happy you called. I need to hear a friendly voice."

"Problems?"

"No, not now. Last night I visited with an old acquaintance. Someone I knew before the war."

"Was she happy to see you?" Annie was a very perceptive lady.

"She did remember me, but we just don't have anything in common anymore." Mike said as he rubbed the stitches on his head.

"I would say I'm sorry to hear that, but it would be a lie."

"Truth be told, Annie, I regret we did not have the opportunity to properly say goodbye."

"Mike, I have some news for you. I have been offered a job at the switchboard in New Orleans. I won't accept if you tell me to turn it down."

154

"Are you certain you want to move to New Orleans? You don't know anyone here."

"I know you."

"You don't really know me. What does your family think of you moving? What about Summer and April?"

"Summer and April are all for it. I haven't told my father, yet, but I've been living in a boarding house for two years and he hasn't visited me once."

"If Summer and April are for it, then by all means come down. Tell me when and I'll pick you up at the train station."

"The telephone company has a boarding house for the operators, so I will not need a place to stay," Annie said softly.

"When do you think you will come down?"

"It won't be for a month or more. Lots to do before I can get away from here."

"That works for me," Mike laughed. "It will take me at least that long to make this house presentable. Are you certain about this?"

"Are you certain I will be welcome?"

"You will be most welcome, but it is a big thing to move across the country."

"Mike, you are talking to a gal who took off for Cuba on a lark. Moving to New Orleans is less of a risk than that."

"You weren't planning to stay in Cuba, though you almost did."

"All I need to know is: do you want me to do this?"

"I would be disappointed if you didn't," Mike said. He was afraid to sound discouraging, but he didn't want Annie to change her life without proper consideration.

"That's close enough for me. My time is up. Goodbye, Michael Demill Josef Rodriguez Robert Stone."

.

CHAPTER 11

Dorn reappeared at Mike's door carrying a canvas sack. Once inside, Dorn opened the bag to reveal a Luger and two boxes of cartridges. The weapon was in excellent condition and showed no signs of wear. Each box contained twenty-five rounds.

"I have had a chance to talk to some gentlemen pertaining to your proposal of providing spirits," Dorn said. "They will tell me in a few days if we might do some business."

"Once they are satisfied I am who I say I am, how much are we talking about?" Mike said.

"Enough to fill that little lorry you have every week," Dorn laughed, "and that is only if we do not sell beyond the Channel."

"That would be about four hundred quarts of rum at eighteen dollars a quart," Mike said. "Can you manage those quantities?"

"Child's play," Dorn said. "You could make more if you could get some good whiskey."

"There's whiskey and then there's good whiskey," Mike said. "I can provide very good rum. The whiskey that's being moved about this town might as well be turpentine. I will make a few contacts and see you tonight to arrange delivery."

"Come over about six tonight. Mary will set the table with some of her famous stew. We can work out the details then."

*****

Mike sat at a table on the levee-side banquette of the Café du Monde. It was a location that was obscured by the café from pedestrians and vehicles moving along the heavily traveled Decatur Street. It may even have been the same table where he had first met Moreno.

Mike had called Manual Moreno's office soon after Dorn brought him the Luger, now tucked safely in his belt behind his back. William, Moreno's office man or butler, had answered the telephone. Mike asked to speak with Moreno and was told to hold for a moment. Mike could hear some discussion in the background. When William returned to the line he said, "Mister Demill, Mister Moreno will meet you at the Café du Monde at noon."

He watched the river traffic as he waited. The superstructure of ships could be seen above the levee and the sounds of a busy port filled the background.

Suddenly a vision intruded into Mike's mind. The mud and soot-covered face of a young man stared up at him with accusing eyes. The eyes were dead. Mike had hacked the man, really a boy, to death with a shovel. Screams and explosions drowned out all other noise.

"Demill," someone was yelling, "Demill, get to the nest and help push the Krauts out. Get that gun back in this fight!"

The man yelling was a lieutenant. Mike could not remember his name. The "nest" was a machinegun position that had been overrun by a sudden advance of the Germans.

The assault had failed when the Americans killed the few soldiers of the first wave to reach the trenches. Now alerted, American and French artillery rained down on the second and third waves just emerging from the German lines. Those men would not even reach the American wire before falling back.

Before that day, the war had been an adventure. It was uncomfortable, cold, wet, and certainly frightening. At the same time, it was exhilarating. Firing on distant figures, patrolling beyond the trenches, comradeship and shared hardships sharpened his feeling of being alive.

But the day he killed that German boy with an entrenching tool it all became unspeakable. An old French sergeant had once told him the secret to survival, over a bottle of stolen cognac. "Never hate your enemy," the old man had said. "It will be your undoing. Hate will propel you to do foolish things. Understand him? Yes. Kill him? Every chance you can. But do not waste energy on hate."

Visions of what he had done, and failed to do, haunted Mike. He could go for days without thinking of the war when, suddenly and without warning, brief flashes of isolated memories would push into his mind. The times when he killed with his hands, times he failed to prevent the death of comrades, would rush into his mind without warning, unwelcomed.

Try as he might, he could not remember the names of the men in his platoon. Men he had lived with, some had been killed before his eyes, and he could not remember a single name. They were just faces.

The recollection of marching past Ynes Marie and Camille was the worse. Those were the only two names from his service in France he would never, could never, forget. He had used her then abandoned her and her child. His mind told him there was nothing he could have done. It was war and he was not free to save Ynes Marie or Camille. The memory still caused his stomach to turn.

He could not remember leaving the front. He had been hiding on the overturned root-ball of a great tree, surrounded by a misty fog, shooting gray-clad figures wearing gasmasks as they passed under him. He needed to reload. He had fished several brass shotgun shells from his pocket and was feeding them into the gun's chamber when the world suddenly changed.

A blinding flash of light overwhelmed the field around the root-ball. A roaring sound accompanied the light, and all perception was suspended. He could see nothing, no land, no craters, no gray-clad soldiers. He could hear nothing, no screams, no explosions, nothing but his own ragged breathing.

The noise subsided, and the blinding light transformed into a white place, not a room just a place enveloped in sweet-smelling fog. A woman began to take form a few feet from him, her features coalescing out of the white mist. He could see strands of her white hair drifting from under her shoulder-length lace shawl. She wore a flowing, loose robe cinched at her waist with a woven cotton belt. She was seated on nothingness, her hands folded on her lap. She looked to be very old and frail.

"It must seem to you that you are meant to be alone, Miguel," she said in Spanish. Her voice was surprisingly strong. Her accent was one of an *Isleña*. Beyond the woman he could see an open doorway flooded with a blinding light. The silhouettes of people moved in the distance.

Mike tried to speak, but he could make no sound.

"You are alone again. Your companions have all been sent into the next world." The woman's thin hands moved as if she were brushing something away and the doorway closed. "You are to remain here."

"Why?" Mike managed to croak.

The old woman shrugged.

"Who are you?" Mike asked.

She smiled and pointed up. Mike's gaze followed her finger.

He was staring at the ceiling of a rail car, the sound of train wheels clacking beneath him as he lay on a stretcher.

No longer was he a member of the 11th Regiment, the "Wandering 11th." Now he was alone. He was baggage being hauled back from France. Mike closed his eyes and forced the unwelcomed recollections from his mind.

"Good afternoon, Mike." The greeting was in Spanish. The speaker was Manuel Moreno.

Mike stood. "Good afternoon, *Señor* Moreno. Thank you for meeting me on such short notice."

Moreno took a seat at the table. "Sit, Miguel. In truth, I was intending to call you. I have much news. Let us order and then we can talk."

The coffee and beignets arrived. The waiter recognized the need for confidentiality and withdrew into the café.

Manuel began. "On the matter concerning the Texan, your uncle and cousin have made it clear to everyone on the island that your actions prevented cold-blooded murder. The Haden brothers cannot act against you. Should they do so, they would not be able to bring one drop of product into New Orleans."

The "Texan" was Karl "Porkins" Portman, the gunman hired by Danny Haden to hijack the shipments of competitive bootleggers.

"D. A. Roberts can do nothing because there is no physical evidence linking you with Portman. He could manufacture evidence, but the community knows the truth and he would lose all support."

Mike was relieved. "Do you think it is safe for me to return to Saint Bernard?"

"That is not so clear. Roberts has begun a political campaign joining with others across the state to oust the remaining incumbents. He has filed indictments against his political opponents for imagined crimes. None will lead to convictions, but the harassment has worked. The Haden brothers are protected, although the attempt to hijack my shipment was a blunder that will not be repeated."

Almost every citizen with a boat and a knowledge of the coastal waterways was involved in bootlegging. It was an accepted practice. Hijacking was a different thing, particularly armed hijacking. A citizen might be killed. A family might lose loved ones. That would not be tolerated.

"The Texan was living with a widow," Moreno said. "He was good to her and supported her children. She had a small mortgage on her house. I have purchased the mortgage and canceled it. Tomorrow, I will send her the cancellation documents. After tomorrow, you should have no trouble if you return to Saint Bernard Parish."

"I asked to meet with you, *Señor* Moreno, for reasons of business," Mike said. "I have a buyer for quality rum or imported whiskeys. The quantity is not great, a few hundred liters a week, but the market will not compete with other importers."

"How is that so? Even now, the Hadens threaten certain customers to not buy from us."

"My buyers are influential men in the Irish Channel." Mike did not need to say anymore.

Moreno nodded his head. "I will tell Mister Leeds to expect you to call upon him. We have enough to provide you with a month's supply. The price, for you, will be nine dollars a bottle." Moreno paused to sip his coffee. He looked up from his cup. "Are you interested in another trip to Cuba?"

"I am free to go when you require it," Mike said. His mind ran the calculations. His cut of the profits would be over five hundred dollars a week. Most doctors did not make such a sum. In two or three years, he could own his own fleet of trawlers.

"There is one other thing," Moreno said as he scooted his chair back from the table. "There is talk that John Haden will run for Sheriff in the next election. With Robert's support and his gambling profits, he might win. It will be hard to be in our business if that should happen."

Hard was an understatement. It was one thing to have to dodge or bribe law enforcement in order to do business, it was quite a different thing when the organs of law enforcement were competitors in your enterprise.

"What do you plan to do, should that happen?" Mike asked.

"I have given it much thought. I think I shall withdraw from the business and concentrate on my real estate holdings. The price of fur is favorable and trappers who lease from me are doing well."

Moreno bit off the corner of a beignet, chewed gently and closed his eyes, savoring the sugary flavor. He sipped some more of his coffee before continuing.

"The Hadens have introduced a violent ruthlessness that is disturbing. We have been importing things for generations and each man was free to bring in what he wished without fear of being attacked and robbed. Now, there is no respect for the people. No longer is it a matter of supporting families. It is money, only money.

"Gambling has made the Hadens wealthy, but this prohibition thing has exposed their greed. They are becoming recklessly dangerous, as you discovered at the Fisherman's Canal landing. I do not want to be involved in such violence against my neighbors. Leasing land and brokering furs does not involve such uncivilized behavior."

*****

Mike pulled up to the warehouse next to the railroad at the head of Fisherman's Canal. He had added slatted sides to the flatbed of his truck. The slats were removable, so he could revert to an open bed anytime he wished to transport lumber or other oversized loads.

The large vertical freight doors lifted as he approached, revealing the darkened interior of the warehouse. George Leeds waved him into the darkened bay. Once Mike was in, the doors were lowered, and the warehouse lights came on.

Several men stood around a loading dock next to a stack of crates. Each crate had the words "Conthigerni Produce" stenciled on four sides. Conthigerni Produce was well known throughout the city and was considered by most to be the top provider of farm produce to markets in every neighborhood. A small truck loaded with such crates would not draw a second look, even from old man Conthigerni himself.

After guiding Mike up to the loading dock, Leeds invited him up to the stack of crates to inspect the cargo. The crates were of a size that could accommodate four of the squat two-liter bottles. Mike's purchase was fifty crates.

"Sample your shipment?" Leeds asked.

"Just one," Mike said. Leeds pulled the soft wire loops holding the lid to one of the crates and pulled out a bottle Mike recognized. They were a part of the shipment he had escorted from Cuba. The seals were in place, but exposure to the seas had washed away the picture of the bull stomping the broken sword and the proclamation: "Toro Negro, two quarts of Cuba's finest rum."

Mike broke the seal and tasted. It was smooth, potent, unadulterated product. "This will go under the seat of my truck," Mike said. "If you would be so kind, please have the men load my truck."

The crates were loaded in neat rows and strapped down to prevent unnecessary force on the truck's side slats. The load stacked three high in a pyramid shape and gave all the outward appearance of a load of vegetables bound for market.

The truck strained under nine-hundred pounds of rum; her leaf springs nearly compressed to the axle. A full load of produce would have been less than a third of that. Yet no one gave Mike and his laboring truck a second glance.

Avoiding the major boulevards, Mike drove along residential back streets to the border of the Irish Channel. Dorn climbed into the passenger side of Mike's truck at the corner of the streets Felicity and Annunciation.

"True, and your little truck is earning her keep this day" Dorn said. "Turn upriver on Annunciation." Directions in New Orleans were always related to the Mississippi River. Streets ran parallel to the sinuous river or perpendicular to it. One either traveled "up" or "down" river or "to" or "away" from the river.

Dorn directed Mike onto a driveway to an open lot surrounded by a high, wood fence. A dozen or so cars, handcarts and a few wagons were gathered in the lot. Dorn had the assembled men form a circle around him.

"Gentlemen, this fellow with me is Mike Demill. He is with us. The price is fifteen dollars for a two-quart bottle of rum. This is pure, un-watered Cuban rum. You pay me, cash only, even for my brother. I will give you a slip of paper with the number of bottles Mike is to hand down to you. First come is first served. When we are done, we are done. I will accept orders for future shipments. Any questions?" The only reaction to this announcement was the appearance of paper bills in several hands and jostling to form a queue.

Mike climbed onto the bed of his truck and began to untie the lashings. As each man approached, he showed Mike the slip of paper and Mike handed down the appropriate number of crates or, sometimes, a bottle at a time.

Cars, carts, and wagons began to flow out onto Annunciation Street, some going upriver, some down. In less than a half-hour Mike was sitting on the empty bed of his truck surrounded by empty produce crates.

Dorn, holding a leather satchel bulging with bills hopped up to join him. He shook the satchel and it tinkled with the sound of coins.

"Some pay only with silver," Dorn explained, "no faith in government paper, it is."

"I can understand how some could be of that opinion," Mike said.

"Well," Dorn handed Mike a roll of bills, "here is your share, one thousand, four hundred, eighty-five dollars. That's one hundred and ninety-eight bottles at fifteen dollars apiece, divided by two. Your share would have been fifteen hundred even, but you set one aside for yourself as did I."

Mike and Dorn together had paid Moreno eighteen hundred for the rum. Mike's share of the profit was nearly six hundred dollars. Each of the buyers had paid the owner of the lot one dollar each for the privilege of being there. A few more sales like this and Mike would be acquiring more real estate.

"If you do not mind my saying so," Dorn said with a nod toward the roll of bills Mike was tucking into his coat pocket, "There is a fine bank in this city, the Hibernia Bank. You might consider opening an account with them. It is a fine name, they have."

"The day is still young. I think I will go there now."

"That is excellent. And with your permission, I would like to ride along with you. I have my own deposits to make," Dorn said.

It was the first time Mike had opened a banking account and he was required to meet with a bank officer. Dorn, it seems, was long accustomed to banking. He marched up to a teller and deposited six hundred dollars of his share of the day's take. "Need to keep some pocket money handy," he had said with a wink. "Mary might be requiring some groceries."

More likely, Sinn Féin had a cut of the proceeds, Mike thought. Dorn waved goodbye while Mike was still filling out papers with one of the bank officers. He would also be keeping some pocket money for contingencies. From that day forward, Mike never had less than one hundred dollars on him at any time.

*****

The week passed quickly. Mike hauled lumber to construction sites across the city. He left the house before the sun was up and returned after dark. The Doons did not contact him during the week, for they had a similarly hectic work schedule. Sometimes, when he came in the back door, he would notice washing hung out to dry or hear bustling in the neighboring kitchen.

One thing that Mike had difficulty adjusting to was the nearness of others in the city. The Doons shared half of the bungalow which had thin walls. He could hear conversations, though too muted to understand, and movement through some of the neighboring rooms.

The money he made in drayage went into the bank. Ever distrustful of banks, Mike scanned the papers every day for real estate sales in anticipation of the next time he would be able to convert cash into property.

Often, Mister Cotton would converse with Mike as he and millworkers loaded the truck.

"You need to get into the stock market, my boy," Cotton would advise in a hushed conspiratorial voice, apparently fearing his employees would hear. None who worked at the mill, save Cotton himself, set aside enough money to consider investments.

"The money I make in stocks is grand," he would brag, "I even have mortgaged my house and put that money in the market. My return is double the note. I just keep putting it in and it grows like a great pig. Work with me and I can invest your money as well, for a small fee. We can both get rich."

"No, but thank you Mister Cotton," Mike would say. "I like my money in my pocket, not some New Yorker's."

That Saturday it rained. Great cloudbursts were followed by an incessant drizzle. With no hauling to do, Mike spent the morning sitting on his front porch drinking coffee, rocking gently, and watching the rain alternate from heavy to almost a trickle.

A covered, horse drawn coach stopped at the corner. Mary and Dorn Doon climbed out into the misting rain, crossed the planks serving the pedestrian walk and hurried up to the porch. Dorn was carrying a canvas shopping bag filled with produce.

"Good morning, Mike," Dorn said. "I feel as if I am in the Emerald Isles again. Such a sweet, cold mist, it is."

"Good morning Dorn, Mary," Mike said. "No work this day?"

"It is a new idea we are promoting, Mike," Dorn said with a wink. "Forty hours of work a week. Saturdays are ours and Sundays are for God."

"It will never catch on," Mike said. "Can't have people lay about all day. Idle hands, you know."

"You feel that way because you work for yourself. You can skip a day when it pleases you," Mary said.

"Yes, ma'am. That is so," Mike said as he sipped his coffee. "I was raised trawling for shrimp or dredging oysters. It is work that allows you to make your own schedule, provided you attend to the seasons, mind you. Monday through Sunday has no meaning when working the sea. I hope to return to it when I can."

"Speaking of the sea," Dorn said, "can we join you for a cup?"

"You are welcomed," Mike answered as he began to stand. "This is the last of my morning brew. I will put a fresh pot on."

"You will do no such thing," Mary chided. "I will put on a pot enough for a proper conversation. It will have an Irish flavor to it, it will." She took the bag from Dorn, who unlocked the door and let her into their quarters.

Dorn pulled over another rocking chair, next to the small table Mike had for his coffee. "Are you sincere about your desire to return to the sea?" He said.

"As much as it pertains to working the Gulf and marshes, I am," Mike sensed a purpose to this conversation.

"This is the kind of day that brings me back to Cork County," Dorn said. "Cold, soft rain. Clear, pure air." He took a deep breath. "The rain has washed away the stink of the city. I grew up on a farm, you know."

"Do you think you will ever go back?" Mike asked.

Dorn's face grew dark. "When we have rid the land of the Black and Tan. When the Brits are gone, and Ireland belongs to the Irish again. When we are no longer slaves in our own country. I live for that day."

Moments passed in silence and Mike watched as Dorn forced his dark mood away. Finally, the man's face brightened.

"Let us discuss your return to the sea," he said with a smile that bore no hint of being forced. "That prospect is much more likely, I am thinking."

"I have been saving for a boat. A blue water trawler, but small enough to chase the brown shrimp when they are in close. Fifty, maybe sixty foot, not some great steam trawler, but a small powered one with a ketch rig so I can sail her when the wind is right."

Mary arrived with a tray of coffee. Mike noticed there were three cups, so he pulled another chair to the table for Mary to join them. Mary set three cups and saucers on the table and poured three steaming cups of coffee. She looked about quickly and produced a flask from an apron pocket.

"Irish sweetener," she said as she added a dash of caramel-colored liquid to each cup. "It is the only civilized way to have a cup, don't you think?"

Mike smelled the sweet aroma of rum wafting from the cup Mary offered him. "Thank you, Mary," Mike said. 'It is a fine wife you have, Mister Doon."

Mary sat and lifted her cup to the gentlemen in a silent toast. She sipped and looked sternly at Dorn, who cleared his throat.

"Ah, yes," Dorn said. "Touching on the sea and trawlers. We, Mary and I that is, have an acquaintance who is a builder of fishing boats. Irish boats, that is. He is of a mind to build a boat here. He would like it to be along the lines of your local trawlers, for the boats here are adapted to local conditions."

"I am in no position to commission a trawler," Mike said. "My hope was to buy a used one and refurbish it."

"That would be what one would expect, "Dorn said. "But the only used trawlers on the market today, we checked, are sail or sail converted to power. My friend desires to build a power trawler, using one of those new, compact diesel tractor engines. Built for power from the keel up, maybe auxiliary sail. A boat fit to run the shallows and get to sea for a few days as well."

"An admirable enterprise," Mike said. "I can less afford that than a converted schooner."

"Well then, hear us out. Our friend is in need of a man who knows how the local boats are built. A man who knows the ways of the bayous and can advise him in this construction. Would you be interested?"

Mike was indeed interested. Ever since seeing the use of engines in cars, boats, and armored vehicles in France, he had toyed with the idea of a powered lugger specifically built for trawling shrimp. Something better than a converted sailing schooner or coastal dredge powered with a Popping Johnny. Powered fishing boats were too new to be on the re-sale market and most available sail to power conversions were poorly done.

Dorn could see Mike was interested. "My friend proposes that you assist him in the design, others will do the work and provide the materials, selected by you. Your compensation would be a part ownership in the vessel and the opportunity to buy out the other owners at a later date."

"Your friend is not going into the trawling business, is he?"

Dorn smiled. "Not likely. What we want is a boat that looks like a trawler and even one that can trawl, but one that can run the blue water when the need arises."

"What size are we talking about?" Mike leaned in. He noticed both Dorn and Mary were beaming with anticipation.

"You advise. Sixty foot seems right."

"What would be my share?"

"One third."

"That is very generous for just offering advice," Mike said warily.

"That it is. There will be something else."

"And what would that be?"

"We need a captain to run her. A man known to be a fisherman, wise in the ways of the coast of Louisiana," Dorn said.

"And willing to meet a ship or two in blue water," Mary said.

"I will not be in competition with my friends, Dorn. The traffic in such goods has drawn the interest of some very bad people. I must stick with those who provided you with spirits."

"We are not interested in bringing contraband in," Dorn said. "We will be bringing goods to sea."

"Goods," Mary added, "that need to arrive elsewhere - discreetly."

"Perhaps, you can combine the businesses. We bring things out for my people and you bring things in for your people. Give it a thought."

"How much does your friend plan to spend?"

"Can we say in the neighborhood of eight thousand dollars?"

Mike was startled. That amount would buy two, maybe three used trawlers.

"That will buy a lot of boat," Mike said.

"True enough," Dorn said. "But we will be needing a lot of boat."

"When do you need an answer? I must talk to my friend." Mike was not going to commit until he talked to Moreno.

"No time in particular. Give it a week. If it is agreed, I will make the necessary introductions," Dorn said.

"Let us have a fresh cup of coffee and toast to new opportunities," Mary said as she reached for the pot.

CHAPTER 12

Mike watched Cass in the soft light. His heart was racing as she slipped her blouse over her head releasing her firm breasts. She quickly covered herself with the blouse, laughing softly, her green eyes sparkling with mischief and desire. *God, how I had loved her!*

Mike shook his head to suppress the memory. In many ways these recollections of Cass were more disturbing than the haunting flashes of combat images. He had been in love and he was certain Cass loved him. Then came the draft notice.

Cass refused to speak with him or even see him after he was drafted. She refused to answer his letters, even those he had written from the hospital. She could not have loved him then, maybe she never did. How could she call him a liar, push him away so resolutely, rage at him as she had in the Orion Club if she had loved him?

No one could love him now. His torso was scarred, disfigured, diseased with weakened lungs. Except Annie had seen his scars, watched him hack up discolored spittle, and she was planning to come to New Orleans. His feelings for Annie confused him. Annie was different.

He shifted the truck into neutral and coasted along the street until he reached the address Dorn had given him. A meeting had been arranged with the Irish shipwright to discuss a building proposal. Dorn said he would be there when Mike arrived. "Knock just one loud rap," Dorn had said, "and we will know it is you."

Mike parked the truck and climbed down from the cab. He looked up and down the street. It was nine o'clock at night, cold, rainy and no one was about. No one sat on their porches to enjoy the evening. Mike thought that absence to be odd.

He walked up the creaking steps to the house, across the porch to the door. He had been listening to a muffled conversation behind the door that ceased when the steps creaked. He lifted his hand and gave the door one strong rap.

A man appeared from an alley beside the house and stood next to the porch facing Mike. Mike turned right to face him, but the man said nothing. Sensing something, Mike turned around to see another man posed next to the porch to the left. The door opened.

"Michael," Dorn said, "I am pleased you decided to come. Step in."

Dorn moved to the side to allow Mike to pass, leaned out of the doorway, his head swiveling about before stepping back inside to close the door. The room was dark when Mike came in, but a light switched on when Dorn closed the door.

There were two other men in the room seated at a large table. A single lightbulb swung gently over the center of the table, the switch chain slightly ticking the bulb. The men stood.

"Michael Demill," Dorn said, "I would like you to meet Mister Brian Boru," Dorn gestured toward the man to Mike's right, who nodded, "and Mister James O'Gara." The man to Mike's left nodded.

"Brian is our shipwright," Dorn continued. He did not explain the presence of O'Gara.

"Please, have a seat," O'Gara said, indicating the chair opposite the table from his own.

Mike took a seat, his back tingling for he had been placed with his back to the door. He nervously glanced back over his shoulder and Dorn, seeming to sense the cause of Mike's discomfort, leaned against the door and folded his arms.

Boru cleared his throat and unrolled some papers. "I would like to hear your opinion on these sketches, Mister Demill. They are crude renditions, but a man familiar with vessels, as I am led to believe you are, should be able to decipher their meaning."

The plans were far from crude. Mike was accustomed to shipwrights who built their boats without plans. Using the shape in their minds and large carpenter's square, an *Isleño* would construct a deep-water lugger or coastal dredge from a stack of cypress lumber and brass fittings.

Mike noticed the plans also contained calculations on the needed horsepower, shaft angle and propeller specifications. "I know nothing of the engine requirements," Mike said. "Every lugger I have ever worked on was sail powered."

"Fair enough," Boru said, "but tell me of her lines."

"I would suggest she is too deep in the keel. Shallow shoals abound. Perhaps more flare from here," he touched a place on the sketch about one third the length back from the bow, "all the way aft. Lower gunnels slightly. We will not be asking her to run the kind of seas encountered off Ireland. Nets must be played out and retrieved so high sides and stern work against the purpose of the boat."

Boru penciled a few lines on the drawings. "How is this?"

"Better," Mike said, "perhaps if we move the pilothouse forward...." Mike took the pencil and drew a few more lines.

"I see," Boru said. "That changes the slope of the shaft and the placement of the engine, or rather the engines."

"Engines?" Mike asked. The only engines he had seen in fishing lugers, aside from the huge ocean steam trawlers, were powered by single tractor or automobile engine.

"Yes. As you can see, the boat I propose is fifty-seven feet at the waterline. She would need a robust engine with a deep shaft. If we use two Gray-Beall four-cylinder marine engines, we can shallow-up the keel and she will not draw as much. Two counter-rotating shafts at forty horses each. She will do twenty knots, I'm thinking. The engines will run on petroleum, kerosene or alcohol."

The discussions went on for more than three hours. Finally, Boru straightened up, collected the papers, and announced. "I think I have an understanding of what is needed, Mister Demill. I shall produce a revised set of drawings and we can go over them again."

"What do you think, Brian?" O'Gara said, slightly startling Mike. It was the first time the other man had spoken in three hours.

"The man knows his boats," Boru said, "but he has never had a minute's formal training. We will build the boat, but the only role Mike is suited for right now is to pilot her."

"When we finish with Mister Demill," O'Gara said, "he will be able to repair every stick and build the engines from scratch. That is, if he accepts our proposition."

"And what is the proposition?" Mike asked.

Boru looked at O'Gara and nodded.

"It is this," O'Gara said. "You will assist in construction by delivering materials, including the engines, and offer insights pertaining to hull shapes, rigging, and such. We will provide funds for the materials, workmen for the construction and a boatyard. For this you will receive one third ownership and captain her for such excursions we may require."

"Where is the boatyard?"

"Milneburg Jetty."

Mike offered his hand, "And I can buy out the remaining two thirds for five thousand dollars?"

O'Gara took Mike's hand. "Done and done."

The Milneburg Jetty was the perfect location for the construction of a shrimp trawler. The railroad that ran from a loading island out in Lake Pontchartrain to docks on the Mississippi River was falling into disuse because of the construction of the new Inner Harbor Navigation Canal-named the Industrial Canal by the people of New Orleans.

After completion of the canal and lock system some time in a little over a year, coastal goods and produce that would customarily be off loaded at the lake end of the jetty and transported to the river or market by rail could be shipped directly to the riverfront through the new lock system.

The anticipated decline of the traffic on the Milneburg Jetty caused the owner of the railway to concentrate on laying new rails to tie into the New Orleans interior lines. The reduced traffic on the jetty provided a secluded location for their temporary boatyard and a means of bringing heavy timbers and machinery to the work site.

Mike found himself without any spare time as he continued to operate his small trucking service while assisting in the building of the boat. He toyed with the idea of buying a second truck and hiring a driver to expand his business.

*****

On Monday, March 20th, Moreno sent a message to Mike asking for a meeting and on that same day Annie called to say she was coming to New Orleans. She sounded excited and upbeat at the prospects of moving south. "It will be worth it just to get out of the snow," she said. "I have never experienced a winter without snow."

The Cumberland Telephone and Telegraph Company sponsored a boarding house for all the girls that worked as operators but did not live with their parents. There were no married women working for the company. If a female operator married, it was cause for termination. If an operator lived alone or with someone not her parent, it was cause for termination.

Annie's train was scheduled to arrive at eleven Saturday morning. The boarding house had a room reserved for her and she gave the address to Mike. It was on the same block as the switchboard building, well within walking distance even in the rain, for the sidewalks were covered.

"I am familiar with the building," Mike said. "After I help you move in, we can have dinner at Turci's. It is a fine little Italian restaurant on Decatur Street. We can walk there from the boarding house."

"I would like that very much, Mike," Annie said softly, "but I will have a curfew. We must take care I do not miss it on my first night."

"What about other nights?"

"I will have to weigh my options if such possibilities arise," Annie said.

After his conversation with Annie, Mike felt a happiness he thought he would never experience again. He grabbed his coat, for a steady drizzle was falling, and headed to his truck. It was parked in the garage he had built from recovered lumber. A thick coat of ivory-colored paint hid the mismatched ship-lapped walls.

Manuel Moreno was waiting for Mike at his usual outside table at the Café Du Monde. A wide awning protected the single table from the light rain.

"*Buenas tardes, Señor* Moreno," Mike said. Their conversations were always in Spanish.

"It is nearer to evening, Mike," Moreno said. "Though the days grow longer."

"How is your family? All in good health, I pray," Mike said.

"Yes, thank you. And how have you been?"

"Busy, as you know. I am building a boat. If I am not hauling contracted freight, I am bringing materials to the boatyard."

"Yes, I have been told you are building a fine boat. Over twenty *varas*, they tell me."

"Yes, sixty feet. Twin engines. She will be very fine."

"And very expensive, no doubt," Moreno observed. "Perhaps you would be interested in another import contract."

"I am."

"Do you remember *Señor* Phillipe Dugas?"

"The massive Frenchman who works for *El Señor* O'Neil," Mike said. "I remember him well."

"Conditions in Cuba have become slightly - unsettled. A temporary situation, I am assured. Something about new appointments and establishing relationships. Which is to say, certain bribes will take time to become effective. Until then, I dare not send you to Cuba. Dugas is coming here, well, to Mobile at any rate, to meet you."

"When?"

"The twelfth of April. Come by my office at noon on the eleventh. William will give you tickets on the L&N Railroad to Mobile and back. He will also give you a satchel you will give to *Señor* Dugas. In return, you will receive a packet for me."

"Is that all I am to do?"

"No. Once I have reviewed the packet, I will need your services to direct several boats to a location I will provide you. When this will all occur has not yet been determined. Late April is likely. Your payment will be twice that of the previous trip."

"My boat will not be ready by April," Mike said. The first week in August was the earliest possible launch date.

"That is not a problem. I will provide five boats, each with a captain and a crew of two."

"*Isleños?*"

"Of course. Now enjoy the beignets. I find them to be particularly good today."

Mike was relieved. He had worried that the job Moreno required would conflict with Annie's arrival. He had the rest of the week to make himself and his house presentable. He left the café and went directly to Maison Blanche to purchase some dress clothes. All he had were work clothes. He had to throw his one decent suit into the trash after the incident at the Orion Club.

He left the store with two casual suits called "Wash Suits," one 3-piece suit, several ties, shirts, and a Bangkok straw hat. He had spent nearly eighty dollars and was a little embarrassed by his extravagance. Still, he did not want to meet Annie looking like a dock worker. It would make a bad impression on the housemother at the CT&T boarding house.

The next day Mike arrived at the lumberyard early to make a few deliveries. After the second load he returned to the yard just as everyone was breaking for lunch. He sought out the rail crew that operated the little switch engine that shuffled flatcar loads of logs and lumber about the mill.

He pulled the engineer to the side and pushed a twenty-dollar bill into the man's hand and said, "Jake, how would you like to earn this and another just like it?"

"I won't kill nobody, but forty bucks will get a man beat real proper," Jake said as he looked about to insure this was a private conversation.

"Nothing so fine as that," Mike said. "I have a shipment coming in on the Illinois Central tomorrow. Do you know the men at the switchyard?"

"Aye, us engineers are as thick as thieves, we are."

"I have arranged for the yardmaster to put a car on the old Milneburg spur at two tomorrow morning. Can you bring your switch engine through the city and push the car to the lake?"

"Hell, Mike, the I.C. line serves our lumber yard. I can have them drop the car at our siding when they pass the yard and bring it out to the lake from here. I'll call the yardmaster and square it with him."

"Perfect, the other twenty will meet you at the Milneburg Jetty tomorrow. She'll be bagged with a half-gallon of rum."

"Now, Mike, my boy, that's very generous. I have to ask, is there anything improper about what's on that car?"

"Would it matter?"

"Not a whit, I would just like to know."

"It's all as legal as can be. The car has two heavy marine engines on it, and I don't want to have to handle them more than need be." *And I don't want others to see me with marine engines.*

"Marine engines? You in the boatbuilding business too?"

"Nope, just drayage. I would have to make two rough trips along that ragged side road along the rail spur to get these engines to my customer. This way I can deliver them straight from the Michigan factory in the original shipping crate, impresses the money boys."

Mike made two more lumber deliveries and then carried a load of his own cypress timbers and planking out to the boatyard. The road that ran along the side of the rail spur was rutted, pitted and treacherously narrow. The lights on his truck swept back and forth, up and down as he bounced along at a snail's pace.

The left edge of the road pitched down into the muddy water of the lake and the right pushed up against the ends of the railroad ties that jutted out from the oyster and clamshell bedding of the rail line. The boatyard was little more than a wide spot in the narrow road at the base of the loading dock at the end of the line.

The boat was taking shape. The shipwrights and carpenters were loading their tools into a large locking shed under the watchful eyes of Brian Boru. The man turned to watch Mike drive up, directing where to place the truck.

"Before you men head in, unload this lumber and lay it out for tomorrow," Boru said to the workers. He turned to Mike. "When will I see the engines? I need to have them to make the cradle."

"They will come in on this rail line tomorrow. If we play our cards right, we could have the remaining lumber and fittings brought in by rail as well."

"How did you manage that?" Boru asked. "The rail clowns I talked to didn't want to send a train out here. They will be pulling up the rail in two months."

"I negotiated with a friend to run the little lumberyard switch engine out here. It's light and it should have no problem pushing a single car out to us. We will just have to be satisfied with deliveries at two in the morning."

"That's great. We have no lay-down area, otherwise we would have brought everything we need in by barge. As it is, we can only bring material here as it goes into the boat. Slows the work, but we will have most of the bulky stuff done before the rail is gone."

"If we can convince the gandy crew to pull up the ties with the rail, we could haul on the old rail bed instead of that joke of a road," Mike said. As long as they held a lease from the railroad on the boatyard, they would have access. After the boat was in the water, the lease lapsed, and Mike would be shopping for a berth.

Mike walked the length of the boat. The keel and cross ribs clearly defined the final shape and Mike loved it. *She will be clean, swift, and seaworthy.*

"What do you think?" Boru said, startling Mike, who had not heard him walk up.

"She will be the envy of everyone on the bayou," Mike said. What had required three boats could easily be carried in this boat. She was no heavily armed ex-patrol boat like the powerful Cuban *La Abeja*, but she could carry the same cargo and do so in water much too shallow for Captain Solis' blue-water gunboat.

"Time to go, boss," one of the carpenters called out. "We have the lumber unloaded and we can hear the beer calling."

"Climb onto the truck bed, gentlemen," Mike said. "I'll give you a ride to the front." Because of the limited space, the workers had to walk a mile from main road to the boatyard. Catching a ride at the end of a hard day, rough as it may be, was welcomed.

Boru climbed into the truck cab uninvited, and Mike started the trip back to the main road.

"When will she be put into the water?" Mike asked.

"Late April, we will slide her into the lake. We will finish her out while we tighten her joints. First week of June, she will be ready to put to work."

"That is good. I would not want to have an unfinished boat on the slips when hurricane season comes around."

"There is one bit of business we need to decide upon before we close the hull," Boru said. "What are you going to name her?"

Mike thought a while. "*El Solitario*," he said.

"*El Solitario*. What does that mean?"

"The Loner."

.

CHAPTER 13

Mike met Jake, the switch engine operator, at one in the morning. He had decided to ride with the engines out to the boatyard and help winch the engines from the railcar. Jake could then return the car to the lumberyard siding. Mike was uncomfortable leaving four hundred dollars'-worth of engines and marine transmissions sitting on an unattended railcar on an abandoned rail line.

The I. C. freight train arrived at the lumberyard at a quarter past one. Five flatcars piled high with logs and one with four crates were shunted into the lumberyard spur. Jake signed the receipt for the timbers and Mike signed for the crates. Once the I.C. train was clear of the siding, Jake culled out the flatcar with Mike's crates and pushed it onto the main line.

"The main line will be clear for four hours," Jake explained. "Plenty of time to get your engines out onto the Milneburg Jetty." Jake was able to navigate through the city on the rail beltway with reasonable ease. Mike would hop down whenever they approached a switch that needed to be thrown, run ahead of the slow-moving car, throw the switch, and clamber back on as Jake chugged by.

Once they were on the Milneburg Jetty, Jake pushed the little switch engine to full speed, eight or nine miles an hour. The full moon reflected off the lake waters on either side of the railway and shone along the rails, unaffected by the oil lamp on the front of the engine. Jake applied the brakes and they squealed to a stop near the toolshed at the boatyard.

Mike used some planks to form a ramp down from the flatcar. He and Jake levered an engine on the ramp and slid it down to the ground. Mike shifted the planks to the second engine, and it was easily moved to the ground. The transmissions were somewhat lighter and were easily levered to the ground.

"I can take them from here, Jake," Mike said. "Look in that bag I put behind the engineer's seat. You'll find what was promised."

"Call on me again any time, Mike. I like your rates."

Jake put the engine in reverse and puttered back up the jetty. Soon the sound of the switch engine faded away and Mike found himself alone with the full moon setting over a millpond-smooth lake. It was stunningly quiet. He wished Annie were with him to share the scene.

He raked a pile of wood shavings together to form a bed under the shelter of the uncompleted hull. He pulled a blanket out of the tool shed and spread it out over the shavings. While he made himself comfortable, he looked up at the planking of the boat *El Solitario*. She was going to be magnificent. As he was admiring the fine workmanship of the tight planking just above his head, he fell asleep.

*****

The call of seagulls woke Mike. He rolled out from under the shelter of the partially completed hull of *El Solitario* and stumbled to the edge of the sheet piling that formed the quay at the lake end of the jetty to relieve himself.

The sun had not yet cleared the horizon, but the pre-dawn light and clear sky softly presented every detail of the quay, birds, and lake. The workers would be arriving shortly to resume work on finishing the hull. The plan was to complete the hull, decking, shafts, propellers and mount the engines and transmissions before sliding *El Solitario* into the lake. The rest of the finishing work would be done moored to the dock.

Mike walked to the lake end of the quay. The lake beyond the line of sheet piles was a vast, smooth stretch of water. There were no boats in sight. The next land was over thirteen miles away, well over the horizon. Lake Pontchartrain was more of an inland sea than a lake.

The corner of the quay held a trash pile which included an assortment of beer and whiskey bottles. Most were broken, but some were not. He selected a few unbroken bottles and place them on the top of the sheet pile of the quay.

Mike walked ten paces away and pulled the Luger from his belt. A tiny lever on the top of the receiver was raised, indicating a round was in the firing chamber. He aimed at the first bottle on the left, thumbed the safety off and pulled the trigger. There was an audible "click" and nothing else.

Mike had thoroughly field stripped and cleaned the pistol the night Dorn had given it to him. He had been impressed with the quality and unused condition of the pistol. Perhaps the ammunition had been compromised. He worked the slide and caught the cartridge out of the air.

He thumbed the safety on, belted the pistol and examined the primer on the back of the cartridge. There was no indentation from a firing pin. He drew his pistol and fired again with the same result. No discharge and a cartridge with an undented primer.

Mike heard the men walking to the boatyard, so he pocketed the cartridges, thumbed the Luger to safe, returned it to his belt at the small of his back and walked over to *El Solitario* to meet the workers.

"Look, we have the engines," Johnny said. He was the foreman of the five laborers hired by Boru. Mike only knew him as "Johnny."

"Johnny," Mike said as he walked up to the group as they admired the crated engines. "When is Boru supposed to be here?"

"Anytime now, boss," Johnny said. "He is bringing a load of hardware to mount the engines along with two shafts, packing and propellers. She is starting to look like a proper boat."

Mike looked up the railway toward the main road. He could see a truck working its way along the rutted excuse of a road. It was a large truck that bounced and swayed perilously close to the edge of the drop to the lake. Mike waited until the truck stopped at the boatyard.

Boru climbed down out of the passenger's side of the truck and shouted to the driver to unload the shafts. The driver set the brake and waved some of the workers over to give him a hand. Two steel shafts and a grate were strapped to the flatbed.

"Did you look at our engines?" Boru asked.

"Wouldn't know what I was looking at," Mike said. "They and the transmissions are still packed in the factory's crates."

"Well let's take a look while the men get the shafts and propellers unloaded," Boru said. He reached into the cab of the truck and brought out two wrecking bars. He gave one to Mike and gestured toward the crates.

They removed the tops of the crates, but left the engines mounted on their factory pallets. They pulled the transmissions out of the packing crates and moved them to the storage shed.

"I'll examine the engines later and get the boys to pull them out completely. They look to be in fine shape," Boru said. "We will not mount them until we are finished with some of the reinforcing on the keelson and rider plates for the engine mounts."

"I'll catch a ride to the front with your driver," Mike said. "I have to get my truck at the lumberyard and make some deliveries."

"I will see you at your place tonight," Boru said as Mike climbed into the truck.

On the ride back to the lumberyard Mike contemplated what he would say to Dorn about the Luger but decided not to say anything until he was able to do a full break-down of the weapon, not just the field strip he had performed when he cleaned it.

He was familiar with the weapon. The men of the 11th Regiment had several Lugers taken from German dead. The men squirreled the contraband pistols away in their kits, hidden from officers who would confiscate them in an instant. Mike had had the opportunity to learn some of the weapon's eccentricities. Unlike the Colt .45 Model 1911, the Luger was not very tolerant of dirt. Perhaps grit was the problem.

Boru and O'Gara were meeting at his house tonight, so cleaning would have to wait until they were gone. Until then, he had deliveries to complete, and he was picking Annie up at the train station on Saturday. Suddenly, Mike's life was becoming very hectic.

*****

It was midnight before Boru and O'Gara finally left Mike's house. The time had been spent reviewing the preferred placement of the engines, transmission, and the slope of the propeller shaft. Both men argued in terms of mathematical equations that mystified Mike. Eventually, a consensus was reached, the rum bottle emptied, and the shipwrights departed.

Mike pulled a chair close to the table and placed the Luger on it. He quickly unloaded, and field stripped it. It was clean and appeared to be in fine condition.

He unscrewed the pin keeper and removed the firing pin and examined it carefully under the light. The serial number on the pin matched that of the receiver as did every other major part of the pistol, meaning that this was a pistol that had not been repaired since it was produced.

Mike noticed something about the end of the firing pin. The texture of the very tip of the pin was not the same polished, smooth surface as its base and shoulder. He rubbed it with his tongue. It was definitely rough. Someone had ground down the tip of the pin.

The work was done so well, that a simple inspection would not have indicated the alteration. The pin was shortened only a little, but enough so when the hammer fell, the shoulder of the pin struck the chamber wall before the tip could strike the cartridge's primer.

No one could have known the pistol was inoperable until an attempt was made to fire it. Mike had been carrying a useless weapon. Had he been required to defend himself with it, it would not have fired. His anger at Dorn faded and was replaced with a calm calculation.

In the morning, he would visit pawn shops or gun stores for a Luger. Abused, war worn pistols, cobbled together by some Doughboy from parts picked up on the battlefield were not uncommon. He would find the cheapest one available and hope it had a complete firing pin.

The next day, Mike made a lumber delivery to the Poydras Street Wharf. After unloading the truck, he diverted from his route back to the lumberyard to pass a gun and knife shop on Camp Street. He found a place to park and ducked into the shop. A small bell tinkled when he opened the door.

A gray-haired man shuffled from a rear room to the service counter. "Can I help you?" He said as he wiped his hands with a rag.

"I am interested in obtaining a German Luger," Mike said.

"As a collector?" Mike detected a slight accent, perhaps German.

"No, the condition is not that important. Any old hopper will do."

"So, it is spare parts you need. Why did you not say so straight away?"

"I didn't know if parts were available."

"My name is Fritz Hoffman, by the way. And you are?"

"Michael Demill. My friends call me Mike."

"What outfit did you serve with, Mike?"

"The 11th Infantry. Is it that obvious?"

"Only Doughboys call the Luger a 'Hopper'," Fritz said. The "hopper" nickname came from the operation of the pistol's slide when fired. Instead of coming straight back, as with the .45, a toggle popped up on the top of the receiver as the bolt retracted and cycled a fresh cartridge.

"Then, my friend Fritz, what I would like to buy is a firing pin."

"Do you have the Luger with you?"

Mike pulled it from his belt, removed the magazine and worked the action to show it was not loaded and handed it to Fritz.

The old man worked the action, dry fired it and then field stripped it so quickly it seemed that the pistol fell apart.

"This weapon is in perfect condition!" Fritz exclaimed.

"I thought the same. Now pull the pin," Mike said.

Fritz pulled a screwdriver from under the counter and removed the firing pin from the carrier.

"It looks fine," he said.

"Compare it to another pin, if you have one."

Fritz walked into the back room as he examined the pin. He reappeared with the receiver of a Luger that was pitted and lacked a grip. He removed the pin from that weapon and held it beside the pin from Mike's gun.

"*Verdammit!*" Fritz exclaimed. "Your pin has been shortened by a millimeter!"

"Rendering the weapon useless," Mike said. "How much for the pin?"

"One dollar," Fritz said. "And I will clean the pin and install it for you, Mike."

Mike put a silver Peace Dollar on the counter.

Fritz pocketed the dollar and scooped up the disassembled pistol. "Come to the back, Mike." Fritz waved Mike past the counter and through a door to a workshop. The workshop was a jumbled collection of tools, gun parts, rags, brushes, and several scarred, oil-stained tables.

Fritz waded through the shop to a table with a power polishing wheel mounted on one corner. He flipped a switch and buffed the replacement pin, moving it around on the spinning felt wheel with his bare hands, occasionally inspecting the effect of the work on the pin.

Satisfied with the polishing, Fritz reassembled Mike's Luger using the good pin. He pushed the magazine into place and walked over to a long, steel tank that occupied one wall. He chambered a round and pointed the pistol into a pipe that protruded from the top of the tank. He thumbed the safety off and fired three quick shots in succession. Mike was surprised at the relative quietness of the muffled report.

Fritz noticed Mike's curious expression. "The tank contains water, and the pipe has heavy canvas curtains to reduce the sound of a gunshot." He set the safety, removed the magazine, and worked the action to empty the chamber. He gave the pistol and magazine to Mike.

"Want the old pin?" Fritz said.

Mike began to say no, and then changed his mind. "Yes, please," he said, holding out this hand.

A bell jingled, and Fritz said, "I have a customer. We go out front."

The customers were two New Orleans Police officers.

"Thank you, Mister Hoffman," Mike said as he slipped the pistol and magazine into his pocket and worked his way around the counter and toward the door. "Officers," he said as he touched his fingers to the bill of his hat. Anyone not tipping his hat to an officer would likely get a nightstick jabbed into his ribs. The policemen simply nodded and glared.

*****

Annie waved to Mike as she stepped down onto the platform for the Illinois Central, track number three. He hurried to her, holding his new Bangkok straw hat. He planned to take Annie out to eat that evening, so he was wearing one of his new suits.

He reached her and was suddenly confused what to do. Should he kiss her hello? They had never been intimate, though they shared a ship's berth. Shaking hands seemed too cold, so when he reached her, he embraced her.

"Michael, is that how you greet me?" Annie said into his ear. She pushed him away just a little, laughed and kissed him on the lips. Not a quick peck, but nothing lingering, just a nice gentle kiss. The kind of kiss a wife would give her husband. Mike's head was reeling. It felt so natural.

Annie wore a gray traveling duster over a green and white laced smock with an ankle length dress. The dress had white and green pleats that matched her smock. Her hat was white, broad-brimmed and decorated with a green ribbon. She wore long gloves and a pair of laced, over-the-ankle traveling boots. Mike knew she had been traveling for more than a full day, but she looked wonderful.

"Where is your luggage?" Mike asked. He was careful not to fully break the embrace. Her body felt magnificent pressed against his.

"I have a trunk and one suitcase in the baggage car," she said. "We will need a porter. I am afraid the trunk is fairly large. You are not here in a car, are you?"

"No. I have my truck. If the trunk is small enough for two porters to lift, it will be no problem."

They started toward the baggage car, Annie walking next to Mike, her arm around his elbow. She walked so lightly Mike wondered if she were skipping.

"How was your trip?" Mike asked, just to have something to say.

"Oh, it was horrid. The sleeper car pitched back and forth until I thought I was on the *Garanhão*. To tell the truth, it made me miss you." She gave him a little tug on the arm. "Every bridge we crossed looked as though it would be swept away at any minute. The rivers we crossed were all torrents. It frightened me a little."

They reached a cluster of passengers and porters at the baggage car vying for room and the opportunity to retrieve luggage. A grey-haired porter pulling a hand cart leaned toward Mike.

"Please, describe your bags for me, sir."

"One steamer trunk and one suitcase," Annie said. "When they were loaded, I saw the man put them in the corner," she pointed, "with the suitcase on top. I tied a green ribbon to the suitcase."

"I think I see them, miss. Let me fetch them out." The porter shouldered his way through the wide car doors and reappeared pulling a trunk with a suitcase on top.

"Yes, those are mine," Annie said.

"Yes, miss." The porter loaded the bags onto the hand car. "Where to, sir?"

"Follow me," Mike said. "I'm parked out front."

The porter, with a little help from Mike, loaded Annie's trunk onto the truck's flat bed and strapped it down. It was heavy and solid. Mike wondered what she could possibly have that was that dense. The suitcase was strapped behind the trunk. Mike tipped the porter one dollar, which was four times his usual tip.

"Thank you, sir," the man said. "That trunk must have a load of bricks, but you ask for Sam next time you are here. I would be glad to help you again."

Mike helped Annie into the cab of the truck, which required some climbing, and then jumped up into the driver's seat.

"This is an interesting cab," Annie observed.

"The original cab was crushed by a net full of freight. The owner repaired it with scrap wood. Looks like hell, but I got her cheap and she works hard. Are you hungry?"

"I had a nice lunch on the train, thank you. What I would like right now is a nice bath. That train was filthy. Then we can go to that Italian place you talked about. What was the name?"

"Turci's on Decatur Street. You will love it." He started the engine. The noise in the open cab discouraged conversation. "We can talk more at the restaurant," Mike half shouted as he drove along Saint Joseph Street toward Camp.

They arrived at the boarding house and Mike pulled off the street into the old carriageway for the building. He helped Annie down and escorted her into the building. The housemother was sitting behind a desk in the reception area.

When she saw Mike, she scowled and growled, "I am Madam Toups. Who might you be?"

Mike recognized a slight French accent, so he said, "*Mademoiselle* Annie Norwak *est ici.*"

Madam Toups brightened considerably and responded in French. "We have been expecting Miss Norwak. I have the register book here." She opened a ledger and indicated a line and said, "Please sign here, Miss Norwak."

Mike smiled, "Miss Norwak is from Chicago. Please use English."

Toups' mood darkened again. "Sign here Miss Norwak," she said. "Here is our rule book. Curfews are strictly enforced and absolutely no visitors except in this lobby and in my presence."

The telephone company ran a tight ship. None of its ladies would be accused of improprieties. Not on Madam Toups' watch. That was made clear.

"We have a cart for Miss Norwak to use to bring her trunk to her room. I will assist her," Toups said as she gestured for Mike to leave.

Mike spoke in French, "I would like to call upon Miss Norwak this evening after she has had time to settle in and refresh herself. I would like to bring her to a restaurant for dinner. Is that permitted?"

"Yes, of course," Toups replied. Conversing in French seemed to lighten her mood. "Curfew on Saturday night is half past twenty-one, unless working the night shift, of course."

Turning to Annie, Mike said, "Madam Toups tells me the curfew is nine-thirty tonight. May I call on you at five and take you to Turci's? It is less than a five-minute walk from here."

"I look forward to it," Annie said. "That will give me sufficient time to make myself presentable." Mike thought she looked perfect right now. A little disheveled maybe, certainly dusted with soot, but perfect.

Mike wheeled the cart out to the truck, loaded Annie's things and brought the cart into the office area where Toups took over and shooed him away.

*****

Mike met Annie in the foyer of the boarding house at five. Toups lectured Mike, in French, about the importance of making curfew and how Annie had yet to appear for the first day of her job and how she would not have an opportunity to work without a good report from Madam Toups.

They walked along Chartres Street arm in arm. Mike pointed out the more interesting buildings as they strolled along in the fading light. Mike would glance toward the subject of interest, such as the Cabildo, and when Annie turned to study the building, Mike would study her.

Her dark, almost coal black hair, was nearly hidden by the small-brimmed hat she wore. Her high cheekbones, full lips and mildly rounded face accentuated her long nose which showed a hint of having been broken at some time. Her hazel eyes sparkled with intelligence and vitality. Her smooth white complexion was without blemish save a tiny straight scar just below her left cheekbone. Mike believed her to be singularly beautiful.

They cut over to Decatur Street at Ursulines Avenue and into Turci's on the corner. They were seated immediately. The table shown to them was next to a window looking out onto Decatur Street and along the back wall. It was a perfect location for quiet conversation. Mike offered Annie a seat facing the window and took the one against the wall for himself.

The waiter brought two menus, single sheets of handwritten items with prices, and placed glasses of water on the table. He lit a candle in the center of the table and announced that he would return to take their order.

Annie looked at her menu and asked, "What is a muffuletta?"

"It is a large sandwich made with Italian bread, sausage slices, olive oil, vegetables and other things. It is very good, but one should be enough for the both of us."

"I would like to try one."

"Muffuletta it is. Now tell me about your decision to move to New Orleans."

"What is it you would like to know?"

"Well, first of all, how did your father and brothers take the news?" That first night aboard the ship Annie had been indisposed, but on the following night she and Mike had talked at length about their lives and dreams. He had come to think of Annie as a friend.

"Well, as you know, my mother died when I was very young so there is just my father and brothers."

"No close friends, other than Summer and April?"

"Not really. There was a fiancé, but it ended badly."

Mike smiled, "I am sorry it ended badly."

"Liar," Annie laughed, "Or at least, I hope you are just being gracious."

"I said I was sorry it ended badly, not that it ended."

"Did I tell you what my father and brothers did for a living?"

"I think you said they were police officers."

"Yes. What I did not have time to tell you is that my father is the Chief of Police for Cicero."

"What does the chief think about his only daughter moving to New Orleans?"

"He said, 'If that's what you have a mind to do, go ahead'."

"And why did the daughter of the Chief of Police for Cicero decide to move to New Orleans?"

"Because of a very unusual man I would like to know more about."

"Who is this unusual man?" Mike asked teasingly.

"A rumrunner by the name of Josef Rodriguez, or was it Robert Stone? But the man that really intrigues me is Michael Demill."

Mike's heart leaped. He had not really believed Annie was moving to New Orleans just because of him. This confirmation rattled him.

Annie saw his expression. "Am I being too forward?" She asked. "Summer and April both accuse me of failing to be coy."

"I find a direct approach to be much better than coy and conniving," Mike said. "And let it be known that I am most interested in learning more about Annie Norwak, adventuress and accomplice to rumrunning."

The waiter appeared, and Annie ordered the muffuletta with two plates. Mike added that they would like two cups of *succo d'uva*.

Once the waiter had retreated Annie asked, "What is *succo d'uva*?"

"It means 'juice of the grape.' I hope you will like it."

The muffuletta arrived along with two coffee cups of dark red wine. Both were delicious.

Mike paid the bill and they walked onto a Decatur Street that was somewhat darker than when they arrived. It was early yet, but they would have to go directly to the boarding house to make curfew.

They cut across Decatur and down Saint Philip Street toward Chartres. Two men stepped out of an alley to block their path. Mike reached for his pistol and turned to look behind him. It had been his experience in France that hooligans would openly block your path and, while distracted by their demonstration, an accomplice would accost you from behind.

His move proved wise. Two men emerged from a doorway but halted when they saw Mike facing them. Mike pulled his Luger and held it along his leg. The men turned and hurried away.

Mike turned back to confront the other two men. The pair were standing in the walkway with their hands raised above their heads. Mike glanced at Annie, who had a revolver pointed at the pair.

"Well, gentlemen," Mike said. "I recommend you run now before the lady decides you are up to no good."

They hurried across the street and disappeared into an alley. Annie slipped her pistol back into her purse and looked at Mike. "A gift from a friend," she said.

They reached the boarding house with a few minutes to spare. Before going inside, Annie stepped in front of Mike.

"There is something else I have to tell you," she said. "On the train down from Chicago I saw two people in the dining car that might be important to you."

"Who could possibly be coming from Chicago that would be of interest to me, except a dark-haired, well-armed Polish lady?"

"Stop joking," Annie said seriously. "My father is Chief of Police and I have been to his office many times. One of the criminals working in Chicago is a man named Jules Ruttan. He goes by the name 'Bumper.' He is a killer for hire. He was traveling with his girlfriend, Myrtle."

"Why does this concern me?" Mike asked.

"It concerns you because the gossip on the train was that he was coming to New Orleans to help someone corner the importing business. Does your friend in the importing business want to take over someone else's share?"

"No, if anything he is looking to get out of the business."

"Then, Michael Demill, you had better find out who is trying to take over and protect yourself." She kissed him on the lips and then took his hand. "Let's go see if Madam Toups is waiting for us."

CHAPTER 14

The following weeks were a blur of activity. Annie, being the new girl on the switchboard, was required to pull the graveyard shift while Mike trucked goods all day and worked on the boat most evenings. Sunday afternoons provided the only opportunity for them to enjoy some time together.

Mike looked forward to these excursions with great anticipation and planned special sights to see each time. He and Annie would walk arm in arm, chatting and laughing. Mike hoped that the affection he was beginning to develop for Annie would be reciprocated.

During their usual evening phone conversation one Friday night, Annie announced that the phone company had hired three new girls, and she was off the graveyard shift.

"We can have a more normal life now," Annie said. "We will be able to go to the theater or dances."

"Or," Mike said, "I can bring you to sights a little further from downtown."

"Sounds like you have something in mind."

"This Sunday I would like to show you the Saint Bernard Parish Church and Cemetery on Bayou Terre Aux Boeufs. My people settled in the Parish about a hundred and fifty years ago. Lots of history there."

"That was a long time ago," Annie said. "My grandparents were still in Poland only fifty years ago."

"We will take the train, because the road is not in good shape with all the rain we have been having. We can walk to the Rampart Station from your place and spend the day on a train ride through the country."

"That sounds like fun. What time?"

"I will come by at nine in the morning. If it is raining, we might do it some other time. I'll bring a basket with some wine, bread and cheese."

The weather was cool, if not downright chilly, with a dry north wind when Mike called on Annie Saturday morning. Madam Toups met Mike in the reception area and they both waited for Annie to come from her room.

"Where do you intend to go today?" Madam Toups asked. She always spoke in French to Mike, claiming "The Americans have turned New Orleans into New York."

"We shall go to the cemetery in Terre Aux Boeufs," Mike said using the French name for Saint Bernard.

"The cemetery," Madam Toups exclaimed with a smile. "I did not realize." Couples in New Orleans often courted in the cemeteries. Toups appraised such an outing a serious step.

Annie appeared wearing a green ankle-length skirt, laced walking boots, a square-necked print blouse with large bell cuffs, gloves and a wide brimmed hat sporting a flower and feather decorated band. Mike was struck by her beauty and grace. She presented an air of reserved confidence that Mike could not explain.

"Good morning, Mike," Annie said. She gestured with a shawl and a duster which she carried over one arm. "Do you think I shall need these?"

"The shawl, certainly. It is dry but blustery this morning," Mike answered. "The duster, I can fold and carry on the basket.

The wind is such that I do not think soot from the engine will be a problem."

He took the duster from Annie, folded it neatly and placed it on the basket beneath the carry handles.

"When may I expect your return?" Madam Toups said. She used English, so Annie answered.

"Before curfew, I am certain," Annie replied. "More than that, I cannot say."

"We will return on the last train up from Shell Beach," Mike said. "That should be about eight in the evening."

"*Voir que vous faites* (See that you do)," Toups said, with a wag of her finger.

They walked the short distance from the boarding house to the Rampart Street stop. It was a cool dry morning, unusually so for early April, and quite a change from the last few weeks which were rainy, overcast, and gloomy. Delighted with the weather, Annie and Mike walked briskly, Annie was almost skipping, to the stop just as the train to Shell Beach pulled up.

The line to Shell Beach passed through most of Saint Bernard Parish, paralleling first Bayou Terre Aux Boeufs and then Bayou La Loutre before running along Bayou Yscloskey to the site of the old fort on Lake Borgne at Shell Beach. The train consisted of three enclosed box cars for freight and three passenger cars. The canvas sides of the passenger cars had been rolled up so that folks rode in forward facing bench seats open on all sides.

A conductor with a change dispenser on his belt walked along the landing collecting fares. Each time he collected a fare he would place a small step at a vacant row and help people aboard. There were no walkways along the coach and if someone wished to change seats they would have to wait for a stop, get down, walk to the desired bench and clamber back aboard.

"Two for Saint Bernard Cemetery," Mike said when the conductor approached.

"Yes, sir. Round trip?"

Mike nodded.

"That will be four bits, sir," the man said. He perforated a pair of tickets with a small hand punch and gave them to Mike. "This way, please." He placed the step opposite the first bench on the last car and offered a hand to Annie. Bunching her skirt in one hand, Annie allowed the conductor to assist her up to the bench. Mike followed and placed the basket on the seat beside him to discourage others from joining them.

"Best seat on the train," Mike said. "Far enough from the engine that there will be little chance we will get a dusting of smoke and with the room between us and the car ahead, we will enjoy an open view of the countryside."

"Help me with my hat, please," Annie said. "I want to tie it in place with this ribbon." She had placed a wide, lacy ribbon over the crown of the hat. While Annie held the wide brim down at the sides, Mike tied the ribbon beneath her chin. The result reminded Mike of nuns he had seen in France whose habit shielded their faces so much they could only see straight ahead.

"Does it look too severe?" Annie asked. She looked at Mike, her faced framed as if it were a portrait.

He didn't know what "severe" meant in the context she intended so he simply blurted, "You are beautiful."

"Flatterer," Annie replied. She smiled, and her eyes twinkled.

The train jerked ahead and began to roll. Smoke poured from the stack on the small engine and was quickly wafted away from the following cars. The tracks ran along the center of a wide right-of-way with macadam roadways on either side for vehicles and pedestrian walkways. Although it was Saturday, the roadways were busy with horse drawn wagons and automobiles.

The line made a bend to the right, matching a turn in the Mississippi River far to their right and unseen. Annie noticed that the street signs now read "St. Claude." They crossed several rail junctions running to and from the river.

At one junction Mike commented, "That's the line to the Milneburg landing."

"Is that where you are building your boat?"

"Yes."

"I would like to see it some time."

"Perhaps next trip," Mike said. "Or after we have put her in the water." He was not certain how his partners would react to him showing a stranger around the boatyard.

The train trundled across a low bridge. The land was a forest of draglines, cranes and construction barges digging a great canal as far as they could see to the left. To the right a wide basin had been carved out of the riverbank where the canal intersected the Mississippi River. The steam shovels working on the locks adjacent to the rail line generated billowing plumes of acrid smoke. Ladies and gentlemen alike on the open coaches covered their faces with handkerchiefs.

"I am amazed at how fast the construction is going," Mike said. "It connects Lake Pontchartrain with the river and, in doing so, connects all of the Gulf Coast. It will be finished within the year, or so they say."

Soon they passed a military installation. A formation of soldiers was parading about in an open field braced by majestic brick buildings.

"Jackson Barracks," Mike commented. "We are crossing out of Orleans Parish. Once we pass the stockyards, we will be in Saint Bernard Parish where we will pass through a switching yard that will put us on the Mexican Gulf Railroad. That is the line that runs all the way to Shell Beach. There were plans to continue the line across Lake Borgne to Bay Saint Louis, but wiser heads prevailed, and the plans were abandoned."

The train passed into cultivated plains with vast stands of trees toward the north. A great sawmill covering acres of land worked huge logs of cypress carried in by a web of small gauge rail lines that radiated out into the stubble of stumps and brush that had once been forest. A deafening noise, smoke and dust once again filled the air causing passengers to huddle and cover their faces until they were beyond the work area.

"Look back toward the river," Mike said, his lips almost touching Annie's ear to be heard above the noise of the train and sawmill. "In just a little while, you will be able to see the tip of the obelisk that was set to mark the site of the Battle of New Orleans."

"You mean to tell me the Battle of New Orleans was not fought in New Orleans?"

"Not really," Mike said. "The battle was fought on a plantation owned by the Chalmette Family. I guess it is about three or four miles downriver from New Orleans."

They passed through a variety of vegetable farms, pastures, and some sugar cane fields. The great cypress forest was just a green tree line to the north. The railroad slowly converged with the Mississippi River until it ran along the toe of the levee with stretches of pasture or fallow sugarcane on the left.

"Growing sugarcane died here after the war with Spain," Mike explained. "The Civil War hurt the cane industry, but

Cuba now produces so much cane that the locals can't compete."

They came to a canal with navigation locks connecting it with the Mississippi. The rail line ran on the top of the riverside flood gates and a roadway ran along the top of the canal side of the lock basin. When the flood gates were closed, trains and vehicles could cross the gates and when the gates were open for boat traffic, land transportation had to wait.

The train slowed to a crawl as it crossed the flood gate. There were gaps in the rails to allow for the operation of the gate and the potential for derailment was great.

"If you look left," Mike said when they were in the center of the floodgate, "you can see up the canal. That rickety boathouse just past those fallen willows used to be where I lived right after the war."

"It looks – rustic," Annie said.

"It is a squalid dump not fit for human habitation."

They rode along in silence for a while until they reached a switch in the rail. One set of tracks continued along the river while another line turned east. The train was sent onto the eastbound line where it ran more or less parallel to a bayou on the south. Small houses with subsistence vegetable farms lined the track. People working in the gardens paused to wave at the train. Annie waved back.

She watched a man walking beside a team of oxen. The man urged the animals along with slight taps with a long, thin pole. The oxen were pulling a wide, flat sled heaped with cabbages along a path that was a muddy quagmire.

Mike noticed Annie's interest in the slow-moving sled and said, "He's headed toward the freight landing. When this train returns, he will sell the cabbages to a produce agent from the city. They call this place 'Terre Aux Boeufs,' meaning 'The land of the oxen,' because the people here are so skilled at breeding draft animals."

The bayou meandered south away from the railroad and then suddenly turned sharply to pass under the rail and follow along on the north side of the train. They had been racing along at twenty-five miles an hour or more, but now the trained slowed. Annie could see a church steeple in the distance. There was a landing coming up and there were people waiting for the train.

"This is our stop," Mike said.

The train came to a stop. Mike stood and the conductor, who had been riding in the back of the last car, scurried forward with the step. Mike climbed down, set down the basket and turned to help Annie down from the car.

With the train behind her, all Annie could see was a cemetery on the north side of the landing. When the train pulled away, she saw that the land south of the railway was wooded. A narrow roadway divided the cemetery. She could see lines of tombs fronting the road like houses. Beyond the tombs, she could see the steeple of a wooden church. A bell began to ring.

"We are in time for Mass," Mike said as he took Annie's arm. He guided her along the road, across a wooden bridge and then up to the church. Buggies were tied to rails and people were going into the church. Mike placed the basket on the corner of the porch and escorted Annie inside, guiding her to a pew in the rear.

A family, a man, woman and two teenagers, a boy and girl, occupied a portion of the pew. The man looked toward Mike and pushed his family over to make room for the couple. Annie whispered a "Thank you" to the man, who nodded and whispered, "*De nada.*"

The Mass began with the Latin prayers no different than the Catholic masses in Cicero, Illinois, and very familiar to Annie, but when the reading of the gospels began, Annie was surprised to hear Spanish, not English. When it was time for communion, Mike moved out into the aisle to allow the others in the pew to go to the altar, but he did not. Annie had expected Mike to follow her. She looked back at Mike who smiled and gestured for her to continue to the altar.

After mass, the entire congregation collected in front of the church to talk and exchange family news. Mike guided Annie to a small gathering of happily chatting people which included the family who had shared the pew with them. He embraced the man and then the woman, muttering something in Spanish that Annie could not hear clearly.

Mike brought Annie to his side and said, "Tío Geronimo, Tía Isabella, I would like you to meet my friend, Miss Anastazja Norwak, Annie to her friends, of Cicero, Illinois."

"*Mucho gusto,*" Geronimo and Isabella said in unison.

Annie gave Mike a curious glance. She did not remember telling him her true name.

Mike continued, "Annie, this is my uncle, Geronimo Demill and his wife, Isabella. That young man over there," he gestured toward the teenagers that had shared the pew, "is their son, Pedro Demill, and the young girl, I do not know."

"She is Maria Lucia Rodriguez," Isabella said in heavily accented English. "She is Pedro's *novia* — how do you say? Special friend."

The teenagers were engrossed in a conversation beyond the gaggle of parishioners. Geronimo called to the youngsters, "Zapato, Lucia, *ven aquí, por favor.*" The couple ceased their conversation and, hand in hand, walked over to Mike and Annie.

"Miss Anastazja Norwak," Geronimo said as the couple approached, "I would like you to meet my son, Pedro, who is called 'Zapato,' and his *novia*, Maria Lucia Rodriguez, who is called 'Lucia.' Lucia, this is Zapato's cousin, Miguel Demill – Mike to his friends."

Annie said, "I am pleased to meet everyone. Please call me 'Annie'." There was an awkward silence until Mike said, "I wanted Annie to meet some of my family and I thought you might be here today. We are here to visit the cemetery.

"Oh," Isabella said and then she caught herself. Bringing a girl friend to visit the cemetery implied that Mike entertained very serious intentions.

"You will find it most interesting," Geronimo said. "It holds many of our ancestors. I think the first burial here was in 1781 or so."

Annie smiled, "Ever since coming to Louisiana, Mister Demill, I have been confronted with nothing but amazing sights."

"Please call me Tio Geronimo. Everyone does, even those who are not my nephews or nieces." Geronimo said.

"But, please, allow me to introduce you to some more of our people," Isabella said taking Annie by the hand. "The men can talk fishing or business or whatever foolishness men talk about." She led Annie toward other clusters of conversation followed by Zapato and Lucia.

"She is a beautiful lady," Geronimo said.

"Yes, she is," Mike said.

Geronimo looked around before he said in Spanish, "The people understand why you did what you did. You saved my life, Nephew. Mine and the life of young Zapato there. You will not have trouble here."

Mike sighed, "Thank you, Uncle." He nodded toward Pedro "Zapato" Demill. "Tell me how he came about the nickname 'Zapato'?"

Geronimo laughed. "One day when we were culling a trawl, Pedro stepped on a catfish. The spine stung him good. For the rest of the trip, he works with one shoe on the sore foot. Everyone started calling him 'shoe' and it stuck."

"Manuel may have some more work for us," Mike said.

"I am ready. We must be more careful. The Haden brothers have been hijacking some shipments. They even tried to stop a boat in Black Lake. Luckily, some others happened into the lake, saw what was going on and intervened." He paused and said in a lower voice, "I heard they have brought in a gunman from Chicago."

"I know. His name is Jules Ruttan. A very bad man."

"Chicago is in Illinois, is it not?" Geronimo asked, glancing toward Annie and the crowd of people Isabella had gathered to meet her.

"It is."

"What do you know of Annie, besides the fact she is very pretty?"

Mike thought for a moment. "Not much. She is the daughter of a police chief and I trust her with my life." He watched Annie laughing and chatting. She glanced over to him and smiled in a way that made his heart flutter.

"Let us hope you are not blinded, Miguel. The heart has made a fool of many a good man."

Suddenly the image of Cass leapt into his mind, her face distorted in hatred. "Son-of-a-bitch," is what she called him. Why had she changed so much? The surprise and disappointment of the memory caused his face to darken.

Annie separated from the cluster of gossiping ladies and came back to Mike, her face reflected concern.

"Mike, are you alright?" she whispered, her lips touching his ear.

Mike pushed the dark thought away and smiled. "Yes, Annie. I am fine. Let's tour the cemetery. My Aunt will wear your ear off if we give her a chance."

"Go take a walk through the cemetery," Geronimo said in English. "I will try to corral Tía Isabella."

Mike embraced Geronimo, waved goodbye to Isabella and the others, collected the basket, and held out an elbow for Annie. She put her hand in the crook of his arms and they headed across the bridge to the cemetery.

"Oh, Mike," Annie said. "I just love your family. They are all so -," She paused, looking for the right word, "- real."

"Real is what we all are," Mike laughed. "You will find a great lack of pretention among the *Isleños*."

"Tell me about the *Isleños*," Annie said.

"I am an *Isleño*," Mike said. "I grew up not far from here in a fishing community. When Spain controlled Louisiana, the King of Spain wanted to help the Americans during the Revolutionary War. He recruited settlers from around the world to come to Louisiana to serve in his army and to populate the land. One of the places he recruited from was the Canary Islands. Thousands of Islanders, *Isleños* in Spanish, came here starting in 1778.

"Spain declared war on England and the army in Louisiana drove the British off the Gulf Coast and cleared the Mississippi River, so supplies could be brought to Washington's western armies. Let me show you a tomb of particular interest."

He brought Annie over to a brick structure covered in plaster and whitewashed in the typical New Orleans tradition.

The front of the tomb was covered by a marble slab with rows of names engraved on it.

"There," he said, touching the top name on the marker. "He was my grandfather's great-grandfather."

The slab was inscribed:

"Don Diego deMelilla
Sargento del España
nacio 15 Julio 1748
murió 22 Septiembre 1814"

Annie removed her glove and traced the name. "He lived to be 66," she said. "A long time for that era."

"He outlived four wives. Louisiana was a wilderness and life was hard, particularly for women. My grandfather, Doramas, changed his name from deMelilla to Demill."

"Why did he do that?"

"He was on the wrong side during the Civil War. He changed his name to avoid – trouble, returned to Saint Bernard and became another fisherman among the *Isleños*."

"But wasn't everyone in Louisiana a Confederate? Why did he have to hide?"

"The Confederacy wasn't the side he was on. His family was in the shipping industry, river boats and rail. The Civil War took everything.

My grandfather's family supported the Union. They provided steamboats, trains, and material in exchange for promises of compensation. The compensation never came. Competitors in the shipping business with greater political influence blocked all attempts to pay for family resources consumed by the Union war effort.

After the war was over, Federal actions brewed resentment and lawlessness. There were riots and lynch mobs, very bad times. Some people in Louisiana did not forget that the deMelilla family had supported the Union. My grandfather changed his name and hid among the *Isleños*."

"I had no idea," Annie said.

"Come, there's more to see." Mike led Annie along the row of tombs. Annie read the names as they walked. "It is as if we were in Spain," she said. "Rodriguez, Hernandez, Campo, Zerpas, and Espinosa. It just goes on and on."

"This next marker is for Pedro deMelilla. He was Don Diego's son and the first Commissioner of Police for New Orleans. He died the year that America purchased Louisiana. It was his son, Bartolomé, a war hero in his own right, that founded the shipping company. I don't know where Bartolomé is buried."

They walked a little further. "And here is my grandfather, Doramas and my father, Diego," Mike said.

Both names were on the same marble slab, along with several others. Annie guessed the others were wives, siblings, or cousins. She noted that Doramas Demill died in 1875 and Diego Demill in 1910.

Annie said, "The only family plots I can visit are my grandparents and my mother. In Cicero, we bury our dead deep and leave a headstone. Down here, you use little houses of brick."

"Let's go over to that bench and see what we have for lunch," Mike said. "I know the wine is good, but I haven't tried the cheese. I also have some bread and sausage. I understand you folks in Illinois are fond of sausage."

They sat at a bench tucked between rows of tombs. Mike placed the basket between them. He opened the wine, pulled two glasses from the basket, and poured a little for Annie to taste.

"My, that is good," she said and held the glass for Mike to fill. He poured himself a glass of wine, sipped some and set it down to slice the bread, cheese and sausage to make sandwiches. They talked for a while discussing the food, the weather and commenting on the beauty of their surroundings.

Mike cleared his throat and said, "Enough of this. I brought you here to – uh – talk about us."

"Is there an 'us,' Mike?"

"What do you mean?"

Annie sighed. "Well, we have hardly even kissed. I kind of don't know where I stand. I thought maybe I was too forward, and it put you off. I am beginning to think something is wrong with me."

"What?" Mike exclaimed. "Wrong with you? God, Annie, you are perfect, well, except for your taste in men, that is. I can't believe you moved to New Orleans just for me."

"What other reason could there be?"

"I don't know. I'm just not good at this stuff." Mike was turning red.

"What stuff is that?"

"Aw, Annie," Mike wiped his face with his hand. "I love you and it scares me. I look at myself and all I see is a shot-up rumrunner with bad lungs. I don't understand what you see in me that is worth anything."

"I will tell you what I see, Mike," Annie said. "I see a strong, brave man who risked everything to save a stranger. I see a man who makes me feel special. I see a man who went through hell and came out an angel. I see the man I love. Now, the next thing you need to do is kiss me. I promise, I will not break."

CHAPTER 15

Mike leaned his right cheek against the padded headrest of the wide bench seat of the Pullman Coach. The steady click of the iron wheels against the rail joints was mesmerizing. Gazing through the glass, he watched as the crowded streets and clustered buildings of New Orleans melted away into scrubby brush, violated remains of cypress swamps and finally, marshland.

Mike had walked to the streetcar line on Saint Charles Avenue before dawn that morning, his fisherman's senses alert to the lack of wind. He had decided to leave his truck home and take the streetcar to the L&N station. He planned on being gone for only one night, but one never knew. He had promised Annie to call her when he reached Mobile. If the schedule changed after meeting with Dugas, he could call again.

The Louisville and Nashville line followed a route as close to the coast of the Gulf of Mexico as was possible. It departed New Orleans in a northeasterly direction, skirted the shore of Lake Pontchartrain, turned east, and ran along the narrow strip of land that divided Pontchartrain from Lake Borgne. The rail followed the coast, occasionally crossing waterways or passing close enough to open water for passengers to catch glimpses of boats working their nets, before plunging into a terrain of gnarled pigmy oaks, tall cane, and brush.

The elegant, fully enclosed coach had two rows of padded, forward-facing bench seats nearly four feet wide. The aisle between was narrow, sacrificing ease of movement between seats for the more valuable space devoted to passenger comfort. The large windows were partitioned into moving panes, permitting the opening of the lower half or upper half depending upon the passenger's desires and the engine's smoke discharge.

It was a calm, clear April day so the windows were closed, top and bottom. Because it was calm, the smoke from the engine hung in the air and stretched along the full length of the long line of cars. Mike's view through the window was mottled with gray puffs of smoke. Had the windows not been closed the car would have been filled with ash and choking smoke. He hoped that a morning breeze from the gulf would arise and he could open a window, smell the salt air.

He rode one of three-day cars, the first car behind the coal car and subject to the densest discharge from the engine. Following the three-day cars was the dining car and then two sleeper cars for long distance travelers. The kitchen and service car came next. Sleepers could order breakfast in bed or were treated to the aroma of hot food being carried forward from the kitchen car.

The last car was the executive suite. It was a combination sleeper, dining and office car designed by L&N big wigs. When not occupied, passengers holding sleeper car reservations were offered a guided tour of the executive car.

Mike remembered the excursion he and Annie had made to the Saint Bernard Cemetery. The little open passenger cars with the hard bench seats and the decades old steam engine were almost antiques when compared to this modern passenger train. Yet, that short ride would be something he would never forget.

Nor would he forget their first kiss as lovers. Deep, passionate and, unfortunately, interrupted by other couples walking through the alleys of tombs. Annie and Mike had dined nearly every night since, exchanging their past and hopes for the future. It was a friendship that had matured into a courtship. Each evening ended at the boarding house lobby. That last aspect, Mike hoped, would change soon.

Mike decided breakfast was in order. He placed his hat on the seat, to indicate he was returning, picked up the satchel William had given him and headed toward the dining car. The first day car was less than a third full, so the likelihood of some other passenger taking his seat was small.

He worked his way through the other day cars toward the dining car. The number of passengers increased with each successive car because seasoned passengers wanted to be both further from the smoke-billowing engine and closer to the dining car. He had timed the trip for a late breakfast when the dining car would be sparsely occupied.

During the trip to the dining car, Mike made a mental note of the people occupying each of the day cars he passed through. Four men in the first car were obviously traveling salesmen. They had their sample cases on the seats next to them and each had his hat pulled low, sleeping. The passing scenery was boringly familiar to them and held no wonderment.

There was one young couple, newlyweds Mike thought. Aside from being very young, maybe teenagers, they were crowded together, almost snuggling, engrossed in conversation and laughing. Mike wondered if that was how he and Annie looked sitting on that bench in the cemetery.

Two families occupied the last four bench seats in the first car. The adults were gathered on the left side of the train while the children, a half-dozen boys and girls, scrambled for places at the right windows, and calling out sightings of boats when patches of open water appeared.

The second car contained more couples, fewer lonely salesmen, and no families. The third car was nearly filled with a glee-club from Newcomb College of New Orleans. All young ladies escorted by a spinster cadre and grim-faced fathers. The chaperones glared in unison at Mike as he maneuvered through the narrow aisle.

Once in the dining car, Mike took the first table to the right. He sat at the chair nearest the window where he had a clear view of the car as well as both entrances.

The waiter approached and asked, "What will you have, sir?"

"Are you still serving breakfast?"

"Yes, sir." The waiter produced a menu card and gave it to Mike. "Breakfast will be available for another half hour. After that, the kitchen will be closed for two hours until the noon service."

"Coffee, please." Mike glanced at the card. "I'll have the ham and scrambled eggs."

"Cream or sugar with your coffee?"

"No, thank you."

"Will that be all, sir?"

"Yes, thank you.

The waiter collected the menu card and hurried off toward the rear of the train. He paused as he passed another couple finishing their breakfast as if to see if there would be anything else. The man answered something, and the waiter scribbled on a note pad before disappearing into the kitchen car.

There was something about the couple that troubled Mike. Neither of them looked toward him when he entered and even now, they kept their faces turned away. He remembered where he had seen them before.

When he had stepped onto the L&N platform in New Orleans, they had been at the far end of the platform, near the ticket office. The instant he showed his ticket to the L&N conductor, the man rushed into the ticket office. Mike had thought nothing of it at the time. But now the couple was at the rear of the dining car and avoiding eye contact.

The man was stout and wearing an expensive suit. His shirt was high collared with a fat tie and a tie pin that sparkled distinctly across the dining car. The lady was dressed in a slim "flapper" dress that shimmered with rhinestones. She wore a rimless box hat with a frilly white veil across her forehead. The man rose, pulled the chair for the lady and they both left toward the sleeper cars without so much as glancing in Mike's direction.

Mike ate slowly while he considered the possibility that he was being followed - or was he just imagining things? He ran down a list of conditions.

Question: How did they know he was going to Mobile?

Answer: They didn't. They must have followed him from his house, maybe shadowing him in a car as he rode the streetcar. When he went to the train station, they had to wait to see which train he boarded and then hurry to get on board.

Question: How do they know where he is going? The train stopped at five towns before Mobile and a dozen after it. This particular train went all the way to the east coast.

Answer: Every stop, one of the followers would have to step down onto the platform and see if he got off. If he didn't, they stayed aboard.

Question: Why didn't they just sit in a day car where they could see him?

Answer: They couldn't chance him noticing them.

He finished his breakfast and decided to put his theory to a test. The Stanton stop was coming up. Mike returned to his seat and moved from the right side of the train to the left. The upcoming station would be on the left.

The conductor walked through the day car announcing that Stanton was next. The train squealed to a stop. The engine belched a great plume of steam and hissed. Mike opened the bottom half of the window and leaned slightly, moving one eye clear of the window frame until he could see the length of the train.

There was the mystery man standing on the bottom step of the last door of the last sleeper car. He was watching the landing intently. Five minutes later, the conductor called out "All aboard" and waved an unlit lantern toward the engine. The train's whistle blew three short blasts and the steam pistons puffed.

Mike watched as the man stepped back into the sleeper car. He had not been imagining things after all. The question now was: "What to do next?"

The train would arrive at Mobile right at dusk. He was to meet Dugas at the Pinto Island ferry landing and return on the night train to New Orleans. The Pinto Island ferry landing was on the opposite side of the L&N rail line from downtown Mobile. Anyone departing the train station and heading toward the ferry landing would be obvious.

He thought about waiting until the last moment to exit the day car but decided to act in a way that didn't reveal he knew he was being followed. He would have to lose or confront them before meeting with Dugas.

The conductor walked through the day car announcing, "Mobile Station in five minutes. Please gather your things if you are getting down at Mobile."

Mike moved to the aisle with the leather satchel on his lap. The train slowed, jerked, and then screeched to a halt. Mike moved to the end of the car just as the conductor folded a small step down from the doorway. No one else in the car came to the door. Mike stepped down and moved to the center of the landing, glancing left and right to get his bearings.

He saw the man at the step of the last sleeper car return into the car and reappeared with the woman in the sparkling tight dress. They had no luggage. This must have been a last-minute thing, or when they started following him, they didn't think he was headed out of the city. Poor planning on their part or a lucky break for him.

Next to the landing was the typical brick train station that was a combination waiting room and ticket office. More than two dozen people, men, women, and children, came out of the station house and queued up at the day car Mike had just exited. The conductor was punching tickets and helping ladies up the step. Once the last of the queue was aboard, he looked the length of the train.

The conductor waved the lantern, which was now lit for it was growing dark, and shouted, "All aboard." He stepped onto the landing of the doorway to the day car and pulled up the step to its vertical position across the bottom of the door.

Mike walked over to a small news stand next to the entrance to the train station. He watched out of the corner of his eye as the woman in the glittering dress pretended to be waving at someone on the train. He decided to call the pair "Jack and Jill." They were having an awkward moment. If Mike lingered where he was, they would have to pass close to him to enter the station. If they stayed where they were they would look very out of place. Nobody stands on a train platform when no train is expected.

The newsboy perked up as Mike approached. "Need a paper, mister?"

Mike looked at the rack of papers, pretending to decide if he wanted one. The boy continued his sales pitch. "They got some barnstormers in town, mister. I got tickets for the show. Friday's show is only a quarter."

Jack and Jill walked toward the station entrance and passed Mike just as he said, "Give me a ticket to the Friday show," loud enough for them to hear. It was only Wednesday.

Mike turned slightly and touched the brim of his hat and said, "Evening, ma'am, sir."

Jack nodded but averted his eyes. Jill made no acknowledgment at all. Jack was a hard-looking man, maybe thirty or so. Dark eyes, heavy brows and a black felt fedora pulled low. Jill was movie-star beautiful, mid-twenties. Blond wisps escaped her hat. She wore shoes with thick heels that clunked as she walked on the wood deck of the platform.

Mike turned to the newsboy. "What is the best hotel in town?"

"The Progress, sir. Go to Water Street, it's just behind the station and go right two blocks to Dauphin Street. It's on the corner."

Mike flipped a half-dollar to the kid who caught the coin in midair. "Keep the change."

"Thanks, mister."

Mike walked through the station house and out onto Water Street. A sign across the street had the words "Pinto Ferry" printed above an arrow pointing left. Mike crossed the street and turned right. The Progress Hotel sat on the far corner of

Water and Dauphin. There was a uniformed doorman at the entrance portico.

"Afternoon, sir," the doorman said. "Will you be staying with us tonight?"

Mike nodded, and the man held the door open for him to enter. Mike crossed a plush lobby that reminded him of the Hotel Grunewald in New Orleans. He stepped up to the registration desk.

The man behind the desk said, "May I help you sir?"

"I would like a room, please."

"Yes, sir. How long will you be staying?"

Mike place his satchel at his feet and glance toward the entrance door in time to see Jack speaking with the doorman.

"Three days."

"Excellent, sir. We have several rooms with a wonderful view of the bay available. Thirty dollars a night."

"I would like something on the west side. I hope to sleep late. Nothing too high. I have an aversion to rooms up high."

"In that case, sir, room 220 should do. Twenty-two dollars a night. One night in advance."

Mike pulled out a clip of bills and peeled off the cash. The clerk spun the register around and Mike signed it, "William Dobbs." There was a space for hometown, and he wrote "Chicago" in that space. There was another space for a telephone number, but he left it blank.

The clerk pulled a key from a pigeonhole and gave it to Mike. "The stairs are on your right. One flight up. 220 is just to the left of the stair landing. Please, enjoy your stay with us, Mister Dobbs."

Mike took the key and picked up his satchel. He turned to go to the stairs and noted that Jill was seated on one of the cushioned chairs in the lobby and Jack was standing over her talking to her. Mike wondered how much money the clerk was going to demand before telling Jack his room number.

Mike found the room, went in, and locked the door. He crossed the room to the window opposite the door and slid it open. He looked out into an alley about ten feet below the windowsill. Crossing back to the door, he placed his ear to it and listened. In just a few minutes he heard the clunk-clunk of Jill's shoes pass his door and stop. There was the sound of a key in a door. It had to be the room next to his.

The Progress was a fancy hotel that had a water closet for every room. There was a small tub for bathing, a basin with hot and cold running water and a toilet. Mike turned on the cold water and let it run. The water closet for the room next door likely shared a wall with this room.

Mike went back to the window and dropped the satchel into the alley. He climbed out of the window, hung from the sill for a moment and then dropped to the alley below. He gathered up his satchel and walked briskly out of the alley onto Dauphin Street. He turned right to Royal Street, which ran parallel to Water Street, and went the six blocks to Canal Street, wondering why the street names were the same as New Orleans. The Pinto Ferry landing was at the bay end of Canal Street.

At Canal Street he headed for the bay, crossing the railroad and the small sliver of land on the bay side of the railroad to the ferry landing. The ferry had just completed the last crossing from Pinto Island and a steady stream of workers from the boat works on the island were headed home. The ferrymen were securing the vessel for the night.

He went to a small office building on the south end of the landing. It was dark and unoccupied. He waited until the landing was vacant, the voices of the last workers to depart fading into the west. He listened to the slap of wavelets and the distant sounds of traffic on Water Street.

"*Tu es en retard*," said a dark, massive shape that moved out from behind the building.

Mike responded in French, "Friend Dugas. I am late. I was followed from New Orleans. It took some time to put the hounds off the scent."

"Who was following you?"

"I do not know. A man and a woman."

Dugas leaned out from the shadows and scanned the land to the west and said, "That is not a problem for me."

Mike offered the satchel to Dugas who took it and placed it on the windowsill of the building. He opened the satchel and felt inside. Seemingly satisfied, he closed the case again and produced a thick envelope which he gave to Mike.

"There are three drop-off locations identified in the packet. The time is noted in the papers. The ship will arrive at the first location at twenty hours, twenty-six April.

"Three drop-off locations are quite a lot."

"It is a large order. Three times the last one you escorted." Dugas leaned closer. "I hear you might have problems with hijackers."

Mike nodded. "Yes. If our captains see somebody, they will just trawl for shrimp and the ship will not find anyone at the rendezvous points."

"Then the hijackers, if they are smart, will not try anything at sea. No place to hide, no?"

"Everyone will return by a different route. So, the hijackers would need to discover where we have unloaded the boats and intercept our trucks on the road between dock and warehouse."

Dugas waved his hat toward Pinto Island and Mike heard a boat engine start. "Then make the trip to the warehouse as short as possible."

"Good advice," Mike said.

A boat pulled up to the far side of the moored ferry. Dugas offered his hand to Mike. "Take care, my friend. I look forward to doing business with you in the future."

Mike took Dugas' massive hand, "Goodbye and give my regards to *Don* Sebastian."

Dugas nodded, turned sharply, crossed the deck of the ferry, and lightly jumped down into the boat. Mike was impressed at how spry the big man was. The boat powered away into the dark.

Mike stepped into the shadow along the wall of the little office building that Dugas had occupied and began his wait. The west bound L&N was due along at seven and Mike had the ticket in his pocket. No need to visit the ticket office.

He wondered who those people were that were following him. Did they know he carried payment for a shipment of rum? The payment was not in cash, too much volume. It was a single stone, a diamond worth a quarter of a million dollars. He hadn't seen the stone. He hadn't even opened the satchel. The diamond was sealed in its own miniature case. Dugas knew what that case and the seals that bound it should feel like.

Were the followers interested in robbing him? If so, how could they have known he carried such a valuable thing. Had they simply known he worked for Moreno, watched him get the satchel from William and then waited for him near his house? Did he manage to throw them off his trail at the hotel?

A train whistle blew in the distance and Mike could see the light of an engine coming from the north. That would be the west-bound L&N coming down Mobile Bay.

He left his secluded spot and hurried up to the railroad. An old trail followed the rails on the bayside of the line. It was lower than the raised railroad, so he was hidden from people across the rails on Water Street. He reached the station at the same time the L&N stopped at the passenger landing.

Mike walked along the stationary train, hidden from the station house by the engine and coal car, to the first day car. The conductor was on the other side of the car helping passengers on and off. Mike grabbed the hand holds next to the closed door, pulled up and pushed the door open. He stepped into the car and the door sprang closed.

He went into the day car. A few passengers who were not getting off were scattered throughout the car. Some were sleeping, most were looking out the windows toward Mobile. He stood back and scanned the windows. He didn't see any shining flapper dresses on the platform.

He took the first open seat, wedged his back against the wall of the coach and waited for the conductor to come through the car to check tickets and punch any he might have missed.

A large man backed into the car. Mike eased his hand behind his back and gripped the butt of his Luger. The man turned around. He wasn't the man Mike had nicknamed "Jack."

The train jerked forward and began to gather speed. Mike stood and went to one of the windows facing the station. He looked at the crowd of people milling toward the doors of the station house. He glimpsed a sparkling dress move from the far side of the building and join the crowd from the train. Jack and Jill had been watching the people board the train and they were still in Mobile.

CHAPTER 16

It was six Thursday morning when the westbound L&N pulled into the station. Mike had slept well on the wide bench seat of the day car. He had deliberately taken the first seat of the first Pullman after the coal car so that no one had to pass him for any reason. He had been confident that Jack and Jill were still in Mobile…. at least for another eight hours until the next westbound L&N came through.

The train slowed slightly and entered a tight turn, awakening him. The conductor came into the day car from the rear of the train, stirring the few passengers at the back of the car. He tottered up the aisle to Mike.

"New Orleans Station, sir," the man said.

Mike had just enough time to walk the five blocks from the L&N Station at the foot of Canal Street to Annie's boarding house and catch her before she left for work at seven. He hoped they could share a breakfast at a small café next to the Cumberland Telephone and Telegraph building. She knew of his trip to Mobile, of course, but he had not been able to call her during his absence. Not hearing from him would have concerned her.

Mike entered the reception area of the boarding house and greeted Madam Toups in French.

"Good morning, dear Madam," he said. "Has Miss Norwak left for work?"

"Good morning, sir. Miss Norwak went into the dining room just this very minute. I will go get her before she gets seated." Madam Toups hurried down a hall and moments later Annie appeared.

She was dressed for work. Ankle-length yellow dress, tight at the waist, wide and billowing at the shoulders, with triple buttoned cuffs at the wrist. She wore laced over-the-ankle boots, tanned gloves, and a wide brimmed hat, which she carried at her side. Her expression transformed from joy to concern and stopped at exacerbation. She was beautiful.

"You did not call," she said.

"And good morning to you as well," Mike responded. "May I buy you breakfast? I promise it will surpass the porridge served here."

Madam Toups, who had followed Annie into the room, cleared her throat.

"My apologies, Madam," Mike said.

Annie said, "Breakfast and an explanation. I was worried sick."

Mike smiled widely and offered his arm. "I will do all I can to satisfy your concerns."

Annie put on her hat and took his arm. She could not maintain her frown. "Oh, Mike," she said. "What am I to do with you?"

He led her out of the boarding house to the breakfast café next door. He selected a table, as was his habit, near a window but not so close as to be seen from the street. He assisted Annie into a chair and then sat opposite her, his back against the wall. Annie, having been raised in a family of police officers, did not find Mike's seating habit unusual.

The waiter welcomed them as regulars and Mike asked for a double order of ham and eggs. "I haven't eaten since noon yesterday," he explained. He waited until the waiter had gone before beginning. "I do apologize for not calling you. It was unavoidable. I had no time before or after my meeting."

Annie sighed. "I don't know if it would have been better if you had not told me anything about having to go out of town. I had supposed the trip was a 'Josef Rodriguez' venture. Your expression tells me I am right, so you understand my concern. I was expecting a call from you about seven or so yesterday afternoon."

"And I had planned to call. It was supposed to be a short trip, and it was. I have been on the train for all but an hour of the time between when I departed and now. When I was in Mobile, I had to spend some time, ensuring 'Josef' had a secure meeting. There was no time to call."

"And what caused you to have to spend this extra time?"

"I was followed."

"Who followed you?"

"I don't know. They began to follow me as soon as I left the house."

"They? How many are 'they'?"

"Just two. A man and a woman." Mike laughed, "I began to think of them as 'Jack' and 'Jill'."

Annie's face became very serious. "Describe them for me."

Mike shrugged. "The man was wide, heavy and dark. Maybe thirty or forty. He wore a heavy trench coat and black felt fedora. The woman was young, very attractive and wore a sparkling, shimmering flapper dress."

Annie said, "Was she blonde?"

"I think so. She had a small hat and veil."

"Mike, remember when I told you about the hired gunman Jules Ruttan and his moll, Myrtle?"

"You think the man was Ruttan?"

"Myrtle is a blonde and flashy, very much the flapper. They are quite notorious in Chicago."

"Well, as hired gunmen go, Ruttan is a poor planner. They began to follow me at my house, but they were very unprepared for a train trip to Mobile. Once in Mobile, it was child's play to lose them."

Annie said, "My father does not think Ruttan is a poor planner. I talked to him last week and he tells me that Ruttan and Myrtle are suspects in two killings for hire. The bootleg activities in Chicago are becoming very organized and violent."

Mike brushed his mustache with his left hand. Annie recognized the gesture as a nervous habit. He said, "Time was when the bootlegging activity here was a simple matter of supply and demand. Now threats of hijackings and strong-arming customers are beginning to be a problem. Just last week, Doctor Zerpas was attacked on his way to visit patients."

Annie asked, "What do doctor visits have to do with bootlegging?"

"Some of the remedies Doctor Zerpas carried in his medical case were bottles of wine and rum. Those medications expanded his practice quite a bit."

"I think you changed your routine yesterday. They weren't prepared for a train trip because they were not expecting you to go out of town. Every other workday morning you take your truck to the mill."

"Well, they will be in Mobile or on the train until two this afternoon. That is the time the next L&N is due in from the east."

"Mike, you must be cautious. Ruttan is no one to be taken lightly."

"I'll talk to Moreno this morning right after I walk you to work. He will know what to do."

"You might consider another line of work. The money is not worth your life."

Mike smoothed his moustache. "I have been planning to end my involvement and stick to trucking honest loads or shrimping."

"Anything that insures you will come home at the end of the day."

"That narrows it down to trucking," Mike said with a wry smile. "Shrimping has its hazards. I could buy several more trucks with my share of this work."

"You can only drive one at a time."

"What I can do is buy several and hire drivers. The Irish and Italians are always looking for work."

"That would make you a businessman."

Mike chuckled, "I would have to hire a manager. My business skills are lacking. If you know anyone who would like to leave the switchboard for a better paying job, tell me."

Annie blushed. "Promise you will tell me first when you decide. I would be very happy if this were your last run."

*****

"Mister Moreno has been expecting you," William said when he answered Mike's knock at the door. He led Mike to Moreno's office and indicated a chair opposite the desk.

"Mister Moreno will be here shortly," William said, and he disappeared.

The door behind the desk opened and Manuel Moreno stepped in. Mike rose to greet him.

"*Buenas tardes*, Miguel," Moreno said. As always, the conversation would be in Spanish.

"Good afternoon, sir." Mike pulled the envelope Dugas had given him from his coat pocket and proffered it to Moreno.

"Ah, good. The resection information," Moreno said as he accepted the envelope. "I take it you had an uneventful meeting with our friend from Cuba?"

"The meeting was uneventful, but the trip was not."

"How so?"

"I was followed by two people, a man and a woman employed by the Hadens, I think."

"Why do you think this?"

"A friend of mine from Chicago, who is well connected to the police there, told me of a man named Jules Ruttan. This Ruttan and his woman, Myrtle, are notorious gangsters. Both are believed to have arrived in New Orleans. The people that followed me matched their descriptions."

"The friend from Chicago would be Annie Norwak?" Moreno asked with a smirk.

Mike blushed slightly, "Yes, sir. Her father is the police chief of Cicero, Illinois. It is very close to Chicago."

"It is more than simply important to have friends in law enforcement," Moreno said. "It is vital. When did you discover this?"

"Just before I boarded the train to Mobile. I was able to evade them in Mobile before meeting with Dugas. I expect they will return to New Orleans on the afternoon train."

Moreno opened the envelope and examined the information contained within. Mike could see the papers were covered with abbreviations and numbers.

"I will need you to organize our fleet of boats. This might be my last large import. The Hadens seem to be embracing more than just importing rum. They have expanded into gambling and prostitution and have demonstrated a tendency toward violence. Many who work with me are friends and relatives. I do not want to place them or their families in danger."

Mike said, "The greatest danger is the truck haul between dock and warehouse. I might have a means of ensuring security."

"I would welcome any new ideas. By the way, your share of this shipment will be twice as much as the last." He handed the papers back to Mike. "You are investing the money wisely, I believe."

Mike said, "I am investing in real estate and, perhaps, trucking."

Six thousand dollars would buy a lot of trucks and, possibly, a warehouse to operate from. If Moreno withdrew from the importing business, Mike might operate a smaller version on his own. Small enough to escape notice of the Hadens. The impulsive Danny was the one to be concerned about. John Haden was a thinker, an organizer.

Then again, Manuel Moreno was perhaps the wisest man Mike ever knew and he was leaving the business. Annie had expressed opposition to his continued involvement in this particular version of the importing business. Her concerns had to be considered.

Moreno said, "William will contact the captains for this job. Nine boats all together. With such a large shipment, I expect we will not be able to keep it entirely a secret. The Hadens know of all the probable routes we might take once we have the goods ashore. We will have to be creative."

*****

Mike stepped aboard the *Captain Robin*, his uncle's boat at a fisherman's village on Bayou La Loutre called Yscloskey. It was six in the morning of the twenty-sixth of April and a light, persistent rain was falling. One of the complications encountered during bootlegging operations was the weather. Ships at sea would not, could not, alter the assigned arrival times. Miss the rendezvous and you miss the delivery. No refunds.

He had driven his truck to the Yscloskey landing because the train from New Orleans was no longer operating. A large leak had developed in the Mississippi River Levee at Poydras. The railroad engineers feared a breach in the levee would sweep away the tracks and maroon their engines outside of the New Orleans rail network, so rail service was canceled until further notice.

Mike was barely able to get his truck through the water that rushed over the roadway at Poydras where the rail left the main line along the river and headed east for Yscloskey and Shell Beach. In less than a mile from the river the escaping flood waters had been confined to Bayou Terre Aux Boeufs. The water levels fell rapidly as the flood dispersed across the adjacent swamplands.

"How was the levee?" Geronimo asked the moment he saw Mike step aboard.

"Leaking badly. There is a split in the levee right where Bayou Terre Aux Boeufs used to meet the river and water is rushing through."

Geronimo looked west as if he could see the river levee a dozen miles away. He said, "If she gives, all of the Poydras junction will be flooded. We will never be able to move our cargo up that road."

Mike nodded. "True, but we were never going to use the road through Poydras. Too many people expect us to truck everything into New Orleans from Yscloskey, Delacroix or Violet. When we rendezvous at the Chandeleur Islands, I will give the captains their resection bearings for meeting the freighter and then I will tell all where we are going to go to port."

Geronimo said, "Fisherman's Bayou will be too small for our numbers."

"That is true as well. And it would take an army to protect both the landing and the warehouse. We are not taking such an obvious route."

Geronimo shrugged. Once the cargo was delivered to a dock, his job was done. It was up to Mike to shepherd the cargo past possible hijackers. Law enforcement, New Orleans, and Saint Bernard, had been given a cut and would be no problem.

Mike asked, "Where is Zapato?"

Geronimo said, "He will stay here in Yscloskey with the rest of my family. He will be needed if the levee fails."

Mike thought a moment, "You are high here and far from the river. Even if the levee fails, high water will never make it this far out into the marsh." Fear of hijackers was the real reason Geronimo had left his son behind. Mike knew and understood. The shooting at Fisherman's Bayou had shaken everyone.

Geronimo said, "If the railroad is swept away, they will never rebuild her. We will not be able to go to New Orleans."

"Buy an automobile and learn to drive. I did."

*****

They had over fifty miles to cover to reach the Chandeleur Islands. At least half of that was down the circuitous Bayou La Loutre. Mike expected to meet the other boats at five in the evening. Plenty of time to distribute rendezvous information and plan for the trip back.

Geronimo started the old tractor engine that served as the *Captain Robin's* power plant. He directed the boat east along Bayou La Loutre at a leisurely pace. They passed many docked boats and fishermen's houses as they moved down the bayou toward Chandeleur Sound and the Gulf of Mexico.

Mike wondered how many of the people they passed would report to the Hadens. An ambush of returning boats laden with rum and hemmed in on the narrow bayou would be a simple matter. Mike had learned many lessons in the trenches of France. He had learned them well because he survived. Soldiers on patrol never returned along the same route they followed to go out.

The bayou ahead was a grey sheen between dark masses on either side. Some fishermen's houses leaked soft light from lamps or stoves. Behind him the wake of the *Captain Robin* spread slowly toward the banks, catching what little light there was and forming a silvery "V" pattern.

Other boats began to appear on the bayou behind them and Mike could see indications of the dying wakes of boats ahead. The night changed to grey as dawn drew near. He could count seven boats now, five astern and two ahead. There were no signals of any kind between the boats. All exhibited stealth and purpose, as if a military operation were underway.

Once it was full light, Mike had identified all the boats running down the bayou with the *Captain Robin*, except for two. These were likely boats headed out to the sound for a day of fishing. Of the twelve boats contracted to meet the freighter, six were with him now.

At eleven in the morning the small fleet passed the mouth of Bayou La Loutre and into the open waters of Chandeleur Sound. Unrestricted by a narrow bayou, Geronimo pushed the throttle forward until the *Captain Robin* was doing twelve knots – full speed.

The remainder of the boats increased speed as well and spread out across the open water. The two unidentified boats veered off to the south, presumably for a day of fishing, or to prepare a welcoming hijack for returning boats.

At two in the afternoon, Geronimo shouted to Mike over the pop-pop of the engine. "I can make out New Harbor Island now."

Mike nodded in confirmation. New Harbor Island was an interior island of the Chandeleur chain, and the designated rendezvous point for the convoy. Here Mike would verify the captains present, form three groups, assign each group to a freighter rendezvous location and issue instructions to return to New Harbor Island with their cargo.

As they neared New Harbor Island, Mike could see six boats anchored in the protected bay of the island. These were Moreno's contracted skippers. The entire fleet of twelve was now accounted for. Geronimo slowed as he entered the cluster of anchored boats. He eased the *Captain Robin* close to the *Reckless* captained by "Jo-Jo" Gutierrez. Mike stepped across the gap and handed Jo-Jo a packet of papers and informed him of the three boats that were to accompany him.

Mike returned to the *Captain Robin* and the *Reckless* started her engine and motored slowly to collect her three partners. They had the furthest to go. Their meeting point was twenty miles away and south of Ship Island. They had to be on station for an eight-p.m. meeting. They would just make it.

The next group was to be led by "Bebedor" Alayon, captain of the *Pastor Larenzo*. Mike made the same sort of presentation of papers and the *Pastor Larenzo* motored away to collect her three companions. Her destination was only twelve miles away just east of a gap in the Chandeleur chain. Bebedor would anchor on the west side of the pass and wait until his appointed time.

The three remaining boats would accompany the *Captain Robin* to the third freighter drop point. That last point was only five miles away, just beyond another small pass through the chain. Their meeting time was three in the morning. They would take the remaining cargo and, if some others missed their rendezvous, they would ferry the excess cargo to a hiding point on one of the nearby islands.

If all things were timed correctly and went according to plan, twelve boats loaded with rum would be at New Harbor Island at sunrise. Mike knew that things rarely go as planned.

*****

Two in the morning presented a dead calm sea, an overcast sky and clear air. The lights of Mike's resection lines were easily identified. The *Captain Robin* waited, engine idling, at the designated parcel of open water.

A little after two, Mike could hear the thrum of a freighter somewhere off to the north where a black mass obscured the horizon. Geronimo could hear it as well and asked, "Should I show a light?"

The three boats had been at station without showing so much as an anchor light. A dangerous thing to do even in the open sea outside of busy shipping lanes.

"Anchor and navigation, please," Mike said. The *Captain Robin* and the other three boats each turned on a white anchor light, a red starboard light and a green port light. In seconds, the black mass blocking the horizon displayed lights as well and the thrumming sound, which had been the great propeller of the ship, ceased.

The calm seas would make the transfer of cargo much easier. There would be no need to drop a net of cargo into the water to be hauled into the shallows before loading onto the boats. Tonight, the cargo would be lowered to the boats and stowed.

Geronimo maneuvered to a gangway landing suspended from the side of the freighter. A very large figure was waiting as the *Captain Robin* bumped alongside.

"*Bonjour, Monsieur* Dugas," Mike said as he stepped from the boat onto the landing. The conversation was to be in French.

"Good morning, Mister Demill," Dugas said as he offered a hand, which Mike took. "Your other boats met us and accepted cargo without incident. One of the first four boats had engine trouble, so we distributed some of the excess cargo to the three working boats, some we saved for the four boats of the second rendezvous, and the last of the excess we will load to these four."

"Any messages from the others?"

Dugas said, "Only that the boat with engine trouble headed back toward New Harbor. Captain Gutierrez plans to take her in tow during their return if repairs had not been successful."

Mike said, "The *Captain Robin* will be the last to accept cargo. I need to be aboard her to help. I'm the deckhand."

"Then I need to give you this now. It is a message from *Don* Sebastian. He wants to continue what has proven to be a rewarding business." Dugas removed a small envelope from his coat and gave it to Mike.

"Do not open the letter until you arrive in New Orleans," Dugas said.

Mike stuffed the envelope into a pocket and said goodbye to Dugas. He climbed aboard the *Captain Robin* just in time to assist Geronimo emptying the first sling of crated rum bottles and store them away. The boat's holds were full after another half dozen sling-loads of the cargo.

The other three boats were waiting just inside the pass through the island chain and all four set out for New Harbor Island at a moderate speed. Sunrise was two hours away. They and daylight should arrive together at New Harbor.

The *Reckless* and the *Pastor Larenzo* were lashed together when the *Captain Robin* rounded the shoal and entered the little bay formed by the crescent shape of the islands. Mike could see that all the boats were circled around the center core of lashed trawlers.

Mike sighed in relief and said, "Tio, let's see what Jo-Jo and Bebedor have to say. Now it will all be timing."

"Are you to tell us where we are bound?" Geronimo asked.

"Now is that time. Let us join Jo-Jo and Bebedor."

Geronimo coasted up to the pair of boats and added the *Captain Robin* to the raft. Jo-Jo and Bebedor clambered over to Mike and shook hands in relief. Offloading from a freighter in open sea is no casual task.

"What is the condition of our engine problem?" Mike asked.

Jo-Jo said, "It was the *Nuestro Hermano*. We had to drain some water out of the bottom of the fuel tank. She's running fine now. Do you want to shift some cargo to her?"

"No time. She can run with us empty and be available for emergencies. Do you know the Milneburg Jetty in Lake Pontchartrain?"

Both men nodded their heads. The Milneburg Jetty had been one of the key docks for produce from the North Shore and Gulf Coast.

"The jetty has been closed for a year," Jo-Jo said. "The new canal was going to put it out of business, so the railroad company quit the jetty."

"They quit it but have not yet pulled the rails. That is where we are bound. We are going to load our cargo onto freight cars that will meet us at Milneburg at eight tonight."

"That will give us about thirteen hours to make a hundred miles," Bebedor said.

"Ninety miles," Mike corrected. "Three freight cars will be there at eight. We have most of the night to load them."

"How did you get railcars?" Jo-Jo asked.

"We need to get to Milneburg by eight tonight. That is all you need to know. We need to know of any boat that cannot make six knots, for any reason, well before we make the Rigolets."

"We can all easily make six knots, as long as the seas cooperate," Bebedor said. Jo-Jo nodded in agreement.

"Tell all the captains to spread out. No need for everyone to maintain sight of the others. I don't want it to look like an invasion when we make the pass or approach the landing. If you don't see freight cars on the jetty, anchor in the lake and wait. Otherwise, tie to the quay and load the cars. The train engineer, Jake, will oversee loading the cars. Any questions?"

Jo-Jo said, "The *Nuestro Hermano* should run last to help a boat with problems."

"Good thinking, Jo-Jo. Make it so. Anything else?"

No one spoke.

Mike said, "Then good luck. And tell each captain he can keep a case of rum to do with as it suits him. A pleasure doing business with you."

New Harbor Island echoed with a dozen engines starting, anchors being weighed and shouts of encouragement to deckhands.

CHAPTER 17

Mike watched the low silhouette of Half Moon Island slip by to the north. A few dots danced on the horizon to the west. Some were faster members of his fleet; some were others about other business. To his east he could see a few more specks. The group had done a good job of spreading out across the sound.

The test would come when they passed through the Rigolets into Lake Pontchartrain. A dozen shrimping boats lined stem to stern in the narrow pass would attract attention. The small fleet had to pass under two railroad drawbridges which would require time to open for the boats. Timing was vital. Darkness would be required for them to offload unseen at the Milneburg Jetty.

Jake would wait at the rail switch with the freight cars. He would not begin to push the cars onto the Milneburg spur until all the boatwrights working on the *Solitario* left the quay. Even if some of the boats were delayed, everything should proceed automatically.

Geronimo nudged Mike's elbow. He pointed his chin south and said, "Somebody is interested in us."

Mike looked south. A boxy shape on the horizon seemed to hover off to port. It was slowly growing larger but stayed almost perfectly two points forward of dead port. Slowly the box transformed into the bow and cabin of a large boat on a line to intercept the *Captain Robin*.

"Do you know her?" Mike asked.

Geronimo stared at the boat. It was not a lugger, and it threw a wide spray from the bow. He said, "She must be doing ten knots."

"No chance we will outrun her, loaded as we are." Mike said. He looked east to see where others of the fleet were. None were very close. "We are on our own, Tío."

Geronimo said, "Take the wheel." He ducked into the cabin. Mike grabbed the wheel and glanced east. If they could stall until one of the other boats caught up it might help.

Geronimo emerged from the cabin with two Springfield rifles. He said, "I believe you know how these work," and handed one to Mike along with three stripper clips of cartridges. Mike held the wheel with an elbow and checked the chamber. It was fully loaded.

Geronimo said, "Never again will a man point a gun at me or mine. It is a bad feeling." Mike nodded.

Geronimo squinted at the approaching boat. "I know her," he said. "She's the *Isle of Hvar*. That fat man at the wheel would be Red McDae."

"I have met Captain McDae," Mike said. "What is he doing this far east?"

"Looking for us, I think. He runs for the Hadens, last I heard."

The *Isle of Hvar* was closing fast, and Mike could see two others aboard the boat. The two deckhands were brandishing pistols.

Mike said, "I will give them a hundred yards before I make it clear we are not interested in a conversation. Keep steady on your heading. If I need your help, I will sing out."

Red McDae leaned out and cupped one hand to his mouth. He shouted, "Stop your engine, Demill." About one hundred yards separated the boats.

Mike knelt and put the Springfield to his shoulder. He put a round into the side of the *Isle of Hvar* about where he suspected the engine to be. The reaction was instantaneous. Red pulled back on the throttle and the two deckhands dove behind the bulkhead. Mike gave them four more rounds in quick succession and stripped five rounds from a clip into the rifle.

"Keep your distance, Red," Mike shouted. They were more than two hundred yards apart now. The *Isle of Hvar* had gone dead in the water. Mike stood and watched the wallowing boat. One of the deckhands came up shooting his pistol. None of his rounds even came close to the *Captain Robin*.

More than three hundred yards separated the boats now. Mike lowered the rifle to his side. "What was he thinking, Tío? Did he think a couple of pistols would frighten us?"

"Miguel, none of us had ever been armed with more than an old shotgun. We just smuggled in rum like everyone else. Then the Hadens decided gambling and whores were not enough for them. Now they run rum, rot-gut whiskey, and hijack honest bootleggers. They have made what we do dangerous work," Geronimo shrugged. "More people are going to get killed if it keeps up this way."

Mike and Geronimo watched as the *Isle of Hvar* got underway, turning west. She moved at a greatly reduced speed and billowed black smoke.

"You stung them good, Miguel," Geronimo said. "Next time they will not be armed with pistols alone."

"We are going to have to make certain there is not a next time, Tío. I think *Señor* Moreno is right. Time for a new line of work."

The *Isle of Hvar* had disappeared over the horizon when the navigation posts marking the entrance to the Rigolets, a narrow pass into Lake Pontchartrain, came into view.

Mike said, "We are right on time. I think it will be about five more hours and we will make the Milneburg Jetty."

"I think so as well," Geronimo agreed. "I recognize two of the boats ahead of us and one about a mile behind us. It should be full dark in five hours, perhaps less. I think we will be able to deliver our cargos before midnight, provided your freight cars are there and the Hadens are not."

*****

The *Captain Robin* was the eighth boat of the flotilla to tie to the Milneburg Jetty. Three more boats bobbed in the lake waiting for space to dock. Two others had already off-loaded and, along with the cargo-less *Nuestro Hermano*, were on their way back through Lake Borgne to Yscloskey. Mike relaxed for the first time in days. All twelve boats were accounted for and the cargo delivered, less a crate for each captain and one for Jake.

A little switch engine sat hissing patiently as the cargo was loaded from both sides into the freight cars under Jake's frantic direction.

"How does it go, Jake?" Mike asked.

"Three cars, two sides each — that's six doors I have to watch at one time. We can't have the crates stacked too high, but if they ain't high enough we will have a hell of a time stacking more on the ones in the back."

"I will leave you to your work, Jake." Mike said. He walked over to where the almost finished *Solitario* was moored. O'Gara had posted a guard to watch the boat when work was not being done, which was most nights. The guard was a round-bellied, red-faced Irishman everyone called Patty-O.

Mike found Patty-O sitting on a nail keg at the bottom of a plank gangway onto the *Solitario*'s deck, a burning kerosene lamp at his feet.

Patty-O stood and squinted as Mike came into the lamp's circle of light. His face changed from one of challenge to one of greeting. "Ah, Mister Demill," he said, "For the love of Christ, what is going on? I thought I would have to fend off this mob by me self."

"Just some fellas moving freight. Friends of mine."

"Well, they gave me a fright, I will tell you that. And just so you know," Patty-O continued, "Just about quitting time some railroad gents came by. They said the company will begin pulling up the rail first of next week. Going to use it elsewhere over by the new canal, so they say."

"Well then, we have finished the heavy trucking for the boatwrights just in time," Mike said.

"You haven't been here for the last two days. Mister O'Gara says that they will box her compass come Monday."

Boxing the compass was the last step in preparing a new vessel. The process consisted of running the boat along lines of known bearing and adjusting the reading on the compass to match the known heading. The adjustments were made by shifting a few small iron bars about the exterior of the compass housing to counteract the magnetic influence of the boat.

"If that is so, she will have her shake-down well ahead of schedule," Mike said.

"First week in March, says Mister O'Gara."

Geronimo walked up. Mike could see the railcars behind his uncle. The loading activity was beginning to slow, and Jake was closing doors. Geronimo said, "We are done here and ready to go."

"Go back without me," Mike said. "I will ride back with Jake."

"What about your truck?" Geronimo asked.

"I will come get it when I can. It is safe where it is for now."

Geronimo embraced Mike briefly. "*Ve con Dios, sobrino* (Go with God, nephew)," he said.

"*Que Dios guie tu mano* (May God direct your hand)," Mike answered.

He watched Geronimo untie the *Captain Robin*'s lines and clambered aboard. The engine started with the distinctive "pop-pop" sound of a "Popping Johnny." The boat pulled away slowly. It and the others were soon lost in the early morning darkness. Sunrise was in four hours and by that time Geronimo, along with several others from the fleet, would be entering the Chef Menteur Pass bound for Lake Borgne and home.

Mike turned to Patty-O. "If you see O'Gara or Boru today, tell them I will call tonight, if you please."

"I will do that, Mister Demill, but I will not see them today. Sunday, don't you know? Anything else, sir?"

"No. That will do for now."

Mike hurried to join Jake at the switch engine. He climbed up on the engineer's platform and stood behind Jake. The machine did not have a proper operator's cab, just an open deck with a bench. An open bin behind the engineer's station held enough coal to fuel the engine for several hours of operation. When working in the lumber yard the engine had to take on water and coal about twice a day.

Jake pulled a few levers, opened the fire box door, and tossed in a half-dozen shovel-loads of coal. He latched the fire box closed and bumped a lever with the palm of his hand. The engine inched forward, jerking each time a coupler lost slack and a burst of steam shot out of the drive cylinders.

"She's earning her keep this night," Jake said proudly. "I reckon we can do fifteen miles an hour to the main line and after that twenty to the warehouse."

"You can just drop the cars at the siding. There are a dozen men waiting to unload her," Mike said. "We will cut you free well before the five twenty-five deadline you gave us."

"I didn't 'give' nothing," Jake said. "The IC will be coming through then and if we ain't off the main line when she does, you will have rum spread from Elysian Fields to Canal Street."

Jake's worries proved to be unfounded. They made the railroad siding by one of Moreno's warehouses without incident. Jake uncoupled the three cars and chugged off for the lumberyard with an hour to spare. The freight cars were empty before dawn.

*****

Mike got home just in time to call Annie before she left for work. She had scheduled a Sunday shift three days ago knowing he would be gone for a few days. Her plan was to have a full day off when he returned.

"Finished so soon?" she asked. "Did everything go well?"

"Better than expected," Mike said. "All went smoothly."

"Well, while you were gone the levee at Poydras split. A great torrent is pouring out. I was afraid you would not be able to get back." Annie knew Mike had gone to Yscloskey, but she did not know he had planned to return to New Orleans by boat.

"It was leaking badly two mornings ago. The road was barely passable. Good thing that I left my truck in Yscloskey."

"It's much more than a leak now," Annie said. "The riverboat *Capital* has even scheduled sightseeing trips to see the crevasse from the river. They are charging a dollar for a one-hour excursion."

"Then, why don't we take a ride tomorrow. You have the day off and I need to sleep tonight. I have been up most of the last two nights," Mike said.

"As have I. Oh, Mike, I could not help but worry."

"Well relax and worry no more, my dear. I will check the paper in the morning and come and get you about nine. Then we can decide when we will see the crevasse."

"I will not completely relax until I see you again in the morning."

"Until nine tomorrow then," Mike said.

"Until then," Annie said. "And, Mike," She paused.

Mike said, "And what, Annie?"

"I love you, Mike."

"And I love you. How could I not?"

Mike hung up. He had one more chore to do before turning in for a much-needed sleep. He went to the kitchen, put three measures of coffee in the percolator of an enamelware pot, added water and set it on the stove. He went to the bathroom, shaved, and washed his face.

Returning to the kitchen, he poured himself a cup of the dark coffee and chicory brew. He made a sandwich with a slice of smoked ham. He sat at the kitchen table, sipped the coffee, ate, and thought. The encounter with Red McDae was no small matter. Things were beginning to escalate.

At eight he called to see if he could arrange a meeting with Manuel Moreno. William answered Mike's call and said that Mister Moreno would like Mike to come to his office for ten.

Mike stepped out onto his porch and checked his surroundings as he placed his hat firmly on his head. The street was clear of vehicles except for an Overland sedan parked across the intersection. This was a working-class neighborhood. Few here owned cars.

A man was seated on the driver's side reading a newspaper. Mike laughed to himself. The man had been perfectly positioned to follow Mike's truck as it crossed the intersection.

Plans often fail when confronted with the unexpected. Mike did not have his truck. He was going to walk to the streetcar stop on Saint Charles and the sedan would look mighty conspicuous puttering along at a walking pace.

Mike left his porch and stepped onto the sidewalk. He watched as the man peered over the top of the newspaper. Mike laughed and waved toward the sedan. The paper shot back up to cover the man's face.

Why am I worried over these clowns? Mike thought. Then he admonished himself. Overconfidence is a fatal flaw. He walked on and heard the sedan start and then cross the intersection behind him headed downriver. *No doubt to report a change in plans.*

William answered the door at Moreno's office. "Mister Moreno will see you now," he said. When William pronounced "Mister" it sounded like "Master."

William led Mike back to Moreno's inner office and announced, "Mister Demill to see you, sir."

Mike stepped in and William closed the door. Moreno was seated at his desk, stacks of ledgers to his left and his right. He stood and walked around the desk.

"*¿Miguel, cómo te fue* (how did it go)?"

"All has been delivered, sir."

"I know. I have been informed. I want to know how things went between the freighter and the warehouse."

"The Hadens had a screen of boats set across the sound. I think they intended to follow us to a landing and then call ahead to set an ambush."

"And what caused their plans to fail?"

"I drove off the Haden boat and it did not follow us to port. And we did not cross the sound, we came in through Lake Pontchartrain."

Moreno said, "It is good that you did. The levee failed at Poydras and the roads are flooded four feet deep at the junction. You would have been trapped at Yscloskey and vulnerable."

Mike said, "So I have been told. When I drove to Yscloskey two days ago the levee was just leaking, and the road was flooded ankle deep."

"How did you drive off the Haden boat?"

"They came too close, and I put a couple of rifle rounds into her engine compartment."

Moreno nodded grimly, "It is becoming too violent, this business." He held out a thick packet to Mike. "Miguel, here is your share. Invest wisely, for I will not arrange for any more imports if the Hadens are in the business. The people that work for me are family. I cannot risk their lives."

Mike accepted the bulging envelope and placed it in his pocket without opening it and said, "Then you will not object if I do some importing on my own?"

"Just do not use my people. I intend to concentrate on my properties. Trapping leases are very promising. The price of furs has advanced greatly."

"I thank you, *Señor* Manual Moreno, for the opportunity of working and learning from you," Mike said as he offered his hand.

Moreno took Mike's hand and then briefly embraced him. "Think long, Miguel, before you decide to go against the Hadens. Call upon me if there is anything I can do."

*****

Mike left Moreno's office and walked to a small café that specialized in serving the surrounding office workers. He bought a newspaper and selected a table in the corner where he sat with his back to the wall. He ordered toast, bacon, and coffee.

Only two other customers were in the small dining area seated on the far side of the room. Two lawyers, by the look of them, quietly discussing business. Mike could not hear what was being discussed, but one appeared bored and spoke little while the other was animated and talkative.

Mike pulled the envelope that Dugas had given him when the *Captain Robin* met the freighter. It had been two nights ago, but he had not had the opportunity to open the envelope. It felt like a letter.

He slit the seal with a butter knife to find a single hand-written page in Spanish. It was from *Don* Sebastian O'Neil.

"Señor:

I pray that this letter finds you in good health. I have been informed that our mutual friend has decided to cease our business arrangement. This is unfortunate but understandable. In business, an honorable Don must consider those who depend upon him before he considers himself.

I offer you the same arrangement if you are interested. Come to see me and we will discuss the details.

SO"

The letter contained no return address, no names, nothing but the message in flowing Spanish script. It would require a trip to Cuba if Mike decided to continue in the special importing business.

Mike then removed the thick folder of cash Moreno had given him. He counted the neat tightly wrapped stacks of twenty-dollar bills. Each banded stack contained one hundred notes and there were five such paper-wrapped stacks.

He opened the newspaper to the front page where there was a lengthy article on the crevasse at Poydras. The swiftly rising waters had marooned over two thousand people. Some were escaping by going east to Yscloskey where the flood receded rapidly as it poured out into the Gulf. Others had taken small boats upriver to New Orleans. There had been no loss of life, but automobiles, trucks and railcars were rendered inoperable.

He saw the advertisement by the Steamer *Capital* for a trip to witness the crevasse. It would depart daily at two-thirty p.m. and return at six p.m. There was a telephone number, but no price listed for the ticket. Mike supposed they were still trying to gauge demand. He would call when he returned home.

He turned to the real estate section. He had ten thousand dollars to buy property. He did not trust banks, and cash was too easily stolen. Land, on the other hand, produced revenue and retained value.

On a whim, he searched for commercial property. Perhaps he would buy a few trucks and hire drivers. He saw one place advertised that interested him. It was a two-story building on the corner of Saint Claude Avenue and Tupelo Street. The ground floor was a warehouse or retail store, and the second floor was a residence.

It was less than a half-mile from Saint Bernard Parish. The asking price was five thousand five hundred. Mike decided he would call them as well. He could buy two more rentals or one rental and several trucks with the remaining money. The important thing was to convert the cash to real estate.

He folded the paper and placed it under his arm just as the waitress brought his order to his table. He ate slowly, thoughtfully. He did not know what he was going to do. The possibilities seemed endless, the variables imponderable.

The waitress returned after he had finished and asked if there were anything else he wanted. He thanked her, and she placed his bill, seventy-five cents, on the table. Mike pulled out a dollar and sat it under his coffee cup.

As he was preparing to leave the table, he glanced through the window. There was a newsstand across the street. Jules Ruttan was buying a paper. Mike looked for Myrtle, but Ruttan seemed to be alone.

CHAPTER 18

Mike sipped the last of his coffee as he considered the possibilities. Ruttan and Myrtle, Mike had to stop thinking of the two as Jack and Jill, must not have realized they had been detected following him to Mobile. Ruttan, and possibly Myrtle, had followed him from Moreno's office. If they suspected Mike knew they were trailing him, Ruttan would not be lounging around in the open.

The street was busy. Automobiles, wagons, and carts clattered along the narrow, brick-paved roadway. The sidewalks on either side bustled with pedestrians. Not the place for a confrontation. Ruttan must believe he and Myrtle were unknown to Mike.

Everyone seemed to know, or at least suspect, the cargo Mike brought in was the last. The Hadens must know by now that Moreno was abandoning the bootlegging business. Why would they, and therefore Ruttan, concern themselves with following him?

Perhaps Ruttan suspected Mike had been paid and was carrying several thousands of dollars. Was simple robbery the goal? No. Busy streets and the likelihood that Mike was headed straight to the bank made robbery a poor choice.

Mike decided this had to be personal. Perhaps revenge for Karl "Porkins" Portman, the hired gun that Mike had been forced to kill to save Geronimo and Zapato. John Haden would have written that off as a cost of doing business. Porkins had been sent to kill and hijack but failed.

Danny Haden was another matter. Danny would have taken the failure as an affront. It had to be Danny who brought Ruttan and Myrtle down from Chicago. Danny wanted Mike killed, not simply robbed. Mike had to be killed to make a statement to the other free-lance bootleggers. The Hadens intended to control rumrunning along with gambling and prostitution.

Mike felt inexplicably calm and relaxed. Somehow, he was relieved. Now that he knew why, he would be able to better plan his response. He watched Ruttan reading the newspaper or pretending to read it. Mike finished his coffee and walked out onto the street.

Mike turned left, in the direction of his bank. Ruttan was across the street, still pretending to read the paper. By the time Mike reached the end of the block, Ruttan was following him on the opposite side of the street.

Mike stepped down from the curb to cross to the next block when he saw Myrtle. She was on the sidewalk of the next block and walking straight at him. She wore a short, tight yellow dress – a flapper style. Her narrow-brimmed hat included a lacey veil which did nothing to hide her sparkling, mischievous green eyes.

She firmly held her purse in front of her waist with both hands. She was walking close to the building side of the walkway and increased the sway of her hips. She glanced coyly at Mike, inviting conversation, as the distance between them closed.

The Hibernia Bank, Mike's bank, happened to be on that block. The high front doors were between them. Mike reached the doors first. He doffed his hat, opened one of the doors and held it for Myrtle and said, "Going in, Miss?"

Myrtle's expression was one of surprise and uncertainty. "No, thank you, sir." She paused, stepped to her left and walked past Mike. Her elbow brushed his arm slightly as she passed. Her perfume was distinctive and alluring, easily suppressing the unpleasant odors of the city street.

Mike watched her continue along the sidewalk. He could see Ruttan as the man stepped into the street, preparing to cross and intercept Myrtle. Mike went into the bank. He did not get into the line for one of the tellers. He went over to the office reception.

The business receptionist was a young man. Mike would have been surprised if the boy were older than eighteen.

"May I help you, sir," the boy squeaked.

"I am Michael Demill," Mike said. "I would like to see Mister Andrew Galway." Galway was one of the bank managers and a man recommended by Manuel Moreno as being particularly discreet.

"Wait here please, sir." The young man walked to a rear office door, knocked, and then opened it slightly. He stuck his head in and said, "Mister Michael Demill is here to see you, father."

Mike did not hear the reply, but young Galway returned to him, pulled open a low gate in the railing separating the office area from the bank floor and said, "This way please, sir."

Galway met Mike at the door to his office. "A pleasure to meet you, Mister Demill," Galway said as he shook Mike's hand and directed him to a chair. Mike heard the door close behind him. "Mister Moreno has spoken highly of you. I am happy to finally meet you."

"Thank you, sir. Our common friend recommended you to me for occasions when deposits are significant, but short term."

"Yes, precisely. No need for our clients to push large sums of cash across a teller's counter in full view of strangers. How may I help you?"

"I have ten thousand dollars to deposit in my account. It is my intention that this money will be used within a month to purchase real estate in the New Orleans area. John Eiseman will be conducting the acts of sale."

Mike placed the envelope of cash on the desk in front of Galway. Galway opened the envelope and counted the contents. "I could recommend several stock investments for you," he said as he counted. "The stock market is rising at a phenomenal rate."

Mike was amazed that Galway was able to count and converse at the same time. He was certain he would never be able to do that.

Mike said, "Thank you, but I much prefer real estate or investment in my own enterprises."

Galway laughed, "I see that you are a student of Mister Moreno. The man is a financial genius, but he only dabbles at the corners of the stock market. I urged him to mortgage his properties and invest in the market. The return would far outstrip the loan interest rates." Galway stuffed the bills back into the envelope. "Ten thousand it is."

He pushed a button on his table. Mike heard a bell ring beyond the door. In moments, the door opened, and the young Galway asked, "Yes, father?"

"Andy, please bring me a deposit form and receipt pad." Evidently, young Galway was a junior. Andy returned in seconds with the requested items, gave them to his father and left the room.

Galway filled out the deposit slip and tucked it into the envelope with the cash. He filled out the deposit receipt and handed it to Mike along with a pad of counter checks.

"Please use these particular counter checks for your large transactions. Eiseman will expect you to use only these checks or cash."

Mike placed the receipt and counter checks in his coat pocket. He stood and offered his hand. He said, "Thank you, Mister Galway," and walked toward the door. Galway came around his desk and opened the door for Mike.

He said, "Are you certain we cannot interest you in some investments in stocks?"

"I am certain. Real estate, trucks, or boats. I will put my money into things that I can put to work. A pleasure doing business with you, Mister Galway."

"I hope we can continue to do so, Mister Demill."

Andy held the small gate open for Mike as he walked out of the office area. Mike stopped before exiting through the gate.

Andy said, "Sir, did you forget something?"

"Andy, is there a rear door to this bank?"

"Yes, sir."

"Where does it lead?"

"The door exits onto Exchange Place, sir."

"Could you show me out that way?"

"Yes, follow me, please." Andy led Mike to a small hall between two offices. The hall ended at a door with heavy bolts. Andy pulled the bolts free and tugged on the door. It opened slowly.

Mike said, "Thank you, Andy." He stepped out into a narrow roadway, almost an alley, with small shops or back entrances to businesses along Royal or Chartres Streets. Andy struggled the door closed and Mike could hear the bolts shoot home. He walked along Exchange Place, crossed Canal Street, and continued to Eiseman's office on Common Street.

Hilda, Eiseman's receptionist was at her desk. She looked up and smiled broadly. "Good afternoon, Mister Demill."

Mike was flattered she remembered his name. "Good afternoon Hilda. I am happy to see you as well."

"Thank you, sir. I am afraid Mister Eiseman is not in. He has left for the day."

"Could you tell Mister Eiseman that I will call to make an appointment for some real estate transactions?"

"Of course, sir."

"If I may, I would like to make a few telephone calls before I leave."

"Certainly, sir." Hilda pointed to a telephone on the wall of the reception room. "You may use that telephone."

"Thank you, Hilda." Mike referred to a paper he pulled from his pocket and unfolded. The first call was to reserve tickets on the riverboat to see the crevasse. The rest of the calls were to schedule visits to several properties listed for sale.

Mike finished his calls, thanked Hilda, and walked out onto Common Street. The afternoon traffic of pedestrians, automobiles and wagons was building to the quitting time peak. He looked carefully and did not see Ruttan or Myrtle. No doubt, if they were still interested in him, they would be somewhere close to his home.

No more ducking out the back, Mike said to himself. *The next time I see either one of them there will be a confrontation.*

*****

Mike walked upriver on Common to a used car lot. He had noticed last week that there was a Ford Model "T" flatbed for sale. He hoped it was still there. Two trucks can be the beginning of a drayage fleet, if that was the way he decided to go. The truck was still for sale and he bought it, after extended negotiations, for an even three hundred dollars.

When he arrived home, he circled the four blocks common to the intersection at his house. He noticed nothing out of place. He pulled into his garage. The floor was dirt and he had never bothered to add doors. Those would come later, should he ever store anything in the place.

He saw that the Doons were home, or at least one was. The light in their kitchen was on and he could hear a radio playing. It was Friday evening, and both should be home from their jobs by now. He climbed the rear steps to his half of the back porch and stepped into the screened area. As he was unlocking the back door, Dorn came out onto his half of the back porch.

"Where have you been, Mike?" he asked. "The boys and I were getting worried."

"You should not have been. I told O'Gara I wouldn't be back to the boatyard until Sunday," Mike said. He opened his door and paused halfway in. "Why don't you come over in a moment and we can talk about the boat."

"I will do that. I will bring some of the apple pie Mary just made. Will half an hour suit you?"

"That will be fine."

Mike walked from the rear to the front of his house checking every room. He opened the front door and checked his mail. Mail delivered to his home was something new to Mike and sometimes days would pass before he remembered to check the mailbox. It contained the water, electrical and telephone bills, it was the end of the month.

I am becoming the thoroughly domesticated man, he thought.

Mike made himself a sandwich and sorted his mail. He answered a knock at the door. It was Dorn, as expected. He was alone.

"Mary sends this pie with her regrets," Dorn said as he offered a small dish with a large slice of hot apple pie. "She has too much to do, and she finds our boat conversations to be tiresome."

Mike said, "Come in. We can sit at the table. Did you not bring some pie for yourself?"

"No. I have had more than enough." Dorn moved to the table.

"Then let me offer you a wee glass of rum."

Dorn smiled. "I never turn down money or rum." Dorn seemed tired or upset over something. Mike poured two glasses of rum and placed one before Dorn. He took the chair opposite Dorn. The hot pie and rum were wonderful. A combination Mike vowed to remember.

Dorn sipped his rum and shook his head, deep in thought.

"What is it, Dorn?"

"First light Sunday, O'Gara and Boru want to meet you at the boatyard. You are to take the *Solitario* out into the lake. They will go with you. He says you are to box her compass, shake her down and run her until her tanks are empty. We have leased a slip on Bayou Saint John. O'Gara will show you where. A truck with fuel will meet you there when you are done."

"It will take two days at full speed to run her tanks dry," Mike said.

"O'Gara said she will have five hours of fuel in her tanks."

"Well, that should be more than enough to shake her down," Mike said.

"Now the other thing. We are going to make a run into the gulf. You are to tell us when we need to leave. That will be from the Saint John slip to Cat Island. We will be meeting a freighter south of the island at four o'clock in the morning on the eighth of May."

"What are we picking up?" Mike asked.

"Not picking up, my boy-o. We are delivering."

"What will we be delivering?"

"No need for you to know," Dorn said. His face was grim.

"I need to know the weight. It affects the speed and fuel consumption."

"Say nine tons," Dorn said. "O'Gara said she'll tote that much with ease."

Ten tons would have been the *Solitario*'s reasonable limit, twelve in a pinch. Nine tons was no problem. He estimated she could do ten knots, maximum. That would be eight hours running time at full throttle, better to figure on ten hours in case there was a sea running. They would need to depart Bayou Saint John by six in the afternoon on the seventh, a Sunday. Not a problem.

*****

Mike picked up Annie at noon on Saturday. The steamboat trip was scheduled to start at two-thirty. That would give them time for a casual lunch and maybe a walk along some of the shops in the French Quarter. He had reserved the tickets by telephone. They cost five dollars each, more than the cost of a good dinner.

Annie met him in the lobby of the boarding house. She wore a business dress. It consisted of an ankle length maroon skirt with matching jacket trimmed in white piping. She carried a shawl over one arm in case it should prove cool on the river. A wide-brimmed straw hat trimmed in flowers, white blouse, maroon bow tie, and laced boots completed her ensemble. She was dressed perfectly for a day walking the French Quarter or observing the sights from the deck of a steamboat.

She was a very different person, Mike thought, from the young flapper on a lark when they had first met. It had been less than a year, yet somehow, he felt as if he had known Annie all his life.

"You certainly look beautiful," Mike said. "Ready to see the crevasse?"

Annie blushed slightly. "Thank you, kind sir. Do we have time for lunch and maybe a stroll along Decatur or Chartres?"

"It was my intention we do so," Mike replied. "The *Capital* will depart the Toulouse Street wharf at two-thirty. Plenty of time for a leisurely lunch and walk."

The *Capital* was tied to the Toulouse Street wharf by her starboard side, facing upstream. She was a sternwheeler and would not readily answer the helm if she were to leave the dock with her stern to the current.

The river beyond the boat was churning, flowing faster than Mike had ever seen. Occasionally, a log or massive root ball would roll to the surface only to disappear in a few hundred feet. The riverboat was moored to the pier, but the water rushed by at three knots or more. Plenty of speed for steerage.

He stepped up to the ticket window and announced his name. The clerk leafed through a stack of papers, pulled out two small cards and said, "Yes, Mister Demill. That will be ten dollars, please."

Mike paid and turned to escort Annie aboard.

"Mike, ten dollars is a lot of money for a riverboat ride," Annie said.

"The fare includes a meal and the chance to see a once in a lifetime spectacle. I am certain you will enjoy the excursion."

Annie held Mike's arm. "I only know I will enjoy being with you," she purred. The young girl he rescued from Cuba was gone and a woman had taken her place. Mike was in awe of the transformation.

They walked up the forward gangway and into the main room of the steamboat. It was a dining room/ball room. On typical excursions, the *Capital* offered dinner cruises. This was not a typical outing, and the dining room was crowded with tables and chairs, covering the entire space, even the dance floor. There must have been a hundred passengers. Evidently, five dollars a head was not too much for many sight seekers.

The forward double doors to the observation deck were open and a cool, wet wind swept across the room. Mike chose a table out of the main draft. Menus were on the table anchored by the silverware, lest they blow across the room.

A whistle blew two short blasts, the gangways were raised, and the *Capital* got underway. The slap of the paddlewheel and chug of the long drive arm below the dance floor could be heard and felt.

"Let's go out on the deck, Mike," Annie said. "I have never seen the city from the river."

The fore deck was crowded. A man with a bull horn was announcing the sights as they slid by. The steamboat had crossed the river and was descending close to the right bank.

The man with the bull horn said, "Across the river to our left, you can see the entrance to the new shipping canal. The locks at the river are the largest in all of Louisiana. Downriver and next to the canal you can see Holy Cross College, a boarding school. It was formerly an orphanage run by the Ursulines nuns.

Mike glanced at Annie. She was on her tiptoes, holding her hat in place with one hand and thoroughly mesmerized by the sights that slid by.

Next came the Army post called Jackson Barracks. The guide said it had been established on the exact location of

General Jackson's reserve post during the Battle of New Orleans.

Next came a wide abandoned cane field next to a massive building. The building was a sugar refinery owned by the American Sugar Refining Company out of New Jersey. Smoke poured from tall, white stacks and a tangle of rail lines separated the building from the river.

They passed the Chalmette Slip, where Annie had come ashore from the *Garanhão do Mar* four months ago. It did not seem possible that so much had changed in only four months.

A stunted obelisk poked up from the trees just past the Chalmette Slip. The guide announced that the obelisk marked the actual site of the American lines during the Battle of New Orleans. Then came endless stretches of woods, fields, and farms. Annie was taking it all in without a hint of being bored.

Mike said, "Remember the Violet Canal? We crossed it on our trip to the Saint Bernard Cemetery. There are the locks where that canal enters the river." He pointed to a cluster of buildings on either side of an entrance to a canal.

"Ladies and gentlemen," the guide bellowed through the megaphone. "If you listen closely, you may hear the roar of the water pouring through the crevasse. Straight ahead the river bends to the right. The crevasse is in the bend of the river."

They could hear a muffled growl over the incessant beat of the boat's great paddlewheel. The sound grew until it was a deafening roar. The guide shouted through the megaphone, but Mike could only hear snatches of what he was trying to say.

The *Capital* cruised by the crevasse on the far side of the river, then she crossed the river and ascended closer to the east bank. She was headed upstream in a fast current, so she was traveling more slowly. The roar was nearly deafening.

Mike could see a missing segment of levee, perhaps a hundred feet wide. Water poured through the gap and rushed over the land beyond. The surface of the water undulated, like a great rumpled carpet, in a standing pattern. It reminded Mike of the wake from a large ship.

Mike thought the gap would have made a difference in the water height of the river. It did not. The surface simply dimpled a little at the crevasse. The river below the break was the same angry rush of water it had been at New Orleans.

Beyond the gap and rushing water, Mike could see buildings submerged to the middle of the windows in chocolate-brown water. He could see some small rowboats or pirogues loaded with dark forms, household goods perhaps, crossing the flooded area far beyond the initial rush of water.

"What a horrible sight," Annie gasped. "What are all those poor people to do?"

"They will have to build again. What else can they do?"

They watched in silence as the sight fell astern. Soon the noise died and then the gap in the levee was lost around the bend in the river. The guide invited everyone into the dining hall for supper. Because of the furious current, the trip back to New Orleans would take almost three times as long as the run down to the crevasse.

Mike seated Annie to his left and picked up the menu. There were only two entrées offered. Steamed shrimp or steaks.

"I think I would like some shrimp," Annie said.

"Shrimp it is, for us both."

A man and a lady, perhaps his wife, stepped up to the table. The dining room had filled.

"May we join you?" the man said. "There seems to be few spare tables."

Mike looked up and then stood. "Certainly, sir. Please do."

The man sat to Mike's right and his wife sat across from Mike, to Annie's left.

"I think I know you," the man said. "Perhaps you remember me? I am Fritz Hoffman, the gunsmith."

"I do remember you indeed, Mister Hoffman," Mike said. "I am Mike Demill in case you had forgotten my name. May I introduce my – friend, Miss Annie Norwak."

Fritz stood and bowed slightly, "A pleasure to meet you, Miss. This lady is my wife of twenty-five years, Gertrude."

Mike and Annie answered, "A pleasure to meet you." Almost in unison.

The meals arrived on large carts which were wheeled to each table and from which portions of shrimp or steaks were placed before the diners. Annie and Gertrude hit it off right away. Each questioning the other about hometowns, Chicago and Bromberg, a town near the Polish border. They laughed as each tried to use what little Polish they knew.

"I think Gertrude has made a friend," Fritz said. "All of our children have grown and gone. I think she is a little lonely, yes?"

"Annie is a good friend to have," Mike said.

*****

After the *Capital* had moored, "good nights" were said all around. It was growing dark when Mike walked Annie through Jackson Square before turning toward her boarding house. It had been a wonderful evening and he was most reluctant to say good night.

"Let's sit here in the park for a minute," Mike said. He chose a bench across from the entrance to the Cathedral.

"Mike, I had a wonderful time," Annie said. "I think I shall never forget such a sight."

Mike swallowed hard and lightly held Annie's hand in his right. Her eyes were sparkling in the lamp light.

"Annie," he started. "I mean, Miss Anastazja Norwak. I do not want to say good night." He brushed his moustache with his left hand, then held Annie's hand with both of his.

"What are you trying to say, Michael Demill?" Annie said with a smile, "on such a fine night."

"I am trying to say that now that I have the means to… I mean, I am a man of property now and…"

"And what, Michael?"

"I am trying to ask you if you would marry me, Annie," Mike said. "Annie, it has been a long time since I have been this nervous."

"Of course, I will marry you, silly. Why do you think I came to New Orleans in the first place? I was about to ask you myself if you took any longer."

*****

Mike woke early Sunday morning. He wanted to see Annie again, but she would be working. They had settled on an August wedding. Annie had a family to notify, and she wanted Mike to go with her to Cicero to meet her father and brothers.

Mike had to go to the Milneburg Jetty to run the *Solitario* through her paces. He wolfed down some slices of cured ham, climbed into his new truck and left before sunrise. According to the evening edition of yesterday's newspapers, the road at Poydras would be flooded for at least a week. Once the river fell and the road to Yscloskey was open, he would have to go with someone to fetch his old truck.

The railway was gone from the Milneburg Jetty. The rail workers had pulled up the ties and graded the old railbed into a smooth road. Mike was the first to arrive. Patty-O had watched Mike drive up to the boatyard and greeted him as he stepped from the truck.

"Life must be good," Patty-O said. "New truck, new boat. Sweet." He pointed south, "Yonder comes O'Gara and Boru."

Mike turned to see a set of lights appear at the south end of the road. He could not tell if it was a car or a truck. The lights were too far away.

"We will see soon enough," Mike said.

The lights proved to be a town car carrying four men. O'Gara, Boru, Dorn and a fourth man Mike did not recognize stepped out of the car. No introductions were made. The fourth man climbed behind the wheel of the car and drove back south without saying a word.

O'Gara asked, "You ready to box her, Mike?"

"I am. I have a chart of a dozen runs between landmarks around the lake. We can box her a point at a time," Mike said.

"Good. Give your truck keys to Dorn here. He will bring it to the slip at Bayou Saint John. We will not be back here."

Mike placed the keys in Dorn's hand. "See you this evening, Mike," he said. Then he said, "With me, Patty-O."

Patty-O got into the passenger's side of Mike's truck and Dorn took the driver's seat. He drove off with a wave to O'Gara and Boru.

"Well, what are you waiting for, Mike?" O'Gara said. "Get aboard and put fire to the engines."

Mike spent the better part of the next five hours running lines of known bearings and adjusting the compass to match. Then he ran her full speed, both engines at their safe maximum revolutions per minute. Then he ran her on one engine, then the other. He put her through her dockside maneuvers, alternating the engines in reverse, slow forward, portside reversed while starboard forward. Mike was able to make the boat move sideways, like a crab. The *Solitario* performed wonderfully. She was the finest boat Mike had ever been aboard, and she was one third his!

"That should do it, Mike," O'Gara said. "Let's bring her to the slip on Bayou Saint John."

The *Solitario* was in the middle of Lake Pontchartrain so Mike took the heading of south and noted the lights along the south shore. The cluster of lights furthest to the right would be the entrance to the Southern Yacht Club and the West End Hotel. The glittering lights just east of the Yacht Club would be the new Spanish Fort Resort situated on the west side of the mouth of Bayou Saint John. The Spanish Fort Park and Hotel sat about five hundred yards further inland. Remains of the long jetties protecting the entrance to Bayou Saint John jutted out into the lake. Further to the east was the Milneburg landing.

The Spanish Fort Resort was a complex of amusement rides, such as a Ferris Wheel reputed to be a miniature of the great Chicago Wheel, a dance hall, and restaurants.

The Spanish Fort Hotel had been restored from a fire but was struggling under the competition of the Resort. It was a wooden building, two stories tall with an annex perched on pilings that jutted out onto the waterway on the east. The Hotel sat several yards from the west bank of the bayou. There was an electric tram that brought revelers from the city that ended on the west bank of the bayou. A crude road ran along the east bank beginning at Esplanade. Most patrons preferred to take the tram because drinks, disguised as coffee, were provided once the coaches left the city station.

Mike eased through the navigation buoys that defined the entrance channel and idled down the quarter mile of protected waterway. They passed the main resort practically under the bandstand. Music was pulsating across the lake and it seemed to Mike that the buildings themselves bounced to the beat.

Mike eased the *Solitario* into a slip O'Gara pointed out on the east bank opposite the tram turnaround. The slip served three piers, one to the north, one to the south and one at the east end of the slip. Three fishing camps of two or three rooms each were perched on a small berm of higher land. The last camp was nestled against the crude dirt road. Mike's truck was parked next to this last building.

Men were waiting to tie the *Solitario* to the southern pier. Mike nudged her gently toward the waiting men until O'Gara and Boru tossed mooring lines and the boat was secured to the pier. After shutting down the engines and going through the routine of securing the boat for the night, Mike accompanied O'Gara and Boru into the camp.

"Well, Mike," O'Gara said. "Sit down and tell me what you think of her?"

Mike pulled a chair out from the only table in the room and sat down. Dorn appeared from a back room and placed four glasses of rum around the table. Everyone took a seat and looked at Mike."

"She is a fine boat, gentlemen. She did all I asked and did it well."

"Can she carry nine or ten tons of cargo?" Dorn asked.

"Easily, and in a heavy sea, if it comes to that," Mike answered.

"Good. When shall we need to depart from here for the May trip?" O'Gara asked.

"Six in the evening of the seventh would be enough," Mike said.

"Good. See you here then," O'Gara said.

"I would like to take her out for a few runs before then," Mike said. "We are going to be asking a lot of her, so I need to know she is up to it."

O'Gara looked at Boru and nodded.

Boru said, "That will be fine. Anytime you want until the first of May. From then on, I want her here in her slip. Understood?"

"Understood," Mike said.

"Come on, Mike. Give me a ride home," Dorn said. He tossed back the last of his rum and put the truck key into Mike's hand.

Mike closed his hands on the key and finished his rum as well.

"See you on the seventh, Mike," O'Gara said. "We will have her fuel tanks topped off, galley full and cargo aboard."

Mike and Dorn left them sitting at the table and watching intently as they left.

It was two in the afternoon by the time Mike pulled into his garage. Dorn climbed down. "See you later," he said. He went to his back porch and entered calling out to Mary.

Mike walked around his truck to look it over. All appeared in order, so he headed for his back porch.

Someone called out from the street, "Michael Demill?"

Mike turned around and walked to the street where three men were waiting. "Yes, what can I do for you?" he said.

The men wore dark suits, fedora hats and scuffed shoes. Two were skinny and the one in the middle was wide. When Mike walked up, the two skinny ones stepped aside and bracketed Mike.

"Are you Michael Demill?" the fat one said.

"I am. What do you want?" Mike said.

"Michael Demill, I am Sergeant Abraham Macy. You are under arrest for murder."

CHAPTER 19

Mike felt his arms being grabbed by strong hands. The men to his left and right, policemen he guessed, grabbed his wrists and elbows.

"Turn him around," Macy said.

The men holding him circled, causing Mike to turn about. Macy patted him down and found the Luger tucked behind Mike's belt.

"Turn him," Macy said, and Mike was spun around to face the sergeant. Macy looked intently into Mike's eyes while he sniffed the muzzle of the Luger. The man could not conceal a look of disappointment. "Cuff him."

In a choreographed set of moves, the men holding Mike's right arm placed a handcuff on Mike's wrist. The man holding his left wrist grabbed the loose cuff and locked it on Mike's left. Macy waved a hand over his head and Mike heard a car drive up.

"Frederick, bring him to the box. Frank and I are going to search his place. Just because this pistol has not been fired, it doesn't mean the murder weapon isn't here." Macy pocketed the pistol and walked toward Mike's house with the other policeman.

Frederick spun Mike around and pushed him toward a black Chevrolet sedan, opened the rear passenger side door and pushed Mike in, banging his head on the frame in the process. He pushed Mike across the seat and got in next to him. The driver turned around and said, "Where's the sergeant, George?"

"Checking out the house. The gun the guy was carrying was cold. Bring us to the blockhouse. Macy will meet us there."

Mike had no idea where the "blockhouse" was located. He knew there were several police precincts, each commanded by a captain, but he was ignorant of the precinct boundaries or arrest procedures. Dorn had talked of being "booked at the eighth," but said little about what took place. He did say the New Orleans police's treatment of arrestees were mild compared to the "Black and Tans" of Northern Ireland. "The New Orleans guys only slap ya around a bit," Dorn had said, "nothing like the Brits."

The blockhouse proved to be a squat, brick building attached to the Eighth Precinct headquarters. It appeared to be much older than the headquarters. It had barred windows without glass panes and a heavy iron door. Frederick hauled Mike out of the sedan and pushed him toward the door.

The sedan sped away as Frederick banged on the door. It creaked open and Mike was pushed inside. The room was dimly lit. Mike, Frederick and the man who had opened the door were the only occupants. A table and chairs occupied the center of a large, bare room.

A row of four cells crossed the far end of the room. Each cell was separated from the room, and each other, by flat iron bars riveted into a lattice work of six-inch openings. There was no furniture in the cells, just bare brickwork floors.

"Who is this?" asked the man who had opened the door. He was a fat man, with a protruding belly that hung over his belt buckle. He moved with a shuffling, hobbled gait because of a deformed right foot.

"Demill. Macy pinched him for murder," Frederick said. "Put him in a cell until Macy gets here to interrogate him."

Mike was forced into the first cell and locked in. They did not remove the handcuffs. The cell smelled of sweat, urine, and shit. Mike leaned against the bars. The brick walls were sweating a moldy grime that ran down in rivulets.

Mike turned his back to the bars and called out, "Frederick, can you take off these cuffs?"

Frederick laughed, "Do you hear him, Owen? He don't like the cuffs."

Owen snarled at Mike, "It's Detective Frederick to garbage like you. Shut your face."

Mike leaned his back against the bars and closed his eyes. What was going on here? It could not be about Porkins. Macy had checked to see if the Luger Mike carried had been fired recently. That made no sense if this was about a shooting months ago.

A half hour passed. It must be near two or three in the afternoon. Mike's stomach growled. He hadn't eaten since breakfast. Annie would be going off the switchboard at nine and she would be expecting him to call her at the boarding house.

Someone banged on the iron door and Owen hobbled over to open it. Macy pushed in followed by the other officer. Frederick and Owen both stood. Macy walked over and tossed a revolver onto the center of the table.

"Colt Army .45 revolver," Macy said. "A real antique. It was stuffed under the mattress in the bedroom. It has been fired in the last two days, still had three spent cartridges in the cylinder."

"Open and shut case," said the officer with Macy.

"Not yet, Peterson," Macy said as he sat on a chair at the table. Owen was on his left and Frederick on his right. Across from Macy a four-legged stool stood where a chair should have been.

Macy said, "Owen, get Demill over here where we can talk."

Owen hobbled to the cell door accompanied by Peterson. Owen opened the door and Peterson pulled Mike by his elbow and forced him to sit on a four-legged stool at the table facing Macy. The legs on the stool were uneven, forcing Mike to lean to one side to steady himself.

Macy said, "Where were you today, Demill. We had to wait by your place since dawn."

Mike shrugged, "On my boat, working."

"You have a boat?"

"I'm building one. Today I was shaking her down," Mike said.

"I have you cold, Demill. I have an eyewitness that saw you do it and I have the gun you used. Just make it easy on everyone and tell us why."

"Why what?" Mike said.

"Why did you shoot him three times?" Macy said.

"Shoot who?"

"You didn't know who it was you killed?"

"I have killed a lot of people, mostly Germans and years ago. I did not know their names. I haven't killed anyone recently."

"You know we have a witness that saw you," Frederick said. Macy glared at Frederick but said nothing. Frederick got the message and shut up.

"You do not have a witness that saw me do it because I did not shoot anyone," Mike said. *Except that hijacker, Porkins,* he thought.

"Whose pistol is this?" Macy said, pointing at the Colt.

"I don't know," Mike said.

"Alright, then tell us this: Where were you yesterday at four o'clock in the afternoon?"

"Yesterday? Saturday?"

"Where were you?"

"I was on the steamboat *Capital*, looking at the crevasse in the levee at Poydras."

"Anyone with you?"

"My fiancée, Annie Norwak," Mike said. It was the first time he had referred to Annie as his fiancée.

"Not good enough, Demill. Your fiancée would swear to anything to save your skin."

"There had to be a hundred people on the boat with me."

"We can't interview a hundred people, Demill," Macy said.

"Fritz Hoffman and his wife, Gertrude were with me. We ate dinner together," Mike sighed. He smiled inwardly at his good luck in meeting Fritz.

"You mean the gunsmith?" Frederick said, drawing another glare from Macy.

"That's him. The gunsmith on Camp Street. You guys must know him."

"Peterson, get Kepler and a car. Go to Hoffman's house. See what they remember about yesterday."

Peterson muttered under his breath as he went out. Owen forced the door closed again.

They sat around the table for twenty minutes. No questions were asked. No one moved. Macy just worked his jaw as if chewing leather and stared at Mike.

Someone banged on the door. Owen opened it and Peterson stepped in. He walked to Macy and said, "Hoffman lives in an apartment over his shop on Camp Street, not five minutes from here. He and his wife were home. I talked to Hoffman downstairs while Kepler talked to the wife upstairs. They both said they were with Demill and his girl on the riverboat from a little after two in the afternoon until nearly seven last night."

"This stinks," Macy said. "Someone is messing with me and I do not care for it."

"Someone is messing with you!" Mike exclaimed. "I am the one cuffed and locked up. I don't even know who it is I'm accused of killing."

Macy looked at Mike for a moment and then slowly said, "Julius Ruttan, a businessman from Chicago, Illinois."

Mike tried not to show any expression, but Macy was too good an interrogator. He said, "You knew Ruttan." It was not a question.

Mike said, "Only by reputation. I have seen him on the street, but I never talked to the man."

"So, tell me, Demill. How did a man you never met get shot three times with a large caliber weapon and I find a Colt .45, practically smoking, in your house with three spent cartridges in the cylinder?"

"I do not know."

"He was shot to pieces at four o'clock yesterday, in broad daylight, in my city and with witnesses. How do you explain that?"

"The witnesses were mistaken," Mike said with a shrug. If he and Annie had not met the Hoffmans on the *Capital*, he would have never been able to defend himself.

Macy leaned back. There were several more plausible explanations. "Take off the cuffs," he said.

"What?" Frederick said.

"You heard, George. Get those cuffs off Mister Demill."

Mike stood, and Fredrick unlocked the cuffs. Mike rubbed his wrists and flexed his fingers. He said, "Can I have my Luger back?"

Macy shrugged. He appeared deep in thought as he dug the pistol out of his pocket, dropped the magazine into the palm of his hand and jacked out the chambered round. He gave the pistol, magazine, and the round to Mike. "Do not leave town, Mister Demill. I may have more questions for you."

Mike pocketed the items and walked to the door. He looked at Owen, who cursed under his breath, hobbled to the door, and opened it.

Mike said, "Thank you, Owen."

"That's Officer Peters to you, Demill."

"Thank you, Officer Owen Peters," Mike said, and he walked out into the fading Sunday afternoon light.

Owen closed the door and Frederick said, "Why did you let him go, Sarge? I mean you had witnesses and the gun!"

Macy glared at Frederick and said, "First, when I am interrogating a suspect, you keep your mouth shut."

"Alright, alright, I'm sorry, but why let him go?"

Macy checked off on his fingers as he counted, "One: He didn't do it. Fritz was with him at the time of the murder. Two: I don't have a witness. I just have an anonymous telephone call. It now appears most likely the anonymous 'witness' is the killer. Three: Demill is up to his neck in something. Four: Somebody has it in for this guy and I'm not going to find out who that is if I keep him locked up. Five: I'm going to have some of our people follow him and see what happens. I can't have him followed if he is rotting in that cell."

Macy thought for a long time and said, "Frederick, I want you to check with the boys at the Ninth. Demill's accent sounds like he's from bayou country. See if they know of him. Demill is into something and my guess is bootlegging. Anyone down there that has a boat and access to a bayou is into bootlegging."

"He said he was on his boat all day," Frederick said.

"Like I said, add one of these bayou rats and a boat and you will have a bootlegger. See if those guys at the Ninth know where Demill keeps his boat. We need to go over it every time he brings it in."

*****

Mike walked to Saint Charles Street and caught the streetcar. He got off at the Jefferson Avenue stop and walked the few blocks to his house. Mike circled his block twice but saw nothing unusual. He checked on his truck once more. Someone had gone through the leather pocket on the steering shaft and left the registration and bill of sale papers on the seat. He returned the papers to the pouch.

He walked up to the back porch of his house. The back door was opened slightly. He pulled it open and saw the lock had been broken. He cursed Sergeant Macy under his breath. His house had been unlocked the entire time he had been in police custody. Burglaries were a common thing, so Mike hurried in to check his possessions.

The contents of the kitchen cabinets had been spread across the floor. Mike held his breath and thought about his operating cash. The small metal box hidden in the kitchen behind the wall boards, and the one thousand dollars in it, was undisturbed.

He checked his bedroom. The mattress had been thrown to the floor. All the dresser drawers were out and on the floor upside down. No other room in the house had been visibly disturbed. Evidentially, Macy had stopped the search once they found the revolver, wherever that was.

There was a loud knocking at the front door and Mike left the mess to answer the door. It was Dorn.

"Mike, where have you been?" Dorn asked as he pushed his way into the house.

"I was arrested," Mike said, "in the backyard right after you went in."

"Arrested! Why? Who arrested you?"

"A cop named Macy said I killed someone."

"I know the bloke. A hard man, that one," Dorn said. "Why did they let you go. I ain't never heard of Macy letting anybody out without first he gets worked over."

"Luckily, I could prove I was somewhere else when the guy was killed."

"Who was the guy that got killed?" Dorn asked.

"A guy named Jules Ruttan. Know him?"

"Can't say that I do," Dorn said. He was staring at Mike in a curious way. He shrugged, "Well, you are out. We can't let anything get in the way of our May thing."

Dorn left, and Mike picked up the phone. He knew Annie was working the long-distance switchboard. He picked up the handset and toggled the cradle three times. An operator came on and said, "Number Please."

Mike said, "Long distance, please."

"One moment, please." There were a few clicks and Annie came on. She said, "Long distance. City, please."

"Annie, can I see you tonight?"

"Mike! Have you finished working on the boat?"

"Yes. Can I see you tonight?"

"I am off in one hour. Meet me at the boarding house. We can talk there."

"I will meet you at the front of the switchboard office."

"Mike, is something wrong?"

"I will tell you all about it when I pick you up."

"Mike, you are scaring me."

"Nothing to be frightened about, Annie. I just need to talk to you as soon as I can. See you at the front door. Goodbye." Mike hung up.

*****

Mike was standing by the passenger side of his new truck when Annie came out of the switchboard building at nine o'clock. She hurried up to him, concern and worry on her face. He kissed her before she could say anything and opened the door to the truck.

Annie paused. "Mike, what is happening?"

"Get in. I will tell you all about it while I drive you to your place."

"Mike, the boarding house is two doors away."

"I will take the long way around. I will have you to the lobby before Madam Toups begins to wonder where you are."

Annie climbed in and Mike hurried around to the driver's seat. He put the truck in gear and started off at a walking speed. There was no traffic, and he was just going around the block.

Annie said, "you must tell me what is going on, Mike."

Mike sighed, "Somebody killed Ruttan, and the cops thought I did it."

"What?"

"Jules Ruttan was shot to death and somebody told the police I did it."

"Who?"

"I don't know. I don't think the cops know either."

"When was he shot?"

"That's the good part. Ruttan was killed around four in the evening yesterday while we were on the steamboat."

Annie leaned back. She was the daughter of a police chief. She knew how it worked. If someone said they saw a shooting, whoever they identified would have to prove otherwise.

Mike continued, "I told them about meeting Fritz and Gertrude. They verified we were on the boat."

Annie moved closer to Mike and kissed his cheek. "Don't ever scare me like that again," she said.

"I had to tell you before Sergeant Macy or one of his detectives paid you a visit. I did not want you to find out that way."

Mike made the turn at the corner.

Annie said, "I was the one that warned you about Ruttan and Myrtle. Macy would have started out questioning me about Ruttan and if I knew him. It would have been awkward, to say the least. A good cop can pick out a lie, usually."

Mike made another turn. He said, "Somebody is making trouble for me. They want me out of the bootlegging business."

Annie didn't say anything. Mike made the last turn. The boardinghouse was just ahead. Mike slowed to a stop.

Annie said, "I still want to marry you, Mike. But there is something you need to know about me before you do."

Mike furrowed his brow. "I know all I need to know about you, Annie."

"I was married before," she said, "well, not really married. I lived with a man."

"Ancient history," Mike said.

"You told me all about your past," Annie sighed. "I did not tell you a thing."

"I told you most of it, not all. It is the past, Annie. I do not care."

Annie looked at Mike, a tear trickled down her cheek. "His name was… It doesn't matter what his name was. I was pregnant. He got drunk, beat me up and I lost the baby."

Mike put an arm around Annie and pulled her close. She cradled her head against his shoulder. "I was sixteen, Mike. I was just a stupid girl. My father found out and my ex-boyfriend disappeared. Years later, I got a job, made friends. I convinced them to take a trip with me to Cuba, on the sly. A crazy, silly thing. I thought it would make me forget."

"Have you forgotten, Annie?"

"A woman can never forget a lost child," she said.

"What I mean," Mike said, his voice was very soft, "can you leave the past behind and marry me?"

"Do you still want to?" Annie said. She had not moved her head from his shoulder and was staring blankly out the windshield.

"I am not marrying a silly kid from Cicero," Mike said. "I am marrying the lady, Anastazja Norwak. That is all there is to it."

Annie sat straight up. "Mike, let's go in. I need to tell Madam Toups I am checking out."

Mike was startled. "Checking out? Are you leaving?"

Annie had climbed out of the truck. "They don't let married women work at the telephone switchboard," she said, "or rent at their boarding house."

Mike climbed down, "So what are you going to do?"

Annie laughed, "One of two things. I am going to live with you until we are married, or I am going back to Cicero."

Mike hurried after her as she walked toward the boardinghouse. "Good thing I brought my truck," he said.

CHAPTER 20

Mike opened his eyes and stared at the indented pillow next to his head. The sounds coming from the kitchen must have awakened him. It was the first night in a long time that he had not dreamt of the trenches in France or of a lonely, desperate widow and her little girl.

He had expected Madam Toups to be angry when Annie announced she had come to collect her things, leave the boardinghouse, and quit her job as a switchboard operator. The opposite was true. Madam Toups laughed. She hugged Annie and then Mike.

"I was wondering if something was wrong," she said. "Perhaps, I think, I have lost my touch. I expected this news two weeks ago, me." Madam Toups addressed Mike in French, "If you do not marry this girl and keep her, you are a great fool." Mike agreed.

Mike rolled out of bed and stepped around piles of baggage and discarded clothes. Last night had been wonderful. They both had been enthusiastic, uninhibited, yet deliberate and unhurried. It was as if they had been lovers for years.

He found his trousers and slipped them on. He went to the bathroom, brushed his teeth, shaved his chin, and combed his hair. He laughed as he looked in the mirror at the weathered, scarred, mustachioed man looking back. *What does she see in me?*

Annie was in the kitchen cooking ham and eggs. She was wearing a house robe cinched with one of Mike's belts. Her hair was tied back in a bun. The table was set for two, though the flatware was blatantly mismatched. She looked up and smiled when Mike came to the kitchen doorway. *God, she is beautiful*, he thought.

"Good morning, Annie," Mike said.

"Good morning, Michael," Annie replied. "I hope you like ham and scrambled eggs. It is all I could find." Mike saw the hint of a blush cross her cheeks.

"I am amazed you found that much. I am not in the habit of keeping a well-stocked icebox."

Annie picked up the plates, one was plain white, the other had a blue pattern around the rim, and placed unequal servings of breakfast on each. She put the larger portion on the table in front of the chair against the wall. The other portion she placed at the opposite setting.

"Breakfast is served," she said, gesturing for Mike to take the seat against the wall. He scooted the chair back and sat.

Annie took her place; her face lost the smile. She said, "Any regrets, Michael?"

"I have yet to taste my breakfast," he said. He noticed tears were welling up in Annie's eyes.

He quickly added, "I have absolutely no regrets, Anastazja. None whatsoever. Do you?"

"Only one," she said. She played with her fork in the eggs.

"What is your one regret?" Mike asked.

"That we waited so long – that I waited so long."

"We will have to make up for lost time then," Mike said with a wink. "We have work to do."

"I just realized," Annie said, "It's Monday and I have no job. But you must get to work. Are you late?"

"I work for me," Mike said. "I have no pressing hauling contracts. We have the day to do several things that need to be done."

"What are those things?" Annie asked.

"Well, we need to go to City Hall and register for a marriage license."

"I would like more than a civil marriage," Annie said.

"If you agree, we will have a proper church marriage in Cicero. But I think a civil marriage now is important."

"Why are you in such a hurry to make an honest woman of me?"

Mike ate some of the breakfast. "This is very good," he said. "It is more than that, Annie. I have money and will have several properties by the end of the week. You need to be my wife to insure you keep what we have should something ever happen to me."

"Oh, Mike," Annie said. "Are you in trouble?"

"I am not certain, but one never knows. Put that aside. Do you know how to drive?"

The sudden change of subject surprised Annie. She paused and said, "No, not really. I have watched my father and you drive, but I don't think I could."

"Then driving lessons are first. I plan to open a trucking business, short hauls only. I would like you to learn. We teased about you running the office, but now it is serious. You need to know how to drive so you can better manage things."

"Is this your idea of a romantic breakfast?" Annie said.

"This is my idea of making up for lost time. After breakfast, we can put your things away, bathe and dress for town. The driving lessons will happen on the way to city hall. Tell me now if this is going too fast for you."

"It's not that things are going so fast. I just can't believe how fortunate I am. I am afraid I will not prove good enough," Annie said.

"So, there it is. You think you don't deserve me, and I know I don't deserve you. We are perfectly matched," Mike laughed. "Tell me what you want, Annie."

"I want to be your wife, Mike. I want you so badly it frightens me."

"Well, then it is decided. One thing my granddaddy always told me, 'Never look back. You can only move forward from where you are.'"

*****

Annie's driving lesson began in the garage. Mike walked her around the truck pointing out features, inside and out. He explained the functions of each. "It is not important to remember everything this first time around. Eventually, it will all become second nature. Make certain nothing is in front of or behind the truck or leaning against it."

"When do we start the engine?" Annie said.

"Get into the driver's seat," Mike said. "There are several things you need to do before starting the engine."

Annie stepped up onto the running board and slid into the driver's position, her hands on the steering wheel. Mike stood on the running board next to her where he could touch all the mechanisms as he explained them.

"First you must always make certain the hand brake is set," Mike tapped the tall lever coming up through the floor. "Grab it with your full hand and squeeze. Pull it all of the way back and release."

Annie gripped the two levers on the brake and squeeze them together. She felt the lever release. She pushed forward and then pulled back. When she let go, she felt it lock in place.

"You have just set the brake and put the transmission in neutral. Neutral means the engine is disengaged from the tires. Never start the engine or turn the hand crank unless this brake is set."

"This is the spark," Mike touched a small lever coming from the left side of the steering shaft. He reached across and touched a similar lever on the right side. "This is the throttle."

Mike stepped off the running board and went around the truck and climbed into the passenger's seat.

He said, "Push the spark lever all the way up."

Annie pushed the left lever up.

Mike said, "Good. Now set the throttle at about one quarter of the way down from the top and turn the key to the 'battery' setting."

Annie did as instructed.

"Now step on the starter button and release it when the engine starts."

Annie did so, and the engine sputtered to life. Mike leaned close to Annie's ear, so he did not have to shout over the sound of the running engine. She smelled wonderful.

"Slowly advance the spark until she runs smoothly. Experiment with the spark. Advance and retard it while you listen to the engine. Decide where it needs to be to run smoothest."

"Now what?" Annie asked, her hands gripping the steering wheel so tightly they shown white at the knuckles.

"Move the hand brake forward one notch," Mike said.

Annie adjusted the hand brake and the truck rocked forward a little.

"Now, to put the truck in low gear, step all the way down on the clutch."

Annie did so, and the truck lurched forward. She pulled on the hand brake and the truck stopped with a jerk.

"Good reflexes," Mike said. "You know how to stop. That is more important than knowing how to go. Nobody's coming on the street, so release the hand brake and drive onto the street. Turn the wheel to the right as you get to the street, so you will be headed toward Saint Charles."

Annie guided the truck onto the street and weaved left and right as she learned the steering response. Fortunately, there was little traffic. In less than one block, she had the truck puttering along at five miles per hour or so.

"Good," Mike said. "Now advance the throttle and spark to increase your speed."

Annie moved the appropriate levers until the truck was hurtling along at nearly fifteen miles per hour.

"Now, slow down and stop."

Annie slowed the throttle, pulled back on the hand brake and the truck skidded to a stop.

"It will get smoother with practice," Mike said. "Now get her going again and when we turn onto Saint Charles, I'll show you how to get into high gear."

Annie drove the truck up to City Hall and skittered to a stop in the roadway. The drive along Saint Charles from

Leontine to City Hall on Royal Street, six miles, had only taken fifteen minutes. Annie shifted into low and guided the truck into a place along the curb using the foot brake. She set the hand brake and switched off the engine.

Mike said, "You are a natural driver, Annie. I've known soldiers in the army who never could get the hang of it."

"Don't tease me, Michael. I watched you hanging on for dear life."

"I was just keeping myself aboard."

Annie laughed. "That is a story," she said. "Now we need to go to the Clerk of Court before you come to your senses and change your mind."

*****

Thursday, the fourth of May, Mr. and Mrs. Michael Demill walked into the law offices of John Eiseman to close on the acts of sale for a duplex at 4617 Laurel Street and a commercial building on the corner of Saint Claude Avenue and Caffin Avenue.

Hilda stood as they entered the office.

"Good morning, Hilda," Mike said. "I would like you to meet my wife, Annie."

"Mrs. Demill," Hilda said as she reached out her hand. "It is a pleasure to meet you."

"The pleasure is mine, Hilda. Please call me 'Annie.'"

"I would offer you some refreshments," Hilda said, "but the attorney representing both sellers is waiting with Mister Eiseman in his office." She stepped over to Eiseman's door, rapped gently and then peeked in.

"The Demills are here, sir."

"Show them in," Eiseman said from beyond the door.

Mike and Annie entered the office. Eiseman was behind his desk and another man sat in a facing chair. Both stood as Annie and Mike came in. Eiseman walked around from behind his desk. "First, I must congratulate you on your marriage." He shook hands with Mike and turned toward Annie. "I assume this lovely lady is the former Anastazja Norwak."

Mike said, "Annie, this is Mister John Eiseman. He will handle our acts of sale."

"A pleasure, ma'am," Eiseman said. He took Annie's fingertips in his hand and bowed slightly.

"May I introduce you both to Mister David Rothschild? He holds the power of attorney for both of the vendors." Rothschild nodded.

"Please have a seat, Mrs. Demill," Eiseman said as he indicated a chair next to Rothschild.

Annie hesitated. "I am certain you gentlemen have business to discuss. I can wait in the reception area and visit with Hilda."

"My dear Mrs. Demill," Eiseman said. "We cannot proceed without you. This is Louisiana, real estate transactions require the consent of both spouses."

Annie sat, a little overwhelmed at suddenly being in the middle of business transactions. Eiseman passed some deed documents around. In every document the "vendees" were listed as "Anastazja Norwak, wife of / and Michael Demill." Mike had explained the purchases and the sale figures, but now it was happening.

The property at 4617 Laurel Street was purchased at two thousand seven hundred fifty dollars and the Saint Claude property was purchased for six thousand dollars. Annie had never seen more than a hundred dollars in one place and now, in two transactions, she was listed as having paid nearly ten thousand dollars. She signed the documents in amazement.

"You are my wife, Annie," Mike had told her when he explained the purchases. "What was mine is now ours."

*****

Annie drove home. Mike insisted she needed the practice. She was becoming quite an accomplished driver and smoothly shifted gears, advanced the throttle and spark appropriately and learned to shift to neutral before braking.

"Next, we will practice backing up," Mike said. "You will be a certified trucker before the end of the week."

Annie laughed, "Driving is not so hard, but loading and unloading might require more muscle than I have."

Mike said, "What do you say? Let's visit our new properties and take inventory on what is required to make them habitable?"

"Shopping? One of my favorite things."

"Tomorrow and Saturday, I have some contract hauls to make, so we need to get it done today." Mike paused a moment, then continued, "Sunday, I have to take the *Solitario* out with the Irish Channel boys. I won't be back until Tuesday morning."

"Are you importing anything?"

"No. I am bringing them to meet a ship."

"Mike, you don't need to import anymore. It is getting too dangerous."

"That it is," Mike agreed and changed the subject. "We need to see if the new properties are ready for tenants. We can place advertisements in the papers next week. If the waters have gone down, we need to drive to Yscloskey and pick up the other truck."

"What we need," Annie said, "is a business plan."

"I confess," Mike laughed. "I married you for business reasons. I would like you to manage the books, if you think you can."

"I can manage the books," Annie said. "But I need you to run the business, so be careful Sunday. Just for business reasons, of course."

When Mike had inspected the new properties before offering to buy, he had not paid much attention to anything other than structural fitness, location, and size. Annie found needs Mike would never had considered, such as interior wall coverings, kitchen appliances and washroom fixtures.

The duplex had all the modern conveniences including gas hot water heater, gas stove, indoor plumbing, an ice box, electrical lighting, and area gas heaters in the bedrooms.

The commercial property had a first floor that was a completely open warehouse space and an apartment on the second floor that lacked electrical wiring but was fitted with gas lights. Mike thought it would take little to convert the building to electrical lighting.

"I will talk to the priest at Saint Maurice Church to see who is looking for work," Mike said. Saint Maurice Church was less than a half-mile from the warehouse. If they hired locally, the employees could walk to work saving both time and money.

"How many are we going to hire?" Annie asked.

"One at a time. I think we will work with two trucks until we get on our feet. After that, we will see what happens."

On Sunday, Annie and Mike attended the eight o'clock Mass at Saint Maurice Church. Attendance at Mass would introduce them to the neighborhood and afford them a chance to develop a sense of the community. Annie had suggested they move their residence to the warehouse apartment once it was made livable and Mike had readily agreed.

After mass, Mike and Annie introduced themselves to the priest and talked of their plans to open a business. The priest for the morning mass, Father John Corning, a short, jovial man of about sixty, was also the pastor.

"Oh, you've bought the old Castro Livery," Father John exclaimed. "Old man Castro made the finest wagon, carriage and leatherworks there. He died two years ago. I heard his sons had the place up for sale."

"It did not seem to have been a stable," Annie said.

"Oh, he never boarded his animals there. He also owned a stable and pasture in Saint Bernard Parish. His sons kept that."

"If you could, Father, we might be looking to hire some good men, family men," Mike said.

"Does it matter if they are Irish or Italian?" Father John asked.

"None of that matters. We want men who are willing to put in a fair day for a fair wage," Mike said.

"Will you pay Negroes and Irish the same as everyone else?"

"Good work for good pay. Don't send us any lost souls, Father. We want to build a solid company," Mike said.

"I will send a list to the old Castro Livery on Wednesday."

*****

Mike had kissed Annie goodbye at five in the afternoon. He said he would be home Tuesday and suggested Annie spend Monday shopping for herself or for things the new properties needed.

"Mike, please do be careful," she said. She pretended she was going to turn in early, but Mike knew that she would be up until midnight.

"I will be most careful, *mi querida* (my dear)." He wished he could find the words to quell her fears. As he drove away from the house, he saw lights come on in the kitchen.

The truck bounced along the clamshell surfaced roadway on the east bank of Bayou Saint John. Several boathouses and camps populated the land between the road and the bayou. The road dodged around a large island with large, expensive homes and, closer to the lake, the foundations of an old fortification hastily thrown up at the beginning of the Civil War.

As he neared the boat slip, he saw the very old foundations of the original Spanish Fort across the bayou next to the Spanish Fort Hotel. There was little left except for foundations. Most of the bricks and all the timbers were gone, rotted away, or taken by scavengers.

The camp next to the boat slip was crowded with three large trucks. Several men were scurrying between the trucks and the *Solitario*, loading crates under the supervision of O'Gara. Their activities were partially masked by the rag-time music flowing from the resort across the bayou. Mike parked his truck along the edge of the roadway.

"I like a man who is prompt," O'Gara said as Mike walked up.

"Is she fueled and provisioned?" Mike asked.

"Topped off and provisions enough for three days, though you should be back here Tuesday morning," O'Gara said. "Brian is directing the storage of our cargo. He knows his business, no fear on that regard."

"I would like to see how she rides before we get into a sea."

"Plenty of time for that," O'Gara said. "Are you armed?"

"Yes, I have the Luger Dorn sold me and there is a Springfield stored near the wheel."

Dorn and Mary stepped out of the fishing camp. Seeing Mike's surprise O'Gara said, "Mr. and Mrs. Doon will be accompanying us. Counting Brian Boru and myself, you will have four passengers for this run."

"No problem," Mike said. "We have room for twice that number."

Brian Boru climbed out of the *Solitario* and walked up the wharf, shooing drivers and laborers back along the way. "The job is done lads. Come to the cabin and I will pay you off. Then it is on your way."

A dozen men, wiping sweat from their faces followed Boru to the cabin and trailed in behind him.

"Once Brian is done with business, Captain, we will cast off. Best warm the engines."

Mike boarded the *Solitario* and opened the engine covers. He checked the oil, fuel lines and belts, and smelled for gasoline vapors. The electrical connections were clean and firm. Unlike truck engines, these had been converted to marine use by eliminating the radiator in favor of connecting the cooling lines to sea water by fittings through the hull. All was in good order.

Mike started the port engine first, settled it into a smooth idle and then fired up the starboard engine. He adjusted them into harmony. He stood at the exterior wheel and watched the rudder indicator as he turned the wheel left and right.

The *Solitario* had two operator stations, complete with wheels, transmission levers, throttle, spark, and choke controls for each engine. One station was in the cabin for foul weather operation and the other was on the deck against the rear wall of the cabin. The rear wheel station provided a clear view of the sides and aft parts of the boat and was ideal for trawling, loading, and docking.

Mike closed the engine covers and walked to the rear storage hatches to check on his cargo. He reached down to unlatch the forward cover when O'Gara called out.

"No need for that, Mike. Brian has it properly lashed. Let's get under way. If she needs a load shift, Brian, Dorn and I can do it."

"Well, we are ready," Mike said. He helped Mary down from the pier and Dorn jumped aboard after his wife.

Mike said, "If you would rather be out of the wind, there is comfortable seating in the cabin. It is going to be eight hours out and eight hours back, a long ride."

"I would prefer to stay on deck with Dorn, if it is all the same to you," Mary said.

"Fine with me. It may get a little wet," Mike said.

Boru and O'Gara clambered aboard after casting off the bow and stern lines. Mike turned the wheel to port, levered the port engine into reverse and forward on the starboard. The *Solitario* crabbed neatly to port away from the wharf. Once in the slip, Mike centered the wheel and slipped the starboard engine into reverse. He backed out of the slip and, once in the bayou, shifted the engines into forward and headed north on the bayou. Guests at the resort crowded the porch to watch the *Solitario* depart. Some ladies waved their handkerchiefs.

"They must thing we are making a bootleg run to the north shore," Mike said. Much of the booze consumed at the resort was "moon shine" shipped in from the north shore of the lake. Boats would slip between the piers of the resort kitchen and lift jugs of whisky up through hatches in the floor.

Mike left the rear pilot's station when they were well away from shore and went into the cabin to resume control of the boat. He opened the window in front of the wheel and eased the engines up to cruising speed.

The day was beginning to fade. Dorn, Mary, and O'Gara had retreated into the cabin with Mike. Boru remained on deck seated on a hatch cover and squinting into the wind. He ignored the slight spray that occasionally drifted across the deck.

They reached the Rigolets at sunset. The other boat traffic in the pass was coming in. The *Solitario* motored along at a moderate speed, passing shrimp boats and few pleasure crafts. The delays at the drawbridges were minimal. As was the custom, people aboard the passing crafts waved at each other as if seeing old friends.

O'Gara stood next to Mike then leaned over and asked, "How do you think we are doing, Captain?"

"We are on schedule. We will be idling on station by four in the morning, no problem," Mike said.

The rest of the evening Mike handled the helm while his passengers talked quietly at the rear of the cabin. Boru had joined the rest around one in the morning. Eventually, Mary and Dorn went forward to the bunks while O'Gara and Boru snoozed sitting around the galley table.

Mike slowed the engines to idle and shifted to neutral at four o'clock in the morning. O'Gara and Boru woke with a start and Mike could hear Mary and Dorn bustling about the forward compartment.

O'Gara stumbled to Mike's side. "See anything?"

"There is a freighter just off the bow and dead in the water," Mike said as he pointed to a dark mass blocking out the horizon straight ahead.

"That's her," O'Gara said. He grabbed a kerosene lamp, lit it, and went out onto the deck followed by Boru. He must have signaled the ship. No more than a minute after his going on deck, the freighter lit her anchor and running lights. Mike could see a gangway and landing lowered from her starboard side, the downwind side.

Mike steered up to the platform and two men came down the gangway to catch the *Solitario*'s mooring lines. The seas were calm, and the ship was stationary. Mike decided it was safe to leave the wheel and went on deck.

Boru was unlatching the hatch covers and the men from the freighter were signaling the ship's deck crane to lower a hook. Boru jumped down into the hatch and fed the hook into a pair of cargo net loops. He scrambled out of the hold and one of the deck hands signaled to the crane operator.

A cargo net packed with long, drab boxes lifted out of the hole and was drawn up to the freighter. Seven more such operations were required to empty the *Solitario*'s bays. Eight tons of cargo gone in eight lifts - one ton per net. Mike figured the cargo must have been something very solid.

The freighter's deckhands climbed onto the landing and up the gangway. Mike watched Mary, her arms full of baggage, step onto the platform where she was joined by Dorn. Boru climbed up onto the platform and held the single line keeping the *Solitario* in place.

O'Gara walked over to the platform and turned to look at Mike, who was not ten feet away. "Well, this is goodbye, old friend," he said. He pulled a pistol, a Police .38 Special, from his belt.

"Why the pistol?" Mike asked.

"Simple, my friend. We can't trust you," O'Gara said. "The coppers never take a bloke in and then release him unless there's been a deal."

"This isn't Ireland, and our cops are different," Mike said.

"Sorry, Mike. I truly am."

The boat lurched. O'Gara stumbled and grabbed at a stay to steady himself. Mike pulled the Luger from his belt and pointed it at O'Gara.

O'Gara caught his balance and said, "Won't do you any good, Mike. I gave that Luger to Dorn when we first met. We didn't know Dorn then, so we gave him a pistol that wouldn't work, matter of trust, you see. Later we gave him a Colt and he sold the Luger to you."

O'Gara straightened his arm and pointed the pistol at Mike's face. Mike shot twice and O'Gara, his expression filled with shock, fell to the deck, still gripping the 0.38 Special. Boru dropped the mooring line and fumbled for his own pistol. Mike shot him twice before the man had the pistol clear of his pocket. Mike aimed at Dorn.

Dorn was frozen on the gangway. Mary, clutching her possessions, was only a few feet further up the steps. Mike lowered his pistol. He could not fire without the risk of hitting Mary. He watched as the boat and freighter drifted apart.

Boru rolled off the platform and into the sea. O'Gara lay on the deck of the *Solitario*. He moaned, rolled onto his side, and pointed his pistol at Mike, his hand shaking. Mike and O'Gara each fired their pistols at the same time.

CHAPTER 21

Mike opened his eyes. He was lying on his stomach, the left side of his face pressed against the floor. It was a tile floor, not the deck of the *Solitario*. He looked horizontally across the floor and he could see a wall and a floor-to-ceiling window. Long sheer laced curtains admitted a faint light, maybe daylight, which outlined the glass panels. He tried to reconcile his last memory with what he was seeing.

Someone said, "*Hola*, Miguel."

Mike pushed himself into a sitting position, facing the window. The room seemed to rock slightly as he tried to clear his head. He attempted to examine the rest of the room. The window he saw when he first opened his eyes was bracketed by two others, identically sized and curtained.

To his right was a closed door between two large portraits, one of a man and the other of a woman. Both were dressed in fancy, antebellum clothes. To his left was a fireplace containing dying embers. A flintlock musket fitted with a bayonet was mounted over the mantel. A large clock was on one corner of the mantel and a vase of flowers on the other. The clock had the hour hand pointing to five. There was no minute hand.

"Do not attempt to stand too quickly," the voice said. "I fear you may still be too weak." It was a woman's voice, perhaps an old woman and she spoke in Spanish. Her accent was heavily *Isleña*. She was behind him.

Still sitting, Mike pushed himself around to face her. The woman was sitting in a high-backed chair. She had a long robe wrapped around her, covering her from her neck to the floor. She wore a white cotton nightcap pulled down to her ears and thin wisps of white hair curled from under the edges. Her hands were open on her lap, palms down. She was more than merely old, she appeared to be ancient. Her eyes were closed and sunken. She was blind with age, Mike thought.

Mike managed to say, "Where am I?"

"The answers to some questions only serve to confuse."

"Who are you? How do you know my name?" Mike attempted to stand, but the floor seemed to tilt, and he flopped back down.

"Your name is Miguel deMelilla, but you call yourself Michael Demill. You are the one known as '*El Solitario*.' I know you better than you know yourself. My name is Fior deMelilla y Steward Roundtree. I am sister to your grandfather Doramas. You may address me as 'Saberia.' Everyone, even my children, call me so."

"If he were alive," Mike said, "my grandfather would be over a hundred years old." Mike's head spun. "How can this be?"

"He would be one hundred six to be precise," she said. She raised one hand to her cheek. "I am afraid that would mean I am ninety-six."

Mike tried to stand again and managed to get to his feet. He stumbled toward the fireplace and steadied himself by placing a hand on the mantel. He noticed that there was a pistol on the mantel, the butt canted toward him. It was a Colt's Dragoon. He could see silvery primers nestled on the cylinder's nipples. The .44 caliber pistol was loaded.

Mike felt for his Luger behind his back. It was not there. He looked across the floor and he saw the pistol on the floor near where he had been. He had not noticed it before.

"I do not understand what is happening," Mike said. The room continued to gently tilt back and forth.

"With time, you will understand. Come here and let me examine your wound."

"Wound? What wound?"

"Feel your head."

Mike touched his forehead and swept his hands back. His head began to throb, and he felt a long gash along his temple. His hand came away sticky with blood. He walked over to Saberia and knelt beside her chair.

"Put your head here," Saberia said, patting her lap.

Mike complied. He placed the uninjured side of his head on the old woman's lap, facing toward the room. The light in the room had improved and he could see a pool of blood on the floor near the Luger. He was certain the stain had not been there before.

"Be still, Miguel," she said. She put her thin, almost skeletal hands on his head. She traced the long gash in his temple with one fingertip and as she did, the burning sensation subsided.

"You have been fortunate," she said. "The bullet slid along your hard head but did not break the skull. Small wonder, that. Stand. I am done."

Mike stood and felt his scalp. The wound was there, but the bleeding has stopped. "What did you do?" he asked.

"Nothing. Are you thirsty?"

Mike licked his dry lips. "Yes, very much," he said. He had not felt thirst until Saberia mentioned it.

"Would you like some wine? We have a very fine red."

"Yes, thank you very much."

Saberia reached out with her left hand and took a small bell from a table next to her chair. She flicked her wrist and the bell tinkled. Mike could hear footsteps and the door between the portraits opened.

A girl of about ten or so came into the room. She was petite, quite pretty, barefoot, and very black. She had a red ribbon in her braided hair and wore a dress fashioned from a flour sack. The girl touched the hem of her dress and curtsied. The girl used English. "What do you want of me, *Doña* Saberia?"

Saberia spoke in English as well. "Grace, will you please bring me a glass of red wine."

Grace curtsied again and said, "Yes, *Doña* Saberia." She left the room but left the door open. Mike could only see a wall beyond the door. Grace had turned left upon leaving the room.

"Grace is such a sweet girl," Saberia said. "She is also very smart. Her family has worked for me for decades, since her father was that age. They used to live downstairs, but now that I am feeble, I live downstairs and Grace lives upstairs with her family. Time has turned the world upside down. Her father wants me to teach her French, so we can send her to study in Paris. Do you think Paris has recovered from the war?"

"I would not know," Mike said.

"We will send her when she is fourteen."

Mike was drawn to the portraits. He edged forward to examine them more closely.

"Do they look familiar?" Saberia asked.

Mike thought, *how can a blind person tell what I am doing?*

"I do not think so," Mike said. The woman was beautiful, with the kind of beauty that exuded power. She was fair, red haired and green eyed.

"My mother," Saberia said. Mike did not understand how she could tell he was looking at the portrait of the lady. "She was *Doña* Anna Steward y O'Brian deMelilla."

"My father is on your left. *Don* Bartolomé deMelilla y Bourg, *El Tigre – El Tigre de Nueva Orleáns.*"

Mike shifted his attention to the portrait on his left. He could see a resemblance to his own father, except this man had a great scar across the left side of his face.

"They owned a shipping company and built this house. The war took all they had except for this house."

Grace came into the room with a wineglass held gently between her hands. She walked slowly, and the dark wine sloshed about, but did not spill. She handed the glass to Saberia and asked, "Is there anything else you desire, *Doña* Saberia?"

"No, thank you, child."

Grace curtsied and walked past Mike without even glancing his way. It was as if she was not surprised to find a bloody man in the room. Grace closed the door as she left.

Mike said in English. "She was named well, for the service was gracefully rendered. She did not question my presence."

Saberia laughed and switched back to Spanish. "That is because you are not here. Had you been here, we would not have been able to keep her from asking a thousand questions. Grace is forever curious."

"What do you mean?" Mike looked around the room. "I am here."

Saberia lifted her hands. "Be quiet and listen. I have been blind from birth. My mother was injured in an explosion when she was pregnant with me. The blast took my vision but gave me a greater gift. I will tell you two things. First: A priest will seek you out. You must grant the favor he asks. Although the request might seem simple to you, it is very important to me. Second, you must name your son Bartolomé."

Mike shook his head. "This cannot be! I do not have a son and why would a priest seek me out for anything?"

"Anastazja Norwak carries your son," Saberia said. "Now tell me you will do as I request."

I must be dreaming! This is all a dream, Mike thought.

He said, "*Obedeceré* (I will obey)."

"Good, good," Saberia sighed, relief playing across her wrinkled face. "Now go, lie on the floor next to your pistol. Close your eyes and all will be answered to you."

Mike stumbled across the swaying room, dropped to his knees and, placing the uninjured side of his head against the floor, lay in the blood stain.

He heard Saberia call to him from the chair. "*Ve con Dios* (Go with God)," she said.

He closed his eyes.

*****

Mike opened his eyes again. His face was pressed on the gently rocking deck of the *Solitario*. He could feel the rhythmic vibrations of the idling engines beneath him. He could see O'Gara's body twisted into a lump and in a pool of blood against the gunnel, still clinging to a revolver. The corpse was missing half of its skull.

Mike struggled to his feet. Night had given way to a gray dawn. At least he thought it was dawn. He had no idea how long he had lain on the deck. He stumbled to the pilot station and checked the compass. The *Solitario* was facing west, and the graying sky was toward the stern. It was dawn. Mike had been unconscious for about two hours.

He scanned the horizon. Nothing was in sight. No boats, no ships, no shoreline, just an endless stretch of open water. There seemed to be a light breeze from the north, so it was likely the boat had drifted south during the last few hours.

His first reaction was to put the *Solitario* into forward and power north to find landmarks. He resisted the urge. There were things he needed to address first. The Luger was not tucked in his belt and he walked around the deck until he found it where it had slid under the lip of the port engine cover.

He thumbed the magazine release and dropped it into his palm. A nine-millimeter round sat at the top of the stack. He could see another round beneath. One in the chamber, at least two in the box made for three rounds. He remembered firing five shots, maybe six. The Luger initially held nine rounds. One in the chamber and eight in the magazine.

He tucked the Luger into place behind his belt at the small of his back. He still had the Springfield stored in the cabin with thirty rounds of 30-06 ammunition. He vowed to carry extra cartridges and a spare magazine for the Luger in the future.

He went to the corpse. A canvas day bag lay at the feet where O'Gara had placed it when he drew his pistol to kill Mike. Blood pooled around the base of the bag and a crimson trickle led to a scupper. Mike pulled O'Gara's body until it lay flat on its back.

He pried the revolver out of the corpse's hand and tossed it overboard. One of O'Gara's coat pockets was stuffed with a wad of pamphlets extorting war against England. Mike tossed the papers overboard. Another pocket produced a badge embossed "Deputy Sheriff – Orleans Parish." Mike tossed this overboard as well.

The trouser pockets produced a box of ammunition for the Police Special, a money clip of American twenty-dollar bills, a clip of British currency, and five wadded one-dollar bills. He put the dollars in his pocket and tossed the British notes overboard. He checked the seams of O'Gara's clothing for hidden stashes but found nothing. He pulled the body to the gunnel and rolled it into the sea where it floated next to the drifting boat.

The day bag contained several banded straps of twenty-dollar bills. Mike counted ten straps making twenty thousand dollars. He transferred the bills to a drawer in the pilot's station.

He found the swab bucket and filled it with sea water and thoroughly washed his face and wound. He splashed the bucket of water across the blood-stained deck. Four spent cartridges from the Luger were flushed through the scuppers along with clots of blood.

Several more buckets of sea water were required to flush away all the blood and bits of scalp. Mike scrubbed the deck with a broom as he sloshed it with seawater and finally swabbed the deck with mop and soap.

He could not find any place where a bullet had struck the deck, gunnel, or cabin. The bullet that grazed Mike's head must have gone into the sea. The shots into O'Gara must have remained in the body or they too had gone into the sea. Mike regretted not examining the body more closely before committing it to the deep.

It was full daylight by the time Mike was ready to get underway, although the sky was overcast and threatening. Using the exterior pilot's station, Mike shifted the engines into forward and, running at idle, pointed the bow to the north. He looked back to see the dark splotch that had been O'Gara bobbing in the chop. It disappeared after the boat had gone less than a hundred yards.

Mike left the deck station and went into the cabin to use the controls protected from the weather. He pushed the throttle and adjusted the spark until the *Solitario* was running comfortably at twelve knots.

One hour of running due north and Mike began to see the outline of an island on the horizon. In another half-hour, he identified the wide east-west spread of Horn Island. He turned the wheel slightly to the starboard and made for the pass between Horn Island and Petit Bos Island. He intended to re-fuel at Pascagoula and call Annie before heading west along Mississippi Sound and home.

A rain shower swept across the *Solitario* as Mike emerged from the pass into the sound. The rain beat down furiously, obscuring the shoreline ahead and forcing Mike to throttle back to dead slow. He had tilted the front windowpane down to keep the rain from flooding in until there was only a small slit for him to look through.

The rain passed, and the sky turned blue. Mike pushed the dripping window fully open. Buoys, including a few new green cans, were just to his left. These marked the channel to Pascagoula. Though blinded by the dense rain, he had managed to hit the channel dead on. He entered the mouth of the Pascagoula River and continued inland for nearly a mile until he was in the shadow of the L & N bridge over the Pascagoula River.

On his train trip to Mobile, he had noticed that there was a lot of new construction along the east bank of the Pascagoula River. The west bank remained marsh or swamp while the east bank had roads, buildings, and docks. One of the docks, the one just south of the railroad bridge, was clearly public and had several fuel pumps.

He eased up to the pier and moored behind a trawler, the *Three Brothers*, taking on fuel and ice. A sweating, scarecrow of a man working the fuel pump for the trawler waved Mike over.

"What do ya need, friend?" the man said.

"Gasoline," Mike answered.

"No ice?"

"No. Just gasoline."

"I will get to you as soon as I'm done with John."

"That is fine. Do you have a telephone?"

"Yes. In there," the man tossed his head toward a small store on the land side of the pier. "We got one of those fancy pay telephones. You can get the coins you need from the clerk."

"It will be a long-distance call to New Orleans."

The man laughed. "In that case, you better get quarters from the clerk," he said.

Mike entered the store. A young man behind the counter said, "Can I help you, sir?"

Mike dug one of the rumpled dollar bills he had taken from O'Gara out of his pocket and slapped it on the counter.

Mike said, "I want to make a long-distance telephone call."

"Where to?"

"New Orleans."

"A dollar will get you three minutes," the clerk said as he swept the bill from the counter and replaced it with three quarters and five nickels.

Mike walked over to the telephone hanging on the wall next to the door. He put a nickel in the slot and spun the crank.

A switchboard operator came on the line and said, "Number Please."

Mike said, "I would like to place a long-distance call, please."

"What city, please?"

"New Orleans."

"Please deposit forty-five cents."

Mike did so, and he could hear chimes as the coins dropped down the slot. There were some clicks as operators plugged in the appropriate wires and a new voice said, "New Orleans, Number, please.'

"Touro 1587," Mike said.

"Thank you, sir. One moment, please."

Mike heard a few more clicks and then the regular, intermittent buzz of a ring signal.

Annie picked up after only two rings. "Hello?"

"Good morning, Annie," Mike said. "I was worried you might be out shopping."

"I just walked in," Annie said. "Where are you?"

"I am in the thriving port city of Pascagoula."

"I have never heard of Pascagoula. Why are you there and when are you coming home?"

"I am just refueling. I will be home about four in the morning tomorrow. The job took a little longer than I thought, and I didn't want you to worry."

"I am going to worry until you are here with me."

"Annie, I am coming home with an empty boat. There is nothing to worry about."

"Who is with you?"

"No one."

"No deckhands?"

"No. Trust me, it will be fine."

"This is going to take some getting used to," Annie said.

"What is?" Mike asked.

"Being married to a boat captain. It is like being a policeman's wife. Worry is always there."

"I love you, Annie. I will always come home to you."

"I love you, Mike. Please be careful."

"I will see you tonight."

"Goodbye, Mike," Annie said.

Mike said, "Goodbye, Annie." The line went dead.

Mike went back outside. The pump attendant was climbing out of the *Solitario*. He waved Mike over. "I checked both tanks," he said. "The starboard tank can take thirty gallons, the port tank maybe thirty-two."

That was just over half of the *Solitario*'s capacity. He had had enough fuel to return to Bayou Saint John, but just enough.

"Good, Top the tanks off, please."

"Let me tell the clerk what you are getting. You will pay him." The attendant stuck his head in the door of the store and shouted, "Sixty-two gallons gasoline for this gentleman, Jack." He hurried back to the pumps. Mike went back into the store and paid the clerk fifteen dollars and six cents. Expensive, but then, dock-side prices were always high. The clerk handed Mike a hand-written receipt and said, "Thank you, sir. Please come again."

By one o'clock that afternoon, Mike had turned the *Solitario* west as she cleared Singing River Island. He watched the lighthouse on the island slide by on his starboard. In the old days, folks wanting to take a boat east or west along the Mississippi Sound would camp on the island and hang a light. Passing boats, if they had room, would stop and pick them up.

Mike estimated he would make the Rigolets Pass at eleven that night and Bayou Saint John at three in the morning. Considering the extra time spent drifting about unconscious and making a re-fueling side trip, he was right on schedule.

It was a half past two when Mike slowed the throttles and eased into the slip at Bayou Saint John. The *Solitario*, empty of cargo, had made good time with the engines running at a comfortable eighteen-hundred revolution per minute and consuming fuel at a rate of about a gallon and a quarter per hour.

Mike shifted to neutral when he was well away from the slip and went to the exterior pilot station. He guided the coasting boat slowly toward the pier. No one was on the dock to help him moor so he had to run from the pilot station to the mooring lines as the boat gently bumped the dock.

As he was lashing the lines to the mooring cleats, a dozen men carrying lights and guns rushed out from between the fishing cabins shouting, "Police! Hands in the air!"

Mike held his hands up.

A big shadow separated from the crowd and walked up to Mike. Sergeant Macy said, "Good morning, Mister Demill."

CHAPTER 22

Mike, unmoving, held his hands up as one of the officers circled behind him, checking him for weapons. Macy watched Mike's eyes during the process looking for indications of alarm or concern. The officer pulled the Luger from Mike's belt and sniffed the barrel.

"Got a pistol here, Sarge. A Luger and it has been fired recently."

"How recently?" Macy asked, never letting his eyes stray from Mike's.

Mike could hear the Luger's magazine released and the slide toggled to remove the round from the chamber. Then came the sounds of rounds being stripped out of the magazine.

"Been fired five times," the cop said, "assuming it was fully loaded."

"I do not think Mr. Demill is the kind of man to go around without a fully loaded pistol in his belt," Macy said. "What was it they say in the army - 'A full box and one in the pipe'? Isn't that right, Mr. Demill?"

Mike didn't say anything. He wanted to point out that right now his pistol had only three in the box and one in the pipe, but he decided to do the smart thing and just answer questions.

"Where were you?" Macy said.

"Just now?"

"Yes, just now."

"I was running my boat on Lake Pontchartrain."

"We will see," Macy said. "Search the boat, men."

Mike watched as men opened hatches, engine covers and went into the cabin. He could hear them ransacking the berths and opening the galley cabinets. For reasons he did not understand, they didn't open the small drawers where the charts, sextant and other navigational equipment was kept or search small recesses. They ignored the drawer next to the pilot's station where he had placed the bands of bills before tossing O'Gara's bag overboard.

When they were finished ransacking every large storage area they could find, one of the officers, Mike recognized him as Detective Frederick, said, "He ain't carrying no cargo, Sarge. We did find this." He propped the Springfield rifle on his thigh.

"Out all night and carrying no cargo," Macy said. "What were you doing, Demill?"

"I was working on my navigational skills."

Frederick slapped Mike across the back of his head and snarled, "Show some respect, you trash."

"I was working on my navigational skills, Sergeant."

"Do navigational skills include firing a pistol?"

"No, Sergeant."

"Why has your pistol been fired recently?"

"I was shooting rats, Sergeant."

"Rats! On your boat?"

"No, Sergeant. Rats in the water trying to get on my boat. May I put my hands down and turn off the engines?"

"Stay up here on deck," Macy commanded.

"I can shut the engines down from there," Mike said as he nodded toward the exterior pilot's station.

"Go ahead," Macy said.

"But move real slow," Frederick added.

Mike turned off the engines and when he turned around both Frederick and Macy were crowded close to him, forcing him to lean back.

"I am not finished, gentlemen," Mike said. He moved toward the engine covers shouldering his way through several officers. The searching officers had unlatched the engine covers, so he propped them open. He said, "Didn't your daddy teach you to latch all covers?" He touched a few hoses and checked some clamps. He was really looking for any mischief done by the search party. He said, "I want the engines to cool so I can do some maintenance."

"Worry about that on your own time," Macy growled. "We have more questions for you."

Mike looked around and asked, "Where is Jonesy?"

"Who is Jonesy?" Frederick said.

"The old man who looks after the camps. He makes sure nothing gets stolen and the boats stay properly moored. He lives in that first cabin," Mike said, pointing with his chin.

"He is waiting in there," Macy said. "One of my officers is keeping him company. We can all join them. I am not finished with my questions."

"Whatever you say, Sergeant," Mike shrugged. He turned to Frederick. "Put the rifle back where you found it."

Frederick sneered, "You talking to me, trash? That's not how you talk to me, boy-o."

"Detective Frederick. Would you please return my rifle to the rack in the cabin?" Mike asked.

Frederick looked at the rifle then tossed it into the water. He glared back at Mike, a twisted smile across his face.

"Come on, Demill," Macy said. He pulled Mike by the shoulder and directed him up onto the pier. Pushing Mike in front, they all trouped up to the first cabin.

Macy opened the door without knocking and pushed Mike inside. Jonesy was standing at the window facing the slip. He was stooped, his white hair and beard glistened in the lamplight in contrast to his leathery, black skin. His hands were cuffed behind him. Detective Peterson was standing next to him, a hand on Jonesy's shoulder.

"Uncuff the boy and send him out," Macy said.

Peterson unlocked the cuffs and pulled them off Jonesy's wrists. He grabbed the old man by the collar, walked him to the door and pushed him out.

"You do know that this is his home, don't you?" Mike asked.

"He will get over it," Peterson growled.

"Where did you get the cut on your head?" Macy asked.

"I did not duck sufficiently."

"Looks more like a graze wound than anything else to me," Macy said. "Have you been in a gun fight?"

"In France? Many times."

"Not in France, fool. Here, in this country, within the last two days."

"I have had no gunfights in this country in the last two days," Mike said. *International waters are another thing.*

"You know, when we arrest someone, they usually ask what they are being arrested for," Macy said. "You didn't. Why is that?"

"Am I under arrest?"

"What do you...," Frederick started to speak, but Macy cut him off.

"No, you are not under arrest," Macy said.

"Well, there you are, Sergeant," Mike said.

"What does that mean?"

"I am not under arrest, so I can hardly ask why I am under arrest when I am not."

Macy rolled his eyes and let out a puff of breath. "We came here because we had information that you were carrying a large shipment of rum. Rum you picked up from a freighter in the gulf."

"You have been misinformed. Was it the same person who claimed to see me shoot that fellow from Chicago? Somebody's making a fool of you, Sergeant."

Macy's face began to turn red. "Where were you today around noon?"

"Pascagoula Landing," Mike said.

"Where is that?" Frederick barked.

Mike looked at the detective and said, very slowly, "On the Pascagoula River in the town of Pascagoula, Mississippi."

"That is your story," Macy said. "Prove it."

Mike reached into his pocket but stopped instantly when at least three officers pulled their revolvers.

"Easy," Macy said. "Take your hand out of your pocket very slowly."

"Don't you trust Frederick here to do a simple weapons search?" Mike asked. Frederick slapped Mike across the back of his head. Mike stared at Frederick as he produced the receipt from Pascagoula and handed it to Macy. *There will come a time, boy-o.*

Macy read the receipt and then pocketed it in disgust. "I will verify this. For all I know, you a have a pad of blanks you can fill in whenever you need it."

"I am not that smart, Sergeant."

"Well, you think you are, Demill. I am going to be all over you like a coat of paint. You will slip."

"You have the wrong man, Sergeant. I'm just a working man trying to make his way."

"Let's go, boys," Macy said. The officers trooped out until it was just Mike and Macy in the room. Macy stared at Mike for several moments until Mike said, "Anything else, Sergeant?"

Macy let out a "harrumph" and slammed the Luger down on the table. He dumped the magazine and cartridges on top of the gun. The loose rounds rolled about the tabletop. One fell to the floor. Macy stormed out and headed for the row of police cars lined up on the clamshell roadway. Mike came out of the cabin and looked for Jonesy. It was dark, but the setting moon cast enough light to see.

Jonesy was wading in the slip next to the *Solitario*. He stopped, ducked under the water, and came up with the Springfield.

*****

Mike pulled into the garage at his house at two o'clock in the morning. He was beyond tired. He pulled a small leather satchel from the seat next to him and headed toward the back-porch half expecting Annie to be waiting at the door.

She was not waiting at the door. Annie was in the kitchen brewing up a pot of coffee and frying some ham. She walked to meet him in the hall when she heard him come in.

"Sorry I am so late, *mi querida*," Mike said.

Annie stepped into Mike's embrace, kissed him, and then gently touched the wound along his hairline.

"I know you tried your best, *querido*," Annie said. "The police came by earlier, so I expected them to have delayed you for a while."

"Did they talk to you?"

"No, they just drove by the house twice about one in the morning. I'm a policeman's daughter. I know how they work. They were checking to see if you were home. Had you been here, they would have rousted you here. Come, sit down, eat, and tell me what is going on. I think I need to know."

Mike didn't move toward the table. He embraced Annie again and said, "Yesterday, I was finishing a commitment made months ago. The one that would leave me owning the *Solitario* full and clear."

"Something to do with the Irish Republic Movement."

Mike stepped back and held both of Annie's hands. "Yes. You remember O'Gara and Boru."

"I remember you speaking of them. I wouldn't know what they looked like."

"They were some kind of officers in the Movement."

"Were?"

"I brought them along with our tenants, Dorn and Mary Doon, to meet a freighter in the gulf. We were carrying ten tons of cargo packed in crates."

"What was in the crates?"

"I don't know, but I think it was weapons. After the cargo was transferred to the freighter, O'Gara pulled a pistol from his pocket. He said they couldn't trust me because I had been picked up by the police and then let go. He was very apologetic, but he was going to kill me."

Annie traced the wound on Mike's head again. "Clearly, he missed," she said.

"But I did not. And then Boru tried to pull his pistol and I shot him as well."

"Oh, God, Mike," Annie gasped. "What about Dorn and Mary?"

"I don't think they knew what O'Gara and Boru had planned. I let them go. So now you know it all."

Annie kissed Mike again and held him for a long time. He felt her shiver. She finally said, "Sit down and eat. You must be starved. Then you need to get some sleep."

"What is the news on the crevasse?" Mike asked.

"According to today's paper, the water has gone down enough for the roads to be passable," Annie said.

"Good. First thing tomorrow, we will drive down to Yscloskey and get the other truck. Then we will search for some tenants. I do not ever expect to see Dorn or Mary Doon again."

"Do you think we need to worry about retributions?"

"I don't think so. O'Gara and Boru were very secretive. My bet is no one in the Irish Cannel or even other members of the Movement knew they were Sinn Féin. Nothing can be done about it now."

Mike tossed the leather satchel on the table. "At least, there is compensation for our efforts."

Annie opened the satchel. She fumbled through the packets of cash and gasped, "There must be thousands here."

"Twenty thousand to be precise. We will go to the bank first thing tomorrow."

"We cannot just walk into a bank and deposit this kind of money," Annie said. "It will cause suspicion."

"There will be no questions asked at this bank. I will introduce you to a reliable banker."

"This is all so much, Michael."

"Sorry you married me?"

"No, never that. It is just last year I was a bored switchboard operator dreaming of adventure. And now...."

"If we can begin our trucking business, you might go back to being bored."

"I do not think I shall ever hunger for adventure again."

*****

Andrew Galway, vice president of the Hibernia Bank, stood as Mike ushered Annie into his office. He had been told that Mike had married, but this was the first time he had seen the new Mrs. Demill. He was struck by the confidence of her demeanor, her poise, and her beauty.

"Mister Galway," Mike said, "May I introduce you to my wife, Anastazja Norwak Demill." He turned to his wife, "Annie, Mr. Galway. He is the vice president of this bank."

"How do you do, sir," Annie said. She held out her gloved hand, palm down.

Galway took Annie's fingertips, bowed slightly and said, "Mrs. Demill. I am pleased to meet you."

"Please call me 'Annie,' sir."

"Miss Annie, with your permission," Galway said, "Please have a seat." He indicated one of two chairs facing his desk. He had been advised by lawyer Eiseman that it was Mike's intension to have Mrs. Demill included in all business discussions. Galway thought the idea to be quite unwise, but Demill was a large depositor and his peccadillos had to be indulged.

Annie placed her purse on the floor next to her chair, sat and adjusted a canvass bag on her lap. Mike took his chair and nodded to Annie.

Annie began, "Mister Galway, we have a large deposit to make into our –'special'- account."

"Of course, Miss Annie," Galway said as he fumbled for some forms in his desk drawer. "What is the sum of your deposit?"

"Eighteen thousand dollars." Annie placed the canvas bag onto Galway's desk and slid it toward him.

"We, of course, wish to convert the account into a joint account," Mike said.

Galway opened a drawer and pulled out a file. Mike could see his named printed across the file's tab. "Yes, sir. Easily done." Galway leafed through the file, pulled other forms from his desk, and began scribbling away. Some forms he offered to Mike and Annie to sign. Other forms were torn into strips and placed into a steel bucket next to the fireplace in his office.

Galway finished with the paperwork and opened the bag Annie had presented. He pulled nine banded stacks of twenty dollar bills out of the bag and placed them on his desk.

"We can wait until you verify the count," Mike said.

"That won't be necessary," Galway said. He scribbled away on a receipt form. "I am confident all is in order."

"There is one more bit of business, Mister Galway," Mike said. "My wife wishes to open another account under the name 'Anastazja Norwak.'"

"Yes, of course." Galway fished out some more forms. "How much are we depositing into this account. There is a ten-dollar minimum on all new accounts."

"Two thousand dollars," Annie said. She picked up her purse and fished out a single banded set of twenties. "This will be my regular household account and I expect to make deposits and withdrawals through the regular bank tellers."

"Yes, Miss Annie. You will be able to use our regular counter checks and deposit forms for this account."

"Here are the necessary documents for your files," Galway said as he handed a packet of papers to Mike.

"Thank you," Mike said, and he transferred the packet to Annie who folded them neatly and placed them in her purse.

"Is there any other business you wish to discuss?" Galway asked. "Some investments, perhaps?"

Mike and Annie stood which caused Galway to stand as well.

"A pleasure meeting you, Mister Galway," Annie said as she made her way to the door where she waited for Mike.

"The pleasure was all mine, Mrs. Demill. Good day to you both."

Mike opened the door for Annie just as Andy, Andrew Galway's son, was reaching for the knob.

"Oh," the boy said, startled. He addressed Mike. "I was just coming to tell you someone was asking for you."

Mike wondered why anyone would be asking for him at the Hibernia Bank. Who even knew they were here?

"Where is he?" Mike asked.

"A lady was asking for you, sir. I don't see her now."

"Did you say I was here?"

"Well, I – well she seemed to know."

"A lady asked for me and then, after you came to inform me, she left. Is that right?"

"Yes, sir," Andy said. "I'm sorry, sir."

"Describe her."

"Well, she appeared to be about thirty, thin with short blond hair. Very fashionably dressed. Very attractive."

Mike looked at Annie. "Myrtle," he whispered. Annie nodded.

"Andy, go to the door and tell us if you see her outside," Mike said. The young man hurried to the big double doors at the bank's entrance.

"Should we go out the back?" Annie asked.

"No. I am willing to bet that is where she will be. We are going out the front as if we have not a care in the world.

"She isn't out front, Mister Demill," Andy said when he returned.

"Well then, she missed us, Andy," Mike said. "Good day to you."

"Good day, Mister Demill, Mrs. Demill."

Mike and Annie walked out onto the sidewalk into the bright, cool May morning. Annie had her hand in the crook of Mike's left arm.

"Let's go to Turci's for lunch," Mike said. "Then we can go to Yscloskey to get the other truck. We will store it at the old Castro's Livery for now."

"Turci's sounds wonderful to me," Annie said.

*****

The next morning Mike tried to call his Uncle Geronimo in Yscloskey. The operator informed him that the telephone lines were still down because of the crevasse, so he and Annie set out in the new truck. They stopped at a grocery store and picked up several loaves of bread, canned foods, and other staples which they placed in wooden hampers and secured in the bed of the truck.

They next stopped at a service station and purchased two five-gallon gasoline cans, which they had filled and lashed to the running boards of the truck. They drove along Saint Claude Avenue and stopped at the old Castro Livery to inspect their new property and prepare for the activation of the gas lines and installation of electrical service.

Yesterday, Annie had arranged for the telephone service to be activated. The phone number assigned to the building was Bywater 2222. It was a single line, which cost half-again that of a party line. She had pulled some strings with her friends at the telephone company to reserve the '2222' number.

"We need to re-name the building," Annie said. "Fifty-six hundred Saint Claude Avenue just doesn't flow."

"What would 'flow'?" Mike replied.

"We are going to be a trucking company, so we will need a business name. The building would be known by that name."

"Then what do you propose for a business name? What do all those books you checked out of the library on business have to say?"

Annie smirked, "Those are accounting and business management books." She had been studying several books but "Principles of Accounting" by William Paton was quickly becoming her favorite. "What about 'Demill Trucking?'"

Mike thought for a moment then said, "No. I think something like 'Saint Claude Drayage' or the like would be better."

"I like it!" Annie exclaimed. "I will begin the process of registering our trucking business as 'Saint Claude Drayage,' or the like. Tomorrow, with your permission, of course."

"You will be running the business, Annie. Do as you think best."

"Aren't you going to work at our drayage enterprise as well?"

"Of course, I am. I'll do the hauling, hiring, maintenance and such but I would like you to keep the books, you are smarter than I am." *And I might be gone for long stretches of time on other business*, he thought.

Annie used the telephone in the darkened second floor to call the gas company and make arrangements to meet a representative at the building who would inspect the fixtures and activate service. She contacted the electric company and arranged to have a contractor wire the building before adding electrical lighting. Both actions were to begin Monday morning.

Mike listened as Annie conducted business. He was impressed by her professional and confident manor. She hung up the handset and looked at Mike, "Will you please meet these service people here Monday? I am going to be busy picking out light fixtures."

"Yes, ma'am," Mike said. "Now let's get on the road to Yscloskey and retrieve the other half of our transports."

Annie smiled, "Yes, sir."

*****

The road leading from New Orleans was beginning to form a queue just beyond Jackson Barracks where the new road crossed several rail lines leading to the switching yards. The traffic was heavy and though the roadway was paved with clamshells, road repair equipment traveling to and from the restoration efforts at Poydras left a slick layer of mud across both lanes.

Sheriff Deputies at Poydras directed them onto a makeshift track of oyster shells and planking past the great gouge at the foot of the crevasse. Roadway and rail lines were being re-routed around the lake that had been created.

One of the deputies mentioned that a train engine and several cars had been swept into the new lake. The rail line leading along Bayou Terre Aux Boeufs toward Yscloskey was being abandoned and the rails were in the process of being removed. After traveling east few miles they noticed the damage from the river overflow quickly declined until everything appeared normal.

"Nothing will be left of the railroad to Yscloskey," Mike observed.

"Better for our drayage business," Annie said. "Farmers and fishermen will have to truck their goods to New Orleans."

They reached Yscloskey at noon. Mike drove to his uncle's house and saw his other truck sitting on the edge of the road. He had expected it to have been used during the recent emergency to move people and goods away from the flooded areas. It was not parked where he had left it weeks ago.

He pulled up behind the parked truck. Mike and Annie climbed down and walked to the front door of Uncle Geronimo's house. The door opened, and Mike's Aunt Isabella stepped out to greet them, hugging each in turn.

"I am so glad to see you, Miguel," she said in Spanish. "Tío and Zapato are out fishing. Tío said you might come soon for your truck. We saved many things with it. We have no gasoline, I am sorry. It has little fuel."

"That is not important," Mike said. "I left it here to be used as needed. I have fuel for it. I also have some things for you."

Isabella was particularly grateful for the bread as she had run out of flour days ago. Word quickly spread up and down the bayou that visitors had arrived from New Orleans and soon Mike and Annie were inundated with requests. The local store had not been properly resupplied since the flood.

Rail service, the main source of delivery from New Orleans, was no more and the store owner, Antonio Kreider, had tried to bring supplies in by boat, but the Violet Locks had been permanently closed and were in the process of being sealed. Boats could no longer lock in and out of the river, so a trip to

New Orleans by boat had to go through Lake Borgne and Lake Pontchartrain, three times the distance it had been by river.

"This is an opportunity," Annie whispered. "We need to visit Mr. Kreider and arrange for shipments to his store."

Mike filled the tank on the old truck and topped off the new one. Annie slipped behind the wheel of the new truck and allowed Mike to lead the way in the old one. They stopped at Kreider's store and soon Saint Claude Drayage had its first customer. Kreider had ordered enough supplies to fill the flatbeds on both trucks.

The sun was setting when Mike and Annie pulled the trucks into the Saint Claude building. During the drive from Yscloskey, Annie had become an excellent driver. She had managed the skids, ruts, and frequent shifting with increasing skill.

"Tomorrow we will begin filling the trucks," Annie said. She was almost giddy with excitement. "I'll make a few calls and we can pick up everything tomorrow."

"Yes, ma'am," Mike said. "I suggest we take one truck home, get a good night's sleep and start out first thing in the morning. Mr. Kreider will have his goods by noon tomorrow."

CHAPTER 23

May 1922 proved to be a hectic month for the newly founded Saint Claude Drayage Company. What began as a few deliveries of staples to a local store in Yscloskey grew into similar deliveries to local stores in the village of Delacroix. They also offered deliveries of sea food products to New Orleans retailers. These new clients were combined with local drayage runs for the lumber yard and furniture stores. Both trucks and drivers were operating to capacity.

Annie had acquired an Automobile Operator's Permit from the Road Department after some consternation on the part of the local agents. Only a few women had such permits, and none were proposing to drive trucks. Operator's Permits were only required, but rarely enforced, in New Orleans. No permits were needed to operate motor vehicles in Saint Bernard Parish.

"We need to add trucks and drivers to keep up," Annie said after a full twelve-hour day. "If our service slips, many will buy trucks of their own and make their own supply runs rather than pay us."

"I will talk to Father John," Mike answered. "He promised us a list of people looking for work. I doubt if any know how to drive, but we can train them. We can buy four trucks and hire six drivers. You and I will only drive when we are in a pinch."

"We should concentrate on deliveries to small shops or stores, ones that are unlikely to spend the money on their own trucks and drivers."

"Yes, Ma'am."

*****

Father John was true to his word. Mike and Annie met him at his rectory one Wednesday after morning mass. He produced a list of eight candidates. Those that weren't Irish were Italian.

"Times are hard for those new to this country. It takes some time for them to adjust, but to my mind, employers are missing out on some dedicated people."

"Tell me about these people, Father," Mike said. "I want to know more about them. Who among them do you know well?"

"I know them all very well. Two know how to drive. All are regular attendees at Sunday Mass. They are married men with families. It is a struggle to just feed their children. All are family men except Joey Steward. I would consider it a personal favor if you were to hire him."

"Why Steward?" Annie asked.

"He is only fifteen and recently orphaned. He is a good boy but rambunctious."

"What kind of trouble has he been in?" Mike asked.

"Nothing like hurting people or stealing from folks. He was arrested twice for vagrancy. He has no place to live, Mike. He lives on the street, sleeps in alleyways or in boxcars."

"Send him along with the others," Annie said. "We will hire them all."

Mike looked at Annie and raised an eyebrow.

Annie smiled and said, "*Mi querido*, Trucks don't need to sleep, but men do. I propose we begin operations where our trucks rarely stop, we will just change drivers as need be."

"It is decided, then," Mike said. "Father, please tell the men, all of them, to report to Saint Claude Drayage at five p.m. this Friday. If they want the job of truckdriver, we will put them on at seventy-five cents an hour and train them. Those that can already drive, we will pay eighty-five cents an hour."

Mike and Annie enjoyed a leisurely walk home from Saint Maurice Church. They visited a fruit and vegetable stand on the corner of Saint Maurice and Saint Claude. The owner farmed half of the square and the stand was next to his house. His produce was wonderfully fresh, better than most markets where the harvest was days ago and trucked in.

Annie had selected a watermelon and trusted Mike to carry it on his shoulder.

"We will be home in just a few blocks," Annie teased. "I think you will manage." Mike laughed. The melon was not heavy, and it balanced easily on his shoulder.

The Saint Claude building had become "home." The old livery had been upgraded to electrical lighting. Mike had constructed walls to sectioned off a portion of the ground floor into an "Office" and a "Garage." The upstairs could be accessed by an exterior stairway or a set of stairs leading up from the Office.

The Garage had vehicle doors that opened onto the side street, Caffin Avenue, and another set opening onto Saint Claude. There was a separate pedestrian door to Caffin and an entrance to the office from Saint Claude. Indoor plumbing had been added for the upstairs apartment and for the downstairs "Office."

"We will catch the streetcar to Almonaster after breakfast," Mike said. "There are several car dealers there and we can begin building our fleet two trucks at a time."

"There is room for at least twelve trucks in the garage," Annie noted.

"Then we have the room to grow," Mike said as he squeezed Annie's hand. "But first we need to get our drivers trained and introduced to our clients. All things in due time."

After one trip to the bank and two trips to Almonaster Avenue, Saint Claude Drayage owned six trucks neatly housed in the garage. That afternoon, Mike made a lumber delivery and Annie hauled supplies to a general store in Delacroix. Each used one of the new trucks. The next day deliveries were made using the two other new trucks. There were no surprises or breakdowns, though some maintenance needs were noted.

The evening of Friday, June 23rd, found a cluster of men gathered outside of the Saint Claude Avenue entrance to the office. Father John was there as well, escorting a tall young man dressed in rags and barefoot.

Mike came to the door and announced that he would call in applicants one at a time. He referred to a list in his hand and said, "Anthony Rezzato, you are first. Please come in."

A burly man of about thirty-five years stepped forward. "I am Rezzato," he said. Mike stepped aside to allow Rezzato to enter and followed the man in, closing the door behind them.

Annie sat at a desk with a note pad and Mike directed the man to sit in a chair at the desk across from Annie.

"Good evening, Miss," Rezzato said with a nod. He pulled out the chair and sat.

Rezzato was a short man, maybe five feet six, but wide and heavily muscled. His complexion was ruddy from years of labor and his hands were callused. Annie had expected the Italian to be darker, but that was not the case. His hair was light brown, and his eyes were green. A scar divided his left eyebrow.

"Father John reports that you know how to drive," Mike said.

"Yes, sir. I can drive, and I can repair both automobiles and lorries. I was a sergeant of infantry in the Great War. I was wounded and sent to hospital. I had luck. When I had recovered, the Major of Surgeons put me in charge of the ambulance service. We had horses and wagons, but soon we obtained lorries of many different types. I kept everything running."

His accent was deeply Italian, but his English was good. He had bright, intelligent eyes and an easy manner.

"Where did you serve?" Mike asked, more to draw conversation from the man than from a need to know.

"I was at Isonzo. I fought the mountains, the cold and lack of supplies. All I ever saw of the Austrians were cannon shells that fell like rain. Even at hospital, the shells came,"

Annie said, "We have Ford Model T light trucks. Are you familiar with them?"

"Yes, *Signora*. Your little 'trucks,' as you say, are merely automobiles, not true lorries. They are simple machines to keep running."

"Mister Rezzato, come with me into the garage and examine our fleet," Mike said. He led the Italian through a connecting door to the garage. Once there, Mike asked the man to look over the vehicles while he returned to the office.

"That is an easy decision," Annie said as soon as Mike closed the door.

"I'll tell him to report for work Monday at six in the morning," Mike said. "Only seven more interviews to make."

*****

By eight p. m., five other applicants had been interviewed and hired. Father John had been diligent in sending applicants who were family men and capable. Some would need training and most had a good command of the English language.

The last to be interviewed was Brian "Joey" Steward. "This is Joey Steward," Father John said as he positioned the boy front and center at Annie's desk. The boy was tall, about five-ten and sandy haired. His complexion was fair but darkened with weathering and dirt. His clothes were tattered, and ill fitting. He had a canvas bag which he placed on the floor at his bare feet.

"How old are you, young man?" Annie asked.

Father John said, "He is fifteen, I think, but he swears to be eighteen to stay out of the foster home."

"Father," Mike said, "let Mister Steward talk for himself." The priest looked surprised and began to protest but Mike held up his hand. "Please, Father, give us the room. I will walk Mister Steward back to the rectory when we are done."

"He does not live at the rectory," Father John said, pushing out his chin. "There is no place for you to 'bring' him." Father John opened the door to Saint Claude Avenue. "Goodbye," he said. He closed the door firmly as he left.

"I think the good Father was a little miffed at you, *mi querido*," Annie said.

Mike shrugged. "Tell us, Mister Steward, are you sixteen or eighteen or do you even know?"

"I am sixteen, Mister Demill. I am orphaned, not stupid. Father John had it right. I claim eighteen, so the police just put me in jail for vagrancy instead of some hell hole of a foster home. I do not have a home and I very much want to have a job." The boy's accent surprised Mike. Steward looked like every Irish vagabond on the docks, but he sounded like an easterner, and educated.

Mike felt an instant liking for the boy. He said, "Call me Mike. The lady is Miss Annie to you. Tell us how you came into your present circumstance."

"I was living with my parents in Baltimore this time last year. I was going to school and looking forward to attending a University. I wanted to be a lawyer, like my father. Then my father died. They told us it was his heart.

"Dad had left my mother some money, so I stayed in school. One morning about four months ago, my mother told me not to go to school. She had packed her clothes and told me to do the same. We went straight to the train station with two suitcases and one steamer trunk. We bought passage on the first train out of Baltimore. It brought us to New Orleans and my mother rented a house."

"Did she send for the rest of her things? I know she couldn't fit a household of goods into one trunk," Annie said. It had taken her one trunk and a suitcase to move her things from Cicero, and that was only clothes.

"She told me to forget about the things we left behind. She said I couldn't even write to my friends back home."

"What happened to your Mom?"

"She told me she had a job offer and headed to some place on Magazine Street. Four hours later a copper is knocking on the door. He told me my mom was killed. It was a robbery, he said. I had to go with the policeman to identify my mother's body."

"Oh, you poor boy," Annie exclaimed. "How awful."

"I stayed in the house for two weeks. Then the rent was due, so I put on my best clothes, put some more in this bag, and made out as well as I could with the three dollars I had left. I am looking for a job."

"Can you drive?" Mike asked.

"No, but I can learn."

"Do you know anything about automobiles or trucks?"

"No, but I can learn."

"When can you start?" Mike asked.

"Right now," Steward said. "I can mop or sweep or help prepare the trucks. Whatever you need."

"Don't you want to know how much the job pays?"

"Father John said you were paying the men seventy-five cents an hour. I will work for thirty-five. I really need a job."

Annie looked at Mike and he read her eyes.

"This is what I propose, Mister Steward. We will pay you thirty-five cents an hour and we will provide you with a cot in the garage. You can live here until you are able to afford a better place."

The look of relief on the boy's face was heart wrenching. Mike thought the kid might cry.

"Please call me Joey, Mister Mike. Just show me what you need done. Thanks for the job. I will not let you down."

"Come on with me to the garage. I will show you where you are staying."

Joey picked up his bag and began to follow Mike into the garage.

Annie called to them as they went, "I will bring you some stew. You must be starved. You can eat at the work bench."

Joey said, "Yes, Miss Annie. Thank you."

*****

Saturday morning Mike found Joey sweeping the garage and arranging the few tools in the long workbench along the eastern wall. He had cleaned the windows above the bench and light streamed in.

"Good morning, Joey," Mike said, slightly startling the boy as he was arranging wrenches hanging below the windows.

"Good morning, Mister Mike. I didn't know what to do, so I just started cleaning."

"That's fine, but today we need to take one of the trucks to get some lumber and plumbing to add a workman's washroom. Do you know any carpentry?"

"No, sir. But I can learn."

Mike selected one of the trucks near the vehicle doors that opened onto the side street and gave Joey his first lesson on starting the Model "T." Once the truck was running smoothly, Joey opened the garage door and Mike drove onto Caffin Avenue. Joey closed the door and joined Mike in the cab.

After several minutes of instruction and demonstration, Mike drove to a café where he and Joey enjoyed a workman's breakfast of ham and eggs. When they left the café, Mike had Joey take the wheel. In the ten minutes it took to get to the lumber yard, Joey was a competent, if not expert, driver.

The rest of the day was spent planning and constructing the workman's washroom. The floor of the garage was packed dirt, so Mike constructed a raised wooden floor. Plumbing and electrical ties were simple. The piping to the second floor ran along the exterior of the east wall, so both water and sewer taps did not even require digging.

Annie carried down a lunch to them, so they could continue to work with minimum interruption. The project was completed by nightfall.

Joey tested the faucets and flushed the toilet several times. He looked up at Mike with a broad smile. "Been months since I have seen a proper commode, Mister Mike. It is a wonderful thing."

Annie came into the garage with an armful of towels, folded clothes, and a bucket of soap bars. "Can't have a proper worker's washroom without soap and towels. I brought a washboard for you to do your clothes. You can hang them on a line in the garage to dry. I have some bib-overalls and a pair of work shoes for you."

"Miss Annie, I don't want charity."

"It is not charity. The cost is coming out of your paycheck. Now wash up, put on these things and come up for supper."

"Yes, Miss Annie."

Later that night after supper was done and Joey had gone down to the garage, Mike and Annie sat at the kitchen table enjoying some wine.

"What do you think of Joey?" Annie asked.

"It is clear that you like the boy," Mike joked. "I thought you would try for adoption."

"Don't mock me, *mi querido*," Annie said. "How could I not help him? He has had quite a bad time. There were times when I…" She fell silent.

Mike understood. "And I as well," He said. "To your question, he is very bright, hardworking and not afraid to take on anything. We will see if he sticks."

"Next week we all will be running around like a fire brigade," Annie said. "We have deliveries to make, people to train and a business to organize."

"By the time Friday rolls around, I am confident we will have the rough edges smoothed out." He took a long sip of wine. "Which brings me to some other business."

Annie recognized the tone. "Josef Rodriguez business?" She asked.

"In a way. I am going to move the boat to a different slip. It is too public where she is now and in Macy's jurisdiction."

"Where do you want to move her?"

"We are going to buy a piece of land in Saint Bernard Parish. It is very near the cemetery on the right bank of Bayou Terre Aux Boeufs. The land has a farmhouse near the bayou. An old plantation canal, the Kenilworth Canal, comes up from Lake Leary and ends in an oak grove not far from the house but out of sight of passersby. Most people don't even know the canal exists."

"When is the act of sale?"

"I'll have Eiseman come here Wednesday, unless you have an objection."

"Importing is getting so dangerous, Mike."

"I know. Right now, I am just protecting my boat. I have no trips planned and I will not get involved in large shipments anymore. I will leave that to others. Small, very special imports are another matter."

"When are you going to bring her to the new slip?"

"Next Saturday. Do you want to come with me?"

"Yes, I do."

*****

The following week was as hectic as Mike could imagine. Two of the men, Peter Shalia and James Dunnigan, had New Orleans Operator's Permits. Four could drive, but had no permits and two, Joey and Edward O'Brian, would have to be taught to drive, though Joey was proving to be a quick learner.

On Monday, Mike teamed the two men with permits with Joey and O'Brian and sent them in two trucks to the lumber yard. Loading and unloading would go quicker with two men working each truck and driving lessons would be provided along the way.

Rezzato and the other three unpermitted drivers were sent to the courthouse to get Operator's Permits. The process was simple. The applicant would pay fifty cents and he would be presented with a hand-written permit.

Mike and Annie took two trucks and delivered supplies to stores in Delacroix, Yscloskey and Poydras. The store in Poydras was re-stocking after cleaning up from the flood and it required several trips to complete the order.

By the end of the week, a regular routine had developed. Each permitted driver was assigned a truck. Joey and O'Brian accompanied drivers that anticipated heavy lifting. By Thursday, Joey and O'Brian had their permits as well. Joey was officially eighteen according to his permit.

Annie ran the office, set up schedules, and took orders. Mike bought a car. It was a model "T" to keep maintenance simple. He spent most of the last days of the week visiting clients, checking on deliveries, getting office supplies for Annie and, on Friday, visiting their rental properties.

Saturday was the first day of July. Rezzato, who had become the head mechanic and garage boss, was put in charge of the morning deliveries. Mike and Annie caught the streetcar and headed out to the Spanish Fort Resort.

They transferred from the streetcar to the tram at the end of Lafitte Avenue at Bayou Saint John. Instead of following the bayou, the tram headed west before turning toward Lake Pontchartrain at a drainage canal. It paralleled the canal for a few miles through a swampland of clear-cut cypress before turning east to the Spanish Fort Hotel and Park. Beyond the Park was the new Resort.

The tram to the resort carried few passengers this early in the morning. Mike and Annie enjoyed the privacy of a rear section of the car, which was electric so there was no soot to spoil the ride. Annie was captivated by passing landscape of tall reeds, gum trees, willows and cypress saplings scattered among huge stumps.

"The view is fascinating," she said. "I am curious though, why didn't we just take the auto along the road by the bayou?"

"I don't plan on coming back to this slip, so we would have had to have one of the men drive us out. Secondly, I am certain my friend, Sergeant Macy, has people watching that road. This tram ends on the west bank of the bayou across from the slip. We should be gone long before Macy is alerted."

"So how do we cross to the slip?"

"The caretaker for the slip, Jonesy, is going to meet us in a skiff. Jonesy will be making the trip to Kenilworth. He will be working for me as a caretaker. He will be living in the farmhouse where he can care for the boat."

The tram made a sharp turn to the right and the hotel came into view. It was a magnificent structure with a wide gallery that wrapped around the bottom floor. The windows on the upper floor were open and the cool lake breeze had the curtains billowing out.

As the tram progressed further, the large Ferris wheel and buildings of the competing resort could be seen. It was early in the morning and already there were passengers riding the wide bench seats high into the air.

"Some claim that once you reach the apex of the wheel, one can see the north shore," Mike said.

"Oh, my!" Annie exclaimed. She knew the north shore was over twenty miles away. "Truly?"

"No," Mike said. "I put it down to bragging."

The tram made the stop for passengers destined for the hotel. Mike and Annie stepped down. They were the only ones to do so. Everyone else was bound for the new resort. Mike watched the tram trundle around the left turn and head for the last landing at the lake's shore.

Annie was examining the hotel. "What a magnificent building way out here past the swamps."

Mike shrugged. "It was on the bank of the lake until the owners of the resort began filling in along the old jetty. Now it is land locked and dying."

"How sad."

Mike touched Annie's elbow. "Our skiff is here." He pointed toward the bayou. An old black man was standing in the stern of a boat and sculling it toward the bank. The boat nudged the shore, and the man nimbly left his post at the stern and scurried up to the bow where he grabbed a rope and jumped ashore. He pulled the bow against the bank and waited.

Mike led Annie down to the boat. "Annie, this gentleman is William Jones, 'Jonesy' to his friends. Jonesy, my wife, Anastazja Norwak."

Annie offered her hand. Jonesy seemed not to notice. He removed his cap and bowed slightly. "My pleasure, Mistress Demill," he said.

"Please call me 'Annie'."

"Yes, Miss Annie."

"Jonesy, please help Miss Annie aboard. We need to cross now."

"Yes, Mister Mike," Jonesy said. He held out his hand to help Annie into the bow of the skiff. He guided her to a seat near the bow. Mike took a seat in the center of the skiff.

Once the Demills were seated in the skiff, Jonesy pushed the skiff from the bank and nimbly wove between his passengers to resume his location at the stern. He worked the long oar mounted in the transom back and forth, turning the blade slightly with each sweep so the boat surged ahead.

Jonesy maneuvered into the slip and pulled the skiff to the side of the *Solitario*. He grabbed the gunnel and held the skiff steady while Mike helped Annie aboard the boat. Mike climbed up after Annie and Jonesy maneuvered the skiff into the pier. He secured it to the pier with the bow rope and climbed into the *Solitario*.

"Do you have all your goods aboard, Jonesy?" Mike asked.

"Yes, Mister Mike. I have everything I own down in the cabin."

"Good. Be so kind as to cast off the bow line and stand by the stern to cast off once I have her running."

Mike opened the engine hatch covers. He saw Annie watching intently. "I open the covers to insure there are no gasoline fumes collected in the engine compartment that might explode when I engage the starters. Would you like to start the engines?"

"Maybe next time. I want to see you do it first." The idea of an explosion on a boat was something Annie had not contemplated before.

"Come stand by me," Mike said as he took the controls of the exterior pilot's station. "Watch what I do. It is not much more than starting a car or truck."

Mike started the port engine and then the starboard one. Once the engines were running smoothly, he closed the engine covers and dogged them down. He returned to the pilot's station.

"Cast her off, Jonesy," he said.

Jonesy looped the stern line off the piling and began to coil it for storage. The Solitario had been moored bow-on to the bayou, so Mike shifted into slow forward and headed out into Bayou Saint John.

People sitting on the porch of the hotel waved as the *Solitario* slid by. Annie returned the gesture. The people on the Ferris wheel waved and called out as well. Annie had to pull back the brim of her wide straw bonnet to see the top bench of the wheel. She waved and smiled broadly. *There is something special*, she thought, *about putting to sea.*

CHAPTER 24

The *Solitario* had been fitted with a long canvas awning that covered the deck behind the cabin from the exterior pilot's station nearly to the stern. The awning was flat and seven feet above the deck so the view to all sides was not obstructed and most of the rear deck was shaded from the brutal July sun.

Annie was offered a seat on a wide padded bench in front of the engine cowls, but she preferred to stand next to Mike at the pilot's station. She had secured her wide brimmed straw hat to her head with a scarf and faced forward over the top of the cabin so that the wind caused her to squint. She marveled at the sense of freedom and power of it all.

She leaned close to Mike and asked, "How fast are we going?"

"I would say we are doing fifteen knots or so. That's about seventeen miles per hour."

"It seems so much faster."

"We could go much faster, but it would burn a lot of fuel to do so," Mike said, his voice only slightly raised to be heard over the engines. "It will take over nine hours to get to the

Kenilworth landing, provided we don't encounter rough weather."

"It is all so wonderful," Annie said. "I understand why you love this boat so."

"Would you like to take the wheel?" Mike asked. "Jonesy and I have some work to do around the boat."

"I have no idea where we are going."

Mike stepped back slightly. "Here, stand behind the wheel and I'll show you what to do."

He had her slow the throttles and then bring them back to cruising speed. She turned the wheel left and right to get a feel for how the boat reacted.

"You look comfortable now," Mike said. "See the indicator on the compass?"

Annie looked at the binnacle mounted on the back of the cabin. It had a compass card enclosed in glass and filled with a liquid. A brass cover obscured the bottom half of the compass so that only the forward half could be seen. A line, the indicator, was inscribed on the glass. The line was just to the right of the number "50."

"If you turn a little to the right, you will see the compass turn so the indicator will read a higher number. Left will make the numbers lower. We are running northeast by east. Steer so the compass reads '53.' We will run on this heading for about an hour."

Mike pointed to the right. "See that sliver of the shoreline? If it seems to get closer, steer left slightly."

He pointed left. "Those boats on the horizon to the north are trawling and should not be a problem. Nothing ahead, as far as I can tell. If something happens, just throttle back, I will not be far from you."

Annie could see specks where the water met the sky far off to the left. She supposed those to be the trawling boats Mike had talked about. There was nothing but water straight ahead. The boat ran easily in the slight chop and holding the heading was easy once she got the feel of it.

Gradually, the shoreline to her right seemed to creep closer. She turned the wheel a little to the left until the compass read "40."

"Mike," Annie called over her shoulder. "We are running on a heading of forty and the shore to the right is still getting closer."

Mike stepped up next to Annie.

"We are getting close to Point Aux Herbes. You see that straight line crossing the horizon? That is the North Eastern Railroad bridge. We will follow along until we get to a drawbridge in the railway. They will open the bridge for us when we get there. We may have to wait for a train to pass. I will take her from here."

"I think I see the train now," Annie said as she pointed toward the southwest where a column of smoke rose above a long, black line along the lake shore.

"That is the east bound train. We will reach the south drawbridge shortly after she clears it."

Mike positioned the *Solitario* perpendicular to the drawbridge just as the east bound train steamed across. Three minutes lapsed before the last car cleared the span.

"Give 'm a call, Jonesy," Mike said.

Jonesy put a horn to his lips and blew a single, long blast. It was answered by a blast from the bridge operator's shack. Slowly the bridge began to lift to allow passage of boats beneath. Two trawlers were waiting on the east side of the bridge and, because the tide was running in, Mike maneuvered to the south to allow them to pass under the bridge first. Once the trawlers were clear, Mike powered through.

Annie noticed that the compass heading was ninety degrees when Mike finally set the throttle at cruising speed.

Mike saw that Annie was interested in the heading. "We are bound for the Rigolets Pass," he said. "If we were to head south, we would be at the Chef Menteur Pass. If we were going to Yscloskey, that is the way. We are headed through the Rigolets bound for the Chandeleur Sound.

Passage under the L&N required no waiting time at all. The bridge was a pike span. The movable section was centered on a great base and it was rotated into the open position when they rounded the bend in the bayou.

They continued on a southeast by east heading into the Mississippi Sound for a half-hour.

"Mister Mike," Jonesy called from his position atop the cabin, "I can see Malheureux Point almost dead ahead."

"I see it," Mike called. "There will be a pole at Three Mile Pass. We should see it in a half-hour." He turned to Annie. "We will cut through some little bays to the Chandeleur Sound. It will save time, but we need to be careful. These bays are shallow."

"It all looks the same to me," Annie said. "What isn't open water is tall cane and scrub brush."

"It does look that way. When we cross the Chandeleur Sound we will stop at Grand Gosier Island for a little picnic. How does that sound?"

"A picnic on the boat in the middle of the ocean?"

"No, we will go ashore and picnic on the finest white sand beach you ever did see. It will be noon and Jonesy packed a lunch."

"What did you bring for lunch, Jonesy?" Annie asked.

Jonesy answered without taking his eyes off the horizon. "I got some good red wine, slices of ham and bread along with a watermelon all packed in the galley ice box. Got enough ice to keep it all cool until noon tomorrow."

It took two hours to thread the *Solitario* through the maze of bays and narrow cuts before breaking out into the expanse of the Chandeleur Sound. Another hour and a half passed before Mike eased back on the throttle.

"Grand Gosier Island dead ahead," Jonesy said.

"I thought we were well at sea," Annie said. "It has been an hour since I last saw any hint of land."

"See that small bump in the sea ahead?" Mike pointed toward a part of the sea that had some green turfs on motionless mounds. "That island is five miles long but only three hundred yards wide, at the widest point. The Gulf of Mexico is on the other side. We are going to anchor on this side where we are protected from the surf and go ashore."

"How are we to get ashore?" Annie asked. "Do we have to swim?"

"We could wade ashore. The water will be only four feet deep where we anchor," Mike said. "But you are wearing such a pretty dress and we wouldn't want to ruin your shoes."

Mike slowed the boat just a few yards from the shore of the island. Jonesy tossed a stern anchor over, pulled to make certain it dug in and then set a bow anchor.

"She's set fore and aft, Mister Mike," he said when he was done.

"Give me a hand with the bateau, Jonesy," Mike said as he unlatched a set of hatch covers. He opened the cover to reveal a hole filled with equipment. A small, rectangular boat lay inverted atop the other gear. It was made of a thin cypress planking and the men easily lifted it from the hole and put it into the water. They placed an oar, a folding table and two stools into the boat.

"Only two stools?" Annie asked.

"I'm staying on the *Solitario*, Miss Annie," Jonesy said.

Annie watched the loading process. When she looked over the side, she was surprised to see the sandy sea floor seemingly inches below the skiff. She had become so accustomed to the murky waters of the bayous and rivers inland that the clarity of the water was astonishing.

"It is not always that clear," Mike said. "This time of year, if the currents are right and the winds mild, you can sometimes see the bottom in fifteen feet of water." He held out his hand, "Climb aboard and we will go to the beach."

"Just a minute," Annie said. She unlaced her shoes, removed them, and placed them on the deck. She then reached back between her legs and grasped the hem of her dress. She pulled it forward and tucked the end into her belt, freeing her stockinged legs from the knee down. "No fear of ruing my shoes nor tripping over my dress."

"You remind me of Persian Guards with their great billowing trousers," Mike said. "I admit that I find the look most becoming."

Annie climbed into the bateau and took a seat in the bow. Mike followed her aboard. Jonesy handed down a basket of wine, bread, and sliced ham from the ice box. He made another trip to bring the watermelon. It was cold from lying next to the block of ice in the ice box. Annie insisted he cut the melon in half and keep some for himself.

Mike used the oar to push the bateau to the beach. He didn't row, he pushed against the hard sand until the skiff slid up on the beach. He stepped out and pulled the boat onto the beach. Annie stepped out without even wetting her feet.

"You could have left your shoes on," Mike said.

"And miss the marvelous feeling of warm, dry sand under my feet? I might pull my stockings off."

Mike smiled broadly and said, "Let's go to the far side of the island and set up our table."

They worked their way between small dunes crowned with tufts of grass. The sand was the whitest Annie had ever seen. When they reached the east side of the island there was a gentle surf running along the beach. Mike set up the table and chairs just above the wash line.

The beautiful beach was deserted and pristine as far as Annie could see. She and Mike were completely alone, isolated as if in a dream and the world had transformed into a painting.

To the west, across the island, she could see the *Solitario* calmly at anchor. She could not see Jonesy. He was likely on the rear deck enjoying his meal. To the east the far blue-green sea was alive with a small chop over long rollers that came crashing onto the beach.

The sky was cloudless, and the sun glared down with a blinding light that reflected off sand and sea. Annie was glad she had the protection of her wide-brimmed straw hat and long-sleeved dress. The day was hot, but the wind from the east moderated the heat.

Sand crabs scurried away as foaming sea water surged up the beach and then reversed to chase the receding water's edge. The air smelled of sea, sand, and purity.

"It is as if I am in a dream," Annie said.

Mike handed Annie a glass of red wine. "Come and sit. We have thinly sliced smoked ham and the finest bread you will ever taste."

"Did you come here often when you were a boy?" Annie asked as she accepted the wine.

"Quite often. My father and grandfather would bring wood and we would build a fire to cook fish. Most of the fishermen preferred to eat on their boats and keep trawling. But my grandfather preferred to stop on one of these sand islands. He always chose islands that didn't have trees or heavy brush."

"Why was that?"

"Some islands, like Breton Island over there, have enough vegetation to support rabbits, racoons and nesting birds." Mike pointed to the west. "Where there are animals, there are flies. Nothing ruins a meal as completely as a swarm of biting flies." Annie could not see any indication of an island in the direction Mike pointed, just water.

"I remember how flies used to swarm around the stockyards in Chicago," Annie said. "They were unbearable."

Mike smiled, "My grandfather talked about how vicious the flies were during the summer in Canada. He said nothing down here compared."

"Your grandfather was not born here?"

"He was born in New Orleans. He had distant relatives in Saint Bernard, but his family operated a steamboat company. Then came the Civil War and my grandfather's family sided with the Union. They lost everything. After the war, the family was dispersed. My grandfather changed his name and came here to escape from old enemies seeking revenge. My father and his brothers were born here, as was I."

"Surely the old feuds have been forgotten by now," Annie said. "The Civil War ended nearly sixty years ago."

"There is more to the story." Mike refilled Annie's glass. "It is a story that will wait for another day. It is too beautiful here to speak of bad times."

Annie knew that Mike had a distain for the Federal Government that she had attributed to Southern resentment of defeat in the Civil War. Once she had asked him about his service in the Great War and he simply replied, "I was drafted." Satisfied that she would eventually learn the details, she didn't press the issue.

"What is that?" Annie asked as she pointed east. She had noticed something growing on the horizon.

"It is a ship."

"Are we close to shipping lanes?"

"No. Any ship you see from this island is not headed for anywhere else. It is coming here. It will stop engines and drift. Soon, fishing boats will visit the ship and buy contraband. Cheap stuff, not the quality rum we brought in."

"In broad daylight?"

"Yes. It is international waters, and the only threat is from hijackers. Every trawler captain used to bring cash for just such an opportunity. Hijackers began to intercept and rob trawlers, so the captains switched to working in fleets of four or more.

"More organized importers contracted with distillers in Cuba, so the boat captains need not have cash on them to buy from the ships. Now the hijackers have switched to ambushing the cargo before it gets to the warehouses. Criminals have made the business very risky."

It was time to go. Mike and Annie collected their things and returned to the bateau. The picnic was over much too soon for Annie. She knew the magic of the place and the moment would be something she would carry with her for the rest of her life.

Once aboard the *Solitario*, Mike and Jonesy quickly stored everything away until the rear deck was clear of all clutter.

"Mister Mike," Jonesy said as they opened the engine covers to clear any possible fumes. "I could see some smoke in the direction of Stone Island a while ago."

Mike frowned. "Where? I didn't see any."

"That way, Mister Mike." Jonesy pointed toward the northwest.

"That is in the direction of Mozambique Point," Mike said. Mozambique Point was at the mouth of Bayou Terre Aux Boeufs. "That is where we are headed. Let's get the anchors aboard, Jonesy. We need to get underway."

Annie asked, "Could it have been from a ship?" The direction appeared to her to be open water to the horizon.

"No ships. The water is too shallow. Except for a few holes, Chandeleur Sound is no more than fifteen feet deep. It is a windy day, so exhaust from a shrimp boat would not climb. It requires something larger to make enough smoke to be seen."

Mike turned to a heading of two eighty-seven and throttled forward. Annie noticed the boat's speed was greater than normal.

"Jonesy," Mike said. "Go below and get our rifles. Make certain they are both loaded."

Jonesy disappeared into the cabin and returned with two rifles. One Annie recognized as a Springfield '06. The other was new to her. Jonesy slung the Springfield over his shoulder and handed the other to Mike who set the weapon in a cradle next to the pilot's station.

"What kind of rifle is that?" Annie asked.

"It is a Browning Automatic Rifle - a B-A-R. I never used one when I was in France, but our friend, Fritz the gunsmith, highly recommended it for discouraging boarders at sea."

"A little smoke concerns you so?"

"One very plausible reason for the smoke is a burning boat. It is better to be armed and ready when nothing threatens than to be unarmed when something does."

Annie watched the horizon ahead intently. She had stepped up onto a box next to Mike's position at the pilot's station to gain an unobstructed view forward across the top of the cabin. She had to hold her hat as the wind threatened to pull it free of the ribbon holding it in place.

She noticed a subtle change in the horizon. A thin, gray streak began to develop to the right. Soon the gray was topped by green, and a pole appeared dead ahead. Something was placed on the top of the pole.

"That marks the channel of Mozambique Point, the entrance to Bayou Terre Aux Boeufs," Mike explained. "Fishermen set the pole and the jug on top to help identify the entrance. Stray far from the marker and you are aground."

The green proved to be a sea of tall canes, Mike called them "roseaux," that waved in undulating ripples imitating the waters of the sound. Smoldering wreckage bobbed about the shoreline. The largest piece appeared to be the bow of a trawler.

Mike shifted into reverse and backed slowly away until he was three hundred yards from the shore. The men put the bateau into the sea and Jonesy climbed in.

"After you look at the hull, check the shoreline for signs of people going into the cane," Mike said. Jonesy was going to go alone while Mike kept the *Solitario* positioned.

"We can't see any boats coming out of the bayou from here," Mike explained. "I don't want to be away from the boat if something comes out of the bayou."

Mike and Annie watched intently as Jonesy first visited the remnants of the boat. He was able to position the bateau over the inclined deck and investigate an open hatch. He looked back at the *Solitario* and shook his head slowly.

Jonesy then poled the bateau along the shoreline searching for signs of someone having gone ashore. The tide was low, so any movement from the water would have left a wide trail in the mud. He returned to report he found nothing explaining what had happened, nor any sign of survivors.

"There were some words on the part of the bow," Jonesy said. "I could make out part of the boat's name. It had an 'IN' and then 'TOSS'."

"The *Captain Toss*," Mike exclaimed. "I know the boat. She belongs to John Donavich. He has oyster leases in the eastern part of Lake Borgne fifty miles or more from here. What would that lugger be doing in this part of the Chandeleur Sound?"

"Perhaps he was hijacked." Annie suggested.

Mike thought a while then said, "No. I don't think so. The *Captain Toss* was an inland oyster lugger, converted from sail. She could make no more than eight knots and she was low in the water. Not the kind of boat to make a run into the gulf."

The men stowed the bateau and Mike directed the *Solitario* past the channel marker into Bayou Terre Aux Boeufs. Soon small camps and farms began to appear along the bayou as they motored inland.

"I am going below, Mister Mike," Jonesy said. "If that is alright with you, sir."

"Go ahead, Jonesy," Mike said. "Catch some sleep."

Annie waited until Jonesy was gone and then she whispered to Mike, "Something wrong with Jonesy? He did not look well."

"With good reason," Mike said. "We are approaching Delacroix Island. You will recognize it from your many deliveries there. Twenty-six years ago, the very year I was born, was a time of turmoil. Work and money were scarce, and the sugar plantations were going bankrupt. Politicians blamed freed slaves for the bad economic conditions.

"People would be harassed on the road. Some were even threatened in their homes. The men appointed by the Union Army to keep the peace were ignored or even harassed. Some men went so far as to appoint themselves as judges. It was a rebellion of sorts. My father and grandfather tried to reason with the people. They thought they had succeeded.

"Then a group of freed slaves gathered at a store owned by an *Isleño*. They wanted whiskey, which the man refused to sell. The store, which was also the man's home, was burned and the storekeeper was killed. His wife and child escaped to hide in the sugar cane field.

"A mob formed. People, mostly freed slaves, were attacked. Nobody knows how many were killed. Jonesy remembers when that happened. It was a bad time to be a freed slave in New Orleans and especially Saint Bernard. He is not comfortable this far beyond the city. Resentments run deep."

"But everybody I have met has been so kind, hospitable and willing to share," Annie said.

"A mob is a terrible thing, *mi querida*. Every lie is believed, reason is rejected, and no one listens. Wars are often mob hysteria on a national scale."

"But you fought in a war. You fought for this country."

"I did, but I was under no illusion that what I was doing was noble. I did what I had to do to survive."

Annie was surprised. She did not understand this man she loved. He sounded like a preacher, but she had known him to do, had seen him do, courageous, violent things. He killed Porkins quickly, seemingly without thinking, when his uncle and cousin were threatened. And then there were those two Irishmen.

Mike noticed Annie's expression. He said, "Do you think less of me now that you know I was not an eager warrior?"

"No, *mi querido*," She said. "I think I even love you more." She kissed Mike's mouth - hard.

The village of Delacroix appeared along the bank of the bayou. Most of the homes and all the shops were along the right side of their line of travel. A few buildings, mostly fishing and trapping camps, dotted the left. It was getting late in the day and some boats had returned from a day of fishing.

Mike had the boat running a slow, wake-less speed. People they passed, both ashore and in boats, waved. Annie and Mike returned every wave. Often someone would shout, "¡*Hola, Miguel!*"

"Everyone seems to know you," Annie said.

"They know the boat and have heard of my encounter with the hijackers," Mike smiled. "I am believed to be a thoroughly dangerous man, but on their side."

They approached a wide bayou joining Terre Aux Boeufs on the left. Mike spun the wheel, and they entered this new bayou, leaving the village behind. Mike throttled up to cruising speed as they broke out into a wide lake.

"Lake Lery," Mike said. "We are almost there." He raised his voice, "Jonesy, get to the bow."

Jonesy came on deck, looked about cautiously, and walked around the cabin to the foredeck.

It appeared to Annie that Mike was going to run the *Solitario* into the bank of the lake. She was just about to say something when Mike slowed the boat. Just when she was certain they would strike bottom, a cut appeared angled sharply to the right. The waterway appeared natural but was deep. Mike steered into the bayou.

After a quarter mile or so, Mike slowed until the boat was almost stationary.

"There it is," Jonesy said. He was pointing to an indentation in a flowing sea of roseaux between two clumps of scrub oak trees. Mike nudged the bow into the indentation, and it proved to be the entrance to a canal. He increased the power to a moderate speed.

The tree and reed covered shoreline of the canal swept by. Annie watched as an alligator plunged into the water ahead of the boat. She noticed that the level of the water in the canal seemed to rise as they approached and then fall quickly in their wake. The trees on either bank seemed to reach across the water until she felt she could touch the tips of the branches. *Deepest Africa could not be wilder*, she thought.

"I have to be careful not to go too fast," Mike said. "If I push too much water, she'll bottom out. We have three miles to go."

Eventually the trees on either bank became great oaks and a mud trail appeared on the left side. Mike shifted into neutral and allowed the boat to drift forward. Without the engines pushing against the confined waters of the canal, the stern seemed to rise.

Jonesy scrambled to the left side of the boat just as a piling came into view. He jumped onto a pier and guided the *Solitario* into position. He tied the bow line to a cleat and walked along the pier to receive the stern line from Mike.

Mike killed the engines and climbed onto the pier. "We are here, *mi querida*." He held out a hand to help Annie onto the pier. She stepped onto the dock, which was newly constructed, and walked to the bank of the canal where a dirt road began.

It was not a true road, but a narrow set of ruts through the trees. There were no other signs of civilization.

"Walk with me up to the house," Mike said. "You will soon recognize the surroundings."

The going was not difficult as they walked between the ruts. Several twists and turns prevented Annie from seeing any more than a few hundred feet ahead. Then the road climbed up a long mound that crossed at right angles. It was the foundation of a railroad.

"This is the railroad dump," Mike said. "Look to your left."

The rails and ties had been removed, but the mound of earth that had supported the ties had been smoothed into a road. She could see the cemetery off to the left and the old rail landing. There was a truck parked next to the landing.

"Isn't that one of our trucks?" Annie asked.

"Yes. I had Joey and Peter Shalia drop it off. We needed a way to get home. Come, let me show you the house."

They walked a little further along the road to a small frame house next to Bayou Terre Aux Boeufs. Across the bayou was the road to New Orleans that Annie had driven many times. There was no bridge to the road.

"Jonesy will be living here," Mike explained. "No need for a crossing to the main road. We really don't want visitors. He will have a vegetable garden and we will bring him supplies from time to time. Let's go get the truck and help Jonesy move supplies."

Mike and Annie walked to the truck and started it up. The engine was still warm, so Joey must have just dropped it off. They drove back along the old railroad bed to the crossing and turned toward the Kenilworth landing to help move Jonesy into the house.

CHAPTER 25

Monday began with a flurry of activity. Saint Claude Drayage was gaining a reputation as the people to contact if you needed it delivered today. Before the sun had cleared the horizon, a half-dozen trucks poured out of the garage, destined for points up and down the river.

Two trucks headed for the lumberyard carrying two men each, to have more muscle loading and unloading. The rest of the trucks headed toward the river docks for short haul contracts. Some retrieved stock from warehouses for retailers. One was dispatched to fetch machine parts from a mishandled boxcar left on a siding in the Carrollton Avenue switching yard and bring them to the sugar refinery on Saint Peters Street.

Once the trucks had been dispatched, Annie and Mike were able to enjoy a leisurely breakfast and discuss plans. There was the possibility that two more trucks might be added to the fleet, especially if longer hauls were a possibility. Roadways within the city were often paved with stones, clamshells, or bricks. Hauls outside of the city were a problem. Roads beyond the city were compacted dirt, which meant they were rutted mud trails for most of the year.

The exception to generally deplorable transportation conditions were the narrow paths that paralleled railroad lines. The drainage and maintenance provided by the railroad companies to their lines inadvertently benefited these roads.

Mike planned to follow the path along the now abandoned railroad toward Shell Beach and contact farmers who had relied upon the railroad to bring their produce to market. There was talk of forming a farmers' cooperative to provide transportation for crops. Mike was certain he could offer at least an interim service, or contract as the provider for the cooperative.

Mike was preparing to go down to the garage when Annie stopped him.

"I just read something in the morning paper," she said, "that you need to see." She handed him a copy of the July 3rd Item. The article read:

"Oyster Lugger Disappears.

"The charred wreckage of the oyster dredge 'Captain Toss' was discovered in Black Lake by local fishermen. The lugger was owned and captained by John Donavich, a resident of Violet. When this correspondent contacted Captain Donavich, he refused to explain how his lugger came to be found in Black Lake, a body of water where Donavich held no leases."

"Now that is interesting," Mike said. "I was afraid we might have lost John."

"Do you know him?" Annie asked.

"In a way. He used to accuse me of poaching his leases. One of the Captains in his fleet, McDae, is reputed to run with the Hadens. McDae is a man I am better acquainted with."

"In what way?"

"He tried to intercept a boat Josef Rodriguez was shepherding. I had to fire several rifle rounds into his engine to ward him off."

"Was he trying to hijack you?"

"I did not attempt to verify that fact. He acted like a hijacker, so I warned him away." Mike left off the detail that McDae's deckhands were armed with pistols and fired several rounds in his direction.

"Also, there was an article on the Saint Bernard Parish Road Commission," Annie continued. "It seems the parish government is going to improve the road between New Orleans and the Poydras Junction. The farmers along that route are desperate to keep their crops flowing to New Orleans and the single remaining railroad is not sufficient."

"The farmers pushing for roadwork are the very people I am visiting today," Mike said. "The majority are Italians who bought up strips of failed sugarcane plantations. We have the perfect drivers to serve their needs."

At the turn of the century, landowners of the failed sugar cane plantations hit upon the plan to divide the land into smaller parcels and advertised family farmland for sale. The advertisements were made in Sicily. Nearly a hundred families immigrated to south Louisiana, bought strips of land, and converted the fields from sugar cane to a variety of food crops.

The remaining railroad along the river was dedicated to a paper and lumber group. It would not consider multiple produce stops and frequent trips.

Mike followed the road along the river and had no problems signing a dozen farmers to contracts. He negotiated agreements that were flexible and scheduled transportation dates to meet the seasonal needs of the crops.

Mike ended his sales trip at the Violet Canal Locks. The locks were in the process of being decommissioned. The locking fees paid by barge and other commercial traffic had shifted to the new, larger locks at the Industrial Canal. The Violet Canal would still be the home port for commercial fishermen who, now cut off from the Mississippi River, would need their catch transported to the city.

Mike pulled off the road into a boatyard on the bank of the canal. He could see a large boat under construction. From the shape of her keel and the span of her ribs, Mike knew it was to be an oyster lugger. He walked up to a man directing workers.

"Good afternoon," Mike said.

He spoke in English because that was the language being shouted about the construction area. The man turned around. It was John Donavich.

"Mike Demill," Donavich exclaimed. "I had heard you gave up poaching." He glanced toward Mike's car. "Your new line of work seems to suit you."

"It suits me fine," Mike said. "I had heard you sank the *Captain Toss*."

Donavich's face darkened. "You heard wrong, Demill. I sold the *Captain Toss*. It was her new owner that put her on the peak."

The "peak" was a shoal near Freemason Island in the Chandeleur Sound. Navigational charts sometimes labeled the general vicinity of the shoal as "shell reefs."

Fishermen familiar with the area scoffed at the designation of "shell reefs." Those who claimed to have examined the shoal swore it was a mound of granite blocks coming up through the bottom of the sound to within a few feet of the surface, like the top of a pyramid.

"Sold her?" Mike asked. He could not imagine Donavich selling the old, converted sail lugger. The man had grown up on the *Captain Toss*. "Who bought her?"

"None of your business, Demill," Donavich said. "What brings you here?"

"My business," Mike said. "Saint Claude Drayage. We run a fleet of trucks serving short hauls to and from New Orleans."

"Short hauls, you say?"

"Short hauls, and no load is too small."

"I need fittings, marine screws and hardware for the *Lady Toss*," Donavich said as he tilted his head toward the lugger. "I was going to have to go myself, in a buggy, to the foot of Amelia Street and buy four crates of hardware. It will take me all day tomorrow if I set out at dawn. How long will it take you?"

"Give me the list and I can have those crates here for noon tomorrow, provided Amelia Marine has what you need."

"How much?"

"Let me see the list," Mike said. Donavich handed Mike a rumpled paper with several scribbled notes.

"Sixteen dollars for hauling and three percent financing. We buy the hardware, bring it to you and charge you a three percent mark-up."

"Do it," Donavich said.

Mike called Annie as soon as he could find a telephone. He dictated the list of items, the estimated cost, and the terms of delivery.

"Joey and Peter are due back here any minute now," Annie said. "I can have them go pick these up today and bring them down to Donavich tomorrow. Are you certain Mister Donavich is good for it?"

"I am not worried. If he doesn't pay us, we can sell the parts up and down the bayou for a better profit," Mike said. "I am going to talk to others here at the canal. The loss of the local passenger line has caused a lot of problems that we can fix."

*****

Mike arrived home at seven in the evening. It was July and still full daylight. He parked the car in the garage, and he noticed one of the trucks loaded with marine parts and ready to go in the morning. Joey was not there, but Annie was in the office going over the books.

"How much did we have to pay for the truck load of parts?" Mike asked.

"One hundred-two dollars and eighty-two cents," Annie said sternly.

"So, our bill to Donavich will be-," Mike paused to do some mental calculations, "nearly one hundred twenty-two dollars."

"One hundred twenty-one dollars and ninety cents," Annie said. "I have prepared the invoice. I think it best you make this delivery."

"Yes, Ma'am," Mike smiled. "Still worried about Donavich cheating us?"

"No. I would just feel better if you would do it. Now come upstairs for supper."

"Where is Joey?"

"He already ate and is on another run. We can't seem to keep up with the orders."

"It is a good problem to have," Mike said as he kissed Annie.

After supper, Mike and Annie were sitting at the table discussing the possibility of adding trucks or even buying a lorry.

"After I talked to Donavich, I chatted with some of the laborers working on his new lugger. They told me that Donavich sold the *Captain Toss* to Danny Haden. The way they tell it, the sale was somewhat reluctant. McDae left Donavich's fleet and is working for Haden."

"What does that matter to you?" Annie asked. "Josef Rodriguez has retired."

"True, but if Haden is operating several boats out of Violet, it could be a problem for my friends, particularly if he is still in the hijacking business."

*****

Donavich was true to his word. He paid the shipping costs and financing fee without complaint. He then made a second order twice as large as the first. This time he paid for the parts in advance.

"This is two truckloads of material," Mike said. "The shipping fees will be thirty-six dollars."

"Fine with me, Demill. Just get the stuff to me. Any delay and I might not get my boat in the water in time."

It was July. No oysters would be harvested for two months, but Donavich could not seed his lease sites or work on developing new sites. He would need to enlist other boats come harvest time, though the *Lady Toss* was going to be half-again the size of Donavich's old boat.

Across the canal, about a hundred yards away, Mike could see McDae's boat, the *Isle of Hvar*, moored at a long pier. Two other boats, the trawlers *Rio Perdido* and *Rosa Amarilla*, were moored at the same pier. These trawlers did not have lines or configurations consistent with local boats. They were low in the bow and narrow of beam. Mike guessed they drew five feet of water or more.

A fancy touring car, a Duesenberg, pulled into the loading area next to the *Isle of Hvar*.

"There's Danny Haden now," Donavich said. "Come to check on his new fleet. The man knows nothing about dredging, trawling or seamanship."

Mike had never seen Danny Haden and he watched intently as the driver of the car climbed out and opened the rear door. A man stepped out, straightened his grey, pin-striped suit coat and put on a black fedora. Mike could see the high polish of his shoes and tight pleat of his trousers. A large, sparkling stickpin anchored a red silk tie in place.

"I will wager he will never be aboard one of those boats when they get underway," Mike said.

Donavich grunted his consent.

Haden held out his hand toward the still-open door of the Duesy. A lady's hand appeared. Danny took the hand and assisted her out of the car. She was dressed in a tight, silvery dress, long gloves, and a pill-box hat. It was Myrtle.

"I will be damned," Mike muttered.

"That is an expensive piece of equipment," Donavich said.

"Sure is," Mike said. *So is the car.*

"The flapper is Myrtle Schaumburg, or so they say. Came down from Chicago with a fellow named Ruttan. Danny takes one look at Schaumburg, and Ruttan gets a bad case of lead poisoning."

Now it was beginning to make sense. Ruttan was a small-time killer. There was no way he could compete with the kind of money Danny tossed around. Mike wondered if Danny did the deed himself. He was willing to bet it was Myrtle who called the tip into Macy.

Mike tucked Donavich's parts order and cash into a leather case. He offered his hand to Donavich. "You can expect delivery at this time tomorrow," Mike said. "Now, I think I shall make a sales contact across the canal."

"To that bunch!" Donavich exclaimed. "I have never seen them do a lick of work the entire time they have been berthed in the canal. All they do is lay about and drink beer."

"You can never catch shrimp," Mike said, "unless you pull a trawl."

Mike climbed into his car, placed the leather case on the seat next to him and started his car.

"Be careful, Demill," Donavich said. "That's my money you have."

Mike drove to the road and crossed the canal on the top of the closed inside lock. He turned into the loading area and parked next to the Duesy. Haden's driver took up a defensive position next to the fancy town car to prevent Mike from parking too close.

Mike got out and walked over to the pier where Hayden was eyeing him suspiciously. Myrtle stepped next to Hayden and whispered something into the man's ear.

"What do you want, Demill?" Hayden sneered.

"You have the advantage of me, sir," Mike said. "I don't think we have been introduced."

"I am Danny Haden, and you know it."

Mike touched his hat, "And the lady?"

"State your business, Demill, or I will have you tossed off this pier."

"I was simply inquiring if you would be interested in a hauling service," Mike said. He never let his eyes wander from Myrtle's. She was smiling, almost laughing. Her eyes twinkled mischievously.

"Boys," Hayden shouted over his shoulder, "toss this bum off my pier."

Captain McDae and two very large men climbed out of the *Isle of Hvar* and began to walk toward Mike.

"I will be on my way," Mike said. "I can see that you are not interested in my service." Mike stepped off the pier and began to back toward his car. McDae, followed by his cohorts, continued to advance until Mike reached behind his waist and gripped the Luger.

McDae stopped short. The two men following bumped into their Captain.

"I have a bone to pick with you, Demill," McDae growled. "This ain't over. Not by a long shot."

"Good day gentlemen," Mike said, "and to you, Miss." He tipped his hat and climbed into his car. He drew the pistol and placed it on his lap. No need to give anyone the chance to rush him. He started up the car and reversed out of the loading area.

As he drove across the lock, he looked right to see Donavich shaking his head slowly.

Mike parked in the garage at Saint Claude and entered the office. Annie was sitting at her desk, working away. Mike plopped the leather case down on the desk.

"Donavich's order," he said. "He paid in advance. The financing fee convinced him to avoid owing us money."

Annie looked up. She smiled wanly. Mike sensed something was wrong.

"What is it, Annie?"

"Mike," she said, "I am afraid there will have to be a change in our church wedding plans."

Mike hurried around the desk to hold Annie. He could see that something had deeply affected her."

"Changed in what way?"

"We won't be going to Cicero next month. My father is coming here in two weeks. I talked to Father John. He can marry us at Saint Maurice Church, if it is alright with you."

"Anything you want, Annie. You know that." Mike allowed himself to relax. Changing a wedding date was not important to him, but clearly it was important to Annie.

"Why the change?" He asked.

Annie smiled. "I am going to have a baby."

Mike laughed out loud. "That is wonderful! God, Annie, you scared me to death." He hugged her tighter. "When's the date?"

"July 29th. It is the last Saturday in July. That gives my father and brothers time to come down."

"I meant the date that the baby is due."

"January, maybe February. It is hard to know this early on."

*****

Kuba Norwak, Chief of Police for the City of Cicero, Illinois, sat in the first pew on the bride's side of the aisle. Next to him, sat his sons, their wives, and his grandchildren. It required three pews to fit them all.

Beginning with the eldest, the men were named, Matthew, Mark Luke, John, Paul, and Joseph. Kuba had insisted his children have American names. He started with the gospels until he begat more sons than the New Testament provided books. Anastazja, his only daughter, was the naming exception, a conciliation toward his late wife.

The groom's side of the aisle was populated by Tío Geronimo, Tía Isabella, Zapato and Lucia in the first pew. Behind them sat Fritz and Gertrude Hoffman, Joey Steward, and the rest of the drivers for Saint Claude Drayage. Manuel Moreno sat in the last pew.

Mike wore his best suit and Annie wore a pale-blue, full length gown with a matching veil of the finest lace. It was held in place by a silver tiara. Mike considered Annie to be the singularly most beautiful woman he had ever seen.

The reception was held in the garage. Anthony Rezzato had shuffled the trucks to one side, cleared the work bench and covered it with a white cloth. The fare consisted of a variety of fruits, smoked ham, breads, and sliced roast beef. Beverages included wine, tea, and surreptitious servings of rum.

The introduction of guests required several minutes and, in the case of some drivers, translations. Food and drink flowed, guests mingled, and laughter filled the garage.

Annie had worried that her father and brothers would not readily accept Mike. He did have a slight accent and was a southerner as well. Her fears proved to be unfounded, for it soon became clear that the Chief of Police and his sons approved of Annie's choice in husbands. Perhaps learning that Mike was a veteran of the Great War had influenced their opinion.

Toward the end of the evening, Kuba pulled Mike to the side. "Mike," he said in subdued tones, "I understand you have had a run-in with Jules Ruttan and Myrtle Schaumburg."

"Not much of one. Besides, Ruttan is dead."

"That is what I heard, but Ruttan was not the dangerous one, Mike. It is the Schaumburg woman who you should worry about."

"I don't expect she is much interested in me," Mike said. "I am in the trucking business now. She has taken up with a local money bag."

"Don't let her near you, my boy. The Chicago Police think she killed two men within a span of a month. Both were killed in broad daylight and on a busy street. The Chicago guys couldn't prove it, but they think they know how she did it.

"She would pick a time when the guy was walking down a busy sidewalk, maybe leaving work or on the way to a meeting. She would walk toward the guy, all smiles and flirty. When they got close, she would bump into him.

"She carried a stiletto hidden against her arm. As she collided with the man, she would stab him so fast that the victim did not even realize he had been hurt. In each case, she was well past them and walking away before the victims collapsed to the ground."

Mike's stomach turned. Myrtle had been walking right up to him that day in front of the bank. What would have happened if he hadn't opened the door to the bank? Had that been enough to foil Myrtle's attempt?

Manuel Moreno walked up to Mike and Kuba. He put his arm around Mike's shoulder and offered his hand to Kuba.

"It has been a pleasure meeting you, Mister Norwak," Moreno said in his heavy Spanish accent. "I must be going now and please pardon me. I need to talk to Mike."

"Certainly," Kuba said. "I have to begin gathering my people up as well. Our train departs in five hours. Barely enough time to say our goodbyes."

Mike watched as Kuba walked over to his sons who were all gathered around Annie and laughing.

"Not a loner anymore," Moreno said in Spanish.

"No, that has changed forever, I hope."

"There is to be a shipment to arrive this August. Interested?"

"No, I thank you, but no," Mike said. "I have taken your advice and invested wisely. I am happy with my wife and our business."

"And I am happy for you, Mike," Moreno said. "Perhaps we will have the opportunity to do business in the future. You know how to reach me."

*****

Sunday morning Annie sent Mike out for a newspaper while she prepared breakfast. It had become their custom to enjoy a breakfast together, reading the paper and planning the day. Sundays had one exception. Planning did not involve scheduling trucks, drivers, and routes.

Annie particularly enjoyed the "Item Magazine" portion of the Sunday paper which consisted of short stories. The stories were often romances or mysteries. Sometimes there was an adventure.

"Perhaps you ought to write an adventure for the Item," Mike teased. "One based upon personal experience."

"The editors would considerate it too farfetched," Annie replied. "By the way, I happened to notice something interesting in the 'Diary of Diana' section."

"What section is that?" Mike asked.

"It is the gossip page," Annie smiled. "Here, look at this."

She opened the paper to one of the inner pages. "Do you recognize the 'Bride of the Week?'"

"Is it you?" Mike asked. He laughed and turned the paper around, so he could read it. Under the caption "Bride of the Week" was a full-length photo of Cass Kienson in a wedding dress complete with a long train, veil and showing a high heeled, white boot. She was holding a bouquet of flowers and glaring at the camera. Beneath the photo was the caption "Mrs. Felix York, III, Formerly Miss Chasity Kienson, daughter of Mr. and Mrs. William Kienson of the Garden District."

"Well," Mike said, "I never knew York the Stork was a Felix and the third of that name to boot. Poor man."

"She's pretty," Annie said.

"Pretty girls are everywhere," Mike said. "Beautiful women, such as you, Mrs. Demill, are rare."

"What a honeyed tongue," Annie smiled. Her face developed a serious continence. "I know Manuel Moreno offered you a part of a new importing opportunity."

"Then you also know I turned him down," Mike said. "I think my uncle Geronimo might have accepted. The less I know about it, the better it is for us both. Now tell me about that lorry you have been thinking about."

"Actually, two lorries," Annie said.

CHAPTER 26

The two lorries that Annie decided upon were Mack Model A-B's. They were three-ton trucks, closed cab, open flat bed, and sporting drive shafts instead of chain drives. The load capacity alone tripled the profitability of each trip from lumberyards or docks. Mike called them his "bull dogs" because of the new Mack logo on the hood of the trucks.

The new Mack trucks cost one thousand five hundred dollars, each. Annie was able to pay for them out of the operating capital fund she had established. Everything she did was on a cash basis.

"We will never pay a bank to use somebody else's money," she told Mike. "We will have the banks pay us to use our money; that's the secret."

Another advantage of the Mack trucks was their ability to traverse rough roads. The high bed clearance and reliable shaft drive had the Macks moving lumber and equipment into developing areas where the little half-ton Fords often bogged down.

The rumors of Ford Motors building an automobile assembly facility next to the sugar refinery on North Peters Street were confirmed. Mike contacted the new plant director with the idea of specialized trailers manufactured by Fruehauf of Michigan.

The trailers could carry fully assembled cars, four at a time, to dealers across the Gulf Coast. The logistics of hiring drivers to move individual cars to dealerships as much as a hundred miles away, one at a time, was daunting. Cars would arrive covered in mud or with damage that had to be repaired.

Mike made a pair of visits to the plant managers, and Saint Claude Drayage had a contract by the first week in August, well before construction began on the assembly plant.

Annie decided that they would require seven new Mack semi-tractors for the Ford contract alone. They needed more trucks, more drivers, and more space. The Saint Claude building was to become the short haul, truck farm and urban delivery center under the direction of Anthony Rezzato.

Mike acquired a warehouse on the corner of Aycock and North Peters Streets. It was one block from the Ford facility. It had office space for a staff of six and enough floor space to house a dozen semi-tractors. The open yard next to the building had enough space for thirty trailers. They took on seven new drivers, all Irishmen.

By the third week in August, they had moved the headquarters of Saint Claude Drayage to the Aycock building, Mike called it the "truck barn," and Annie was looking for a house in a nearby residential area. Mike also talked Annie into hiring an office staff and an accountant.

"I don't want you spending days and nights here," he told her, "You are going to need time for yourself. Perhaps you can make some trips with me to visit new clients. I know they will be impressed with the brains of the company."

By the last week of August, Saint Claude Drayage was working out of two locations, had a fleet of twelve vehicles, eighteen drivers, and a half dozen office and maintenance staff. They ran the trucks day and night and still could not keep up with demand.

The house Annie had settled on was a two story on Mehle Avenue less than a thousand feet from the truck barn on Aycock Street. The house was raised so high on piers that they parked the car under the house. It had a cupola on the center of the roof which provided a wonderful view of the Mississippi River and New Orleans.

Their first evening in their new house they lay together on the bed in the upstairs master bedroom. The tall windows were open and a cool breeze from the river swept across them. They had just made love.

Annie nuzzled into Mike's chest.

"I can't believe how lucky I am," she said. "Last year about this time I was looking at a life of tedium. Now, my head is spinning with all the wonderful things that are happening."

"I am the lucky one," Mike said. "Right now, I cannot imagine how life could be any sweeter."

*****

One of the drivers returning from a delivery to the Violet Canal told Mike that John Donavich was opening a marine supply business and boatyard. The oyster lugger Donavich was building, the *Lady Toss*, was such a success that three other oyster dredgers had become determined to retire their converted sail luggers and build their own power boats.

Donavich had accepted construction contracts on two new boats. He decided that he might as well open a marine warehouse and repair company. Donavich Marine was headquartered in the old train station a few hundred feet from the Violet Canal.

Donavich was going to need a steady supply of parts to keep the new business working. Mike met with Donavich and arranged a delivery schedule. As Mike was preparing to leave, he and Donavich were standing near the pier.

"Say, Demill," Donavich said as he pointed to a small boat moored at the corner of the pier, "isn't that your old oyster skiff?"

"I do believe it is," Mike said. "And that man sleeping in her is Francis Ayo." It was hard to believe that a year ago that skiff had been Mike's only possession.

Mike walked down to the boat and squatted at the mooring line. "Not much work for an oysterman today," he said in French.

Francis lifted the big straw hat that covered his face. He broke into a wide smile. "Michael Demill! Man, I am some glad for you to see me, yea," he said in his version of English. Then he frowned. "If you come for the money, I owe you for this boat, I am not ready to pay you today."

"The agreement was you would pay me when you can."

Francis' smile returned. He struggled to his feet and made his way to the bow to shake Mike's hand.

"I have heard you are a landsman now," Francis said, switching to French. It made his headache to use too much English.

"Married and satisfied with life on land," Mike said.

Noise from across the canal made Mike look up. Three touring cars roared into the lot next to Haden's three boats.

Men tumbled out of the cars yelling at one another as they rushed back and forth between the cars and the boats.

Each man, on each trip between car and boat, carried armloads of supplies. On the last trip, each man carried a shotgun. Mike counted nine men, three to a boat.

The only man Mike recognized was McDae, the others were strangers to him.

"Look at that," Francis said. "I know those men. The only one who knows these waters is the Scotsman. Those two other boats are from Texas. None of the deckhands have been out of sight of land."

"I don't like what I'm seeing," Mike said. "They are acting like something is up."

"I will tell you what is up," Francis said. "They are fixing to hijack a load of rum. All those men ever did was hang out on their boats and drink beer. At night, I could hear them all the way down to my place, bragging about how they were going to be the only people bringing in rum."

"Take care, Francis," Mike said.

"Do that yourself," Francis answered.

Mike returned to his car and watched as the three boats in the canal got underway. McDae was clearly in charge as he directed the other two boats to follow him. That would make sense if the other two captains were not familiar with the waters where they were bound.

Mike drove across the canal locks. He stopped in the middle of the lock and watched the three boats powering up the canal. It had the look of a military operation. Mike drove to a store where he knew there was a pay telephone.

The public telephone was in a corner of the store. Mike looked about and did not see anyone nearby. He dug out a nickel and dialed a number.

"¡Hola!"

"Tía Isabella, this is Miguel."

"Miguel! It is so good to hear you. How is that lovely wife of yours?"

"Tía Isabella, I need to talk to Tío Geronimo."

"He is not here, Miguel. He is on his boat."

"When do you expect him to return?"

"Tonight, Miguel. He will be home tonight. Why do you ask? Is something wrong?"

"No. Nothing is wrong. It can wait until tomorrow."

"But, Miguel, you never call and now you need to talk to your uncle."

"It can wait. I must go now. Goodbye, Tía Isabella."

Mike hung up the telephone and fished out another nickel. He dialed another number.

"Saint Claude Drayage," said a female voice.

"This is Mike, Sara. I need to talk to Annie," Mike said the instant the phone was answered. Sara, one of the new office staff, was a little surprised. The other times that Mike had called, he chatted with her a bit before asking for Annie.

Mike could hear her calling Annie to the telephone. "Miss Annie, its Mister Mike. It seems urgent."

Mike could hear the telephone change hands.

"Mike, what is it?" Annie said.

"Trouble for my uncle, I think. Do you remember the job Mister Moreno offered that I turned down?"

"Yes."

"I think Tío Geronimo is making that run now. He could be headed for trouble." Mike filled Annie in on what he had seen and what Francis Ayo had heard.

"If the boats with my uncle split up to make the run in, McDae could intercept them one at a time and overpower them."

"Mike, what can you do? There is no way to warn your uncle."

"I can take the *Solitario* and intercept my uncle before they separate for the run in. If they keep together, they will out-number and out-gun McDae. I have to warn them."

"How can you find them? It is a big ocean."

"I believe they will gather at Freemason Island before the trip in. My only hope is to get to Freemason Island before they leave or before McDae finds them."

"Oh, sweet God, Mike," Annie said. "Please be careful."

"I'm going to warn them, that is all. I have to go."

Mike hung up and sprinted to his car. Fifteen minutes later he drove through the Saint Bernard Cemetery to the abandoned railroad bed. He drove along the bed toward the Kenilworth Canal. Jonesy was standing at the crossing waiting for him. Mike stopped, and Jonesy got into the car.

"Miss Annie called," Jonesy said. "She said you going into some trouble. I put the Springfield and the BAR. in the boat."

"How much ammunition?"

"Two loaded magazines for the BAR. Two is all you got. I got a box of clips for the Springfield."

"How is she provisioned?"

"Full of fuel. Got a barrel of water. Beans, jerky, and bread in the galley. Enough for a week for the two of us."

"You are not going, Jonesy."

"Mister Mike, I sure is."

"Jonesy, you are not going. I don't need a deckhand to deliver a message. I'm paying you to keep the *Solitario* provisioned and ready. You have done that job. You are to stay here. Tell Miss Annie that I will be at Freemason Island or at the New Harbor Islands. If I don't come back, Miss Annie is going to need your help. That is how it is going to be. No arguments."

Jonesy sat in silence until they pulled up to the pier where the *Solitario* was moored.

She was tied to the pier on her starboard side and facing south. Mike climbed aboard, ducked into the cabin, and reappeared with the Springfield. He gave it and the box of clips to Jonesy.

"Cast her off, Jonesy," Mike said.

"I feel like I ought to go with you, Mister Mike."

"No more about it, Jonesy," Mike snapped. "Now cast off her bow line and hold the stern while I start the engines."

Mike opened the engine cowls to allow for any trapped fumes to escape. He was in a hurry, but some things just couldn't be skipped. He brought the BAR up from the cabin and placed it next to the exterior pilot's station. He started the engines, latched down the cowls and nodded for Jonesy to cast off.

The narrow and shallow canal restricted the *Solitario* to a speed just a little over idle. Mike pushed it as much as he could, but he had to reduce throttle every time the canal behind him lost water because of the bow wave being pushed ahead.

It was nearly an hour before he reached Lake Lery and could go to full throttle. Still, it was less than three hours since McDae left the pier on the Violet Canal. The trip from there to Freemason was four hours longer than Mike's run through Mozambique Point.

He powered through Bayou Gentilly and down Terre Aux Boeufs without slowing to reduce his wake. Moored boats banged against their piers and the few folks about gestured angrily. It couldn't be helped. He would only have three hours of daylight left when he made Freemason, not counting the time it would take to find his uncle or other boats bringing in rum.

He broke into Chandeleur Sound and put the compass on sixty-five degrees. There were several thunderheads building toward the east, a common thing in August. These storms proved to be violent and could wreak havoc on a trawler, but mariners easily avoided the isolated thunder cells.

He scanned the horizon for any signs of traffic and saw nothing. He had hoped to see the delivery ship on the other side of the Chandeleur Islands, but the storms removed any hope of picking up that clue to the location of Moreno's fleet. The sea was smooth as a millpond, despite the nearby storms.

Mike noticed a twinkle to his left. He turned slightly to the north. It twinkled again. A glint of sun reflecting off glass, no doubt about it. There was a dark dot, a boat, on the horizon and moving west. He turned to intercept.

As he closed the distance with the boat, he saw three dots further east but closing fast. The first boat changed direction to the south and then southwest. He was headed directly toward one of the thunderstorms.

He is going to try and shake his pursuers in the storm, Mike thought. There was no other explanation. If the three trailing boats had been harmless, there would be no reason to plunge into a storm. Soon it was clear that the lead boat was not going to reach the thunder shower before his pursuers reached him.

Mike adjusted his heading once more. If the other boats held their course, the *Solitario,* the pursued boat and the three other boats would arrive at the same spot in the sound at the same time.

They were close enough now for Mike to see that the lead boat was the *Pastor Larenzo,* Bebedor Alayon's boat. The first of the chase boats was *Rosa Amarilla*. He could not make out the names on the other two boats, but from their lines he decided that the middle boat was the other Texan, the *Rio Perdido*. The last boat was clearly the *Isle of Hvar*.

Mike maneuvered the *Solitario* to pass just behind the *Rosa Amarilla*, cutting off the other Texan. He could see two men in the bow of the *Rosa Amarilla* waving shotguns and signaling for their prey to stop. They were so concentrated on their quarry that they did not seem to notice the *Solitario* closing fast.

The men in the *Rio Perdido* did see Mike and slowed slightly before turning toward him. There were two men with shotguns in the bow of this boat as well. Mike could not discern what they were shouting.

Still, they shouted, waved Mike away and shook their shotguns in the air. Then one put the shotgun to his shoulder and fired. The range was far beyond the reach of a shotgun, about five hundred yards and Mike did not even see where the pellets fell.

The Solitario bounced through the wake of the *Pastor Larenzo* and Mike turned slightly to pass near the stern of the *Rosa Amarilla*. The *Rosa Amarilla* crew had been alerted by the shots and, for the first time, saw Mike closing with them.

The men in the bow lost all interest in the boat ahead and rushed to the stern. They shouldered their shotguns, and they were now within range. Mike crossed their wake just as one of the men started shooting. Nothing hit the *Solitario*.

Mike looped a rope over a spoke of the wheel to free his hands and raised the BAR. He fired a three-round burst; POW - POW - POW; at their engine cover. The men in the stern dove behind the transom. Mike gave them two more three round bursts; POW - POW - POW; a pause and; POW - POW - POW. The *Rosa Amarilla* went dead in the water.

Mike freed the wheel and spun hard to port. He passed close to the *Rio Perdido,* port side to port side. Her men were attempting to fire their shotguns as well, but the churning wakes of the boats ahead was tossing them about like dolls. Mike throttled down and readied his BAR as the other boat slid by.

He sprayed the deck with three round bursts. He saw the man at the wheel go down. He did not know if he had been hit or was just diving for cover. The *Rio Perdido* fell away to her starboard. None of the men in her showed themselves to return fire.

Mike turned to see the *Isle of Hvar* closing fast. He had lost track of McDae's boat during the confusion. He dropped the now empty magazine from the BAR and pushed another in. The bow of the *Isle of Hvar* loomed above the *Solitario.* It blocked the view of the men aboard her. Mike held down the trigger of the BAR and sprayed rounds into the side of the other boat hoping to hit something or someone.

The bow of the *Isle of Hvar* crashed into the *Solitario* just forward of the cabin. Mike was thrown into the pilot's station. Pain shot from his right hand as the BAR was ripped from his grip by the collision. He fell to the deck and watched in wonder as the bow of the *Isle of Hvar* settled onto his boat.

There was a loud cracking sound and the *Isle of Hvar* twisted at the waist as her momentum and still running engines broke her back. McDae appeared on deck with a pistol.

"You!" He shouted. "I am going to kill you, Demill." He fired several shots at Mike. Mike scurried along the deck of the *Solitario* until he was against the side of the *Isle of Hvar* where McDae could not see him. He reached for the Luger in his belt but winced in pain. His right hand must have been broken.

He pulled the pistol out with his left, toggled the safety with his right thumb and squeezed his frame down into a cavity created by the collision. He had practiced shooting with his left when he was in France. He was far from proficient.

This won't do, he thought. *All McDae must do is wait for his other boats.*

The engines of the *Solitario* quit with a hiss. Water had reached them. The engine in the *Isle of Hvar* quit as well. Both boats were sinking. Timbers groaned and popped as they split, and water poured into the broken hulls.

Mike heard another boat coming up to the tangled mess at the stern of the *Isle of Hvar*.

"What happened?" someone shouted.

"We rammed her," came the answer. Mike recognized McDae's voice. "What's wrong with Rider?"

"Engine shot to pieces. He needs a tow."

Mike guessed Rider was the skipper of the *Rosa Amarilla*.

"What about you?"

"We are sinking," McDae answered.

"Climb aboard while there is time."

"First, I have to kill a man," McDae said.

Rather than try and shoot it out with Mike on a sinking boat, McDae could transfer to the one working boat and wait for the wreckage to sink. Then he could shoot Mike in the water if he hadn't drowned.

McDae was an impatient man. Mike heard him stomp across the deck to the gunnel.

"Hear me, Demill?" he shouted. "I am going to kill you and cut you into bait."

Mike squeezed up against the hull of the *Isle of Hvar* where it had crushed the cabin of the *Solitario*. He was hidden from any observer on the deck above.

Two shots from above splintered the cabin of the *Solitario* near where Mike crouched. He looked further aft and saw the BAR laying on the deck against the port engine cowl.

"I see you've dropped your fancy rifle," McDae shouted. It sounded as though he were directly above Mike.

"McDae," someone shouted, "come climb aboard. The boats are sinking, and the storm is getting close."

"Not until I kill this bastard, Tony," McDae said.

"He is dead already, or he will be when these boats go down," Tony answered.

"I need to cut him into bait."

A pair of boots appeared over Mike's head. McDae was preparing to jump down to the deck of the *Solitario*. Mike gripped the Lugar in his left hand and hoped he could get off a few shots. The chances of him hitting anything, off-handed and on a pitching deck, were slight.

McDae's boots dropped a little lower as the man prepared to jump. Mike moved close to the dangling feet. Just as McDae launched himself, Mike swept the boots back with his right hand.

McDae twisted on the way down and fell against the deck on his back with a crash. He pointed the pistol in his hand at where Mike had been seconds before and fired.

Mike, who had thrown himself next to McDae's left side, put the Luger under the man's chin and fired three times. He scrambled back into the shelter of the hull. He looked at McDae ready to fire again, but the top of the man's skull had come off.

"Did you get him?" Tony shouted.

Mike held his breath and listened as feet scuffled to the place where McDae had launched himself.

"McDae, are you alright?" Tony shouted.

Mike leaned out until he could see the head of a man, likely Tony, peering over the rail above. He fired one shot at the head, and it disappeared.

"McDae's dead!" Tony shouted. "As soon as I'm aboard, get away from here."

It was beginning to rain and a bolt of lightening struck somewhere nearby.

"What about the other guy?" someone asked.

"Let him drown," Tony said. "Let's go!"

Mike heard the other boat, the *Rio Perdido*, roar away, fading until all he could hear was the rain hammering down.

A scupper on the deck over his head began to pour rainwater. Mike positioned himself to drink from the stream. He was going to be in the sea soon. If he managed to find a piece of wreckage to hold on to, or if he could swim to an island, he might survive long enough to be sighted by a passing boat.

The August sun glaring down on one of the treeless islands would dry a man up. The thing that killed a man adrift at sea was thirst. Mike drank as much of the rainwater as he could hold.

The rain stopped, but the sun to the west was blocked by the retreating thunderhead. Mike could see east, toward where the Chandeleur Islands should have been. They were too far away to be seen, perhaps five miles or more, he thought.

He did not know precisely where he was. The action had been so sudden and fast moving that he only had a vague idea of where it started. Then there was the storm and the boats drifting while locked together. Freemason Island should have been close and just to the north, but he could see nothing.

The deck below him was now awash. He was going to have to leave the boats soon or risk being trapped as they sank. He would have to swim, but which way? How would he know if he were swimming in a straight line and not in circles?

He eased into the water and swam a little way away from the wreckage. He treaded water about a hundred feet away and watched the boats go under. He hoped that some sizeable piece of wood or an old cask would float up, but nothing did.

He turned in a circle trying to get his bearings. The only direction he was certain of was east, and that was because it was evening. It would be dark in less than an hour. With nowhere to swim to, he slowly treaded water and tried to conserve his energy. Night would last nine hours or more.

The sea about him had been churned up by the storm into steep crests, but now the energy of the storm was gone, and the seas were subsiding. Everywhere he looked, the waves were now small, one-foot high, white-capped pyramids that would appear and quickly disappear.

Except... one place was smooth, or at least, much less agitated. Mike recognized the subtle signs of a shoal, and one so shallow that it would not support the steep chop. He swam for the circle of calmer water.

Once he was in the center of the suspected shoal area, he attempted to tread water. His feet touched a hard surface and he stood. The water was up to his chest, about four feet deep.

He knew where he was. He was on the "peak," the shoal that had sunk the *Captain Toss*. Freemason Island was about five miles east and the nearest Chandeleur Island seven miles beyond that. He was not going to swim anywhere.

CHAPTER 27

Annie hung up the phone. Mike's assertion that he was only going to warn his uncle of a possible hijacking attempt did little to assuage her concerns. There is always some hazard associated with rum running, particularly if you are alone. She called Jonesy to warn him that Mike was going to need the *Solitario* fueled and provisioned.

A half hour later, about two in the afternoon, Jonesy called back to say that Mike had set out in the boat.

"He's got all he needs, Miss Annie," Jonesy said. "I begged to go with him, but he wouldn't hear it, said I needed to stay here. I don't like it, Miss Annie."

"Neither do I, Jonesy," Annie said. "I think I will call Mike's Uncle Geronimo after dark and see if Mike found him. You tell Mike to call me the minute he returns."

"Yes, Miss Annie," Jonesy said, concern filling his voice. "You can count on me, Miss Annie."

Annie then told Sara and the rest of her staff that she expected to be out of the office tomorrow.

"Tomorrow is already scheduled, Miss Annie," Sara said. "We can take care of everything."

Annie went home about six in the evening. There would be about another hour of daylight. She did the math in her head. If Mike had pushed the *Solitario* as hard as she would run, he would be arriving at Freemason Island right about now. If Mike turned around as soon as he reached Freemason Island, he could not possibly get back to Kenilworth until eleven that night.

She was beginning to prepare supper when she felt a sudden rush of fear. It was as if she couldn't breathe. She put her hands on her knees and gasped for air. Slowly the feeling passed, and she was able to walk around the kitchen. She would skip supper.

Annie sat down and watched the clock on the wall. If she did not receive any word by eleven, she would call Tío Geronimo. She started to cry but stopped herself. Crying would not help, and it was going to be a long night.

*****

Mike began to cough violently. He brought up gobs of brown mucus between gasps for air. He had to squat until the water was up to his chin. If such a fit had come upon him while he was swimming, he would have drowned.

The spasms passed, and Mike was able to stand up again. He realized he still had on his shoes. He should have kicked them off the instant he decided to enter the water. It should have been instinctive, but it was fortunate that he had not.

The surface he was standing on was covered in barnacles and oyster shells. Some shells were crushed, perhaps by the impact of the *Captain Toss* when she wrecked. Some were intact. The stone structure beneath this coating of living, shelled creatures was flat.

Mike moved about tentatively. Everywhere the depth seemed to be the same except when he came to the edges of the peak. At the edges, the surface ended abruptly, falling away vertically. He felt with his feet for a shelf or lower surface but felt nothing as far as he could reach.

He returned to what seemed to be the center and looked west. The thunderhead blocked any view of the western horizon. He could not see the setting sun, but it was growing dark.

He looked east and watched as the stars began to appear. It would be full dark in less than a quarter hour. The moon was not up, but a wide swathe of stars covered the sky and provided enough light to see nearby objects, had there been any. The sea was as smooth as glass. He could see no lights on the horizon.

Mike tried to think when the moon was due to rise. Last year, he could have told you the times of sunrise, sunset, moon rise, moon set, high tide.

High tide!

Mike stood still. The water reached his sternum. It was lower, he thought, than when he had first arrived. High tide had passed. Even so, the tidal ranges in the Chandeleur Sound were usually less than a foot and a half. He remembered how he had marveled at the eight-foot tides on the coast of France.

He would not be washed off his perch by high tides. It would take a storm or dehydration to push Mike into deep waters. Either prospect was very likely. Evening thunderstorms, such as the one that had just passed, were common and sufficiently violent to generate five-foot breakers. Mike had little hope of surviving such a storm without being washed into the sound.

Tomorrow, the sun would be relentless. Dehydration may take two or three days, but if he were not found by then, he would eventually lose consciousness and drown. Tomorrow was ten hours away.

Mike waded to a corner, and it was a distinct, right-angled corner, of the shoal. He decided it was a platform, a stone platform. The corners were so distinct, so regular, that they could only have been shaped by the hand of man.

He faced toward the North Star. He felt his way along the eastern edge of the stone slab and determined it was perfectly aligned to north. He started at the southern corner and, placing heel to toe, he began to measure toward the north.

At eighteen feet he came to another corner just as square and abrupt as the one he left. He turned left and following what could only be described as the north edge of the stone, he counted twelve feet before finding another corner.

The west edge of the stone platform produced a surprise. At six feet, he encountered a corner. Turning left, east, he found another corner at six feet that turned south again. Another six feet and the edge turned west for six more feet before turning south again.

The remainder of the west edge was six feet long and returned him to a place six feet west of where he had started. He was so struck by the regularity and consistency of the flat stone platform that he measured it several times before finally settling on a shape.

The platform was twelve feet wide in the east-west direction and eighteen feet long in the north-south direction. There was a six-foot-by-six-foot notch perfectly centered on the west edge. Everything was much too regular to be a natural formation.

Then a thought came to his mind. He went to the notch and felt below the edge with his foot. About eight inches down he felt another flat surface. It was a step. Beyond the first step was another. It was a stairway ascending to the platform from the west and facing perfectly east.

He turned to see the first hint of a rising half-moon. It must be close to midnight, he thought. He had been so absorbed in exploring the "peak" he had lost tract of the time.

Five more hours before sunrise. And then....what?

*****

Annie was startled by the telephone. She must have been dozing. She glanced at the clock as she answered. It was just after midnight.

"Hello?" Annie said.

"Annie? It is Tío Geronimo,"

"Tío! Have you heard anything?"

"I have heard some things," he said. "Bebedor, one of the other captains working with us, was chased by three boats today. He was running to hide in a rainstorm when another boat he did not recognize cut off his pursuers. He does not know what happened after that because he entered the storm."

"Was it Mike?"

"I do not know."

"When was this?"

"Bebedor thinks it was about six in the evening, a little before sunset."

"Then Mike should have returned to Kenilworth by now," Annie said.

"The Kenilworth Canal? Is that where he kept his boat?"

Annie realized that only she and Jonesy knew where Mike had moored the *Solitario*.

"Yes, how long should it have taken Mike to get back?"

"Bebedor said he was a few miles north of Breton Island," Geronimo said. He paused for a few seconds. "Mike should have been able to get to Kenilworth by eleven or so."

"He hasn't returned. Jonesy would have called."

"Who is Jonesy?"

"Jonesy is the caretaker at the Kenilworth house," Annie said. "I don't know what to do."

"Nothing can be done right now," Geronimo said. "We can go into the sound and search tomorrow."

"We need to go now."

"It will do no good to go now. We could never find anything in the dark. I will call some friends, boat captains, and we can set out from here at three in the morning. That will put us into the sound at sunrise."

"I am coming as well," Annie said. She hung up the telephone before Tío Geronimo could object. She gathered a few things, her purse, the keys to the truck she had taken home from work, and, not knowing why, a blanket.

She went down the stairs to the truck. She could see the shadowy form of someone sitting on the truck's running board. Annie reached into her purse and clutched her pistol.

"Miss Annie?" It was Joey.

"Joey, what are you doing here?"

"Miss Annie, I couldn't sleep. You are going to think I am crazy," Joey said. He was almost in tears.

"Tell me what happened."

"I came in after I finished my deliveries today and Miss Sara said there was some trouble. I went home and went to bed." Joey looked about as if to be certain no one else was listening. "I had a dream, Miss Annie."

"A dream? About what?"

"I don't rightfully know. Some old woman kept telling me 'el cumbre' over and over. I think it is Spanish, but I don't know what it means."

"You are coming with me, Joey. Get into the truck. I know someone who can tell us what that means."

The drive to Yscloskey would take nearly an hour and a half. Annie expected to arrive at Geronimo's house about an hour or less before they left to search for Mike. *Search for Mike!* Despair began to creep into her mind, but she forced it away.

She drove toward Saint Bernard Parish with Joey sitting in the passenger seat. He was mumbling "El cumbre," over and over. Annie did not know why she felt Joey's dream was important. Perhaps she was just grasping at straws.

There were no other cars on the road for the first several miles. As they approached the Violet Canal, there were two touring cars parked on either side of the road. The cars were facing down river, the engines were running, but the headlights were off. Men were clustered behind the cars.

One of them saw Annie coming and stepped into the roadway. He held up his hand and Annie stopped.

"Who are you?" the man said.

"I am about my own business," Annie said. "Who are you?"

Surprised played across the man's face. "What are you doing about this late, girlie?"

"None of your business," Annie replied. "Give us the road."

"I do not think I will," the man replied with a smirk.

"You will," Annie said. She pulled her pistol from her purse and pointed it at the man's eyes. "Give us the road."

"Let her go, Danny," said one of the men behind a touring car. "We ain't here for people going down, we are looking for someone coming up."

Annie pushed the truck into gear, and it lurched forward. The man blocking the road jumped aside at the last minute.

"You gotta come back this way, girlie" he shouted as Annie drove past.

"Who were those men?" Joey asked.

"I don't know. They weren't coppers, so they must have been hijackers. We need to get to Tío Geronimo's place, quick."

When Annie pulled up to Geronimo's house, there were three trawlers moored by their bows at the pier. The boats were idling and had their lights on. One was the *Captain Robin*. The other two were the *Pastor Larenzo* and the *Reckless*.

Annie saw Tío Geronimo standing on the pier. She parked the truck and hurried over to the man, followed by Joey. Annie was introduced to the other captains.

"We will leave in a half hour," Geronimo said. "That will put us near Breton Island at dawn. That is where we think Mike was last seen."

"I think Joey has something important to tell you," Annie said.

The men turned to face Joey.

"A dream woke me up," Joey said. He expected the men to scoff at him, but they did not, so he continued. "I dreamt of an old woman."

"Did you know who she was?" Geronimo asked.

"No," Joey said. "I felt like I should have known who she was, but I didn't."

"Is that all?"

"No, the thing I need to tell you is she kept saying 'El cumbre, el cumbre, el cumbre.' I don't know what that means."

Bebedor, who's English was marginal at best, asked in Spanish, "Why does the boy keep saying 'the top'? It doesn't make any sense."

"Maybe he does not mean 'the top'," Jo-Jo said. "He could also mean the English word 'the peak.' Not 'the top,' but 'the peak,' the old woman was trying to tell us to look on the peak!"

"But the peak is twenty miles north of Breton Island," Bebedor said. "We last saw Miguel not two miles from Breton Island."

"You heard the boy," Geronimo said. "He knows no Spanish, but in his dream an old woman would only say 'el cumbre.' We go first to Breton Island, then we turn north to the peak."

*****

Mike watched florescent streaks play around him beyond the edge of the peak. The bursts of light were sometimes followed by swirls or ripples on the surface. The moon light and canopy of stars provided enough light for him to ascertain the slightly undulating surface of the sea about him.

He tried to estimate the passage of time by watching the ascent of the moon and noting which stars disappeared behind the climbing edge of the crescent. The combination of the motion of the stars and the moon confounded him and he quit trying to use them to estimate time.

An old man was sitting in a chair, his head on his chest. The man let out a burst of air in a great whoosh.

Mike stiffened. He had fallen asleep! His left foot was on the peak, but the right hung over the edge. If he had not awakened, he might have floated away. He shuffled back to the center of the platform.

Something black rolled out of the sea to his right and shot a spray of water into the air. It was a porpoise, followed by another and then a third. It was the whoosh of air from the animal's blowhole that had disrupted his slumber. They circled his position for several minutes. One even poked its head above the surface and looked at Mike with its tiny eye.

"Thank you, my friend," Mike said. "You woke me just in time."

The porpoises were gone, and Mike was once again alone in the sea.

He looked at the moon, now almost directly overhead, and tried to guess the time. It seemed like an eternity since he was marooned, but now dawn was maybe two hours away.

He began to systematically scan the horizon, the distinct line where the stars met a black sea. He pictured a compass in his mind. A compass has thirty-two points, and each point of the compass is eleven and a quarter degrees of arc.

He started by facing the North Star. He studied that segment of horizon directly before him for a count of one hundred, then rotate to his right one point of the compass and examine that new sector in the same way. The next time he faced north, a quarter of an hour had lapsed.

The third time he faced about one point north of east, he noticed there were fewer stars on the horizon. The sky was beginning to turn grey as the pre-dawn twilight grew stronger. There was a time when this was his favorite time of the day. Now he welcomed dawn and dreaded full day.

There had not been a breath of air moving all night. By the time his routine had him facing west, a slight breeze skimmed across the water creating slight ripples. If the wind increased too much the resulting chop would make it difficult for searchers to see the insignificant bump on the wide sea that was Mike Demill.

Before he faced north for the fourth time, it was uncomfortably hot. Mike removed his shirt and held it overhead to create a shade. His right hand, which had been severely swollen during the night, appeared to have improved.

His fingers seemed to work but the hand still throbbed with pain and he could not grasp anything tightly with it. He draped the shirt over a forearm and head, switching arms as they tired.

The breeze diminished and then stopped completely. The sea surface was once again dead calm. He was becoming thirsty.

"Too bad," he said. "It is going to be a lot worse very soon. Fourteen hours of daylight to go." *Now I am talking to myself.* "Cursing the broiling sun and dreading another night," he said. He stopped the regimen and began to concentrate on the west. If help came, it would be from the west.

The Chandeleur Island chain was to the east, no boats would be moving there. If a trawler happened by, it would be to the west. The sun would be in the eyes of boatmen to the west until well into the day. After noon, the chances of being sighted from the west improved greatly.

The chances of traffic coming down from the north or up from the south were slight. The shoals and islands associated with Freemason and New Harbor Islands restricted free movement. Even boats destined for these islands would come in from the west or through passes in the Chandeleur chain.

He concentrated on the west and only occasionally glancing in other directions, more out of boredom than an expectation of seeing anything.

It was about ten or eleven in the morning when one such casual glance caught a hint of a speck on the horizon to the south. At first, he was not certain he saw anything, but after a few minutes what had been a speck grew into a box. It was a boat. The hull was still below the horizon, but it was coming directly toward him. Two more specks appeared, one to the left and another to the right of the original.

Mike was so astonished he initially could not move. Then he regained his senses and waved his shirt back and forth in a great arc over his head. He knew that the glint of sunlight reflecting off the wet shirt and tossed water would be highly visible.

He heard a horn. Someone on one of the boats was blowing a horn. The box grew, and the hull became visible, throwing a bow wake. It was the *Captain Robin*. He could see a figure in the rigging, a man, waving.

The boat was three hundred yards from Mike when the engines shut down.

"¿Miguel, *eres tu*?

It was his Uncle Geronimo's voice.

"Yes! Don't come any closer. I am on the peak."

He heard his uncle say in English to others in the boat, "It is Miguel. We have found him."

"Michael, are you alright?" Annie's voice.

"Yes, Annie," Mike managed to shout, though he almost choked with tears. "I have hurt my hand, but that is all."

Someone jumped into the water. Mike feared it was Annie until she shouted again from the boat, "Joey is bringing you a rope and a life ring. We will pull you to the boat."

"Mister Mike, are you OK?" Joey said as he swam up towing a life ring.

"I am fine, now that you have found me."

"How did you find this place?" Joey asked when his foot touched the flat surface of stone.

"It found me," Mike said. With Joey's help, Mike slipped the life ring over his head and slid it down to his chest. Joey grasped the ring's collar rope and shouted, "Pull away. I have him."

Several hands pulled Mike and Joey out of the water, removed the ring from Mike and lay him on the deck. Annie cradled his head on her lap. She held a cup of water to his lips and Mike drank so quickly, he fell into a coughing spasm.

"Not so fast," she admonished. She held a replenished cup to his lips, and he drank more slowly. In the background he could hear Geronimo shouting to the other boats in Spanish. "We have found him! He is well. Let us go home."

The boats roared to life and Mike could feel the comforting vibrations of the engine beneath him. He looked up at Annie.

"I am sorry to cause such worry, *mi querida,*" he said. "I was afraid I would never see you again."

"Oh, Mike, be quiet and rest," Annie said. *I was terrified, not worried.*

"The *Solitario* is gone," he said.

Annie kissed his parched lips and Mike fell into a deep sleep.

CHAPTER 28

Mike sat at his uncle's kitchen table wrapped in the blanket Annie had given him. He felt chilled to the bone even though the sea had been as warm as bathwater. He had slept for most of the three hours the *Captain Robin* required to return to Yscloskey, yet he felt drained of energy.

Tía Isabella insisted on feeding him *caldo*, a seafood and vegetable stew. Between spoons of *caldo*, he drank down water and rum at his uncle's urging. Annie stood behind Mike's chair, her arms over his shoulders, and her hands on his chest.

The room was crowded. Joey occupied a corner with a bowl on his lap spooning in his own share of *caldo*. Several of Geronimo's neighbors, fishermen and their wives, lined the walls or stood in doorways. The room was alive with conversation, all in Spanish.

"The water you need because the salt in the sea steals water from your body," Geronimo said as he pushed another cup into Mike's hands. "You need rum to get the blood moving. It is very important."

Bebedor and Jo-Jo were sitting at the table as well. They were taking turns hammering Mike with questions. What happened to bring Mike to that particular part of Chandeleur Sound? What transpired after Bebedor had escaped into the rainstorm? The details of the collision and being marooned on the peak were reviewed, repeated, and reexamined endlessly.

Bebedor was apologetic at having escaped. "We were unarmed," he repeated. "We did not know it was you, Miguel. Hijackers were chasing us. We had to get away. The storm hid everything from us."

"You did the right thing, Bebedor," Mike said for the tenth time. "I could have escaped as well. None of those boats could have caught the *Solitario*."

Annie recognized the word "*Solitario*" when Mike spoke, and she gave his chest a conciliatory pat.

"My blood was up," Mike said. "I was foolish, and it almost killed me."

"Do not blame yourself, Miguel," Jo-Jo said. "It is the fault of the Hadens. They were going to kill Geronimo and Zapato, but you stopped them. Then they were going to kill Bebedor, and you stopped them. That is what almost cost you your life."

"And next time, you might not live," Bebedor said. "We have to stop the hijackers. We know who they are, and we have to stop them."

"What can we do when the Hadens are backed by District Attorney Ira Roberts?" Bebedor asked.

"Annie, tell Miguel what you saw when you came down," Geronimo said in English.

At first, Annie was startled to suddenly hear English, and it took her a moment to realize Geronimo used the Spanish "Miguel" when referring to Mike.

"I was stopped by some men at the Violet Canal," she said. "They were waiting for someone coming up the road; two cars, six men."

"Did they bother you?" Mike asked.

"Not after I showed them the gift you gave me in Cuba."

Mike smiled. He would have loved to see the expressions on the men's faces when Annie leveled the pistol.

He asked, "What time was this?"

"About two in the morning."

"Was one or both of the Hadens there?"

"I do not know," Annie said. "I don't know what they look like."

"There were two boats that escaped," Mike said, thinking out loud. "One was undamaged and the other may have had engine problems. If they ran due north, even with one boat under tow, it should have taken only four or five hours to make one of the ports on the Mississippi Coast. They left me at six-thirty or seven, just before sunset.

"They had plenty of time to find a telephone and report what had happened. They knew I was alive, but they did not know if the *Solitario* sank, nor did they know if someone had circled back after they left and pulled me from the wreckage."

"And whoever they called had plenty of time," Annie said, "to plan an ambush for you."

Geronimo repeated the conversation in Spanish for the sake of those who were not proficient in English.

"I can have a dozen men, all armed and ready," Bebedor said. "We can shoot Haden's men."

"That will do us no good, even if we killed them all. Roberts will have the law on us," Mike said. "These men have families. They cannot support their children if they are in jail."

"Then what we need to do first is kill Roberts," Jo-Jo said. "We can wait for him at Poydras Junction. He passes there every evening at six or seven. With Roberts gone, we can wipe out the Hadens. Who is with me?"

Jo-Jo headed for the door and every man followed him except Mike and Geronimo.

"Wait," Geronimo called after the mob.

"We will not wait," Bebedor said. "We will not hide in fear from hijackers." The men could not be dissuaded, and they left, some in trucks, but most on horseback.

"What is happening?" Annie asked.

"They are going to kill Roberts and put an end to hijacking," Mike said.

"You must stop them," Annie said. "If a mob attacks the District Attorney, the governor will declare martial law."

"Too late," Geronimo said. "What happens is not up to us anymore."

*****

The Demill family, and Joey, were still gathered in the kitchen when the sounds of hoofbeats could be heard outside of the house at nine that evening. Mike and Geronimo went out to see who it was.

They found Bebedor, Jo-Jo and some of the men. All were disgruntled and downcast.

"What happened?" Geronimo asked.

"Somebody must have warned Roberts," Jo-Jo said. "He left his car in English Turn and had a farmer row him across the river in a skiff. We will wait for another day."

"We acted too rashly," Bebedor said. "We will plan better for the next time."

"We need to think," Mike said. "There has to be a better way. If we have open warfare, the governor will send in the National Guard and they will be on Robert's side."

"Who is the smartest man we know?" Geronimo asked.

"Manuel Moreno." Bebedor and Jo-Jo said in unison.

"Then let us ask *Don* Manuel what to do," Geronimo said. "Mike can call him from here in the morning."

Reluctantly, all agreed to accept Manuel Moreno's counsel on the problem. After all, Moreno's importing business was suffering as much, or more, than everyone else's.

Geronimo's kitchen was just as crowded at seven the next morning when Mike called Moreno.

"William," Mike said when the telephone was answered, "This is Mike Demill. May I speak with Mister Moreno?"

"One moment, Mister Demill." There was the sound of a handset being shuffled about and Manuel Moreno came on the line.

"*Buenos Días*, Miguel." As always, the conversation was to be in Spanish.

"Good morning, sir. Forgive me for disturbing you, but I have a problem."

"I know there has been trouble, Miguel," Moreno said. "I have had many reports, but it is best we meet to discuss this." Moreno never discussed details on the telephone.

"I am at my uncle's house," Mike said. "I may not be able to come to New Orleans."

"Yes, I understand. It so happens that I am meeting Ira Roberts and the Haden brothers at Tee-Ta's. Perhaps you could join us?"

Tee-Ta's was an old barn converted into a barroom and dance hall on Bayou Terre Aux Boeufs about two miles below the Poydras Junction. The owner was Tee-Ta Gutierrez, Jo-Jo's brother.

Mike swallowed hard. Moreno was always five steps ahead of everyone else.

"Yes, sir," Mike said. "When?"

"Today at three in the afternoon. I have guaranteed their safety."

"I will be there."

Mike hung up the telephone and explained the conversation to those in the room who could only hear what Mike said.

"I am going to be there with you," Annie said. She was not asking permission.

"And we will have men in the woods all around Tee-Ta's," said Bebedor.

*****

Mike drove the truck along the bayou road. Annie sat in the passenger's seat while Joey rode in the truck bed, a shotgun across his lap. Two young men, both sons of Bebedor, on horseback and armed with shotguns, followed the truck.

Mike stopped about one hundred yards from Tee-Ta's barroom/barn/dancehall. The south end of the barn faced the bayou. It had two large sliding doors as did the north end. These doors were opened during times of business to facilitate ventilation. The south doors were closed. Mike could not tell if the north doors were closed as well.

When Tee-Ta's was in full operation, the large doors at both ends were opened wide. Music and the sounds of people enjoying life coursed up and down the bayou. Beer, wine, and whiskey were served openly with little regard given to the laws of prohibition. The sheriff was receiving consideration for every drink sold.

Tee-Ta Gutierrez was bi-lingual by necessity. His wife spoke only French and the small village around Tee-Ta's establishment considered French the preferred language. Perhaps it was for that reason the dancehall was considered a neutral meeting site by Ira Roberts.

Between the main entrance and the bayou was a wide clamshell-surfaced parking lot. During hours of operation, it was not unusual for the dancing to spill out of the open barn and onto the parking area. Some of the parked cars were also sources of supply for whisky of higher quality than the fare offered by Tee-Ta's.

There were only two cars parked in the lot. One was an Overland touring car and the other was a Duesenberg. A man was leaning against the fender of the Overland. Mike could see movement in the wooded area north of the barn. It was a man, an *Isleño* by his dress, who edged into a brush-covered tree fall and ducked out of site.

Mike and Annie got out of the truck and Joey climbed down from the bed to join them.

"The man by the Overland is William, Moreno's assistant," Mike said. "The Duesy belongs to Danny Haden."

Mike did not see Haden's driver, if there was one.

He said, "Joey, I want you to stay in the truck. Get behind the wheel and keep the engine running. If something happens, use your judgment and remember we have people in the woods."

"I don't see anybody," Joey said.

"Good," Mike said. He turned to the men on horseback. "Stay where you are and remember we have friends everywhere. Do not get excited and start shooting."

Mike took a deep breath. He looked at Annie. "Are you sure you want to do this?"

Annie nodded.

"Well then, come on, Annie. We have a meeting to attend."

Mike skirted the parking lot and front entrance. He and Annie circled to the east side of the old barn to a doorway hidden against the tree line and a row of outhouses. He paused before opening the door to see where the *Isleños* had positioned themselves. He could see nothing, which was good, if they were there, or bad, if they were not.

The back door opened into a short hall between storage rooms and led to the back of the bandstand. Mike stepped inside and waited until Annie joined him.

"Let's wait a few seconds for our eyes to adjust," he said. The transition from bright daylight to a dingy back room rendered them almost blind. After a few moments Mike's eyes had adjusted.

"You ready?" he asked.

Annie nodded.

"Once inside, I want you to hang back against the wall. With any luck, they would not have seen you come in with me," Mike said.

"Everyone outside saw us both come in," Annie said.

"True, but no one outside is talking to those inside."

Mike moved through the storage area and ducked around the stage. He could see four men seated at a large table. The man with his back to Mike was Manuel Moreno. One of the men on the far side of the table was Danny Haden. The other two, Mike had never seen. He surmised that one was John Haden and the other was Ira Roberts.

"Please, join us, Miguel," Moreno said in Spanish. Mike could see Moreno's face smiling at him through a mirror on the far wall. "I have asked Miguel Demill to join us," Moreno continued in English, "Because I do not trust my English for such delicate; how do you say it, Miguel?"

"Negotiations, *Don* Manuel," Mike said.

"Yes! Negotiations," Moreno finished.

Mike moved to the center of the room and stood next to Moreno at the table. He glanced out of the corner of his eye and saw Annie duck behind a rack of bottles.

"*Las introducciones están en orden*," Moreno said.

"Introductions are in order," Mike repeated. "Everyone here knows *Don* Manuel Moreno. I am Mike Demill."

The heavyset man at the far end of the table stood. "I am District Attorney Ira Roberts. To my left is John Haden and to my right is his brother Daniel Haden."

"My English is imperfect," Moreno said. "I will have Miguel translate my words so there will be no *-¿como dices: malentendidos?* "

"Misunderstandings," Mike said.

"Sí. No misunderstandings," Moreno said, "Very important."

"You called this meeting," Roberts said. "What is it that you wish to discuss?"

Mike translated Robert's words and then listened to Moreno's answer.

"*Don* Manuel says," Mike began, "Your friends, the Hadens, have been engaged in hijackings. Several men have been killed. Until yesterday, all the men killed have been foreigners. Captain McDae was not liked, but he was one of us. This must stop."

"It is Demill here, that has caused the problems," Danny Haden interjected. Roberts gave Danny a hard look, and he fell silent.

"We have fifty men surrounding this place," Mike translated. "We want no more than to conduct our business in peace. We know that the Hadens cannot be trusted to keep their word. But you, Ira Roberts, are a man of honor."

"Are you going to let this Spic talk to us like this?" Danny said as he stood.

"Shut up and sit down," Roberts hissed. "You will get us all killed."

"We are not such fools as to think any agreement reached under these conditions will last longer than it takes for you to reach safety," Mike continued. "Know that I have intervened to save you, Ira Roberts. If this agreement is broken, I cannot save you."

"Your people missed their chance," Roberts said. "I was warned and crossed the river."

"It was I that warned you, Ira Roberts," Mike translated. "If we fail to agree, there will be war. War will bring martial law and the National Guard. The governor may be in your pocket, Roberts, but he will have no choice if there is war."

"Are you going to let this fool hurrah you?" Danny said. "We will cut them off. They will never move so much as another cup of rum."

"John," Roberts said, "shut your brother up or get him out of here."

Moreno spoke and Mike translated, "What Mister Roberts is trying to tell you, John and Danny Haden, is that if the governor is forced to intervene there will be no gambling, no importation of spirits, no prostitution and no protection from the law. Roberts will be gone as District Attorney and you will be out of business, and likely in prison. The *Isleños* will continue to fish and eventually return to bootlegging, but you will be out of business."

"*Don* Manuel, what do you propose?" Roberts asked.

"We propose that the Hadens will refrain from hijacking. We import and sell to the highest bidder. In return, we will not conduct war. If this is agreed to, we will need assurances that you, all of you, will be true to the agreement."

"War is not what I want, be assured of that," Roberts said.

417

"We welcome a war," Danny said. He jumped to his feet again and began to pace the room. "When the dust clears, we will control all of the whiskey that comes into New Orleans, governor be damned."

"That, Mister Roberts," said Mike, "is the real problem. How can you assure peace with a hot head like Danny?"

"This is how," Roberts said. "John, you need assurance that your gambling and prostitution enterprises can continue without interruption. Right now, you must pay me ten percent, bribe the sheriff, and keep paid informants within the State Police to protect your gambling, which is, after all, your real money maker. Bootlegging is small change for you. Be reasonable. Buy your product from the locals and let them be.

"Elections are coming. I will arrange that you, John Haden, are elected sheriff. No more worries about bribes or State Police and I will keep my requirements at a mere ten percent."

"How can you promise that John will win the election?" Danny sneered.

"I control the polls. The vote goes the way I say," Roberts replied. "Controlling the polls is the reason I have the governor's support. I deliver the votes, make no mistake about that. As for you Danny, I know you killed Jules Ruttan. What is more, I can prove it. You will do as I say, or I will have you convicted of murder and imprisoned."

The room went silent. Then Roberts said, "John, this is absolute; Danny will have nothing to do with the bootlegging side of your business and the hijackings will stop."

Danny sat down.

"In return," Mike translated, "we will not make war on the Hadens, we will sell our imports to whoever will pay, including Haden's gambling halls, and we will not kill Ira Roberts."

Ira Roberts leaned back in his chair. "That is crudely put," he said. "What about Mister Demill? He killed Haden's men, the one called 'Porkins' and Captain McDae. I can't just let him return to bootlegging. It would be bad for my image."

"It was in defense of family," Moreno said in English.

"A fact I admit," Roberts said. "I propose that Demill be banned from importing spirits." Ira Roberts raised his voice, "Please join us, Mrs. Demill."

Annie came from behind the rack of bottles, walked to the table and stood behind Mike. She kept her right hand in her purse.

Danny snorted in recognition. "Had I known who you were, girlie," he said, "things might have turned out better for us."

"Shut up, Danny," John said.

"What do you say, Mrs. Demill?" Roberts asked. "Can we be assured that your husband will stay out of our business?"

"I am done with bootlegging," Mike said.

Moreno spoke in Spanish and Mike translated.

"We have the terms. No more hijackings, Danny Haden and Miguel Demill are out of the bootlegging business, and there will be no war, no assassination attempts."

Danny was about to rise again when his brother pushed him back into his chair. "This is a good deal for us," John said. "You nearly ruined it all with your scheme to take over all imports. This agreement keeps us in business and ensures we will have no problems with the law."

District Attorney Ira Roberts stood and walked around the table to face Manuel Moreno. He offered his hand.

"The terms you proposed are agreed to," Roberts said.

"*Acuerdo*," Moreno said.

"It is agreed," Mike translated.

EPILOGUE

The truce between the Hadens and the *Isleños* held until the end of prohibition. The Great Depression, so devastating to the rest of the country, was only mildly felt in the bootlegging industry. The federal government greatly improved the enforcement of prohibition, but never did eliminate bootlegging through the bayous.

Michael and Annie Demill continued to operate a trucking business that survived the depression and prospered thereafter. Annie gave birth to a boy on January 18, 1923. They named him Bartolomé. The man, Bartolomé Demill, joined the United States Army on December 8, 1941. He went on to fly P-38 Lightnings in the North African Theater of the Second World War, earning the flight name of "Mad Bart" and the distinction of "Ace," but that is another story.

There were four additional Demill children, two boys and two girls. Gerome, born in 1925 died of polio at the age of six. The daughters, Mary, born in 1927 and Helen, born in 1932, both married bankers and joined the Garden District elite.

Andrew, born in 1934, inherited the family business in 1970, when his parents retired.

Mike and Annie Demill died on November 1, 1992, within one hour of each other.

Daniel Haden and Myrtle Schaumburg moved to New Orleans and lived as man and wife until March of 1952 when Danny died of complications from a syphilitic infection. Myrtle moved into a nursing home that year and died two years later.

Brian "Joey" Steward served in the Navy aboard an aircraft carrier during the war and enrolled at Louisiana State University on the GI Bill after the war. He became a tenured Professor of Economics at LSU in 1950.

Mrs. Fior *"Doña* Saberia" deMelilla Roundtree died on January 15, 1926, in Saint Francisville, Louisiana. She was reputed to be over 100 years old. More than one thousand people attended her funeral. Some came from as far away as San Diego, California, and must have begun their journey before the lady died.

HISTORICAL NOTE

Any reader of this fiction familiar with the history of Saint Bernard Parish, Louisiana, will notice a striking similarity between the author's characters and certain real persons.

Manuel Moreno in this fictional work is, unapologetically, influenced by Manuel Molero. Molero was an *Isleño* of extraordinary abilities. He was a financial genius who developed a method of accounting that was later adopted by most financial institutions.

He was a bootlegger, landowner, and folk hero. One of his many accomplishments was his intervention between warring parties during the infamous 1926 "Trapper's War." It was, many believe, Manuel Molero who prevented an escalation of an already bloody conflict and brokered a peaceful resolution.

Leander "Judge" Perez was the inspiration for District Attorney Ira Roberts. As District Attorney for both Saint Bernard and Plaquemines Parishes, Perez controlled every aspect of local government. To those persons wishing to know more, I recommend the books:

Leander Perez, Boss of the Delta, by Glen Jeansonne and

Judge: Life and Times of Leander Perez, by James Conway.

John and Daniel Haden are fictional characters and the crimes they committed are fictional. Dr. Louis August Meraux and his brother Claude Meraux were not fictional. Both were close associates of Leander Perez.

The relationship between Ira Roberts and the Hadens was inspired by the rumored, but never proven, relationship between Judge Perez and the Merauxs. Dr. Meraux, supported by the Perez machine, was elected Sheriff of Saint Bernard Parish in 1924 and died in office in 1938. He was able to amass a great fortune and extensive real estate holdings during his terms of office.

It was widely believed that several illegal activities, one of which was bootlegging, enabled Dr. Meraux to gain such wealth in the midst of the Great Depression. Nothing has ever been proven.

Upon his death, Dr. Meraux's son, Joseph, inherited the estate and through frugal business practices, was able to increase his inventory of properties. After Joseph Meraux's death, the estate eventually was merged into a trust. Today, the Meraux Foundation actively supports community development and educational programs in Saint Bernard Parish.

Claude Meraux, many believe, was the person responsible for the murders of two deputies on April 17, 1923. Claude Meraux and several armed associates were escorting trucks of rum when two sheriff deputies stopped the trucks.

The deputies were killed by shotgun blasts from an escort car. Although Claude was certainly one of the shooters, another member of the Meraux gang confessed, declaring he thought the deputies were hijackers. The convicted killer was able to obtain a full gubernatorial pardon a few years later.

The "peak" on which our protagonist survived is fictional. The possibilities of a pre-historic stone structure hidden in Chandeleur Sound is not. Discoveries by the amateur archaeologist, George Gelé include an area of large granite blocks, the largest being 200 by 700 feet, mounded in such a way as to suggest a structure.

Professional archeologists are, of course, skeptical, but recent discoveries in other parts of the world support the possibility of civilizations predating the end of the last ice age.

ABOUT THE AUTHOR

Stephen Estopinal grew up in the Louisiana swamps and bayous of Saint Bernard and Plaquemines Parishes. He is a graduate of Louisiana State University (class of 1968), a US Army veteran (Combat Engineers, active duty: 1969-1971) and is a Retired Licensed Professional Land Surveyor and Civil Engineer.

Mr. Estopinal was a living history volunteer at the Chalmette Battlefield National Park and a black powder expert. His love of history, particularly the history of colonial Louisiana, has prompted him to write a series of novels to bring that history to life. A descendent of Canary Islanders (*Isleños*) transported to Louisiana by the Spanish during the American Revolution, he draws on extensive research as well as family oral history to tell his stories of Colonial Louisiana from a Spanish point of view.

Mr. Estopinal began writing books in 1986 when John Wiley & Sons published his textbook, *A Guide to Understanding Land Surveys*, now in its 3rd edition and required reading at LSU's engineering survey course. His second textbook, written with co-author Wendy Lathrop, *Professional Surveyors and Real Property Descriptions* also published by John Wiley was released in 2011.

The first of his novels was *El Tigre de Nueva Orleáns* published in 2010 and has been approved for sale by the National Park Service at the Chalmette National Park Visitor's Center. It has been followed by a novel every year. *Incident at Blood River* was published in 2011, *Anna* in 2012, *Escape to New Orleans* in 2013, *Mobile Must Fall* in 2014, *Pensacola Burning* in 2015, *Solitario* in 2018, *The Man from Red Hill* in 2019, and *Beneath the Bonnie Blue Flag* in 2021. All of Mr. Estopinal's books are available at Amazon.com in hardcover, paperback or e-book. See Estopinal.com for more about the author.

Made in the USA
Coppell, TX
28 January 2024

28135374R00249